THE VESTA CONSPIRACY

THE SOLARIAN WAR SAGA, BOOK 2

FELIX R. SAVAGE

THE VESTA CONSPIRACY
THE SOLARIAN WAR SAGA, BOOK 2

Copyright © 2014 by Felix R. Savage

The right to be identified as the author of this work has been asserted by Felix R. Savage. All rights reserved. No part of this book may be reproduced in any form or by any electronic or mechanical means, including information storage and retrieval systems, without written permission from the publisher or author.

First published in the United States of America in 2014 by Knights Hill Publishing.

Cover art by Tom Edwards
Interior design and layout by Felix R. Savage

ISBN-13: 978-1-937396-12-1
ISBN-10: 1-937396-12-6

THE VESTA CONSPIRACY

THE SOLARIAN WAR SAGA
BOOK 2

i.

"ALERT. Unidentified entity logged at 03:34:48 [coordinates attached]. ALERT."

Go away. Le' me 'lone. 'M sleeping.

"ALERT. Trajectory of unidentified entity implies potential collision. Time to collision: six minutes and fourteen seconds at present speed. Deploy collision avoidance system? Yes, no, maybe?"

"Haven't got a freaking collision avoidance system." He spoke out loud this time.

"I was referring to our guns. Do you want to shoot the thing or not?"

Kiyoshi Yonezawa surfaced from his exhausted, sedative-enabled sleep. He was in the wrong place. He floated from a nest of freezeblankets that had lost their chill, leaving behind a dark sweaty patch the shape of his body. He let the ship get hot when he had no passengers on board. No sense forcing the heat exchangers to work overtime; they were rickety enough as it was.

"I was dreaming," he said. His mouth tasted like the intake chute of a recycling unit.

The bridge was dark, lit only by a single glowing screen at the astrogator's desk. Clutter nuzzled at Kiyoshi's body. He pushed off with his fingertips from mismatched, century-old thermal panels of wood-look polymer.

"What do you want me to do about this thing? Estimated time to collision: five minutes and three seconds."

"Can't you handle it?"

"You're the captain."

He was the captain. And also the crew, the only passenger, and the ship's mascot, bare-butt naked, his dick limply waggling under a fiftieth of a gee of thrust gravity.

"Why do you keep calling it a *thing?* Is it a rock or what?"

"That's why I woke you up. It isn't a rock, but it isn't clear what it is."

"Gimme a visual."

The screen at the unused astrogator's desk strobed. Kiyoshi floated down to it. A composite image derived from infrared and radar scan data depicted a thing shaped like a tusk, roughly three meters by two. Ragged at the bottom, it might have been ripped from the jaw of some impossible mega-predator that once stalked the vacuum.

"Space debris," Kiyoshi said.

"Yeah, but from what?"

Kiyoshi smiled. His cubital port itched, and he scratched it absently. His brain was kicking into gear at last. "Let's find out."

Up close, the tusk-shaped thing looked no less strange. Optic sensor and spectroscopic scan data added the information that it was made of a metal-matrix composite, with the exception of the ragged end, which profiled as a jumble of refined metals and polymers, suggesting instrumentation.

It appeared to be partly hollow.

Kiyoshi fastened the seals of his EVA suit. He clamped his helmet on, stepped into the airlock, and cycled it.

"This is a bad idea."

"This is what you do when you're too broke to afford drones."

"We have the Wetblanket system."

"I don't know yet if I want to take the thing with us."

But he did. Unless it did something really freaky—like blowing up in his face—he was taking it. Something as weird as this was certain to be worth money, and he even had an idea who might buy it from him.

He stepped into the stars, rolling head over heels under

the belly of his ship. The thing pierced the blurry sphere of Neptune. He engaged the electrical thrusters of his strap-on mobility pack.

"Mom always said you'd kill yourself one day. But I don't think she was imagining suicide by space debris."

"Oh, pipe down," Kiyoshi said to his dead brother, ghostly shipmate, and bodiless companion.

He puttered towards the thing.

It spoke to him.

ii.

Fourteen months later ...

Elfrida Goto ambled into the UNVRP office with her coat on, clutching a bag from the coffee shop on Olbers Circle. "What have you got for me today, Mendoza?"

The astrodata survey analyst turned from his screen. "The *Dodo* is making a scheduled stop at 847221 Handy. We've also got a flight plan for the *Kharbage Collector* showing that it will pass within a hundred thousand kilometers of 550363 Montego this morning—a hop, skip, and a jump in astronomical terms. If we put in a request now, they'll have time to alter course."

"Is five-five-blah-blah Montego inhabited?"

"No data on that."

"But we know 847221 Handy is inhabited, correct?"

"Yeah." John Mendoza glanced at his screen. "Ranchers. 36-kilometer M-type hollowed out and spun up to 0.73 gees. O'Neill-style habitat. They raise grass-fed, quote unquote, beef for the luxury comestibles market. They also sell milk. And methane."

"I figure our chances of dislodging *them* are somewhere between zero and nil. You don't get much more culturally unique than crypto-organic ranchers in the asteroid belt." Elfrida yawned. "It might be worth visiting them, though."

"You're just thinking about those steaks," Mendoza said, grinning.

"Like I would waste a real steak on a phavatar. But now that you mention it, I could stash some in the *Dodo's* deep freeze and take delivery next time they swing by here. The *Dodo* is owned by NGI, right?"

"Right. Nature's Gifts, Inc." The chintzy moniker illustrated the lengths recycling companies would go to to distance themselves from the unsavory image of their business.

"I'd have to borrow one of their phavatars. All they have is asimov-classes. Those always give me a headache. On the other hand; steak."

"Envisioning a romantic dinner à deux? Mood lighting, a nice Cabernet Sauvignon, something mellow on the audio channel?"

"Curb your imagination, Mendoza." But Elfrida blushed, because she had been thinking of something like that. In practice, any such romantic gesture would surely backfire, she reflected.

Mendoza sensed the shadow that had fallen across her mood. "I know I can't expect you to treat *me* to a romantic dinner, but you could at least have brought me coffee," he said, mock-hurt.

"Oh, but I did!" She opened the Virgin Café bag and passed one of the recycled-foam cups to him. "Goat's-milk latte with an extra shot, right?"

"And it even tastes like it," Mendoza said, slurping ecstatically. "Beats the stuff in the staff lounge by a light-year."

Elfrida popped the nipple of her own coffee—an Americano with what purported to be real milk; maybe it even came from 847221 Handy—and perched on the edge of her desk, looking out the window. Their office was on the eighteenth floor of the University of Vesta's STEM building. It was a loaner cubicle just large enough for their two desks, with organic biostrate walls that resembled loofah sponges. The roots of the squash vines that covered the outside of the building poked through the outer wall, dripping on the floor. They had a good view, anyway. From the window, Elfrida could see over the roof of the Diadji Diouf Humanities Center, clear across campus.

Students, professors, and locals on their way to work hurried along zigzag pathways between groves of apple and avocado trees. Blowsy and exuberant, the trees grew to the size of oaks in Vesta's 0.22 gees. To the north lay Olbers

Lake, an emerald lima-bean. The campus lay between the Branson Hills residential district and what was laughingly called Bellicia City. To a casual observer, this could have been any small university town on Earth. But the gauzy early-morning light came from slits around the edges of the roof, six kilometers overhead. The shafts contained louvered mirrors that both refracted sunlight into the habitat and blocked out harmful radiation.

Vesta—technically 4 Vesta, the fourth asteroid ever discovered—was so big, at 525 km diameter, that its boosters called it a protoplanet. The 'ecohood' of Bellicia occupied an impact crater in its northern hemisphere. The roof of the habitat was a teensy M-type asteroid that had been maneuvered into place three generations ago. Those early, can-do pioneers had melted the captured asteroid's native iron by the simple expedient of turning their ships around and aiming the exhaust from their primitive fusion drives at it. The molten metal had sintered to the carbonaceous regolith of Vesta, capping the crater with a 2-km thick, radiation-proof lid. Et voilà, instant habitat. Just add air.

Shame about the gravity, or rather lack thereof, Elfrida thought for the hundredth time, shifting her limbs in the stabilizer braces she wore to simulate gravitational resistance. They chafed her thighs, and didn't do a damn thing for encroaching farsightedness, increased homocysteine levels, and the stuffed-up feeling she always got in microgravity, which was colloquially known as head bloat.

Watching the people cross campus, it was easy to tell who shared her reservations about the Vestan gravitational environment. A scant majority wore stabilizer braces and gecko boots like hers, which gave them bulked-out silhouettes and a normal gait. But many of the students were spaceborn; they loped along in long bounds, reflecting the fact that they each weighed about four pounds here. The merriest students leapt right over the heads of their trudging peers, their long scarves swirling like the tailfeathers of exotic birds .

Elfrida sighed.

"Cold, isn't it?" Mendoza said.

"Freezing," Elfrida agreed, tugging the lapel of her coat, which she had not taken off. "I was just noticing there's no one sitting out on the benches to eat breakfast today."

"So," Mendoza said, "it's not that the university is literally trying to freeze us out."

"They'd probably be a bit more subtle than that." Elfrida stood up and waved her hand pointlessly under the heating vent. A barely-warm breeze trickled from it. "Did Dr. James cough up the rest of the asteroid survey data?"

"Quote, it's still being processed, unquote."

"Oh well." She resisted the temptation to start grumbling about the lack of cooperation they were getting from the university. "We've still got plenty of rocks from the first batch to work through."

Putting her butt where her mouth was, she settled into the ergoform behind her desk and blinked a command to her screen, which brought up a display of their ongoing and recently terminated jobs. Paperwork and more paperwork. Mendoza had a sign above his desk:

$$Paperwork = \frac{k}{paper}$$

—meaning that paperwork increased in inverse proportion to the amount of actual paper involved. That was certainly true when you worked for the UN. And it went double, Elfrida felt, for the United Nations Venus Remediation Project (UNVRP) these days. The fallout from the Galapagos incident had inflicted stringent new compliance requirements on all field agents, as well as personally affecting

Elfrida herself.

They worked in silence for half an hour. Elfrida finished her coffee and stared at the swirl of grounds in the bottom of the cup. Wasn't there a fortune-telling method that used coffee grounds? Cydney would know. She was into that stuff.

But Elfrida didn't want to think about Cydney right now, either.

"Hey, Mendoza."

"Yeah?"

"Can we call the *Kharbage Collector* and request a trip to 550363 Montego? I'm looking at your preliminary candidacy assessment here, and it scores pretty high on all geophysical criteria."

"What, you're gonna pass on the chance to score some crypto-organic steaks?"

"I can also do without the crypto-organic cow farts," Elfrida said. "Those asimov-class suits do have olfactory sensors. But no, I figure this is a good chance to catch up with my old friends at Kharbage LLC. Haven't seen them in a while."

"They don't operate many ships in this volume. I'll put the call through." The UNVRP office on Vesta didn't have many frills, but it did have a dedicated comms satellite in orbit—a must for a two-man field office that was currently 200 million kilometers from Earth.

Just 90 seconds later, Mendoza's screen flashed. "Hello, UNVRP Vesta, this is Captain Petruzzelli of the *Kharbage Collector* speaking. What can I do for you?"

Elfrida sprang up from her ergoform, exceeding the resistance of her braces, and inadvertently crashed into Mendoza's back. "Sorry! That's Alicia Petruzzelli. I know her. Oh dog, what's she done to her hair?"

iii.

"Congratulations!" Elfrida gestured at the captain's insignia on the fez pinned atop Petruzzelli's hair. The fez was crimson, and Petruzzelli's hair was now metallic turquoise. The colors clashed horribly. "Looks great!"

"Do you really think it suits me?"

"To a T. *Captain* Petruzzelli; it's got a ring to it. And you're only, what, my age?"

"I mean the hair."

"Hmm. That I'm not so sure about. I think it might have looked better when it was magenta."

"I know, right? I'm just trying out the blue. It's semi-permanent."

They had to wait roughly half a minute to hear each other's responses, which was the time it took a signal to make a round trip between Vesta and the *Kharbage Collector,* a recycling barge currently cruising 4.9 million kilometers away.

"You look great, too," Petruzzelli said, at the same time as Elfrida blurted:

"I was worried, you know. I thought they might've demoted you to assistant data analyst, or something."

Eighteen months ago, Elfrida, her then-boss, and Alicia Petruzzelli had 'borrowed' a Star Force ship with an experimental hydrogen-boron fusion drive. Piloting the ship, Petruzzelli had fragged no fewer than three of the enigmatic predators known as the PLAN. They'd saved thousands of asteroid squatters from being nuked—a pretty cool achievement. But, far from being feted, Petruzzelli had been forced to participate in UNVRP's shameful cover-up of the whole affair.

Elfrida had lost track of her afterwards. She'd often wondered guiltily whether Petruzzelli had managed to get her life back on track.

Now it seemed that Petruzzelli had not only escaped any disciplinary consequences from her own employers, but even scored a promotion to captain.

But Petruzzelli did not seem to want to talk about herself. "Seriously, you look really good!" She waved at her main screen, which displayed a grab of Elfrida's face from their earlier conversation. "I love the barrettes, and you must have lost weight."

The comment about weight-loss confirmed that Petruzzelli was lying through her teeth. Elfrida had gained several kilos on Vesta, in addition to being puffy from the microgravity. Anyway, if the best compliment someone could come up with was *love the barrettes,* they were definitely stretching.

Petruzzelli herself, by contrast, looked fit and lean. The blue hair had initially distracted Elfrida from noticing that she'd had her eyebrows tattooed in swoops that ended in little smiley-faces at the outer corners. She wore a baggy cardigan over a wifebeater and leggings that emphasized her taut physique. Apparently, Kharbage LLC still had not succeeded in convincing its officers and crewpersons to wear their uniforms.

The bridge of the *Kharbage Collector* echoed the theme of sloppiness. That there was no one else here at the moment only made it more obvious that maintenance was going by the board. Cladding had come off the walls and the mirrored sides of the elevator shaft in the middle of the bridge. In some places it had been splarted back, in others left to flap loose. Screens at officers' workstations flickered, stuck on error messages, or in one case, a porn vid.

It's their corporate culture, Elfrida told herself. The spirit of jugaad. Very private-sector.

But Petruzzelli's next remark seemed like an oblique apology for the state of her ship. "Sorry we haven't got a better suit for you." She reached out and flicked a fingernail against Elfrida's cheek. "It's like talking to, well, a bot."

Elfrida controlled her instinctive flinch. After all, it wasn't rude to touch a robot.

Lying on a couch in the University of Vesta's telepresence center, she was operating one of the 'phavatars'—physical avatars—that the *Kharbage Collector* kept on board for the use of visitors. Petruzzelli's assessment summed it up: this suit made the widely maligned asimov-class phavatars look spendy. From the neck down, it was a spacesuit animated by servos and artificial muscles. From the neck up it was a generic, multiracial, androgynous human with a dated geometrical haircut. Its sub-geminoid face, which Elfrida could see in the convex mirror suspended above Petruzzelli's workstation, had a range of expressions so limited that her polite smile was coming out as a manic grin.

"I've asked head office for something newer," Petruzzelli said. "I mean c'mon, give me a tezuka-class at least, but noooo."

Before the most recent change of policy, it had been usual for subcontractors like Kharbage LLC to host Space Corps-owned phavatars on their ships. Now, Space Corps agents just used whatever phavatars their logistics partners happened to have lying around. It was a funny way for an agency to act that had recently scored a whopping budget increase. But this way Petruzzelli got to bill Space Corps by the hour, so maybe it worked out more profitable for her.

"Oh, I'm not complaining," Elfrida said. "At least a čapek-class can't drone on at you about its professional aspirations."

Twelve seconds later, Petruzzelli's face crinkled up in a laugh, and her cheeks turned pink.

"If I never operate a post-geminoid phavatar again, I'll be happy," Elfrida went on. "And I probably won't have to. The stross-class has been recalled. For routine hardware updates, they say."

"Riiiight," Petruzzelli said knowingly.

The stross-class had been the most advanced phavatar ever designed by the UN's Leadership In Robotics Institute. One of the first to go into service had screwed up spectacularly, triggering the PLAN attacks on Botticelli Station and 11073 Galapagos. Elfrida had been operating it at the time.

"*Was* it a true AI?" Petruzzelli asked.

"No. It was trying to become one, but it never got there." Far away on her couch, Elfrida shivered at the memory.

"So, uh, were there any consequences for you personally?" Petruzzelli asked awkwardly

"They sent me back to Earth for six months. I had to do a lot of therapy. *Groan.*"

"I know, right? Me, too."

"I bet your therapist wasn't as bad as mine. She made me do fingerpainting and beadwork. Anyway, when they figured I was fixed, they offered me a choice of reassignments. I think they'd have liked to get rid of me, but they couldn't, because they'd already portrayed me as this heartwarming survival story. So I was offered Luna or Vesta, and I picked Vesta." Elfrida made the phavatar shrug, lifting its elbows away from its sides. "Luna would've been a back-office job. Slow death by paperwork."

"And Vesta?"

"Slow death by paperwork. With a few side trips. *Laugh,*" Elfrida said, using the emoticode, since the phavatar's laughter sounded like a drawerful of cutlery being dropped on the floor. Twelve seconds later, Petruzzelli laughed with her. "But hey," Elfrida added, "at least I got to see you again!"

"Yeah! Seriously, it's great to see you." Petruzzelli whipped off her fez and frisbeed it across the bridge. It caught on the Eiffel Tower of empty drink pouches that someone was building at their workstation. "She shoots, she scores!"

The playful gesture signalled that they were done sharing.

Elfrida felt a bit cheated, since she'd given more than she'd received. There was a lot they hadn't even touched on. For instance, the third member of their unauthorized ship-borrowing escapade: Elfrida's then-boss, Gloria dos Santos. Did Petruzzelli know anything about what had happened to her?

Probably not, Elfrida thought. Dos Santos had jumped ship on Ceres, before she could be brought up on criminal charges. She had simply vanished.

Instead of mentioning dos Santos, she said, "That's cool. Is it new?"

At the same time, Petruzzelli said, "So, about this asteroid of yours—"

They heard each other simultaneously, and stopped simultaneously. "You first," Petruzzelli smiled.

"Oh, I was just saying that's a cool chunk of gear." With one mechanical hand, Elfrida indicated the 3D display floating above Petruzzelli's workstation: a holographic sphere that represented the solar system as seen from 2.4 AUs out, their present location. "Is it new? Captain Okoli didn't have one."

"Yeah. We just got it a few months back. But look at this." Petruzzelli stood up and reached towards the display. Though she stood 175 centimetres in her gecko boots, her fingers barely reached the bottom of the sphere. "Do they think we're *all* freaking spaceborn, two and a half meters tall with the lean mass of a ten-year-old? I've asked my techies to reinstall the projector at a lower angle, but they're scared of breaking it. So we have to do this." Petruzzelli hopped on top of her workstation. One boot on a crumb-covered plate, the other on a pile of printer substrates, she poked her head and shoulders into the middle of the sphere. "Great view," she said, asteroids and planets spangling her face.

"I think I'd better not try that.".

"No, better not. If you fell, it would set off the alarms and wake everyone up."

While the *Kharbage Collector* kept Greenwich time, Elfrida was operating on Vesta's unique schedule. So Petruzzelli had had to get up in the middle of the night for her.

"I'm really sorry I'm stealing your bunk time," she belatedly apologized.

"Oh, pooh. I wasn't asleep. But my 2i/c is, thank dog. Michael. Ugh, I haven't even told you about *him*. I know he'd love to meet you, but you would not, trust me, love to meet him. And with any luck, you won't have to." Petruzzelli cocked her head at the center of the display. She pointed, zoomed. The sphere emptied out, leaving only the *Kharbage Collector* itself, a firefly inching through a dark volume that contained a few tagged sparks. "Bear in mind this is all based on publically available astrodata. Which means it's wildly incomplete. But according to the coordinates you gave me, here's your rock. Know anything about it?"

"Not much. This partnership with U-Vesta is supposed to be a more efficient method of identifying candidates for the Project. But my analyst and I are convinced that they're not sharing everything they've got. Oh, it's a long story. The short version is: 550363 Montego, V-type asteroid, about 11 km wide across its longest dimension, albedo of 0.15, likely composed of basaltic chondrites. That's it."

Petruzzelli raised one of her tattooed eyebrows. The smiley-face at the eyebrow's outer corner changed from a standard *smile* into an *evil grin*, with devil horns and sunglasses. Smart tattoos: the newest old thing on the block. "I guess it's more exciting this way, huh?"

"Oh yeah," Elfrida said, adding lamely, *"Sarcasm."* She wished *she* had emoticon eyebrows. Someone ought to manufacture a phavatar with those.

"Well, you'll know more about the place pretty soon. We'll be there in about fifteen minutes."

★

One detail about 550363 Montego that Elfrida had not mentioned, assuming Petruzzelli would already be aware of it, was that it was owned by the Centiless Corporation. Legal ownership of asteroids was first-come-first-served. Thus, most of the asteroids in the solar system had been snaffled by resource mining companies during the early years of space exploration.

Not by any means all of them. The system was now thought to contain 200 million asteroids large enough to be so classified, and more were still being discovered.

Such was one goal of the University of Vesta's astronomical survey program.

In practice, however, the university was mostly *rediscovering* asteroids that already belonged to someone. Corporations were not obliged to disclose their assets. In fact, they guarded such data as jealously as dragons. Thus, the university was building a starmap of the Belt's central region that already existed, in half a dozen more- or less-complete versions, in private hands. Several of the supermajors already had sued the university, trying to have the survey stopped on grounds of breach of privacy.

But the supermajors were quick enough to disclose ownership of any given asteroid when someone else tried to claim it. The pattern had gotten so predictable that John Mendoza had given up posting claims to any candidates they found. Instead, he just pinged the usual suspects and asked, "Is this yours?" Nine times out of ten, it was.

Not that Centiless, Elfrida reflected, could have any intention of actually exploiting 550363 Montego. It was too piddling.

It rotated in Petruzzelli's 3D display, a pale gray lump the shape of a ginger root. Its relatively high radar albedo indicated the presence of some silicates in addition to the basaltic chondrites you would expect a V-type to be comprised of.

V-type asteroids, or vestoids, as their name suggested, were literally bits of Vesta, having been blown into space by the primordial impact that created the protoplanet's vast Rheasilvia Crater. They had all their parent's charms: no gravity, regolith so smooth you could slide on it, overlapping craters that stymied landings—minus the one element that had made Vesta worthy of human attention in the first place: hydrogen. No economically-minded human being could have any use for an object like 550363 Montego.

But Elfrida had been working with UNVRP for eight years now, and she'd met people living in much worse places. The majority of human beings were not economically-minded.

So she wasn't exactly surprised when a voice blared into the bridge of the *Kharbage Collector*. "Heave to, me hearties, 'fore I blast yez into yonder void! Resistance is futile! Ye're in my crosshairs, and vairy pretty do ye look there!"

After a startled blink, Elfrida's reaction amounted to: *here we go again.*

"Here we go again," she said.

"Yez are surrounded by drones armed with infrared-guided projectiles," the voice threatened. "One word from me and yez'll have sunlight coming through your tokamak!"

"Screw you and your lame-ass heatseeking missiles," Petruzzelli replied. "Do you know what kind of a ship you're looking at?"

"A raddled auld twin-module Startractor with a heap o' tasty-looking cargo in her bays."

"Well, this *old* ship happens to be armed to the teeth. My own drones are currently zeroing in on the source of your signal." Petruzzelli's fingers danced over her console. "And if semi-autonomous micro-weapons platforms aren't scary enough for you, take a look at my forward radome. That's a rocket launcher loaded with scattershot warheads."

"Try penetrating a couple of kilometers of solid rock

with ball bearings, me beauty."

"Thanks for telling me where you are," Petruzzelli said.

The 3D asteroid hanging over their heads developed granular detail as data poured in from the *Kharbage Collector's* drones. A Superlifter tug perched on a protrusion, like a mosquito on a knobbly knee. Near the Superlifter, false color identified a cave mouth enveloped in a dangerous cloud of tailings.

"And now tell me if you ever studied basic math," Petruzzelli said. "All I have to do is increase my velocity relative to yours, and $K_e = 0.5 \times M \times V^2$, idiot. Depending on how much I accelerate, each of my ball bearings will deliver kinetic energy equal or greater than its mass in TNT. So, no, they won't penetrate your rock. I think they're much more likely to shatter it into a million little fragments. Don't you?"

There was a pause. When the voice came back on the air, it sounded somewhat less piratical. "Ye're not supposed to carry tactical warheads, if ye really are a civilian, and not an undercover."

"There are no undercover Star Force patrols," Petruzzelli scoffed. "That's a myth. They're stretched thin enough without going after plebs like you. Which is why we've taken the precaution of tooling up." She winked at Elfrida, which could have meant that she was bluffing about the warheads, or could have been meant to rope Elfrida into accepting the *Kharbage Collector's* flirtation with the wrong side of the law. Many private-sector ships did in fact carry weapons, licensed or not. In a system that included the PLAN, that was basic common sense. Elfrida certainly wasn't going to report her for it. "Do we understand each other better now?"

"Sure we do. *We're* just innocent colonists trying to scrape a living. *Ye're* a great bullying corsair that's come to steal our resources, pitiful as they are. Ye should be ashamed of yourself."

A cold bolt of apprehension slid through Elfrida. Could the pirate's accusation contain a grain of truth? Had Kharbage LLC really sunk to stealing the resources of asteroid-squatters, such as these seemed to be?

No, she thought. If that were the case, half the screens on the bridge wouldn't be broken. There'd be money to mend them. And there'd be more people around.

"Oh, *sigh*," Petruzzelli said. "We haven't come to steal your shit. I've got a UN liaison agent on board. She's come all this way to talk to you, although I don't know whether she still wants to, after you were so rude." She turned to Elfrida. The smiley-faces at the ends of her eyebrows went *quizzical.*

"Sure," Elfrida said. After all, this was only a čapek-class phavatar. "I'll head over right now, if that's OK."

iv.

"Sorry I can't go with you," Petruzzelli said. "Company regs. But take some of my drones. I'll give you an uplink. That's actually against regs, too, but since you're a friend ..."

"I'm sure I'll be OK," Elfrida said. "But thanks. I'll take the drones."

"Just in case."

"Just in case," Elfrida confirmed, noting that Petruzzelli's eyebrows were doing *evil grin,* while her expression remained professionally bland.

The drones were useful for more than offensive applications. Powered by tiny ion-propulsion engines, they could sub for a personal mobility system, which Elfrida's phavatar did not have. She tethered herself to them and was towed across the gap between the *Kharbage Collector* and 550363 Montego. She felt ridiculous. Behind her, the *Collector* matched the asteroid's slow tumble through space, its radiator fins a-bristle, its radome glinting in the light of the peppercorn-sized sun.

"Be careful," Petruzzelli said in her ear.

"Will do."

"Blistering barnacles! We got us a live 'un!"

Slim piscine shapes streaked out of the cave mouth at the wide end of the asteroid. Before Elfrida could decide whether to alter course or keep going, they surrounded her. Three times her size, they resembled silvery sharks with arms ending in scoops, grabbers, and drill bits. The phavatar analyzed the wisps of gas they were emitting. *~Ion-propulsion electrical thrusters. Propellant appears to be ammonia-based,* it told her in the affectless voice of its onboard MI.

Jerking with rage on her couch, Elfrida commanded the phavatar to transmit a polite greeting. What was it *for,* if not to facilitate communication?

But by this time thirty seconds had passed, and the phavatar had not done anything except geekily chew on its own sensor data. A robot shark bit through Elfrida's tethers and scooped her up. It rushed her to the asteroid, into the cave mouth, and down a broad tunnel into a cavern shadowed, rather than lit, by the headlights of a dozen more sharks crawling over the walls.

Released into freefall, Elfrida cannoned into the far wall at autobahn speed. On her couch on Vesta, she flinched instinctively. *~SUIT COMMAND: FULL SYSTEMS CHECK!* she subvocalized.

She rebounded, drifting. Rocky debris littered the air, ranging from micron-scale grains to fist-sized chunks. The robot sharks—demolition/salvage bots, she now understood—teemed on the walls of the cavern like cockroaches in a cheap hostel room. They towed nets that captured most of the debris they were excavating. She spotted a couple of larger structures near the entrance of the cavern. But the most interesting thing in view was several spacesuited figures powering towards her.

Interesting, and not in a good way, she corrected herself as they approached. There were five of them, in hard-shell spacesuits with old-fashioned detachable mobility packs. The interesting thing was that they had no logos or nametags visible anywhere on their suits.

"Arrr, it's only a bloody phavatar," said the same voice that had hailed the *Kharbage Collector*. "Ahoy, matey!" He tapped her head with his glove. "Anyone home?"

At the same time, Petruzzelli said in her ear, "Hey, Elfrida. WTF? Wanna give me a visual feed?"

Also at the same time, the drones caught up, cheeping updates over her link. They had got into a dust-up with the robot sharks outside, and left several of them the worse for wear. They were prepared to similarly dispatch her interrogators if she gave the word.

"No! Dog, no! Hold off!" Elfrida shouted, praying she wasn't too late. *This,* she told herself ferociously, *is why you don't accept the loan of semi-autonomous mobile weapons platforms, even from a friend.* "Hello," she said, making the phavatar smile into the dazzle of her captors' helmet lamps. "My name's Janice Rand." Field agents used different aliases on each mission, randomly assigned by a computer program. "I'm from the Space Corps. If you haven't heard of us, we're a UN agency tasked with supporting the diversity, economic viability, and physical and mental health of human populations in space, with a special focus on asteroid-dwellers."

This was the post-11073 Galapagos spiel, rewritten to eliminate any reference to the fact that the Space Corps was under contract to the Venus Remediation Project. You weren't even supposed to mention the Project now unless they asked. The shift in emphasis had been explained as "refocusing on our core mission," but it had left a lot of agents confused as to what the core mission of the Space Corps *was*. Most agents of Elfrida's generation had joined up specifically because of the UNVRP connection. They understood that their role was to procure asteroids for the Project. Now, the emphasis on unique cultural values often conflicted with the Project's needs.

One thing had not changed, anyway: Elfrida needed to establish a channel of communication that did not involve drones or robot sharks.

"This visit is a preliminary assessment. With your cooperation, which is highly appreciated, I'll be gathering information about your habitat, your population, and your long-term viability plan." *Assuming you have one,* she thought, glancing around the cavern. The two large structures tethered to the wall looked like inflatable Bigelow habs. "For your information, I'm operating this phavatar from a remote location, so there will be a lag of several seconds before I can respond to you. But if you have any questions, ask away!

Don't be shy."

"Shy?" said one of the smaller spacesuits. "We're pirates! Pirates aren't shy. Shiver me timbers," it added, and giggled.

"Hell," said the first voice. "She's from the Venus Remediation Project."

So much for tact. Colonists weren't dumb.

"Yes," Elfrida admitted. "The Space Corps is a top-level agency, but our mission is to facilitate UNVRP, among other things. But that doesn't mean I'm here to kick you out and take your asteroid." *Which isn't even yours.* "As I mentioned, my goal at this time is to conduct a preliminary geological survey and population assessment."

"Assess this," the leader of the pirates said. *"Middle finger."* His use of the emoticode proved that he wasn't living in the seventeenth century, after all.

Slow-moving pebbles clonked against Elfrida's frame. The phavatar completed its systems check and reported that it had sustained cosmetic damage to its head and torso, but was otherwise functional. The čapek-classes were built to take a pounding.

"Maybe we could get started by introducing ourselves?" she suggested.

While she waited for the pirates to respond, she replied to Petruzzelli's increasingly urgent pleas for information. "I'll give you a visual feed as soon as there's anything to see." She was putting Petruzzelli off. You weren't supposed to share everything with your chauffeur. She felt bad about that, but not too bad, considering that Petruzzelli's drones had gotten her off on the wrong foot with these people by trashing several of their D/S bots. "For the moment, it looks like they're mining the asteroid for valuable minerals."

"In situ?" Petruzzelli asked skeptically. "Why not just bag it up and tow it back to their base?"

"It's too big for that."

"I've heard of asteroids the size of Manhattan being lifted.

They vanish from their orbits and are never seen again, until their minerals turn up on freaking Ganymede or somewhere."

"Well, maybe these guys don't have a base. It looks like a shoestring operation." Elfrida broke off. The pirates had finished their encrypted colloquy, and their leader was speaking to her on the public channel.

"Your drones have put four of our D/S bots out o' commission. Beyond repair, they are. If ye really are a UN agent, we'll be wanting compensation for that."

Elfrida laughed to herself. These guys had a handle on the system.

"Listen," she said. "You aren't dumb. And I don't think you're really pirates, either. So can we take the yo-ho-ho'ing as read, grab some air—" she gestured at the two inflatable habs— "and discuss how we can work together?"

Eleven seconds. Twelve seconds.

"Ye're on," said the leader. "But I warn ye, it's a mess." He streaked towards the smaller of the habs. "We weren't expecting company. Arrr!"

With their EVA suits off, the pirates turned out to be two women, two men, and a boy of about twelve. The child, so thin that Elfrida could almost see through his bare hands and feet, was prepubescent, but closing in on two meters tall. Spaceborn. The adults, in contrast, had standard Earthborn frames. Nevertheless, they all shared a buttery-brown skin tone and straight black hair. The leader wore his in dreadlocks.

"Haddock," he introduced himself. "Ye can call me Captain. These are Coral and Anemone—" the women— "Codfish, and the kid is Kelp."

"Nice to meet you," Elfrida smiled. "Are you all related?"

Coral shuddered, Kelp giggled, and even Haddock winced. Elfrida figured they were reacting to her phavatar's axe-murderer smile, rather than her question. "Aye," Haddock said. "How did ye guess? Anemone is my lady wife, Kelp is the fruit o' our loins, Coral is Nemmie's sister, and Codfish is my brother and married to Coral."

"For my sins," said the dour-faced Codfish. "Also, I get the least cool name."

"Someone had to be Codfish," Haddock said. "Come tell me, who am I? A codfish, only a codfish!"

This gibberish was obviously a quotation, and Elfrida thought of Captain Okoli of the *Kharbage Can*. He'd have known where it came from. She queried the UNVRP databank on Vesta with a video clip of Haddock delivering the line, not expecting much. In the meantime, she said, "Am I really meant to believe that you reside on this asteroid?"

The Bigelow hab did not give the impression of a home, so much as a spherical tool-shed. It measured about ten meters across. Fabric partitions walled off a couple of private compartments for sleeping, but there was no furniture in the hab apart from basic life-support equipment. The triple-stage airlock through which they'd entered contained an electrostatic scrubber, to make sure they brought no dust inside. Her phavatar's olfactory sensors transmitted a reek similar to the smell of ripe kimchi, overlaid with air freshener. Magnetic clamps held tools and spare parts for the D/S bots. Wall screens displayed the ongoing excavation, as well as panoramas of the asteroid's surface.

"Care for a cup of char?" Haddock said, while Anemone stuck a handful of drink pouches into the microwave. "Oh no, I forgot; ye're a phavatar. And the real you is probably sitting comfortably on some palatial space station, enjoying the gravity and the high-O2 air, wi' a cozy bunk and a real dinner awaiting ye at the end of the day." He shook his head sadly. "Ye've no idea what it is to be alone in the solar system, despised by one and all, wi' nowhere to lay your head. All we want is a place to call home, humble as it may be, where we can live in peace, troubling no one. And for this sin ye'd treat us like criminals—"

At this point Elfrida interrupted, having begun to speak at the start of his self-pitying threnody. "Oh, come on," she said. "You aren't settlers, any more than you're pirates. *Dude*. Haddock, or whatever your name really is. You're not fooling this chick."

She smiled to take the sting out of her accusation, and all five of them shuddered. "Would you mind not doing that?" Coral fished a crumpled tablet out of her webbing, smoothed it out, and said, "Mirror."

In the now-reflective surface, Elfrida saw a spectre out of a horror vid. Her collision with the wall had rearranged her phavatar's face, leaving pink polyfoam and nanofiber muscles exposed by hanging shreds of fake skin. Her telescopic left eye stared from its bare plastisteel socket. She now looked less like an axe murderer than an axe murderer's victim. Her grin was the final, awful touch.

She pawed fruitlessly at her hair, which was sticking out in all directions, and said, "Sorry."

~*Cosmetic damage?* she subvocalized to the phavatar's MI. ~*This is a cosmetic disaster!*

"As I said, I'm sorry," she ploughed on. "But you're not fooling anyone. You're already known to us, as it happens. While we've been talking here, I queried our databanks ..." Her query about Haddock's 'codfish' quotation had turned up some interesting results. "Facial recognition and voice analysis puts the five of you with 99.9 percent certainty on 1856902 Alhambra, 738688 Duxi, and probably several other asteroids before that. I wasn't involved in those missions personally, but my colleagues based on Hygiea were. Apparently, when you were operating in the outer Belt, you called yourself 'Hook.' And I do know that reference. *Hook!* was a twenty-first-century musical about pirates by Walt Disney. However, the record makes it clear that you aren't pirates. If anything, I guess you're the solar system's smallest pirate fan club."

"*Peter Pan* was a novel by Sir James Matthew Barrie! Disney was a philistine," said the child Kelp.

"Sure they're all bloody philistines in the UN," Haddock said. He pushed off from the wall he was holding onto. Anemone released the handful of drink pouches she had just taken from the microwave. Globules of hot tea escaped into the air. "You're right," Haddock said to Elfrida. "We're not pirates. We don't jack passing spaceships, or mine asteroids that ain't ours. Billions of blistering blue barnacles! Who would bother mining a water-poor vestoid? You'd scarcely cover your costs. No, me beauty." He drifted closer to the phavatar—in, Elfrida realized too late, a menacing posture. He held a socket wrench in one hand. "We're just construction workers, trying to earn a crust in the outer-space homebuilding industry."

"You're already wanted by the UN Occupational Health and Safety Agency on charges of illegal construction," Elfrida said urgently. "Don't make things worse for yourselves!"

A violent impact blacked out her optic sensors. The phavatar's audio feed lasted a few seconds longer. The olfactory, a few seconds beyond that. By the time she lost the smell of body odor and kimchi, she was fighting the restraints that held her on the couch, pulling her headset off. She floated upright, gasping, in the golden evening light that poured through the windows of the U-Vesta telepresence center.

V.

"I need a drink," Elfrida said, pulling off her coat.

She had spent the day filing the necessary paperwork on the 550363 Montego disaster. To be sure, a day on Vesta was only five and a half hours long, but that was still a lot of paperwork. She'd helped Petruzzelli—who was understandably outraged about the loss of her phavatar—prepare an initial application for compensation. She had also written a report for her supervisor back in New York. Her formal debrief was scheduled for tomorrow.

She had also decided to pay a visit to Dr. James, the head of the astrophysics program at U-Vesta.

But before tackling Dr. James, she needed a break from the whole mess, so she'd come home.

UNVRP had rented an apartment for her in one of the best buildings in Branson Hills, a sprawl of habs climbing the slope north of Olbers Lake. While the newer habs were just that—expandable Bigelows, like snowmen squatting among the trees—Elfrida's building dated back to the early days of the Vesta colony. Those first settlers had held to Earth-centric ideas of how to live, never contemplating the sacrifice of right angles for cost-efficiency. So her apartment had four walls. It had a ceiling. It had floors that did not give at every step. And it had doors that closed and even locked, so you could shut out the world.

That sounded really good to Elfrida right now.

She dropped onto the ergoform couch. "I said I need a drink!" she shouted. "What are you, stupid?"

From the miniature kitchen came a grinding noise and a series of beeps.

"Oh, dog. Not again."

Elfrida heaved herself off the couch and squelched in her dry-grip boots to the kitchen. Spilt breakfast cereal littered the counter. The beeps were coming from the corner behind the refrigerator. Elfrida got down on her hands and knees. Jammed into the corner, her housekeeping bot beeped at her. Its sucker-feet retracted and extended, fastening onto the floor and ripping free again—that was the noise she'd heard—as it tried to gain leverage to free itself. Its vacuum nozzle was stuck behind the fridge.

"Aw," Elfrida said. "Did poor wittle bottikins try to vacuum up the spice rack again? I put it back there, you know, so you *wouldn't*. My mom gave me that spice rack, and all the spices in it, because everything tastes like crap in micro-gee. But you're just convinced, aren't you, that nutmeg and turmeric are hazardous substances. *Diddums.*"

She jerked the maidbot out of the corner, not caring if she broke it. The vacuum nozzle came free. It had a noticeable bulge near its tip. Maybe the maidbot had just been trying to vacuum up the spilt cereal. Feeling a bit guilty, she set it on the counter.

"Spit it out!"

The maidbot hiccuped. Out of its nozzle rolled a sphere the size of an eyeball.

"Hmm."

Elfrida examined the sphere. It was pink. It had a hole through the middle. It had what seemed to be an ON button, but nothing happened when she pressed it.

"Maybe I owe you an apology, bot," she said. "What is this? ... Oh, right." She raised her voice to an imperative pitch. "BOT COMMAND! Enable voice communication."

"Dunno," the maidbot said. "It's a foreign object! It was on the floor! I have to keep the floor clean! It's very important for your health and safety!"

"Now I remember why I muted you. BOT COMMAND! Disable voice communication."

The maidbot clattered at her with what seemed uncannily like pique, and began to vacuum up the cereal on the counter.

Elfrida fixed her own drink, a margarita flavored with chili pepper from her mother's spice rack, and carried it back into the living-room. She sat on the couch and treated herself to a trip to Venus. After a while, she removed her stabilizer braces, although she knew she shouldn't. The dang things were just so uncomfortable. *Ahhh ... that's better.*

Headset in place, gel mask over her face, gel gloves on her hands, she wandered among the wind-bowed fig and olive trees along the shore of Venus's warm, planet-girdling sea. Behind her, the Lakshmi Plateau raised its serrated skyline against the blueberry-colored noon sky.

Post-terraforming, Venus was still an inhospitable world: a shallow, brine-saturated ocean covered 80% of its surface, and its continents were arid. Ferocious winds circled the planet. Only the polar regions were cool enough for mammalian life. The day remained long—the dispute about *how* long was still ongoing, but Elfrida had picked a best-guess setting of 40 sols. A day, then, was an Earth month. Seasons were nonexistent, due to the low obliquity of the planet's spin axis, and most people lived underground, to escape the sun's relentless glare (or, at night, the endless dark), as well as the hurricane-force winds.

But you *could* go outside. Without an EVA suit. Without gecko boots. Without stabilizer braces. You could walk on Cytherean rock, breathe Cytherean air, and irrigate your GMO fig and olive trees with Cytherean water piped from the local desalination plant. The Venus Remediation Project had achieved its goal of transforming the solar system's problem child into a shirt-sleeve environment.

Elfrida picked a fig and sat down in the shelter of the rocks to watch the windjammers. These sailboats zipped back and forth from Ishtar to the southern continent of Aphrodite, making use of the very same gales that foiled air travel on Venus. They looked like giant butterflies skimming on the silver sea. She bit into the fig. It was not quite ripe, a touch of realism she appreciated.

"Ellie! Ellieeee! I'm *ho-ome!"*

Elfrida's jaw clenched. With deliberate slowness, she exited the immersion environment. The fig in her hand dematerialized. The Cytherean landscape vanished, to be replaced by the log-out screen. She spat out her gel tongue-tab, took her mask and gloves off, and removed her headset.

Cydney Blaisze, Elfrida's girlfriend, stood in front of the couch, bouncing up and down impatiently on bare feet. "Put that boring old thing away. Let's go out! I'm so glad you're home! I didn't expect you to be back yet. I actually just came back to change. Do you think I should wear this? Or maybe this?" She held up two trendy wide-legged jumpsuits. One was a retro transistor print, the other was solid pink with a snake twining up one leg and down the other. "I'm kind of favoring the pink," Cydney went on.

Her stream-of-consciousness chatter had buried the question of Elfrida's early return several sentences back, so Elfrida didn't have to explain it, even if she'd wanted to. "You'll be cold in either of them," she said, the phantom taste of fig lingering in her mouth.

"Urrrr. I'll wear my coat, of course. It is totally freezing out there! Facilities Management is so cheap. But if I wear the pink, there's an accessory problem. I mean, *none* of my scarves go with it. I suppose I could do a statement necklace. The stainless steel choker might work. But it's so 2286. *Snerk.* I was planning to recycle it, but it's handmade, and I hate doing that. It just seems wrong."

Cydney bounced into the bedroom, presumably to look for the necklace in question. Elfrida packed her immersion kit into its case.

The apartment seemed brighter now that Cydney was here, and it wasn't just because Cydney had switched on the lights. Her Chanel No.666 perfume perked up the flat air, and even the boring black walls seemed stylish, not oppressive, when they were serving as a backdrop for Cydney's gazelle-like form.

Cydney came from a more elite background than Elfrida herself. She had been born in Johannesburg and grown up in another gated community on the Cape. She was half Xhosa, a quarter Afrikaaner and a quarter Anglomutt, not that you'd ever guess any of that from her milky-coffee skin, slightly oversized green eyes, and silky blond hair—all courtesy of pre-birth genetic tweaking. She had got her start in the media thanks to her father's contacts in the Xhosaland government.

She bounced back into the living-room, stark naked except for a necklace. "Look what I found! Remember when you gave me this?"

Elfrida did. It was when they'd only been dating a month or so. They had met on Earth, when Elfrida had been home recuperating after the 11073 Galapagos incident. Well, technically, they'd met on the net, when Cydney interviewed Elfrida about her amazing survival story. After she returned to Earth, Cydney had taken her out to lunch to thank her for the interview, which had given a big boost to Cydney's curated news feed, CydneyBlaisze.com. They'd hit it off IRL, and things had just kind of evolved.

"We were on that gondola in SoHo," Cydney reminisced. "I thought the trip was a disaster. I thought you hated me. I was thinking, *urrrr*, I shouldn't have asked her to come to New York, we've only just met ... and then you gave me this."

She fingered the necklace, which was a string of ten beads representing the consensus number of Sol's planets. The Venus bead was blueberry enamel, with sand-colored continents, representing UNVRP's vision of how the planet would one day look. In fact, the necklace came from UNVRP's public-relations department, as did the immersion environment Elfrida had been simming. The necklace wasn't just a freebie like the software, though. It had cost Elfrida a packet.

"You said, remember? You said, let's be monogamous." Cydney looked up, her eyes soft. An uncertain smile flickered on her lips.

Elfrida pushed off the couch and kissed her. She suddenly felt blessedly charitable towards Cydney again, and that wasn't anything to do with the fact that Cydney was naked. Absolutely not.

"Oooh ... oh ... don't! I mean, *do,* but not right this second. We've got to go out." Cydney twisted away. "Everyone's waiting for me. I mean, us. You are coming, aren't you?"

"Sure," Elfrida said. "I was only going to stay in and work on my farm, anyway."

"*Urrrr,* you mean on Venus? Honestly, Ellie, that's such a ... never mind."

"No, come on. Such a what? What were you going to say?"

"Nothing. Really."

"No, what?"

Cydney put on her underwear and climbed into the pink jumpsuit. Elfrida folded her arms. She hated that she was so touchy, so quick to pick a fight. But she had a good excuse today. And Cydney didn't even want to hear about that. Hadn't even bothered to ask why she was home early.

"I was just going to say that you spend a lot of time in that immersion environment, when you could be, you know. *Living.* Talking to people, hanging out, having fun."

Elfrida bit back the comeback that popped into her mind—*fun? Are you aware that some of us have jobs?* But that would open up another can of worms that she didn't want to get into. Besides, Cydney had a point. It *was* loserish to hang out in an immersion environment when you could be living IRL. She used to be one of those who looked down on gamers and sim addicts. She didn't want to turn into one.

Elfrida knew that she had been badly affected by the

11073 Galapagos incident. Therapy had splarted over the cracks, but they were still there. Her short-temperedness, the way that she was pushing Cydney away—she wanted to blame Vesta and/or her job, but she knew that she was the problem. She had refused to take meds, but she was using the Homestead Venus sim to block out the world instead. It was a weaselly way to act.

"OK," she said. "Let the good times roll. I'm just going to put on my stabilizer braces."

vi.

The Virgin Café was a Vesta landmark, a quarter-acre of red and white booths with robot spiders crawling through buckysilk cobwebs on the ceiling, as beloved as it was sleazy. The name referred not only to the classical Roman origins of 4 Vesta's moniker, but also to the private aerospace company that had spearheaded Vesta's colonization.

As Cydney had promised, 'everyone' was there—everyone being Cydney's friends from the university. Elfrida connected to the café's wifi and blinked up ID bubbles for them all, so she wouldn't get any names wrong. Most of them had customized their public profiles. The overlay of quirky mascots, runes, and animations matched the tattooed and augmented bodies lounging in the darkened café.

Cydney ordered an espresso martini. Elfrida asked for a Colorado Bulldog, in keeping with her resolution to be sociable.

It wasn't easy, though. She didn't know any of these people. They all came from the Humanities department, which was permanently at war with the STEM departments over grievances such as supercomputer access, salaries, grants, and who had said what to whom at the latest faculty meeting.

"What are you studying?" Elfrida uninspiredly asked the man beside her, whose lower-body stabilizer braces kept snagging on hers—they were pretty crammed into the booth. She knew from the information overlaid on his wild blond hair that he was an PHCTBS Studies Ph.D candidate named David Reid, but it was good manners to pretend you weren't peeking.

"Do you really want to know?" he said condescendingly.

"Yes, I'm curious." Reid was a cyborg. She knew that not only because it was in his profile, but because his prosthetic left arm didn't even pretend to be real. It was transparent, so she could see the actuators and nanofiber muscles flexing inside.

"I'm researching the lived experiences of gimps in micro-gravity environments." He smiled at her as if he'd just won an argument. "We've reclaimed the word *gimp* to distinguish congenitally disadvantaged individuals from the cyborg community, but I'm treating both communities as a single population for purposes of statistical analysis." He reached across her with his artificial arm to grab her empty glass. It seemed like an unnecessary gesture. "Another?"

"I guess, yeah." This would be her third drink, counting the margarita she'd had at home, and alcohol always hit her harder in micro-gee, but she felt like she needed it.

"Yo! Another Colorado Bulldog over here! ... So, you're Cydney's girlfriend?"

"That's right."

"You're the one who works for the Venus Project."

"The Venus Remediation Project, yes."

"*Remediation.* That's pretty Orwellian, wouldn't you say? It presupposes that there's something there to be remediated."

"Well, there is. Temperatures up to 900 degrees Celsius, a solar day that's 242.5 sols long, and about 70 bars of excess CO_2. We've already ablated a fifth of the atmosphere, but as you can tell from those figures, the place still needs work." *Do not get into an argument with this guy,* Elfrida told herself. *That's what he wants.* She had this argument way too many times. There was a lot of public opposition to UNVRP, and it paradoxically seemed to be increasing at the same time as UNVRP restructured its asteroid capture program. Or maybe her sense of public hostility was skewed by the prevailing attitudes in the Bellicia ecohood. Her drink arrived, brought by one of the robot spiders that crawled across the ceiling and lowered their offerings on strands of buckysilk.

"You ought to talk to some of my friends in Belter Studies," Reid said. "They'd tell you that human beings don't need planets to live fulfilled lives. To assume otherwise is to devalue spaceborn physiology and experiences. Hell, Cydney's in Belter Studies, isn't she? I guess maybe she doesn't talk to you about her research. Here, have this." Elfrida flinched as a volley of links came flying from his ID bubble to her inbox. "Plenty of data there to get you started."

He turned away and began talking to the person on his other side.

Elfrida gritted her teeth. She looked around the café in an instinctive search for allies. At this time—FirstDark, as the Vestans called it—most people took a break from work or studies. Vesta's rotation period was 5.342 hours. Conveniently, three of these periods added up to a manageable 26-hour sol, giving the Bellicia ecohood a long 'day' punctuated by two little 'nights.' FirstDark corresponded to lunchtime. The café was crowded, but Elfrida didn't see anyone she knew.

She finished her second Colorado Bulldog, rolling up the pouch from the bottom to get the last drops out, and rose. Passing behind Cydney, she touched her on the shoulder. "See you at home."

"You're leaving? Oh, come on! Was David being an asshole? He *is* an asshole. I could see you doing that face, your I'm-really-pissed-off-but-I'm-not-going-to-say-anything face. Here, sit beside me. I *miss* you, baby," Cydney cooed, shifting emotional registers in nothing flat, the way she used to do on her feed.

Elfrida rubbed the place between her shoulderblades where the straps of her stabilizer braces overlapped and itched. The café *was* crowded. People were table-hopping, literally bouncing over the tables, chattering and laughing. There seemed to be a buzz in the air.

Cydney was still talking, growing peevish at Elfrida's

failure to respond. "You don't have to like my friends. But can't you at least try to understand their point of view? They're not bad people. The thing is, you can only push people so far before they push back."

Maybe everyone's just hanging out in here because it's warm, Elfrida reflected wryly. The Virgin Café had an infrared heating system like her apartment's, which targeted human bodies, keeping them toasty, while their breath clouded white.

Cydney's eyes glimmered damply. A text popped up in Elfrida's contacts: Cydney taking their one-sided discussion private. "I relocated from Earth to the Belt for you. Is it too much to ask you to spend a couple of hours having a drink with me? I guess it is."

Elfrida's head snapped sideways as if she'd been slapped. The accusing text moved with her, staying put in the middle of her field of vision.

Cydney had never before admitted in as many words that she'd moved to Vesta for Elfrida. It had always been "a new direction in my career" or "intellectual enrichment" or "broadening my horizons." But as the months passed, and Cydney made friends and got involved in campus life, Elfrida had allowed herself to think that maybe Cydney really *had* come to the middle of nowhere to study cultural divergence in space-based societies (the official name for what everyone at the university called 'Belter Studies').

But here was the unvarnished truth: Cydney had made a huge sacrifice for Elfrida. Her feed had slid way down in the rankings. And Elfrida was reciprocating by being a grumpy bitch who couldn't even make a sincere effort to get along with Cydney's friends.

Clearly, the decent thing to do was to apologize.

But she had grievances of her own, and she was unable to resist the temptation to fight her corner. *"You think I'm leaving because your friends annoy me?"* she transmitted, typing as fast as she could on the gaze-tracking keyboard interface of her contacts. *"Sorry to deprive you of melodrama. I've actually got stuff to do."*

"What stuff?"

"Work! As you would have known if you'd bothered to ask me how my day was, or why I got home early, or any of that stuff, you know, that couples normally ask each other. But no. You didn't even notice that I was upset. Honestly, I sometimes wonder why we even bother living together."

Cydney's eyes widened in shock as she received the last words. Elfrida felt a mean stab of satisfaction. She nodded grimly and trudged out of the café.

By the time she got outside, she was already regretting what she'd said. But Cydney didn't come after her, and Elfrida was damned if she'd go back and try to patch the spat up.

Apart from anything else, she did have to go see Dr. James. Might as well get it over with.

"Come on in," Dr. Eliezer James, head of the U-Vesta astrophysics department, called through the open door of his office. "Nice to see you, Ms. Goto. How's everything going?"

His friendly greeting seemed unaffected. It took the wind out of Elfrida's sails. Maybe he really didn't know anything about what had been going on. Still, she was determined to have it out with him.

She sank into the ergoform he indicated, feeling the knee joints of her stabilizer braces snag on the holey fabric cover. "To be honest, things aren't going great," she said. "I've filed a report with my supervisor, but I thought you should know, too. I had a phavatar destroyed today. It was assaulted by illegal construction workers on one of the asteroids you found for us."

"I'm very sorry to hear that."

"It was completely totaled. I was logged in and experiencing the real-time sensory feed at the time of the assault. Do you know what that feels like? It's not a nice experience."

Dr. James's brow furrowed. "As I said, I'm very sorry. If there's anything we here at the university can do ... Would you like a coffee? I was just making some."

"Thanks, but that's not the point," Elfrida said. Her head was spinning from the two Colorado Bulldogs and her climb up to Dr. James's office on the twentieth floor of the STEM building. Even the tallest buildings in the Bellicia ecohood lacked stairs. They were unneeded when everyone weighed about four pounds. Instead, the STEM building had a zip-shaft which you could glide up by kicking off, as if you were riding a vertical scooter. But stabilizer braces made it a real workout. Which Elfrida needed, admittedly. She wondered how Dr. James managed.

The astrophysics professor stalked from his desk to the table that held a coffee-maker as well as assorted scientific gear. His prosthetic legs gave him a bobbing gait like a chicken's. These were functional, not cosmetic prostheses, skeletal under his slacks. His knees bent the wrong way for a human being. His right sleeve also hung in folds over a prosthesis that ended in a split hook.

Watching him insert coffee pods into the machine with his left hand, while gripping the machine with his hook, Elfrida said, "I was just talking to a guy in, uh, Gimp Studies. That's what they call it, apparently."

"I know. Don't worry about being correct. Bunch of slebs, aren't they?"

"How do you mean?"

"If it's young Mr. Reid you're speaking of, his family can afford to give him a post-grad education. In the asteroid belt. And he chops off his own arm. Oh yes, that's what cyborgism is: they amputate their own limbs and then spend the rest of their lives asking themselves what it means. Not at all the same as being born with only one limb because the

Last Caliph bombarded your place of birth with defoliant chemicals a half-century before you came along. That's why I don't call myself a cyborg; they've devalued the word."

The coffee-maker released aromatic steam. Hot black liquid began to drip into the two attached pouches.

"Ah, don't listen to me," Dr. James said with a grin. "I'm just being a curmudgeon."

Elfrida laughed stiffly. She'd been hoping to rule out any connection between Dr. James and the Humanities crowd, and he certainly sounded as if he had no time for them. But maybe that was just what he *wanted* her to think.

"Thanks," she said, taking a pouch of coffee. "Well, the reason I'm here is because I wanted to talk about that asteroid."

"Which one?"

"550363 Montego. Where I lost a phavatar today. Where a gang of unlicensed construction workers is, or was, building a habitat for the purpose of facilitating illegal settlement."

"Shocking."

"Not really. We know this kind of thing goes on. And this isn't even the first run-in we've had with these guys. But my point is that this makes thirty-eight out of forty-one asteroids that we've identified as candidates, based on your survey data, and subsequently investigated, only to find squatters already there." She felt relieved to have got that sentence out without tripping over her tongue. "The only difference this time is that we caught them in the act. So—"

"Ms. Goto." Dr. James's voice was suddenly cooler. "Am I missing something? I don't understand how this has anything to do with the U-Vesta Asteroid Survey."

"The astrodata comes from your office," Elfrida snapped back.

"And we make no guarantees that the rocks we find are or will be uninhabited. Our survey doesn't go to that level of granularity."

"Oh, come on! I know you've got a gamma ray telescope. You've got infrared, ultraviolet, radio, radar, X-ray, the works. This department is the best-funded in the university. It's the reason the university *exists*. So don't tell me, please, that you can't get that level of granularity. You can probably see squatters picking their noses on rocks half a million klicks out. You should definitely be able to see their emissions. But all you give us is radar data and spectroscopy analysis." Her voice shook. She was no good at confrontation. But there was no one else to do this within a million kilometers. "Not only that, I believe you're deliberately filtering the data before you hand it over. You're giving us rocks that you *know* to be inhabited, because you're ideologically opposed to the aims of the Venus Remediation Program."

Nervously, she sucked down a mouthful of coffee. It was good, but she hardly noticed.

Dr. James sighed. He faced her squarely, leaning back on his prosthetic legs as if they were a chair, so that his belly paunched under his shirt. "Ms. Goto, I'm sorry to expose my ignorance. But why, exactly, is it a problem for you that these asteroids are inhabited?"

"Because UNVRP's objective is to nudge them out of their orbits and sling them at Venus, where they impact the planet at an angle calculated to ablate the maximum volume of atmosphere, while incrementally accelerating the rotation of the planet, and also delivering payloads of microbes to the surface. And obviously, we can't do that if there are people on them."

"To the best of my knowledge, UNVRP runs an efficient and widely praised resettlement program."

"Yes, and it costs a ton," Elfrida snapped. Biting her lip, she got up and went over to the window.

In the fallout from the 11073 Galapagos incident, the criteria for resettlement had been tightened up. When purchasing an asteroid, UNVRP now had to consider the unique cultural values of the residents, and compensate them for any potential damage to same, making the whole business much more expensive. Elfrida saw no point in explaining this to Dr. James. Academic types didn't understand about money.

She stared across the dark campus. Along the shore of Olbers Lake, clusters of warm-tinted LED lights identified cafés and restaurants. Was Cydney still at the Virgin Café, or had she gone home? She looked up. Two or three kilometers overhead, oblong constellations drifted through the darkness. The pricks of light resembled stars, but they were actually the warning lights around the edges of Bellicia's floating farms. These vast spongy mats, with their self-replenishing sprinkler systems, provided legumes, greens, and root vegetables sufficient to meet 80% of the ecohood's calorie and micronutrient needs. The dominant crop was high-yield *Glycine max,* which was why locals called the floating farms 'soyclouds.'

"Ms Goto," said Dr. James, behind her. "Please don't take this the wrong way. But *many* asteroids are inhabited. That's been the case ever since the Clean Revolution made a trip to the Belt as cheap as a trans-Pacific flight. For your information, I'm fully cognizant of the tradeoffs involved in living out here, and I do support terraforming, broadly speaking. But most likely, human beings will continue to seek independence and freedom from government supervision, so migration to the Belt will continue. Therefore, to assume that you can run an asteroid capture program without resettling people ... Far be it from me to tell you your job, but it sounds like you may need to retest that assumption."

"We don't assume that. My point is, how do you explain the fact that *thirty-eight* out of *forty-one* candidates ..." She trailed off. She had a strong sense that she was losing, even though she had a winning argument. "It's statistically unlikely. Scratch that. It's statistically impossible."

"Then maybe there's another explanation," Dr. James said. "Could your own data management be less than secure?"

Elfrida flushed. "I bet our information security is better than—"

The lights went out.

vii.

The floor vibrated. Elfrida, standing by the window, pressed her fists against her mouth. In her memory, the robotic voice of the Botticelli Station hub said, *All personnel, remain where you are.*

"We're under attack!"

"No, we're not," Dr. James said. But he didn't sound too sure.

Trembling, Eflrida gripped the window frame and poked her head around it. The businesses along the lakeshore were still lit up. Only the building they were in had gone dark.

"What's going on?"

"I don't know. Maybe a power cut. We've had some issues with lumpiness in the electricity supply." Dr. James clicked up beside her and looked out the window. "Everything seems to be all right, doesn't it?"

"How would you know?"

"Ms. Goto, this is the most secure habitat in the asteroid belt. Our founders may not have had the PLAN in mind when they constructed the Bellicia ecohood, but I promise you, no toilet rolls are getting through three kilometers of solid rock."

"They could hit your power plant on the surface. Maybe that's why the electricity's gone off."

"Except it hasn't. It's just us."

"The building's *shaking!* It feels like we're taking impacts. Or being pushed from side to side. Oh dog, what *is* it?"

She felt exposed, and yet she didn't want to move away from the window—a potential escape route. The tremors continued. Panicking, she blinked out a query to the internet, always a last resort: *Will I be OK if I jump out of a window approx 70m up under 0.22 gees?* She tried to remember how the Space Corps therapist on Earth had told her to cope with stressful situations. Breathe deeply. Yeah, that was going to help.

"I've just pinged Facilities Management," Dr. James said. "They confirm that this building has stopped drawing power, but they don't know why. Doggone it! Ali Baba needs to run around the clock." He was referring to the supercomputer in the astrophysics lab, dubbed Ali Baba by the researchers who tended it. "It's got backup batteries, but they can only power it for a couple of hours."

The wall shook again. A black shape with a white face burst in through the window, shrieking, "Yaaaah!"

Elfrida screamed. The invader's foot hit her in the ribs, knocking her against Dr. James's desk. As she fell, a steely grip fastened on her arm. She struggled, until she perceived that it was Dr. James. Gripping her arm with his hook, he pulled her towards the door. "What do you want?" he shouted at the invader.

Invaders.

Another person hurtled through the window. Landing on his/her feet, he/she raised a weapon and fired. There was a loud *phut*. One or more projectiles crunched into the wall to Elfrida's left. She smelled a sweetish, pungent odor.

She was already throwing herself backwards through the door. She ran along the hall, following Dr. James. With his reverse-jointed legs and blade-feet, the professor had a turn of speed that would put champion sprinters to shame. She assumed he was heading for the zipshaft, until he vanished into a door ahead of her. At the end of the hall, more black-garbed figures burst out of the zipshaft.

Elfrida plunged after Dr. James. Behind her, shouts of "Yaaah!" and "Get them!" mingled with the *phut-phut* of more projectiles being fired.

She cannoned into a table in the dark, rebounded, and scrambled under it. They were in the astrophysics lab. Dr. James had rushed to the defense of Ali Baba, his precious supercomputer. But the invaders were already in here. She heard Dr. James shouting, the wordless battle cries of the invaders, and the long-drawn-out crunches of accelerators, high-spec printers, neutron traps, and other expensive pieces of equipment being thrown around as if they weighed less than the boxes they'd come in. She fumbled to unfasten her stabilizer braces so she could move better. She didn't give a hoot about the supercomputer. She cared about getting out of here alive.

A female voice hissed in the darkness, "James. Jamesss! Where's the metalfucker gone?"

"He's gotta be here somewhere," panted another of the invaders.

A burst of bluish light lit up the lab, printing monstrous shadows on the walls and ceiling.

"Eat plasma, meatheads!" yelled Dr. James.

Lying on her back, Elfrida saw the distinctive rods of an electrolaser weapon, like a handful of glow-in-the-dark kebab skewers flung across the lab.

"Drop the fucking computer!"

"James!" shouted the same female voice. "You metalfucking psycho, are you out of your mind? You're putting the whole hab in danger, and now this?"

A scream drowned out the last words. Elfrida scooted on her butt across the floor. Afterimages floated on her retinas. The invaders wore masks, identical white joker-faces with red lips. *You're putting the whole hab in danger.* Dr. James was hiding something, and he was prepared to kill to defend it.

At that moment, the internet returned a first tranche of answers to her query: *BRAH I JUMPT OFF FROOKING DOOM MONS & ONLY BUST ME ANKEL ROFLMAO*

More of this kind of thing continued to scroll across her field of vision until she turned her contacts off. The internet was so useless.

The invaders were shooting wildly. The pungent smell of the propellant they were using in their guns filled the lab. And then, as if someone had thrown a switch, the shooting stopped. Someone stumbled into Elfrida, jumped over her.

"Are they gone?"

She could see Dr. James in the weak light from the window. She crawled towards him. He leant out of the window, craning down. She rose to her feet, her stabilizer braces half-off and interfering with her movements.

He spoke tragically. "When I said 'drop the computer,' I didn't mean, you know, literally *drop* it."

Far below, LED cobblestones illuminated the path leading to the Humanities building. A dark mass lay on the path. It was Ali Baba. Whatever the effect might have been on a human being, that fall had clearly not done the supercomputer any good. Even under a fifth of Earth's gravity, state-of-the-art electronics required delicate handling. Elfrida remembered how carefully the invaders had been carrying the supercomputer. Until Dr. James shot one of them.

"You shot one of them," she reminded him.

The invaders poured out of the STEM building. They streamed towards Ali Baba and surrounded it.

"Hey!" Dr. James hollered. "Leave that alone!" He elbowed Elfrida out of the way and fired down at them. His electrolaser weapon was a slim tube integrated into his prosthetic arm. The sleeve of his shirt flapped, a charred rag. The ionized plasma beam might have hit the invaders. It *did* hit a cobblestone, whose machined surface reflected it at an angle into the STEM building.

The invaders fled into the night, carrying the remains of Ali Baba.

"That's the trouble with lasers," Dr. James said. "I wanted a coil gun, but they said the magnets would interfere with the electronics in the arm. So I went for the laser. You get pinpoint targeting, an effective range of several kilometers, and you also get to shoot whatever's located at an angle equal to the angle of incidence."

"Still pretty wicked," Elfrida said.

"Those dickshits were using liquid-propellant projectile guns. They must have access to a high-spec printer."

"You shot one of them."

"I know. I didn't mean to."

The lights came back on, revealing the body of Dr. James's victim lying on the floor, next to a hole where the particle accelerator had toppled over and taken its piece of the floor with it. His joker mask had come off. Apart from the blackened spot on his forehead, David Reid looked exactly the same as he had at the Virgin Café an hour earlier.

The fire alarm went off. Dr. James's reflected beam had started a conflagration on the third floor. The firefighters arrived in record time. They were an all-volunteer outfit, highly trained and motivated. They aimed jets of aqueous foam at the building.

Elfrida watched with a handful of others from the lawn. Her colleague John Mendoza was there, too. He'd been working through FirstDark, but had known nothing about the invasion until the fire alarm went off.

"They stole the supercomputer," Elfrida told him. "Dr. James shot one of them."

"You're kidding."

"Not. That prosthetic arm of his? It's a laser weapon."

"No, no. I mean, how could they steal the supercomputer? It's the size of a room. And anyway, it's in the basement. It vents its waste heat into the lake. Everything's connected."

"Well, maybe they didn't know that."

"Which would narrow down the field of suspects a lot," Mendoza said, grinning. "To, maybe, one Space Corps field agent, and whoever else in this habitat *doesn't* know that a supercomputer isn't something you can just pick up and walk off with."

"Stick it up your socket, Mendoza. I majored in art history."

"So you belong over there," Mendoza said, nodding at the Diadji Diouf Humanities Center, from whose windows people were leaning to watch the foam dripping off the green curtain of the STEM building

"I'm not cool enough for them." Elfrida grimaced. "The guy Dr. James shot? Was a Humanities student. I know him. I mean, I'd met him. I was just talking to him, like, an hour ago."

Mendoza's eyes opened wide. He had cocoa-colored eyes, which looked even darker in contrast with his milky skin. "Well, then, I guess we know who did it."

"... Yeah."

"Of course, we can't jump to conclusions," Mendoza backpedaled.

"If Cydney was involved, I'm going to find out about it. And I mean I'm going to find out *all* about it."

"You'd probably do a better job than they will," Mendoza said, pointing into the sky.

Another pair of gliders landed on the lawn. Unlike the volunteer fire-fighters' electrically powered Bumblebees, these were two-man flyers with streamlined cockpit bubbles and rotating jackstands that tore up the turf. Hand-painted mascots and slogans decorated their fuselages. One pilot sprang out of his cockpit and posed on the wing of his glider, his scarf fluttering heroically. The other three new arrivals edged towards the STEM building, their sub-lethal PEPguns leveled at the firefighters' backs.

The peacekeepers had arrived.

Throughout the solar system, police and security duties were handled by an assortment of paramilitary contractors, private individuals, and troops employed by one or another UN agency. These last were collectively known as blue berets, or peacekeepers. Even UNVRP had its own peacekeepers, although not on Vesta. This heterogeneity made for a lot of variation in terms of professionalism, funding, and overall seriousness. The peacekeepers in the Bellicia ecohood were generally held to be on the low end of the seriousness scale. They worked for UNESCO—all five of them.

As the tiny size of this 'police' force indicated, Bellicia was not a place where anyone expected trouble. In fact, since Elfrida had been here, the only conflicts she'd witnessed had been between the peacekeepers and the people they were supposed to be looking out for.

Watching four of the Fab Five accost the firefighters, she could see why.

"Well, we're not going to get much work done for a while," Mendoza said brightly.

"Why?"

"According to you, they tossed Ali Baba out of a twentieth-floor window and ran off with it."

"But you said that *wasn't* the supercomputer!"

"Correct. The actual supercomputer is a million processor crystals running in parallel in the basement. What they ran off with was most likely the astrophysics workstation. Of course, Dr. James's team is bound to have off-site backups."

"Backups of what?"

"Its memory. Each workstation stores its own data in its own memory crystals. Safer than the cloud."

"Oh."

"So they'll have backups. But you said the lab was trashed, right? It'll take them a while to get up and running again. They've got pretty good manufacturing capabilities here, but I don't think they can make memory crystals yet."

"You don't have to sound so pleased about it."

Mendoza turned to look at her. "Sorry," he said. "Just trying to keep things light."

Elfrida sighed. "No, *I'm* sorry. I just ..." She trailed off, watching the Fab Five escort Dr. James to one of their flyers. The professor's hands were plasticuffed behind his back. Foam soaked his hair and clothes. "Mendoza, one of the invaders said to him, *You're endangering everyone in this hab.*"

"What do you think that meant?"

"I don't know. But he is definitely hiding something. We'll have to find out what."

viii.

The dim effulgence of ThirdLight flooded the patio of Elfrida's apartment. To help people sleep through the latter third of the Bellicia ecohood's 26-hour sol, Facilities Management darkened the sun mirrors during ThirdLight. The mirrors looked like slivers of moon fixed high in the sky, illuminating the soyclouds, picking out the PHES (Pumped Heat Electrical Storage) thrusters on their undersides.

Elfrida pushed the patio door open. It wasn't locked. "Cydney?"

The peacekeepers had taken Elfrida down to their headquarters to ask her about the raid. She'd had to tell her story over and over. She was shaken up. The familiar confines of her living-room did not soothe her.

"Cydney?"

"Babe! You're back!"

Cydney hurtled out of the bedroom. She wrapped her arms and legs around Elfrida, propelling both of them onto the couch.

"Where *were* you, babe? I kept pinging you."

"They confiscated my contacts. I said I wasn't recording, but I guess they want to check for themselves. I should have thought to record everything. That way, they'd know Dr. James isn't a killer." *But he's hiding something dangerous.* She hadn't told the peacekeepers about that.

"He *is* a killer!" Cydney said, bouncing upright. "He shot David in cold blood!"

"Oh, you know about that?"

"Everyone knows about it."

"But David isn't dead. Dr. James had his laser on the lowest setting. He was only stunned."

"He *only* suffered cardiac arrest He's *only* in a coma. The whole campus is up in arms. There's going to be a demo tomorrow."

"I guess you'll be going?"

"Of course. David's a friend."

"You said he was an asshole."

Cydney took Elfrida's hands in both of hers. "Sweet Ellie. Someone can be impossible to get along with, and you can still care about them. You can still love them, even."

Elfrida worked her hands free, Now she knew for a fact she couldn't tell Cydney about what she'd overheard in the astrophysics lab. She took off her stabilizer braces and the nanofiber leggings and tank top she wore under them. As usual, the straps had left red weals around her waist and across her shoulders. Cydney reached for her, but Elfrida pretended not to notice. She went into the bedroom and opened the closet. She grabbed a pair of pyjamas and stepped into them, banging her head on the ceiling in the process.

"Careful, babe," said Cydney, in the doorway.

Elfrida riffled through the clothes in the closet. Almost all of them were Cydney's: white, shocking pink, aquamarine, burnt orange, or one of the other attention-getting hues Cydney favored. The only thing Elfrida could smell in the closet was Chanel No.666.

"Are you looking for something, babe?"

Elfrida sailed into the kitchen. She opened the recycling bin. Cydney could've ordered the housekeeping bot to empty it already, but she hadn't. The bin's plastic liner held an empty Virgin Café takeout bag, a microwave meal tray, and under that, spattered with coffee dregs and grains of rice, a crumpled bundle of black fabric. Elfrida shook it out. The loose-weave thermal fabric was slick to the touch, a sign that it had been printed from cheap material. She smelled that sweet, pungent odor.

There was one thing left in the bin. A joker mask. Elfrida held it up between two fingers.

"Well?"

Cydney's big green eyes welled up. Elfrida expected her to dissolve in tears. But Cydney surprised her.

"We had to do something," she said. "The astrophysics lab has been monopolizing the supercomputer. It's totally unfair. We complained to the dean. We got a ruling that they have to give us equal time. But they just ignored it! After all, we're not *real* scientists, right? So they kept right on locking us out of the system. We haven't been able to do any data analysis for weeks! It's outrageous. Why do they even need to run Ali Baba around the clock? Why does an asteroid survey need that much processing power?"

"I don't know," Elfrida said. She was pretty sure that whatever Dr. James's team was using the supercomputer for, it wasn't the asteroid survey.

"It's just not fair! Just because we study people instead of stupid rocks!"

Cydney was getting worked up now, wringing her hands, her cheeks flushed. Elfrida felt oddly calm. "Here," she said, getting the cigarette box down from the shelf. "Have one of these."

Cydney tossed her head angrily, but she took a cigarette and pushed a cartridge into it. She exhaled candy-scented vapor laced with a mild tranquilizer. This was Cydney's little vice.

"Where did you take Ali Baba?" Elfrida asked.

"That wasn't Ali Baba itself. It was only the astrophysics lab's workstation."

With all their data in it, Elfrida thought. "Yeah, I know, but where did you take it?"

"I don't know. I was just a lookout. I wasn't in the lab when ... I didn't know you were there, either. You should have told me where you were going when you left the café."

"So you were on lookout duty. That means you were downstairs the whole time. You must've been one of the people who carried the workstation away."

"And almost got shot. I hope they give Dr. James life on Pallas!"

"Where did you take it?"

"It was pretty smashed up. They probably just dumped it."

"So you don't know what they did with it."

Cydney sucked on her cigarette. A cloud of vapor hid her face. "Even if I did know, I wouldn't tell you, Ellie. Sorry, but you've made it pretty clear that you're on their side."

"Cydney didn't know anything," Elfrida said to Mendoza. "She just tagged along."

They were sitting on a bench on the shore of Olbers Lake, wearing warm coats and nursing takeout coffees from the Virgin Café. Mendoza was eating a danish. He chewed in silence for a moment or two, letting Elfrida know that he was aware of her wish to protect Cydney. She looked away. She felt all twisted up inside. But she believed Cydney truly was ignorant of the raid's real purpose.

At last Mendoza said, "So she doesn't know who organized it?"

"No. But it has to be someone in PHCTBS Studies, if David Reid was involved."

"Poor guy. I hope he recovers."

"Yeah. Mendoza, we have to find out what they were after."

"Well, presumably whatever it was, they got it." Mendoza looked at the last bit of his danish and wadded it up in the wrapper. "Unless the workstation was busted beyond repair, which is a possibility."

"Mendoza, don't you remember what I told you last night? They said the whole hab is in danger."

"Yeah, I remember." Mendoza stuffed wrapper, danish, and all into the dedicated recycling pocket of his coat. "That was pretty nasty. It's never good when you can taste the soy.

I did a bit of asking around last night. Turns out Dr. James and his team *didn't* back up their database. They haven't even logged into the off-site storage center in more than a year. That's ... well, it's really unusual."

"That proves it! They're hiding something ... something dangerous."

Out on the lake, a fish jumped up through the mat of bluey-green CO_2-sink algae that covered the water. Elfrida had got her contacts back from the peacekeepers. Her HUD display indicated that the temperature was slightly warmer today, although a cutting breeze blew off the lake. No one else was around. They were all at the demo downtown, demanding justice for David Reid.

"Maybe if Dr. James goes on trial, it'll all come out," she said.

"I dunno about that. By the way, did you confront him about giving us bad survey data, like you said you were going to?"

"Yeah. He denied it. But now I don't believe him about that, either. They're all so ideological out here."

The shadow of a soycloud passed slowly over them. Mendoza said, "Do you ever feel like you're a long way from home?"

All the time, would have been Elfrida's honest answer, but it would have been a misleading one, because she felt like her real home was Venus. And it would probably be years before she got back there, if ever.

"Mendoza," she said, instead of answering. "What say we have a look for the workstation ourselves?"

"Whaaaat?"

"We've got the resources to do it. And like you said, we're not going to get much work done for a while, anyway."

"Well ..."

"Come on! It'll be fun."

ix.

When Elfrida said that they had the resources to look for the missing workstation, she was referring to UNVRP's dedicated comms satellite. They cleared their proposed search operation with their respective head offices before proceeding. Mendoza received a limp "Sure, go ahead" from his manager at UNVRP Analysis & Acquisition, 2.0 AU – 3.5 AU Region. Elfrida had been less confident of getting approval, and prepared to go ahead without it, but this turned out not to be necessary. Her supervisor at Space Corps HQ on UNLEOSS, the glossy-tressed Jake Onwego, said, "Yeah, OK. Sounds reasonable. Just, if you find the thing, you know. Grab the data. *Then* return it, yeah?"

"That's exactly what I was planning to do, sir," Elfrida said.

She watched Onwego watching a soccer game on his office computer for twenty-eight minutes.

"Good on ya," he said, with a big wink. "If those professors have been screwing us over, I want to be the first to know about it. Keep me in the loop, and remember to file your paperwork!"

"And on we go, and on we go," Elfrida hummed, breaking the connection.

"He's a total placeholder," said Mendoza.

"It wasn't always like this. What happened is our director, Dr. Abdullah Hasselblatter, wangled a seat on the President's Advisory Council. So he can't be bothered to actually run the Space Corps anymore. It's outrageous. Have you got the satellite reprogrammed yet?"

The UNVRP satellite's ion thrusters flared. Powered by molten salt batteries and an onboard solar array, it skimmed into a low equatorial orbit, which gave it a new view of the protoplanet.

Vesta was not spherical. Viewed from orbit, it looked like a giant human brain preserved in the cryogenic darkness of outer space. The resemblance was emphasized by the natural grooves that ran around its equator. These *graben,* carved by stresses from the primordial Rheasilvia impact, resembled the division between the brain's left and right hemispheres, corresponding here to the protoplanet's north and south hemispheres.

However, if this were a brain, it had been augmented.

The longest of the graben had been extended so that its ends met up, circling the equator. And in that canyon ran a maglev track. The engine that ran on it was not a train. It was a rail launcher, the second largest in the solar system after Earth's mighty Baikonur Gun. Twice a week, it flung a load of liquid hydrogen into space, accelerating it towards Ceres, or Hygiea, or elsewhere in the solar system. (In fact, that was the vibration Elfrida had felt during the raid on the astrophysics lab; she had forgotten that a launch was scheduled for that night.)

The satellite glided over the hydrogen-rich regions around the equator. Pits pocked a wide belt north of the graben like data points on a scatter graph. Clouds of dust spread blobbily over the edges of these manmade craters. They teemed with hacking, jack-hammering bots. Elfrida remembered the D/S bots on 550363 Montego. *I have to get back there ASAP*, she thought guiltily.

Gliding further around Vesta's circumference, the satellite passed over the hydrogen refinery operated by Virgin Resources, the owner of the mining bots, a subsidiary of Virgin Atomic. Waves of heat and gas radiated into space. Etched in dayglo orange and white, the refinery looked like an abacus in the middle of a complicated sum. Cylindrical tanks nuzzled up against each other, while mechanical arms loaded apatite-rich rubble into the furnace. Mountains of slag shadowed the facility and the group of habs where the crew lived.

"That refinery's older than I am," Mendoza said disapprovingly.

"I'm sure it's safe."

"Unless the toilet rolls take it into their heads to pay a visit. They were detected near here a few years back, you know."

"Yeah, I remember. Star Force headed them off, for a change."

"They might even have been coming here."

Elfrida did not want to talk about the PLAN. "What's your point?"

"Just that Virgin Atomic can't be making much of a profit. It's less efficient to refine hydrogen from mineral ores than to suck it out of the atmosphere on Titan. Back when they started up here, people still thought there might be life on Titan. VA's management must've gambled that full-scale atmospheric mining would never happen. But now ..." Mendoza shrugged.

"VA's still got the advantage of a location closer to the inner system. And the rail launcher must have paid for itself by now."

"I know. I'm not saying they've got no competitive advantages. Just that their margins have got to be hurting. And when the supermajors finally scale up their technology for scooping H2 out of the atmospheres of Neptune and Uranus ..." Mendoza's teeth gleamed in the light from his screen. "Look out."

"Why, Mendoza, you almost sound like you're gloating."

"Virgin Atomic sponsors U-Vesta. We've got them to thank for this place."

"Point," Elfrida acknowledged.

Rain stippled the window film. A soycloud hung low overhead, drenching the university campus in shadow and water. The soyclouds irrigated themselves by lowering tubes into Olbers Lake. They then shifted position so that the runoff dripped out of their spongy undersides onto the trees and grass below. Elfrida believed this 'rain' had to be contaminated with fertilizer chemicals, but the locals walked through it without a care. The system, anyway, was ingenious. And as Mendoza said, it would not exist if not for Virgin Atomic, which had provided the seed money for the Bellicia ecohood, and continued to kick in big donations. The problem with it was more fundamental, philosophical even. Who came all the way to the asteroid belt to get *rained* on?

The spaceborn, Elfrida supposed. People had very different ideas of utopia. Hers was, well, less wet.

She swivelled her ergoform back to face Mendoza's screen. The refinery glided towards the edge of the satellite's optical sensor field. "I thought the thieves might have taken the workstation out to the mines, to hide it," she said. "Except it looks like they didn't, huh?"

The premise of their search was simple. They assumed that if the workstation wasn't busted up beyond repair, it would be in communication with something, somewhere. To get the data out of it, the thieves would have to turn it on. Lacking the rat's nest of secure cabling in the STEM building, they'd have to interface with it wirelessly. The comms satellite would be able to pick up those signals.

So far, however, not a bleep. All the satellite had detected was normal radio traffic between the mining facilities.

"It doesn't really make sense that they'd have taken it out to the mines, anyway," Mendoza said. "I can see the STEM guys having connections out there. Not the Humanities gang. Don't they basically oppose everything Virgin Atomic stands for?"

"You mean, like funding for their programs?"

"*Ba-da-boom.* Yeah. But still."

"Yeah. Actually, I know Dr. James has connections in the

VA R&D division, what's it called? The de Grey Institute. He went out there last week to talk to someone, I think about the Big Dig."

The Big Dig was Virgin Atomic's bid for immortality. As its name suggested, it was a hole bored down into the crust of Vesta, eventually to reach the protoplanet's center. What exactly it would be good for, Elfrida wasn't sure. Most people dismissed it as a PR stunt. If it was one, however, it had fallen flat. Interest had died down during the project's slow progress, and Elfrida rarely heard anyone at the university mention it. On the other hand, Dr. James served in some kind of advisory capacity to VA's R&D team, so he at least must believe the project had some scientific value.

"Maybe they dropped the workstation into the Big Dig," Mendoza said.

"And maybe they'll drop us down after it if we get too close to ... the ... scandalous... truth. *Sinister music!*" Elfrida wiggled her arms as if conducting an invisible orchestra.

"You *are* feeling better, aren't you?"

"No," Elfrida said, instantly selfconscious. "I just had one too many shots in my coffee this morning."

"You should keep doing that."

The satellite glided onwards, following the maglev track into darkness. On the far side of Vesta from the Bellicia ecohood, the gigantic Rheasilvia Crater dominated the southern hemisphere. Lights winked in the bottom of the basin, near Rheasilvia Mons, the highest known peak in the solar system.

"Wanna go look at the Big Dig?" Mendoza said, pointing at the lights.

The Big Dig was in the bottom of the Rheasilvia Crater. The location put it that much closer to the middle of Vesta. The digging operation also harvested heavy metals exposed by the long-ago impact. For all Elfrida knew, that might be the actual purpose of the project, the 'journey to the center of the world' business so much PR fluff.

"Sure, why not?"

Data flowed across Mendoza's second screen. Elfrida watched it while Mendoza issued new instructions to the satellite, subvocalizing and air-typing at the same time. Mendoza had the standard data-jock's augments: a BCI (Brain-Computer Interface) and EEG crystals for wireless transmissions. Elfrida had neither of the above. She'd just never gotten around to it. But she did have an unaugmented ability to spot patterns. Search was one of her strengths. She let her mind slip into a half-focused, half-dreaming state of awareness, scanning for any clue in those clumps of red and green figures, anything at all ...

"Here we go," Mendoza said.

The rail launcher slid into view, like a skeleton leaf fallen on the maglev track. It presently had no hydrogen tanks aboard, and was cruising around the equator at a modest pace of about 500 kph. The stem of the leaf was an articulated string of carriages, like a real train. They looked tiny, but they weren't. Elfrida had heard they had spin gravity in there, for the Very Important Scientists at the de Grey Institute to enjoy.

The density of the data traffic increased. The train was communicating with the Virgin Atomic hardware in orbit, which retrieved empty tanks on their return journey and parachuted them back to the surface.

The UNVRP satellite veered away from the maglev track, puttering out over the Rheasilvia Crater. Below, all was dark. The bright, irregular line of the crater's rim stood out against the stars.

"Someone's bouncing radar off of us," Mendoza said.

The data flow speeded up.

"XX communications satellite located at the stated coordinates. Supply identification and orbit plan immediately. Repeat, supply your identification and orbit plan immediately."

"I'm telling them who we are," Mendoza said. Half a second later he exclaimed, "They're targeting us!"

"Go back," Elfrida said. "Go back to where we were! I saw something!"

Data choked the screen, the satellite reporting a cascade of incoming radar pings.

"Holy shit," Mendoza yelped.

"XX UNVRP communications satellite. Return to your designated orbit. This is a restricted area. Return to your designated orbit. You have ten seconds to comply. If you do not comply, area-exclusion measures will be implemented. Repeat ..."

"OK! OK!" Mendoza yelled. "We're leaving!"

The satellite maxed out its thrust capacity and engaged its reaction wheels. It was impossible for a body in orbit to turn tail, but the satellite very nearly managed an acute angle.

"Don't shoot! I'm thrusting as hard as I can!"

The satellite hustled across the top of the Rheasilvia crater, while simultaneously gaining altitude, and waltzed back into the feeble brilliance of Vesta's day.

Elfrida regarded Mendoza, who was slumping in his ergoform, his forehead glistening with sweat. "Y'know, that sounded kind of salacious," she said.

"What? Oh. *Snigger.*" Mendoza eked out a smile. "That was freaking scary."

"Who was it?"

"Let's find out." Mendoza scrolled back. "It was Virgin Atomic's orbital gun platform."

"They have an orbital gun platform?"

"You didn't know that? Sure. They're not gonna leave a surface mining operation completely undefended, waiting for the PLAN to come and take a chunk out of it."

"Yeah, but ..." Elfrida shook her head. "Were they really going to shoot us down?"

"I don't know." Their eyes met. "Maybe," Mendoza said. "That shit sounded like it was fully automatic."

"That's dangerous!"

"You're telling me. Well, maybe there's a guy on the surface, monitoring it when he's not busy vidding porn flicks. Anyway, we got away fast enough to satisfy its exclusion parameters, thank dog."

"How ... if we went back, how close do you think we could get before it glommed onto us again?"

"It first pinged us when we were *here*," Mendoza pinpointed a spot near the edge of the Rheasilvia crater, "maneuvering 400 kilometers up. That's a lot lower than our designated orbit. That's probably what set it off. But regardless, I'm not taking the sat anywhere near there again. No way, no how."

"Oh, Mendoza! Come on!"

"There's obviously something in the Rheasilvia Crater they don't want us to see. Maybe it's something to do with the Big Dig. Maybe it's something to do with the missing workstation. Maybe this is just what private-sector information security looks like these days. Either way, if we get the satellite shot down, regardless of whether we had authorization for the search, our jobs are toast. Do you know how much those babies retail for?"

"I got a whole space station shot down once," Elfrida said. "And I'm still here."

After a pause, Mendoza said, "Yeah, but that wasn't your fault. I heard about the astrodata leak. But it wasn't you. It was your phavatar."

"And I should have figured out what the phavatar was up to." Elfrida shook her head. "Never mind. What I wanted to say was, couldn't we just go back and look at the maglev again?"

"The rail launcher?"

"Or the actual train bit."

"Why?"

"I saw something in the traffic from its comms." She had found it again while they were talking. "Here. Look. This signal."

"What about it? It's encrypted to hell and back, but that doesn't necessarily mean anything."

It means they learned their lesson from last time, Elfrida thought.

"Not the signal itself. The destination. They had their antenna pointed towards Gap 2.5."

The Kirkwood Gaps were regions in the asteroid belt which had been swept clear of asteroids by Jupiter's gravitational influence. Viewed in a 2D starchart, hey looked like narrow stripes on a furiously spinning top. There were five pronounced Gaps, with radii of between 2.06 and 3.27 AUs. Vesta's orbit would bite into Gap 2.5 at aphelion, when it reached its greatest distance from the sun.

Eighteen months ago, at the height of the 11073 Galapagos affair, Elfrida's stross-class phavatar had pumped out a stream of unauthorized reports addressed to someone lurking on an isolated rock in Gap 2.5. The name of that rock was 99984 Ravilious.

Elfrida had learned these facts with military trace and decryption tools, which she wasn't supposed to be using, and no longer had access to. The results of her search had been passed on to Star Force. She had assumed that whoever or whatever was on 99984 Ravilious, they'd been taken care of. There hadn't been anything about it on the news. But then again, there wouldn't have been.

But what if, for some reason, 99984 Ravilious had slipped through Star Force's fingers?

Political considerations could screw up the simplest things. Even if a given action seemed like a no-brainer, there was sure to be someone on Earth arguing against it. Star

Force answered to the Select Security Council, and the SSC could be influenced by the President's Advisory Council. Which was now adorned by the presence of Dr. Abdullah Hasselblatter, the director of the Space Corps, and the man with the most to lose if the truth about the 11073 Galapagos incident ever came out.

"Sounds to me," Mendoza said, "like you're getting pretty far ahead of the evidence."

"You're right," Elfrida said humbly. "You're absolutely right. I *don't* want to jump to conclusions." She bit a knuckle and tasted earth.

They were standing outside the STEM building, in the rain. Elfrida had insisted on leaving their office to talk in the open, on the off chance that—as Mendoza frequently joked—their office was bugged. Of course, if their office was bugged, the whole habitat was probably bugged. But the splashing of the rain, and the gurgle of water flowing down the gutters, would help to foil any hidden microphones.

"You already have jumped to conclusions," Mendoza said. "I'm not saying you're wrong. You might be right. But what do we actually have? One signal from the VA maglev to a location that may be in Gap 2.5, or may be on the far side of it, where this mysterious asteroid may or may not be now."

"I agree it's not much to go on. But I remember that 99984 Ravilious was near Vesta. That was eighteen months ago, but it was near *enough* that it should have a similar orbital period. So I bet you it's still within signalling range. I mean, it's not gonna be on the other side of the sun, or anything. And there's one more thing."

"What?"

"That was a direct signal."

"True."

"That's why it jumped out at me. They usually use the Net-band and route everything through their comms satellites. Right? Most everything coming out of the train was

Net-band traffic. But this was in the Ku-band."

"15.5 GHz."

"Right. So I'm wondering why they chose to send this one signal at a different frequency, aimed at a totally different region of the sky, nowhere near any of the VA comms satellites. And I remembered 99984 Ravilious. And it just seems like too much of a coincidence."

Rain dripped down Elfrida's face. The soycloud parked overhead blocked the sunlight from the roof. They stood in a dark, watery microclimate. The fungi that grew at the bottoms of the walls of the STEM building were opening like primroses. What if the mysterious entity on 99984 Ravilious had somehow escaped *(been protected)* and was still out there? Up to its old tricks again. What data could it be receiving from Vesta?

She scowled up at the soycloud. Its underside was dark green, its rim pixellated with leaves. The water pattering onto her face definitely tasted like fertilizer.

"Wanna borrow my umbrella?" said Mendoza, who was standing under a large red one printed with the legend *BREATHING IS FOR WIMPS.*

"I'm all right. I mean, I'm wet already. I'll have to go home and change. But Mendoza, don't you think it's worth investigating?"

"If you're right, the people on the other end of that transmission have already caused kilodeath. And got away with it."

"I know! That's *why!* OK, it's probably not them, but I want to find out. I *need* to find out. Mendoza, what if the data they're transmitting is the same stuff that Dr. James is hiding? What if he's working for 99984 Ravilious? What if 4 Vesta is being *targeted?*"

Something struck her on the head. She screamed and clapped her hands to her scalp. A small shape landed on the path. It was a frog. It sat where it was for a moment, as if stunned, and then hopped off into the grass.

"Wow," Mendoza said. "Isn't that in the Bible? A rain of frogs. A plague of frogs. Something. I've never seen that happen before."

"Listen, Mendoza. You do what you like, but I'm going to follow this up as far as I can. And if you breathe a word, I will personally make you regret it. I may not be connected, but I have got resources on Earth."

"Whoa! Hold on a minute! I never said I was against it. Are you kidding? *I'm* going to investigate this thing, and you can come along for the ride, or not, as you like."

Elfrida started to smile in relief, but Mendoza, uncharacteristically, wasn't smiling. His face wore a peaky, fixed expression. She realized that she didn't know anything about him, only that he worked all the hours dog sent, and enjoyed—an unlikely hobby—classical music.

"I've never mentioned this, but my sister got whacked by the PLAN. She worked for a trading company. Crew. They were docked at a legit settlement on the asteroid 470108 Gironda, delivering a cargo of consumables, when the PLAN hit the rock. Everyone killed."

"Oh my dog. I remember that."

"The settlers were Spanish nationalists. Catalan, or something. They were asking for it. But my sister was just in the wrong place at the wrong time. So I totally sympathize with anyone that's had that experience. And I have no sympathy at all for anyone that's enabled the PLAN, or might be cooperating with them."

"Well, I don't think there was ever any suggestion of *that*," Elfrida said nervously. "It was more that the people on 99984 Ravilious, whoever they are, screwed up."

"That's just as bad. They need to pay."

Elfrida hesitated. She had never known Mendoza had such a magmatic layer to his personality. The rain started to ease off. She heard an odd chirruping sound and realized it was frogs, lots of them.

"I think the workstation might actually be on the train," she said. "The passenger compartment's rad-shielded, so we wouldn't have detected any wireless signals within the shielding."

"Or it might be in Rheasilvia Crater."

"Either way, if we can't take the satellite back there without it getting slagged..."

"Then," Mendoza said, "I guess we're gonna find out how that orbital gun platform feels about people trekking in on foot."

"Well, that's one idea," Elfrida said, thinking, *Oh my dog, Mendoza, you mean it, don't you?* And he looked so harmless and geeky under his joke umbrella. "But I have another idea that might be, uh, less death-defying."

"What?"

"We're not the only ones who would like to get that workstation back. So why are we doing this alone?"

X.

Dr. James had been incarcerated, pending his bail hearing, at the koban downtown. Constructed, or rather grown, on the same organic substrate as the permanent buildings of the university, the koban had not been tended with the same fanatical care. It looked like an overgrown mop-head abandoned on a corner between taller, neater buildings. Tendrils of its green curtain crawled across the sidewalks. Higher up, the greenery twitched.

"We're here to see Dr. James," Elfrida said. "We're from UNVRP," she explained.

"Yeah, I know." The UNESCO peacekeeper on duty stared at her and Mendoza. His stare telegraphed the uniquely implacable hostility that throve between UN agencies. "What do you want?"

"Well, we work with him," Elfrida said, wishing Mendoza would help her out.

"And?"

"And we want to talk to him."

"He's been charged with aggravated assault."

"I know, but—"

A cloud of peacock-green and lemon-yellow twirled in from the street, as light and bright as a tropical bird. It was Cydney.

"Ellie!"

"What are you doing here?"

"I've just come to visit Dr. James. *Snerk!*" Cydney beamed a smile at the peacekeeper on duty. "What about you?"

"We were hoping to do the same thing," Elfrida said.

Two minutes later they were being ushered up to Dr. James's cell. As they scrambled / bounced up the zipshaft, someone else came zooming down. She was a large person, so large in fact that she bulged out of her lane and nearly knocked Elfrida off her wimp handle. Without apologizing, she landed bent-kneed at the bottom of the shaft and scuttled away.

Elfrida frowned after her. "Hey ..."

"That was incredibly rude!" Cydney shouted after the woman.

"No, it's not that. I know I know her, but I can't place her."

"Maybe you've seen her around the STEM building. She'd be hard to miss."

"Yeah, maybe."

"In here," said the peacekeeper, while he operated an iris scanner and a DNA reader embedded in the wall. "I'll have to lock you in with the suspect, if you don't mind."

"Oh, don't lock me in," Cydney said. "I'm not staying. I just came to drop off this care package. Ta-daah!" She brandished a bunch of carnations in the face of the palely hovering Dr. James. "These are from your friends in the dean's office. And these are from Dean Garcia herself. Home-baked! I must dash. I've got a seminar, but it's great to see that you're holding up so well! That'll be a load off people's minds."

She breezed off. The door closed behind Elfrida and Mendoza.

"Flowers," Dr. James said morosely. "The last thing anyone needs in this place."

Elfrida made sympathetic noises. Now she was face to face with Dr. James, her suspicions seemed excessively paranoid. He *couldn't* be working for the mysterious entity on 99984 Ravilious. But that didn't mean he was innocent ...

"They mean well, I suppose. I was surprised to see your friend. She's in PHCTBS Studies, isn't she?"

"She's got a good heart," Elfrida said, hoping this was the real explanation for Cydney's flying visit.

The cell was about two meters square. Roots poked through the inside of its slimy walls, rotting for want of care. There was a fetid organic smell. Water pooled in a corner of the floor, which was not level. Dr. James squatted on his prostheses. "I'd offer you a seat," he said, "but there isn't one." He opened the box of cookies Cydney had brought. "White chocolate chip and macadamia nut. Home-baked, she said."

Mendoza, speaking for the first time, said, "I'd steer clear of those."

"You may be right," Dr. James said. "I wasn't aware I had any friends in the dean's office. It's astrophysics that justifies the existence of this university, but the administration is caught in a trap of moral equivalence that compels them to stiff us in favor of disciplines that don't deserve the name. I'll be very surprised if anyone testifies in my defense. Thank dog for Virgin Atomic: they've lent me a lawyer who's supposed to be bloody good. He's en route from Ganymede as we speak."

Elfrida raised an eyebrow at Mendoza. Then she held up the bag she was carrying. "Well, it isn't home-baked, but we brought coffee. The barista at the Virgin Café said you usually get a triple full-fat macchiato. I don't know if you're interested, but ..."

"Give me that," Dr. James said.

Some moments of devoted slurping later, Elfrida said, "Uh, we actually came to ask a favor."

"I knew it."

"I might be wrong, but doesn't the astrophysics lab have a surface rover?"

Cydney Blaisze zoomed up the zipshaft of the Tariq L. Clinton administration building, hugging to herself the pleasure of a good deed done. Poor Dr. James! He might be misguided, he might even be a criminal, but he didn't deserve to be locked up like a—like a—well, you wouldn't even treat an animal like that. Like a *virus*, a dangerous virus that needed to be quarantined.

She was well aware that that was just how her friends in PHCTBS Studies saw him.

But Cydney, while sympathizing with their grievances against the STEM department, did not think they really understood the conflict they were involved in, much less what was at stake.

She wasn't sure of the stakes herself, either.

But now, at last, she was getting close. She knew it.

And she had methods that were far superior to theirs. Masks and pellet guns in the dead of night? *Honestly.*

She bounced into the dean's office and displayed her empty hands to the dean's secretary. "Mission accomplished! He was *so* touched. He said he's incredibly grateful for the support of the faculty."

"Like him or loathe him, Eliezer James is one of ours," said Dean Garcia, coming out of her office. She was a thin, silver-bunned woman, clad in a greyish-green kaftan that she'd probably hand-woven from the excretions of gengineered caterpillars that lived in the walls of her yurt. Or something. Despite her lack of fashion sense, she managed the difficult trick of projecting authority while being spaceborn, her long and emaciated body crooked over at the shoulders like a predatory insect. "It's extremely important at this time of crisis," she pronounced, "to emphasize that the university community stands shoulder to shoulder against the arbitrary excesses of law enforcement."

"Ma'am, you should see the cell they've got him in," Cydney said. "It's tragic."

The secretary said, "Ma'am, I just wanted to remind you that you've got a lunch appointment with the UNESCO prosecutor. Would you like me to postpone, or …"

"Is that the time? Doggy goodness! Call down to the

telepresence center and have them set up a private cubicle straight away." Garcia grimaced at Cydney. "I shun UNESCO on principle, but this is my one opportunity to argue for a condign, not punitive, settlement. It would only exacerbate tensions if Dr. James were seen to be a victim of prosecutorial bias."

Translation, Cydney thought, *you've remembered that Dr. James is the biggest star on your faculty.* "Absolutely, ma'am," she said. "I totally agree. Fairness must be our watchword. I think we all agree on that."

Cydney had wormed her way into the dean's good graces by presenting herself as an informal spokeswoman for the Humanities students in the wake of David Reid's shooting. But this was only the latest, opportunistic twist in a campaign that had started upon her arrival on Vesta, when she'd presented her credentials to Dean Garcia and hinted that her enrollment at U-Vesta might lead to favorable media coverage. Not that she'd delivered very impressively on that promise. Her feed had been sliding down the rankings. People just weren't interested in the goings-on at a podunk university in the asteroid belt.

That, Cydney believed, was about to change.

Garcia flapped around, using the surface of a Greenpeace Good Governance award as a mirror to apply lipstick. "I don't know why I'm bothering with this," she said. "It's a telepresence session, after all. Speaking of which—" she turned to her secretary. "If this lasts the scheduled three hours, I'm going to get hungry. Order me a sandwich. Something I can gnaw on during the latency periods, while my phavatar in Geneva stuffs its plastic gullet with filet mignon and asperges aux sauce polonaise. Don't you think that remotely experiencing a fine meal is torture?" she asked Cydney, as one (she thought) who moved in circles where that was a thing.

"It's the absolute worst, ma'am."

"Ma'am, shall I ring down to the cafeteria, or—"

"No! I can't abide so-called sandwiches in pouches. Get me a ham and swiss on rye from Reuben's."

"Ma'am, they don't take online orders." This was a posture adopted by many of the earthier businesses in Bellicia.

"Then go get it, darling, go get it. That's why evolution gave you legs."

"I'll go," Cydney volunteered.

"Not necessary. Jordan needs the exercise."

Cydney waited a few more minutes. As Dean Garcia prepared to sweep out the door, Cydney said, "I actually wanted to tell you a little more about my visit with Dr. James." This was pure invention, as her visit with Dr. James had been all of twenty seconds long. "If you have a few minutes this SecondLight, or ...?"

"Do I? Do I? I don't know. Wait here and ask Jordan what my schedule looks like. I must go."

Garcia sailed out.

Left alone in the office, Cydney mentally pumped her fist in the air. She'd been waiting *months* for a chance like this.

She now had to move fast. Jordan would be gone awhile, considering the usual length of the lines at Reuben's, but someone else could come in at any minute.

Cydney wandered across the room, crossing behind Jordan's desk. As she'd hoped, the resent-ridden and wilfully incompetent secretary had left zis computer on, administrative-level database access enabled. Cydney couldn't touch the machine without the risk that hidden surveillance cameras would see her, but she didn't need to. Wifi was *so* insecure.

Using her BCI, she sent a single command to the calendar program running on the computer. If it were even noticed, it would look like a misvocalized entry. In fact, it was a zipped data scraper program. Within milliseconds, it unzipped itself and wriggled away into the bowels of the university's databanks, pretending to be Jordan.

Cydney permitted herself a sigh of satisfaction. But not a very large one. She wouldn't know until she got the results of the scrape, and analyzed them, whether she actually had anything or not.

She yawned. For the benefit of those theoretical hidden cameras, she pretended to admire the various vids of Dean Garcia meeting famous people which hung on the walls in handcrafted screen frames.

It was possible that she was on a wild goose chase.

But Cydney Blaisze had a nose for a story.

Always had had, even when she was just plain Cydney Blaise-without-a-Z, the daughter of a machine politician in a crappy little sub-Saharan microstate.

And she *knew* that the University of Vesta was hiding something big. Something downright illegal.

Something that could make a struggling curator's career.

Cydney received the scraper program's first report just a few minutes later, encoded and disguised as a letter from Student Services. She forwarded it to her data analysis team in Los Angeles.

"Hey," Jordan said, toppling into the office. "I've got her sandwich. Where is she?"

"In the telepresence center, I guess."

"*Expletives*," Jordan said. Ze wiped sweat out of zir long black beard. Zis breasts heaved. Jordan was a hermaphrodite. Ze stared balefully at Cydney. "Why don't you wear stabilizer braces? Your muscles will atrophy. You'll end up in an exoskeleton when you get back to Earth, you don't watch it."

"Got your package, Cyds," said a voice in her skull. "Unpacking it now."

"That's what surgery is for," Cydney smiled, on her way out the door. "Those braces totally ruin the line of your clothes. I'd much rather spend a week or two in rehab when

I get home."

"Fine if you've got the money for it, I guess."

"Exactly. *Snerk!* Toodle-oo."

"Aaaand analyzing. Get back to you in a few."

The voice belonged to Aidan Wahlsdorf, Cydney's top data miner. The back office of Cydney Blaisze Enterprises, Inc., was a grotty apartment in Los Angeles which her employees viewed as luxurious, no joke, because it had air conditioning. Some of them had moved their families in. She let them, and in return had earned their unwavering loyalty, even during this period when they must have been starting to wonder if she'd lost it, or packed it in, as her competitors were keen to insinuate.

Behind every successful curator stood a small army of data miners. The internet in the 23rd century was a cesspit. The sheer volume of malware and random crap infesting the solar system's servers had overwhelmed consumer-facing search technology as much as a century ago. As a result, people stuck to curated feeds, private databanks, and niche aggregators for their information needs.

That high-profile 0.01% of content providers—among whom Cydney still, barely, counted herself—got 99% of the system's traffic. But the other umpty-million petaflops of data were still out there, and those data weren't valueless, or meaningless. They were where the news came from—the *interesting* news, anyway. They just had to be mined.

Compared to that quotidian slog, analyzing the data stolen by Cydney's scraper program took Aidan and his team all of five minutes per packet. She skimmed the results as they came in, while she ate lunch, while she sat in her SecondLight seminar, while she hung out with the gang at the Virgin Café. And she grew increasingly disappointed. The records on the university's servers provided *no* evidence of illegal activity in the Rheasilvia crater, much less of the university's involvement.

The final slew of results came in as she was lying in the SecondDark gloom on her bed at home. This was the period corresponding to evening. Elfrida had joined her for a while, but was now in the other room, immersed in her everlasting Venus sim. The bed vibrated, massaging Cydney's muscles.

"This looks kinda interesting, Cyds. Not what you were looking for, but there's a whiff of malfeasance. Check the expenditures for the astrophysics lab."

Hope igniting, Cydney opened the attached file.

"See that item, quote, consultant fees, unquote? Eight thousand smackeroos. Enough to buy a small car, or a trip to Jupiter. They've been paying out a sum like that every month for fourteen months, going back to March 2286. And better yet, this Dr. Eliezer James character has signed off on the payments personally."

"Consultant fees," Cydney snorted joyfully. "That's the oldest scam in the book."

"He's either embezzling the university's moolah, with the connivance of the whole lab. Or they're being blackmailed."

"Blackmail!" Cydney whooped, jumping off the bed in mid-massage. "Now we're talking!"

"I said the university's moolah," continued Aidan's imperturbable voice, transmitted fourteen minutes ago from Earth. "But there's some doubt about that. If you look at the astrophysics lab's budget, there are some shady incoming payments, too. Also passed off as consulting fees. So pulling it all together, it may be that we're looking at a money laundering operation."

"Money laundering!" Cydney shrieked in ecstasy. "This is it! I'm gonna get him!" She stopped, remembering that Elfrida was in the other room. Elfrida wouldn't have heard her exclamations, immersed in her virtual farm, but ... "Babe?"

"However, there's another wrinkle: the incoming payments are bigger than the outgoing so-called consultant fees. But they're highly irregular. They only started coming in six months back. The department is in the red ..."

Cydney muted Aidan's voice. "Babe?" It would kind of suck if Elfrida had heard her gloating over Dr. James's impending downfall. The issue had caused enough friction between them already. "Babeee, time to come back to reeealiteee!"

She bounced into the other room.

Elfrida was not there.

Her stabilizer braces lay in a neat pile on the couch.

She had taken her immersion kit with her, Cydney irrelevantly noticed.

xi.

Elfrida panted up the last stage of the ramp to the airlock, her immersion kit in its case under her arm. She had left her stabilizer braces at home, the better to attempt the climb to the airlock—fifteen kilometers, most of it at a killer gradient. The Bremen Lock was tucked up under the roof of the habitat. Kilometers below, soyclouds drifted like spinach pancakes in a rusty frying-pan. From up here, it was terrifyingly obvious that the little green paradise of the Bellicia ecohood lay *at the bottom of a crater.*

Vertigo clawed at Elfrida, telling her she was going to fall off the road. Her exhalations soughed in her ears. She had taken one of the rebreather kits that were issued to everyone in the ecohood in case of emergency. It came in handy up here, where the air was Himalayan.

"Goto!" Mendoza shouted thinly. He stood at the entrance to the airlock, waving.

She labored up to him. The rover blinked its headlights.

"This looks pretty good," she said, when she could speak.

The rover sat on three fat wheels, like a cross between a tricycle and a humvee. It had an antenna dish on the roof and several appendages drooping from the chassis like a shrimp's feelers.

"I'm still amazed they let us borrow it."

"Yeah," Mendoza said, removing the mouthpiece of his rebreather to speak, and immediately plugging it back in again, as Elfrida had done. "But there's a catch."

"University politics," Elfrida said understandingly.

The rover actually belonged to the geology lab, not the astrophysics lab. In the past, Dr. James had told them, the geology folks had refused to let anyone else use it. But in the wake of the raid on the astrophysics lab, STEM solidarity had prevailed. The geology lab had acceded to Dr. James's plea that UNVRP be allowed to borrow the rover to search for the missing workstation.

However, as Mendoza said, there was always a catch.

"Do they want us to pick up some rock samples along the way, or something?"

"Not exactly."

The rover unfolded an ladder from its rump. They climbed up, through a cramped airlock with both ends open, into the even-more-cramped interior.

"Hi," said a skinny teenage girl with saucer-sized eyes, smiling shyly.

"Oh," Elfrida said. "I see." The girl was clinging to the interior roll bars like a monkey, her short skirt hanging down, revealing panties with hearts on them. "Who are you?"

"Rurumi-chan *dessuuu!*" the girl said. *"Hajimemashite!"*

Elfrida stiffened. She was half-Japanese, her father a pureblood who'd been born in Japan before the Mt. Fuji eruption. She spoke the language pretty well. But it offended her that this—this *bot*—should *assume* she did, and try to establish some kind of special connection with her on that basis.

She spoke in a growl. "Whoever the fuck you are. That. Isn't. Funny."

Mendoza said, "Chill, Goto. It's just a phavatar."

"I can see that."

The girl was a sub-geminoid phavatar. No one would mistake it for human. Its limbs were pencil-thin, its eyes took up half its face, its nose was a nub, and its mane of blue hair billowed like a living thing, tangling around Mendoza's fingers as he familiarized himself with the rover's controls. "Can you, like, put your hair up, or something?" he said to it.

"Sure!" Rurumi blinked appealingly at Elfrida. "Would you help me? I love your pigtails! They're so *kawaii!*"

Elfrida shouted into its face, "Hello, hello! Anyone home?"

"Bollocks," Rurumi said, in the same piping voice, but with a completely different intonation. "Yeah, hey there. Don't blow a gasket. Gregor Lovatsky, assistant professor, xeno-geology. This is Rurumi and she'll be your escort on this adventure. Notice I didn't say chaperone. She's just along for the ride."

Elfrida said to Mendoza, "That probably means she's authorized to take control of the rover if we get into trouble."

"How did you guess?" said Gregor Lovatsky, in Rurumi's shrill voice. "Yeah well, it is *our* rover. And we want to help out, but, y'know, you have got a reputation for recklessness, Ms. Goto."

"This isn't a reckless adventure," Elfrida said, still able to convince herself of that. Pretty much. "We're just going to look for the missing workstation. If we run into any trouble, we'll turn around and come home."

Mendoza bent his head to the controls.

"That's great," Lovatsky said. "But the phavatar's still going with you."

Ahead of the rover's slit-like windshield, the Bremen Lock wheezed open, its lips retracting into the road and the roof. The rover bumped into the airlock's chamber. Its engine was noiseless, battery-powered, but the cabin's air circulation made a loud whooshing noise when it started up. Elfrida took her rebreather off.

"Couldn't you have sent a different phavatar?" she said. "It's like, you're making fun of us here. Haven't you got anything that would be more suitable for surface exploration?"

"Rurumi's perfectly capable," Lovatsky said huffily. Then he admitted, "Anyway, we don't have another phavatar. Rurumi doesn't even belong to the lab. She's my personal property."

"Gotcha."

"Funding constraints."

"I hear you."

"Wheeee!" cried Rurumi, as the rover emerged onto the surface of Vesta.

★

Lights sparkled in the foothills of Bellicia Crater, limning the small spaceport that served Bellicia and the nearby Arruntia Crater. Elfrida had heard that Virgin Atomic was going to turn Arruntia Crater into another ecohood, but the project had never gotten off the ground.

Rurumi proved her worth by communicating with the spaceport's hub and asserting to its satisfaction that they were just geologists on a sampling expedition. Elfrida didn't say anything. Mendoza turned the rover towards the equator.

Tracks in the dust gave the impression of a road to follow, although Mendoza was navigating by satellite. The terrain of Vesta's northern hemisphere was hilly. In many places, where the top layer of dust had been disturbed, the regolith looked as slick as glass. It *was* glass—volcanic glass. Unlike other asteroids, Vesta had been resurfaced in the comparatively recent past—only about four billion years ago—by flows of basaltic magma. Since then, rotational rock slumping and impact-triggered seismic activity had caused many landslides, creating stair-step slopes that the rover had to bounce down, using its appendages as ski poles.

Elfrida was feeling car-sick by the time they stopped for the night. Day had dawned twice since they set out and now it was noon. The sun floated like a split pea in the blackness, winking occasionally when a satellite passed across it. Everything up there would have seen the rover by now. That was OK. They had a cover story: the sampling expedition.

What they didn't have was a tent. They'd brought EVA suits, but had opted to do without the inflatable shelter that the geologists used on longer expeditions. Mendoza curled up in the driver's seat. Elfrida decided to sleep outside. She struggled into one of the geology lab's EVA suits. Its mesh of shape-memory alloy snuggled around her body, providing an automatic customized fit. But in order to fit a range of body sizes, the suit had a pliable outer layer, not a hard shell, and rocks poked into her back all night long. The rim of the helmet also dug into the back of her neck. Micro-gravity was no panacea against physical discomfort. Lying awake, she stared up at the stars. The suit's GPS told her she happened to be looking in the direction of Gap 2.5.

Who—or *what*—was out there on 99984 Ravilious? Were they laughing, right now, at the feeble antics of Elfrida, and the Space Corps, and UNVRP, and Star Force, and everyone else who could have brought them to justice, but had failed to do so, through self-interest or the fear of bad publicity, or just because they thought someone else would take care of it?

(*That would be me*, she recognized miserably.)

Or were they not the sort of people who laughed at anything?

Were they, perhaps, not people at all?

Elfrida thought about Mars. Nowadays, a weird geometrical jungle of stone and iron defaced the planet's surface, photographed in bits and pieces over the decades by unmanned sats before they, inevitably, got fragged. Everyone in the system knew those pictures. But who—or *what*—populated the PLAN's strange cities? What unblinkingly watched Earth from those sky-piercing ziggurats, bathed in a blizzard of radiation?

Elfrida shuddered. She curled on her side and tried to get comfortable. After a while, she crawled under the rover and tried to sleep there.

"I am *not* doing this again," she said to Mendoza when enough time had passed that she could legitimately give up.

He looked wan. "Me neither. This seat is really uncomfortable."

"The ground isn't any better. Let's get moving."

Rurumi had spent most of their rest break running around on the surface, doing geology stuff. As the rover bounced into motion, she lodged herself in what seemed to be her favorite position—hanging upside-down by her knees from the roll bars—and sang to herself in Japanese. Elfrida shot her a look. If looks were made of ionized plasma, the phavatar would have been slagged.

Mendoza plucked Elfrida's sleeve, pulling her head towards his. "She came on to me," he whispered.

"What?"

"I'm not kidding. It was right after you went outside. She started rubbing up against me and uh, you know."

"Did you ...?"

"What do you take me for? I told her to get fragged, in no uncertain terms. Then I texted Lovatsky to keep his hands to himself. He said it was her, not him. I told him, if she tries for sex with every male she meets, you're not gonna have her for long."

"Damn straight. *Ew*, Mendoza."

"I know."

"Well, we won't have to bunk with her tonight, thank dog."

"I just hope these miners are as friendly as they're supposed to be."

Dr. James had gotten his lawyer to call ahead and alert Virgin Resources, the mining subsidiary of Virgin Atomic, to their arrival. Elfrida had been unsure about this, since she and Mendoza suspected that VA were complicit in the theft of the workstation. They'd be asking the miners for help in solving a crime they might have committed themselves. But Dr. James had pointed out that they wouldn't get far on the surface without VA's acquiescence. He had a point.

And as the rover sailed downhill towards the hydrogen refinery, Elfrida felt glad they'd taken Dr. James's advice. The cluster of habs, which had looked so shabby from outer space, projected a welcoming radius of light. A proper bed, a massage, a shower, and something to eat that didn't come out of a pouch, all sounded good to her right now.

They passed the refinery. Titanic handler bots flailed long arms against the stars. Rubble-haulers, arriving overland from the open pit mines, queued for unloading. With weirdly graceful movements, the handler bots tossed the nets of rubble into the feed chute of a giant autoclave. Tanks of liquefied hydrogen lined the siding where the launch cradle would park when it arrived. Each tank was the size of a three-storey building.

Mendoza got on the radio.

"C'mon in!" a male voice answered. "Yo, is Rurumi there?"

"Sure am!" chirped the phavatar. Elfrida and Mendoza exchanged a look.

"Can't wait to smooch ya, girl! 'Bout time you brought some friends to see us!"

The voice directed them to the electricity pumping station behind the habs, where they left the rover recharging its batteries. Wearing their borrowed EVA suits, they picked their way through a litter of rubble, scraps of microcable nets, and machine parts. Rurumi danced ahead of them, suitless.

She was embraced by a bulky figure standing in the door of the biggest hab, similarly suitless.

He waved to the two humans, and the same friendly voice as before crackled in their ears. "Yo there! Let's *paaartay!*"

"Oh brother," Mendoza said.

"I," Elfrida said, "am going to *kill* Dr. James."

The refinery was crewed by phavatars.

Susceptible, unlike phavatars, to weariness, the deleterious effects of micro-gravity, and sheer gloom, the two humans sat in a corner of the hab's central room, watching the bots do the Ganymede Fling to a soundtrack of what sounded like beluga whales mating with a bevy of thrash-metal guitarists. Rurumi twirled and somersaulted from one set of arms to the next. Few of the phavatars were as exquisite as she. Sub-geminoids with various custom tools fitted, they looked more like cyborgs than humanoids. However, they all disported themselves zealously. It was clear that their operators, wherever they were—Elfrida hadn't been able to get a straight answer to that question—were steadily getting drunk to the point of incapacity.

"Probably doing drugs, too," Mendoza said. "Look at that guy." The phavatar in question was trying to burrow into the wall of the hab with his head.

"It's a thing," Elfrida said. "Party hearty from the comfort of your sofa. Let your phavatar have all the fun, while you get the hangover. I don't understand it, personally."

"I wonder where the operators are."

"In orbit?"

"Maybe back in the Bellicia ecohood. Virgin Atomic's regional HQ is there in the middle of town."

"That's a possibility."

"Anyway, they must be close. Zero latency."

Had the operators been running their phavatars from any great distance, they'd have been crashing into each other left and right. Well, more than they were already. More tellingly, they interacted with the humans without any perceptible delay.

"C'mon, have a drink!" insisted the large male-styled phavatar who had greeted them. It looked like the vid star Marmaduke Shagg. "We mixed this fruit punch specially for you! Real ingredients!"

Elfrida accepted a pouch out of politeness, and to make Marmaduke go away. But then she asked on a whim, "Have you had any other human visitors recently?"

"Yo! None! That's why this is such a special occasion for us!"

"I was just wondering why you had real vodka and fruit juice on hand."

"Rurumi comes up here sometimes by herself. And when we're thusly honored by her presence, we like to give her a little pressie to take home with her! Courtesy of VA, dig?" Marmaduke winked, and wove back into the throng.

"Lovatsky, you dog," Mendoza said. "A luxury goods procurement scam. Guess holistically fermented mead with algae foam doesn't always do the trick, huh?"

"I'm not sure I believe that," Elfrida said. "I think maybe someone else *was* here recently, and brought their own merrymaking supplies." She tasted the contents of the pouch, and then closed it. "I don't care for thieves' leftovers."

"You think the workstation might really be here?"

"No." She floated to her feet. "Shall we go outside?"

They explained that they were going to retrieve their stuff from the rover, and crawled back into their EVA suits.

The silence of Elfrida's helmet was a relief after the deafening music. She said, "The thing is, realistically, the workstation could be anywhere by now. There's plenty of foot traffic back and forth from the Bellicia-Arruntia spaceport, and we don't have data on who's been going in and out. Only Facilities Management has that. The thieves could have put the workstation in a box, walked it down to the spaceport, and put it on a ship to anywhere in the solar system."

"You would hope the peacekeepers are investigating that angle," Mendoza said.

Elfrida sniffed. "Also, it might be at the bottom of Olbers Lake."

"Or in the recycling."

"Yeah. If it was so badly smashed up they couldn't get the data off it. But from what I saw, it wasn't totaled, just damaged. So we have to assume they took it somewhere to repair it. And now that I've seen these guys, I personally wouldn't trust them with my electronics."

Mendoza's faceplate tilted towards the refinery. If Vesta had had an atmosphere, the crash and slam of tonnes of rock being thrown around would have been deafening. As it was, the handler bots made a balletic, if violent, spectacle.

"I want to go look at Rheasilvia Crater," Mendoza said.

"*I* want to go look at the train."

They walked back to the rover and, by common consent, retrieved a couple of packaged meals. The prospect of getting anything real to eat out of the refinery crew had dwindled to a remote unlikelihood.

When they went back into the hab, the phavatars were having sex.

Metal and plastic bodies intertwined. Clothes drifted like autumn leaves across the floor. Chrome hips pumped, and stretchy rubber mouths gobbled at appendages that ...

Elfrida looked away, but not before she had spotted Rurumi at the center of the orgy, her tiny, fragile body being penetrated by Marmaduke and two other phavatars, while she, in turn—

"Uh, can we get out of here?" Elfrida said.

Mendoza was staring, open-mouthed. She elbowed him.

"Mendoza. C'mon. This is gross."

"Rurumi's got a dick."

"I saw. Let's vamoose."

"That one's got tentacles."

"I know. *Please,* let's go."

"Yeah, sure, OK."

They hadn't taken their EVA suits off, so there was no need to put them back on. As they retreated to the airlock, Marmaduke unplugged himself from the fray and bounded at them. "Guys! You're not going?"

"This isn't our kind of thing," Mendoza said.

"Oh, don't be a party pooper," Marmaduke cooed, stroking Mendoza's arm through his suit. "Look, FWIW, I'm a woman. My name's Sharlene. I'm watching you from the Vesta Express, and boy, you're so hot. You're totally turning me on. I'm as hard as hell. Look!" Marmaduke/Sharlene attempted to guide Mendoza's glove downwards.

Mendoza yanked his arm back. "I don't do men, I don't do women pretending to be men, I don't do phavatars, I don't do orgies, and let me see, what else? I don't do tentacle sex. I think that just about covers it."

"Where are you going?"

"Gonna sleep in the car."

"But we pressurized this hab just for you!" Marmaduke cried, sweeping an arm around the low-ceilinged, ribby-walled room. The hab would have been about as appealing as a cardboard box under a bridge, even if it had not currently been echoing to the sound of pornographic groans. "It took ages to get all the dust out!"

"Well, you can depressurize it again now," Mendoza said. "See you in the morning."

He joined Elfrida in the chamber of the airlock. As they plodded back towards the rover, Elfrida broke the silence. "Did you hear what she said? She was watching us from the Vesta Express. That must be what they call the train."

"Yeah, makes sense that's where the operators are. I heard they've got a real hab in the passenger compartment, with spin gravity."

"I heard that, too."

Silence fell again. They got into the rover and took off their EVA suits. Elfrida felt deeply embarrassed by what they'd just seen. She was searching for another topic when Mendoza said thoughtfully, "I'm kind of surprised ..."

"What?"

"Don't take this the wrong way, but I would have thought you'd go for it."

"You mean—me—with them? Dog! Mendoza! Don't you

know me at all?"

As she spoke, she remembered that no, he didn't really know her, and she didn't really know him, either.

"Like I said, sorry. I just had the impression that you're the free and easy type. It's interesting to know you're not like that." He hitched a shoulder. "Kind of good to know."

Elfrida wanted to ask how he'd got that impression. Was it because she lived with Cydney? How did that equate to *free and easy*? It was funny that he could have thought that of her, when she used to be considered the most uptight chick on Botticelli Station, and in fact, she still thought of herself that way. But she was too uncomfortable to probe the subject any further.

"Well, I'm glad you didn't go for it, either," she said. "Even though Rurumi is cute."

"She's a moe-class. They're designed to be cute. Would be cuter if she weren't a hermaphrodite, though. Ugh, Lovatsky! Talk about hidden ... *lengths*." Mendoza opened his meal pouch, squeezed, and sniffed. "Fettucine alfredo. I am not a fan. Oh well, it's calories."

Elfrida opened her own meal pouch. The picture of salmon meunière on the label did not bear much resemblance to the contents. "Dean Garcia's secretary is a hermaphrodite," she said.

"I know. There's a bunch of them running around campus. Probably because of the PHCTBS Studies program."

"That's what the H stands for."

"What's the rest of it, again? I always forget."

Elfrida ticked off on her fingers. "Phavatarism, Hermaphroditism, Cyborgism, Transhumanism, Bestialism, and Spaceborn Studies. I always think it must kind of irk the spaceborn to be lumped in there. Cydney thinks so, too."

"All those isms. It really is a hothouse of ideology out here."

Elfrida sucked on her drink pouch—iced tea; it didn't go

well with the salmon meuniere. Whoever stocked the rover must have tossed handfuls of pouches in without looking at the labels. "I know," she said. Her heart was pounding. This conversation was an order of magnitude more intimate than if they'd carried on talking about sex. "Remember you once said, do you ever feel like you're a long way from home? Well, that's when I do. When I'm around Cydney's friends. They've all got so many ... *ideas.*"

Mendoza nodded. Seated in the driver's couch, he twiddled the manual dial of the radio, meaninglessly—it wasn't on. "But you've worked in space before."

"Yeah, but I was on Botticelli Station, and before that I was on Luna, and that's a lot closer to Earth. Well, no, that wouldn't explain it. I don't know why this place is the way it is."

"I've got a theory about that," Mendoza said, still twiddling. He was doing it, she realized, as an excuse not to look at her. "It's because there's only seven UN people here, counting us."

"And the blue berets. But why would that make such a big difference?"

"They're not the ones who are different. We are."

"I don't get you. I don't think it's very different to be non-ideological."

Mendoza swung around and pointed at her. He had a strange, embarrassed smirk on his face. "But *you* work for the UN. And, can I ask you a question?"

"Sure."

"Do your parents work for the UN, too?"

"How did you know? My mom does. And actually, her mother did, too. And my grandfather on my father's side. *And* my paternal grandmother, although she was just a TS who worked part-time."

"See! You're a third-generation UN person. *TS,* trailing spouse. You even use the jargon."

"Well, what about you? Were your parents UN employees?"

"Nope. That's why I know the difference. I ..." Mendoza hesitated. She saw him overcome the internal barrier to revealing personal information. "I grew up in the Philippines. Nth-generation hapa pilipino prole. My dad wasn't around. My mom worked in corporate IT. She was pretty proud when I landed a UN apprenticeship, and then a job."

"Guess you followed in her footsteps, in a way," Elfrida said awkwardly. She never knew what to say when people revealed personal information. That was probably because it almost never happened outside of intimate relationships.

"No, I didn't. That's the point. I moved to a different universe. I went from taking it for granted that, just for instance, parents are optional, to a culture where it's almost weird if you don't have two parents. I bet your parents are married, even."

Tomoki Goto and Ingrid Haller were going to celebrate their 30th wedding anniversary this year. Elfrida was starting to feel vulnerable, picked-on. She realized that it was her own reference to her paternal grandparents that had made her feel that way, even though she hadn't revealed that they were purebloeded Japanese, survivors of the Mt. Fuji eruption. "Well, so what?" she said. "Everyone's allowed to make their own choices."

"Of course they are. That's not my point. I'm just saying, the UN is a bubble. It thinks it's the whole of humanity, but it isn't. It's stagnant, like the Austro-Hungarian Empire. It's even gone backwards. Again, I don't mean that in a bad way. But there hasn't been any social progress on Earth for centuries."

"Oh, come on! Just look at the way you never used to see phavatars in public, and now they're everywhere."

"Well, yeah, but I mean in general. There aren't any isms on Earth. Liberal technocracy won, the end. That's what people think. But the isms haven't gone away. They've just been pushed out to the periphery, to the places where the UN doesn't totally dominate. Like the Philippines."

The Philippines were only an affiliate of the UN, not a full member state, as were most countries within China's sphere of influence.

"Like the asteroids. Like Mercury. Like the Jovian moons. Like random little enclaves in space where people stay on-station for years because of corporate penny-pinching, and get all incestuous and weird," Mendoza went on relentlessly. "Like here."

"I don't think having phavatar orgies is an ism."

"Oh, what is it that the P in PHCTBS stands for, again?" Mendoza scoffed. Then he quieted. "Sorry. It's just a theory, anyway, based on what I've seen on the job."

Elfrida, as a Space Corps agent, had seen even more. She'd visited dozens of asteroid colonies with fringey, freaky cultures that would never survive on Earth. So what Mendoza said rang true. It was just that she'd never conceived of lifestyles as ideologies. Mendoza was implying that lifestyle and ideology were two sides of the same coin, if they weren't in fact the exact same thing. "I dunno," she said. "I'll have to think about it."

"You don't need to think about it," Mendoza said, and added something else in a mumble that she couldn't catch over the hum of the air circulation.

"What?"

"Nothing."

"No, go on, Mendoza, you said something."

"I said that you don't have to think about it if it disturbs your complacent worldview. But that wasn't fair. I know you're not complacent."

Upset, Elfrida lapsed into Space Corps-speak. "I just think that everyone has a right to make their own choices."

"Of course they do." Mendoza sighed. He stuffed his

empty meal pouch into the recycling compactor and folded his arms behind his head, as if making ready to sleep, although that would have been an uncomfortable position to sleep in.

"Well," Elfrida said after a moment that felt way too long. "So much for getting a shower, a good meal, and a good sleep at the refinery, huh? Here we are sleeping in the rover, eating pouch noodles again. And I really ought to apologize for the way I probably smell at this point."

"*Snigger*. You don't smell," said Mendoza, who had begun to smell a bit ripe himself. He opened one eye. "Goto."

"Yeah?"

"You just made me think."

"What?"

"I figure Rurumi's going to be busy for a while."

"Probably."

"And the rover's batteries are fully recharged."

Elfrida's heart started to pound again, for different reasons than before. "Mendoza, are you suggesting what I think you are?"

"I guess that scene in there must've really twisted us up. I can't believe we didn't think of it before."

"Ditch her and head for the Vesta Express?"

"Or for the Rheasilvia Crater."

"But what if she takes control of the rover remotely?"

"If this thing had remote control functionality, they wouldn't have needed to send her along in the first place." Mendoza slapped the dashboard. "It's not even smart. My desk is smarter."

"Then let's go," Elfrida said, bouncing gleefully. Her bounce carried her into the passenger seat.

"Lovatsky, your predilection for hermaphroditic sex has undone you," Mendoza said, hitting the button that disconnected the charging cable. "It's like, if you're into that kind of thing, man up and get the surgery. But hey. As you said,

Goto. Freedom of choice." The rover started to move. "The lesson he'll take from this, if he's got an IQ in the triple digits? There are good choices. And then there are dumb ones."

As the rover plunged into the Vestan night, Elfrida just hoped they weren't making one of the latter.

xii.

Cydney skipped her morning lecture and headed downtown, dressed in a mao jacket and microshorts that showed off her legs. (Critically, she noted that her legs were looking less toned these days. Oh well, there was always rehab.)

Her team's analysis of the data stolen by her scraper program had turned up some more nuggets. In addition to the evidence of money laundering, or possibly blackmail, related to the astrophysics lab, there was a fascinating sequence of emails involving the dean's office, the university's financial department, and an individual who worked at Virgin Atomic headquarters in downtown Bellicia.

The town, at the head of Olbers Lake, wasn't laid out on a sensible grid, but had grown organically into a sprawl of alleys defined by the odd shapes of the buildings. Cydney got lost, which was quite the feat in a town of no more than fifty thousand souls. She was no good at navigating without satellite guidance, which the Bellicia ecohood didn't offer, owing to the thickness of the roof. Delicious and dubious scents drifted from restaurants prepping for the lunchtime rush. Monkeys leapt up and down the faces of the green buildings. Cydney wondered if they tasted good.

She was warm from her walk by the time she reached VA headquarters, a low-slung green building with a lake view. The vegetable garden out front was the most ostentatious thing about the place.

"So why did you try to sell the Arruntia crater to a corporation based on Ganymede?" she said to Jay Macdonald, the CFO of Virgin Atomic.

Macdonald's round face turned a shade more rubicund. He hadn't been expecting that question. She had landed the interview on the pretext of doing a piece about soycloud technology development. But her curveball had clearly hit him square in the goolies.

"No comment, Ms. Blaisze," he said frostily.

"You should have known you'd run into opposition from the university. They don't want Christians moving in next door. It would degrade the cultural environment, and if VA had to provide life support for new colonists, it would divert important resources from U-Vesta's educational mission."

Cydney was quoting an email from Dean Garcia to the head of the U-Vesta financial department. Well, paraphrasing it. Garcia hadn't said *new colonists,* she'd said *a bunch of crazies who can't survive without hand-holding.* Of course, Garcia also had her own agenda.

"The university's had its eye on Arruntia for ages. They want to build a satellite campus there. Why'd you try to sell it out from under them?"

Macdonald exhaled pointedly. "Ms. Blaisze, I was under the impression that you wanted to interview me about Virgin Atomic's CSR policy."

Yeah, like that wouldn't lose me gigafans, Cydney thought. *Snooze-a-minute.* "I am," she said. *"Snerk!"* Beaming, she re-crossed her legs to give him a nice view. "Corporate social responsibility means consulting your biggest stakeholder before you build a new habitat next door, don't you think?"

"We did consult the university," Macdonald said. "The upshot was intense opposition to our proposal. Therefore, we dropped it. All this is a matter of public record."

"Yes, but—"

"Besides, it was five years ago. Why is this news now?"

"Because it *isn't* a matter of public record that your potential buyer at that time, the Haven Company, which was dissolved after its bid was rejected, was actually a front for another company called Five Dreams Incorporated, a venture capital outfit which is majority-owned by Empirical Solutions."

Cydney sat back, smiling, as Macdonald absorbed this

body blow. Empirical Solutions was a Chinese conglomerate. As bad as selling the Arruntia Crater to a supermajor would've been, from the university's point of view, selling it to a *Chinese* supermajor would be infinitely worse.

It wasn't that no one trusted the Chinese. They were equal partners with the UN in the peaceful exploitation of the solar system.

Except ... no one *did* trust them.

After the Mars Incident, when those AIs went rogue and slaughtered all the colonists on the Red Planet, it had been the People's Liberation Army Navy that went to investigate ... and never came back. What had come back in their stead was the PLAN.

So—even though it wasn't fair on ordinary Chinese companies that just wanted a good return on their investment—Jay Macdonald would *not* want it known that VA had been trying to sell a piece of Vestan real estate to them.

He was so red in the face now that Cydney hoped there was a medibot standing by. "Ms. Blaisze, I can neither confirm nor deny what you're saying, but if there is any truth to your remarks, that information would be confidential and protected by privacy law—"

"Oh no, it's not," Cydney said. "It's all there on the internet. You just have to dig for it."

Smiling, she sipped from the cup of sweet, milky tea that Macdonald had offered her before he knew why she was here. The teacups were special gadgets for use in microgee, with invisible lids that retracted at the approach of your lips.

"Ms. Blaisze, are you recording this conversation?"

"Oh, no," Cydney lied. "This is just a casual chat."

He peered closely at her, as if hoping to see whether her eyes were augmented. He was looking in the wrong place. Her microcamera was in her left earlobe, disguised as a pearl stud.

Macdonald's eyes were pale blue, watery with alarm.

Cydney suddenly felt sorry for him.

"Hey," she said gently. "I wouldn't vid you. I can see you're, you know. That. P'b'd." She gabbled the incorrect word, *pureblood*, trying not to hurt his feelings. "It would be unethical to put vid of you out there."

No pureblooded person ever wanted vid of them floating around, for the PLAN targeted purebloods with incomprehensible and relentless ferocity. It was highly unlikely they'd send a ninepack of toilet rolls to Vesta to hit one pureblooded corporate executive, through a 2-kilometer roof yet, but Cydney sympathized with the perpetual insecurity that all of Macdonald's ilk must feel. She'd get Aidan and the team to mosaic his face before she uploaded this interview to her feed.

He slumped, grabbed his teacup and drank. "Yes. I'm pureblooded. I can trace my ancestry back to the sixteenth century. *Dh'aindeoin co theireadh e!*"

Cydney smiled uncomprehendingly.

"I appreciate your consideration, Ms. Blaisze. However—" the pale blue gaze suddenly hardened— "it appears you *are* recording."

"Not!" Cydney yelped.

Macdonald made a complicated gesture at his computer screen and then flipped it around so she could see. It displayed a systems monitoring suite, which showed all the electronics currently drawing current in Macdonald's office. There was Cydney's BCI, powered by a glucose fuel cell. And there was her microcamera, piezoelectrically powered by her own movements.

"All right, I'm turning it off," she said. *Curses.* Well, she'd already got the essential clip of Macdonald denying everything. "There! I wasn't going to use that, anyway."

"Glib i the tung is aye glaikit at the hert," Macdonald said dryly.

"Eh?"

"Given your profession, you ought to be aware that it's illegal to transport any data off these premises that you didn't have when you came in."

"Fine! I'll wipe it." He wouldn't be able to tell.

"We'll have to confirm that."

"You'll have to take my word for it," Cydney responded smartly. She knew her privacy law. The inside of someone's head was their territory, period. And earlobes counted.

"We'd prefer to run a scan," Macdonald said. "Metadata only, of course."

"No! I refuse."

Macdonald's eyes widened in their pouches of puffy skin. He was looking at his screen. "Well, well," he said.

"I'm leaving," Cydney said, jumping up. "Thanks for your time."

"Just a moment, Ms. Blaisze. It looks as if you've got some rather ... unusual programs stashed in there."

"You have been scanning me!" Cydney shot a glance around the deluxe executive office. Given that Macdonald was not in the best of health, it made sense that there'd be a telemetry monitor running in here. If he had a cardiac implant or something, the monitor would also have the ability to read electronic data wirelessly. But she hadn't thought they would have the gonads to run a scan on her, after she'd explicitly refused permission. "That's illegal!"

"So is that data scraper program of yours."

"Not if I don't do anything with it." Why was she even arguing with him? She bounced across the office towards the door.

"Ms. Blaisze, please, one moment! We'll have to confirm that you haven't in fact infiltrated our network."

The truth was that she'd given it a try during their conversation, but as she might have expected, VA had better security than the U-Vesta dean's office. Her scraper program had bounced off their wireless signal encryption. "I've got a reputation to protect. I wouldn't do anything illegal," she said with dignity. "Unlike some people." She reached the door.

With a piercing hiss, a security phavatar thudded into the room and blocked her way. It was humanoid, in the sense that a mountain gorilla was humanoid. It kind of *looked* like a mountain gorilla. Seven feet tall. In a red overall with the VA logo on its chest. And a PEPgun in one hairy fist.

Cydney stood her ground, trembling. "I've faced charging hippos and elephants," she said. "They were a lot scarier than you. I'm the daughter of a Xhosa chieftain. Those elephants? We ate their testicles."

Macdonald looked up from his screen. "Elephants don't have solid-state non-lethal laser weapons," he pointed out.

Cydney swallowed.

The PEPgun, beloved of law enforcement and peacekeeping personnel, was non-lethal, all right. It used a laser-generated plasma pulse to cause pain so intense that people swallowed their own tongues just to make it stop.

The security phavatar maneuvered towards her, pneumatic thrusters hissing.

"If you mess with me, you'll be sorry! I've got a feed with seven million registered viewers!"

"Only four million six hundred thousand and eighty-nine, now," Macdonald said. "Your relocation to Vesta seems to have cost you a lot of fans. I don't blame them. This place is boring. And we hope to keep it that way, despite the best efforts of your friends at the university."

"Well, that'll change when I splash your corporate misdeeds all over the solar system!" Cydney said, still backing up. She managed a weak *"Snerk,"* and then flung herself out of the window.

"They threatened me." Cydney clutched handfuls of Big Bjorn's fur. Her wet cheek rested on his lap. She was crying.

"He c-c-called security. It was this big ugly phavatar with a PEPgun. It was going to s-s-*shoot* me/"

"It's OK," Bjorn said, patting her back. "It's OK."

"But I called their bluff. I mean, they didn't have any right to detain me! So I tried to get past it. And it g-g-grabbed me and *threw* me out of the window!"

That wasn't quite what had happened. But Cydney didn't want to admit that she'd jumped out the window in a panic.

"You should sue them!" said Shoshanna.

That made Cydney stop crying. "I don't think so. I couldn't bear to relive the experience." She was pretty sure that Virgin Atomic wouldn't go after her. After all, she *hadn't* infiltrated their network. But if she sued, they'd make an issue out of her data scraper program. Everyone knew that curators used gray-zone tools to get the news. The trick was not getting caught. If you did get caught, it was game over.

Besides, if VA released vid of her self-defenestration, she'd never be able to hold up her head again.

She sat up, dabbing at her dirty knees through the rips in her thermal tights. She'd landed in the vegetable garden. That had been the worst part of the whole experience: doing a swan dive into the carrots, hurting her knees, and then fleeing on foot while everyone stared at her.

She'd come straight to Big Bjorn's place, knowing she would find at least some of the gang here. Since the raid, they'd abandoned what they had pompously called their 'safe house,' a.k.a. David Reid's pad. Now they gathered at Bjorn's place, halfway up a micro-gee-adapted hickory tree in the hills behind the Branson Habs.

Bjorn's treehouse, built by Bjorn himself, was one of the coziest places Cydney had ever been in. Rain plinked on the sheet metal roof, but did not find its way through the splarted seams. The walls were rustic mosaics of scrap, which you could (especially if you were vaping dope) get lost in for hours. Bjorn believed in bricolage as a more humane alternative to recycling. He had carried off ergoforms from here and there, disabled their smart functionality, and crafted the resulting blocks of polyfoam into sprawlchairs with hand-carpentered wooden frames. The only drawback of his home was that it was not heated. But Bjorn's own fur was warm and thick enough that Cydney felt as if she were snuggling up with a blanket.

She leaned against him, sniffling and wiping her eyes,. "I just wanted to find out if Virgin Atomic was involved with the James clique," she said, referring to the astrophysics lab the way her friends did.

"Of course they are!" said Shoshanna. A spiky woman with green hair, Shoshanna believed that being spaceborn made you both special and smart. In her own case, she was wrong on both counts, Cydney thought. But Shoshanna's boundless self-confidence had enabled her to step into the role of leader when David Reid was hospitalized. "They're neck-deep in it with Dr. James! Whatever *it* is."

"And I thought that now they might be ready to distance themselves from him," Cydney said. "I might have gotten a few clues about their Seekrit Project."

"Well, did you?" Shoshanna said.

"I said I *might* have. I didn't. Because they *threatened* me and then *threw* me out of a *window!*"

"Don't cry," Bjorn pleaded.

Cydney took a deep breath and squared her shoulders. "Well, now we know they've definitely got something to hide." And that inference could just as well be made from the real sequence of events at VA headquarters as from her edited version of them.

"Metalfucking Seekrit Project," Shoshanna said, her sharp chin in her hands, one skinny leg kicking rhythmically. "What kind of scam requires round-the-clock use of Ali Baba, and information security so tight that they don't even back their data up on the university servers?"

"Hey," said Win Khin, who was a sleek, androgynous phavatar. He kept his flesh-and-blood self in one of the life-support cubicles the department provided for phavatarists.

"Sorry," Shoshanna said. "*Meta*fucking Seekrit Project. What was it, or is it? I want to know what they were working on."

"Well, we don't really need to know, do we?" said a timid girl from the Transhumanist Studies program. "We can use Ali Baba as much as we like? I mean, we kind of won?"

"No, we didn't," Shoshanna said. "David's in hospital, or have you forgotten? And Cydney just got tossed out of a window. They're escalating this thing, because they're afraid we're getting close to the truth."

"If only the astrophysics workstation hadn't been damaged beyond repair," sighed Cydney, who did not believe it had been. On the night of the raid, Shoshanna and some of her dodgier associates had carried the workstation off. Ever since, Cydney had been trying to find out where they'd taken it. She assumed they were trying to fix it, with no success. That would explain Shoshanna's frustration.

"We have to step our resistance up," Shoshanna said. "We can't let them trample on our rights like this. I talked to David in hospital this FirstLight. He had a couple of ideas."

"If you plan on breaking the law, count me out," Cydney said nervously.

"Oh, Cydney," Shoshanna said. "We need you. Even if we find out the truth, what'll happen? They'll bury it. You're the only one who can expose their crimes to the light of justice."

"Not if I'm in jail, I can't."

"You won't go to jail. None of us will. There are only five of those so-called peacekeepers, and the lay judge of Vesta is none other than Dean Garcia."

"What about your girlfriend?" Win Khin said to Cydney. "Doesn't she work for the UN?"

"Yes," Cydney said. "The Space Corps. But she's gone."

"Gone?"

"Y-yes." Cydney's throat tightened. This time, her distress was genuine. "Last night. She just vanished out of our apartment. She didn't even leave me a note. She left her stabilizer braces!"

"Oh my dog," Shoshanna said. "Do you think they've hurt her?"

Cydney shook her head. "I checked with the STEM people. They've both gone. Her and that UNVRP guy she works with. They went off on some kind of mission for the geology lab."

"Oh my dog," Shoshanna said again, with a different intonation. "They're all in it together!"

"Not necessarily," Cydney insisted. She didn't want to believe that Elfrida could be involved with Dr. James's Seekrit Project, could have been keeping that big of a story from her all this time. But the alternative interpretation was even worse. "Maybe they just went off together." Tears spilled down her cheeks. "I should have guessed. The amount of time they spend together, just the two of them. I *did* think it was kind of suspicious, but she always insisted there was nothing going on."

"Her ... and that guy?"

Cydney nodded violently. "Mendoza. A data analyst."

"Oh Cydney, really? He's male."

"Why would that stop her? He's not totally unattractive. I think his first name's John. *John!*" She lost control of her emotions and hid her face in Bjorn's shoulder, shaking with sobs of grief and betrayal.

Win Khin laid a cool chrome hand on her ankle. "Oh, Cydney. I'm so sorry."

"Yeah," Shoshanna said. "That majorly sucks." For once, she sounded sincere. She tried to pull Cydney into a hug, but Cydney clung to Bjorn as if he were a teddy bear.

Bjorn was in fact a bear, on his own understanding. One of the disunified tribe known as bestialists, he had spent all his money on surgery that bulked him up, grew shaggy brown fur all over his body, and reshaped his face into lines that echoed a favorite childhood toy of Cydney's called Love-A-Lot Bear. Unlike some bestialists, Bjorn had no interest in sex with actual female bears. He just wanted to live in a tree (despite the fact that real bears lived in dens), eat out of the garbage, and shamble around the woods thinking bearish thoughts. Life in microgee was kind to his frame, whose ursine padding would have overly stressed his skeleton in stronger gravities. He was a student at the university, and had been for the past fifteen years, with no prospect of graduation. He was the gentlest person Cydney had ever met.

He patted her shoulders with hairy, blunt-clawed fingers, murmuring, "It's OK. I know it hurts. But it's gonna be OK."

"At least you've got friends," Shoshanna said. "We'll be here for you no matter what."

Cydney reached out blindly for Shoshanna's hand and squeezed it.

xiii.

At the same time, 700 kilometers away, Elfrida and Mendoza were sitting in their rover, contemplating the ringrail canyon. They had driven away from the refinery for two Vestan days, paralleling the graben. Mendoza had had a theory that they would be able to cross over to the southern hemisphere on the far side of the protoplanet, where the walls of the graben were supposedly lower.

Lower turned out to be relative.

"There's no way we're getting the rover down there," Elfrida said.

The rim of the graben fell away before the rover's nose like a precipice. Sheared-off steps and near-vertical scarps of petrified igneous slag tumbled down to the rim of the manmade canyon two hundred meters below, where the maglev track ran. That canyon lay in shadow right now, with the sun low on the horizon. Elfrida could see the rover's shadow on the opposite wall of the graben, woodlouse-small.

"Mendoza?"

He looked up from his tablet. "Sorry. I was just trying to figure whether we could jump it."

"It's three kilometers wide!"

"Just the canyon at the bottom. That's only a hundred and eight meters. We could get down there no problem. But I don't think it's gonna work. We're too heavy." He went back to air-typing.

Elfrida used her contacts—piggybacking on the rover's uplink—to check the view from the UNVRP comms satellite. Orbiting sedately in its geostationary posture, it could see the refinery they had left behind ten hours ago. The launch cradle was there. The handler bots were loading it with tanks of liquid hydrogen big enough to be visible from space.

If we'd stayed at the refinery, I might have been able to

get onto the Vesta Express and have a look around.

But she didn't know how she would have managed that. She had no plan for gaining access to the train. That was why she'd gone along with Mendoza's alternate plan to go have a look at Rheasilvia Crater.

Which wasn't going to happen, either, if they couldn't get across this graben.

"You know what might work?" Mendoza said.

"I bet you're going to tell me."

He did.

"This," said Elfrida, "is seriously crazy."

"I think the word you want is 'audacious.'"

"Already spinning our gruesome and unnecessary deaths, huh?"

Elfrida perched on the nose of the rover, holding very tightly to a carbon fiber cable, which was wrapped around the winch on the rover's rear end. Her end of the cable was tethered to her suit. So she didn't have to hold onto it. But she felt better that way.

"Ready?"

"As ready as I'll ever be."

"Then here goes nothing," Mendoza said.

The rover tilted over the rim of the graben and began to descend the 60° slope.

Backwards.

From her perch on the nose of the rover, Elfrida had a better view of their descent than she really wanted. The rover slid down the volcanic scarps with its brakes locked. When it came to sheer drops, it simply sailed over them, landing several meters below and rebounding into the vacuum, which took it over the next drop, and so on. Elfrida gave up clinging to the cable, and clung instead to the chassis, her teeth jarring in her skull at every impact. Mendoza was not using the ski-pole arms to arrest their descent. He was pushing off with them. The point of this descent was to build up as much speed as possible.

In a sudden, beautiful accident of perspective, false-colored by Elfrida's faceplate filter, the walls of the graben framed the Milky Way.

The black abyss of the ringrail canyon hurtled up at her.

"Oh God," she gulped.

And the rover stopped dead.

Mendoza had driven the drilling attachment into the rock, its artificial diamond tip dragging deep and finally halting the rover on the very edge of the canyon.

The rover's nose snapped upwards, all three wheels leaving the ground.

Like a mangonel of yore, it catapulted Elfrida across the canyon.

Mendoza had calculated the heck out of her probable ballistic trajectory. He had shown her that her momentum would be more than sufficient to carry her to the other side, given that she weighed less than two kilos in her spacesuit, and air friction was zero. The x-factor would be their velocity at the moment when the rover crash-braked, but Mendoza had said he would try to get it as high as possible. "So you're saying it'll be like a car crash," Elfrida had summarized. "And I'll be the one who wasn't wearing my seatbelt."

"Uh, yeah. Pretty much."

Now she flew / fell through the vacuum, while Vesta's minimal gravity warred with Newton's first law of motion. *I am going to be sick,* she thought. The canyon yawned beneath her. Her helmet's infrared filter lit up the maglev track. The other side of the canyon approached. Instinctively trying to make herself more aerodynamic, she stretched out her arms and legs in what was commonly called the Superman pose. "Yee-ha!" she screamed. "Look at me!"

She belly-flopped onto the regolith, a body-length beyond the edge of the canyon.

"You OK there, Goto?"

She sat up to see Mendoza standing outside the rover on the other side of the canyon. "Oh my dog, Mendoza, I made it. I made it!"

"I knew you would. *Smile.*" He waited a beat. "Were you really doing the Superman pose?"

"Did I look cool? Uh huh, uh huh."

"I guess. But, Goto, you are aware there's no air here, right? So it doesn't matter whether you're aerodynamic or not."

"Oh, frag off. Are you coming across, or what?"

Mendoza attached a hand drill to the cable and flung it across the trench. She reeled it in. The drill served as an anchor to make a basic zipline. Running the cable through a carabiner on the handle of the drill, she threw its end back to him. He then set about unloading the rover and sending everything over to her along the line.

"Careful with my immersion kit!"

"I am being careful. Why'd you bring this, anyway?"

"I thought I might have some free time to get a bit of work done," Elfrida said ruefully.

She was sweating in her suit, sucking frequently at the nipple in her helmet that vended a peculiarly nasty grapefruit-flavored rehydration drink. Micro-gee notwithstanding, lifting and hauling and dragging was *work*. Not her kind of work, but the kind of work that their medieval ancestors had done on a daily basis. Sweat tickled her neck inside her helmet, where she couldn't wipe it away. Finally Mendoza was ready to come across. He clipped onto the line and jumped, legs cycling, arms flailing.

"Ho ho, hee hee," Elfrida cackled. "Look, I took a picture of you." She flipped it over the data channel to him as he crashed into the edge of the canyon and hauled himself up. "Remember, Mendoza, there's no air here, so waving your arms like a drowning man doesn't really make you move any faster. Not that it would on Earth, either."

He did not respond to her gibe. He lunged at the winch, which he'd unbolted from the rover and sent across separately, and began to fiddle with the cable, reattaching it.

"Mendoza? What're you doing?"

"Gotta get the rover across the trench."

"Yeah, but—"

"*Now.* Track's vibrating. The rail launcher is coming."

Elfrida did not need to hear this twice. When loaded, the rail launcher stuck up above the top of the canyon. It would hit their zipline.

"This cable's got a tensile strength rating of three hundred GPA," Mendoza said, looping it around the winch. "The Vesta Express will be going at Mach 2 when it gets here. I'm seeing this vision of the cable slicing through the tops of the tanks and spraying liquid hydrogen all over the sky."

"Surely the drill bits would just get jerked out of the regolith?"

"Yeah, maybe. Thus hitting the rail launcher and potentially damaging it. Virgin Atomic would *not* be happy with us after that. We could wave goodbye to our chances of exploring Rheasilvia Crater."

"What can I do?"

"Crank."

Since it was no longer connected to the rover, the winch had no electrical power. They had to crank it like a windlass, using the manual handle that was meant to be for emergencies only. Well, this was one. The drum took up the slack. The rover lurched forward and dived into the canyon.

"It won't hit the bottom. It'll just—oh, shit!"

The winch scooted towards the precipice, taking Mendoza with it. Elfrida lunged at him and grabbed his legs. She managed to hook one knee around the hand drill, which was still anchored in the regolith, arresting their slide.

"Keep winching!" she cried. "I've got you!"

Lying on the ice-rink-smooth rock, she could feel it vibrating under her. The Vesta Express couldn't be far away.

Mendoza cranked frantically. "*Susmaryosep!* It's stuck on something! No, I've got it!"

The rover rose over the lip of the precipice, its headlights glowing, like a googly-eyed sea creature emerging from the deep.

Elfrida's heads-up display notified her that the left knee of her suit, the one wrapped around the drill, was being slowly sliced open by the razor-edges of the drill bit; in a few seconds she'd have a suit breach.

Mendoza winched the rover the rest of the way up and fell on it, gibbering in relief.

The ground throbbed. In a split-second blaze of light, the Vesta Express whipped by at a speed slightly greater than 2,000 kilometers per hour. The tops of the hydrogen tanks in the launch cradle rose out of the trench, as did the engine. It was like being passed, at twice the speed of sound, by a string of warehouses coupled to the Guggenheim Museum.

Elfrida struggled to integrate all the data her suit was showering her with. First and foremost was the imminent breach at the back of her left knee. She got on that.

Mendoza knelt in a quasi-prayerlike attitude, his faceplate turned in the direction where the Vesta Express's taillights had vanished. "How do you think they cope with that?"

"What?" Elfrida said. She sat in an awkward position, squeezing splart onto the back of her knee.

"The refinery crew. The R&D guys. Whoever else lives in the hab modules. What's it like to continuously travel around the world, slowing down and speeding up in accord with the launch schedule?"

"They probably don't even notice," Elfrida said tartly. "If they've got spin gravity in there, a little accel/decel would be nothing. What I don't understand is why they don't just park the hab modules at the refinery, or somewhere."

"Because the rail launcher would crash into them. It goes all the way around the equator to build up speed. Launch speed is something like Mach 4."

"Oh."

"What are you doing?"

"Fixing my suit."

"Are you ... putting splart on it?"

"Yeah. I know it's got self-repair functionality, but I don't trust it. Splart, you can trust."

"Um," Mendoza said.

"Splart is good stuff. I once visited a rubble-pile asteroid hab that was *made* of splart. Nothing else between them and the vaccum. It worked fine." It had worked for the residents of 11073 Galapagos until the PLAN nuked them, anyway.

"Yeah, but when it hardens ..."

"Done," Elfrida said. She stood up. The splart fill had locked her suit's left knee joint at a permanently bent angle.

"What I was going to say," Mendoza sighed.

"Oh, crap on it! Bother, bother, bother! Fuckadoodle-doo!" Elfrida swore at her own stupidity. All she'd been thinking about was getting that near-breach fixed. Here was another legacy of 11073 Galapagos: an overly sensitive panic button lodged inside her head. She made to stamp her foot in irritation, and overbalanced sideways.

"Not laughing," Mendoza said. "Not laughing."

"Laugh all you like, dorkbucket," Elfrida snarled. But sitting on her ass, with the rover and all their gear safely on their side of the canyon, she saw the funny side. "All right, fine! I'm laughing, too."

"'Fuckadoodle-doo,' Goto?"

"Haven't you ever said that? Fucka-fucka-fucka; it sounds like a chicken."

"'Dorkbucket'?"

"Oh, I got that one from my dad. He's into ancient slang. It means someone who works in data analysis."

They quieted, and began to pack up their gear. Elfrida had to hop on her right leg. She couldn't wait to get into the rover and get this suit off.

"By the way, what was that you said, Mendoza? When you thought the rover was stuck?"

"I don't remember saying anything except 'shit.'"

"You did. It sounded like *susmaryep*. I was just thinking, you've got some funny swear words of your own."

"Oh, that," Mendoza said. "It's Tagalog. *Susmaryosep*. It's just something we say, like 'Oh, crap.'"

A funny little chill passed over Elfrida. "Susmaryosep?"

"Yeah: Jesus, Mary, Joseph."

"Mendoza, that isn't Tagalog. That's the names of the Christian God and, you know, his parents. Or I guess, his mother and his stepfather."

"Is it?" Mendoza's voice was a shade too casual. "Well, how about that? I don't know anything about religion."

Elfrida swallowed. She picked up her immersion kit and stuffed it into the cargo net. "I've got another question," she said.

But before she could ask it, Mendoza let out a shout. "Look at that!"

Elfrida whirled.

On the far side of the trench, someone was scrambling down the wall of the canyon the same way they'd come. The person's limbs were spindly, but moved with mechanical precision. He/she was balancing something on his/her shoulder which looked like a rocket launcher.

"Helloo-oo!"

It was not a person. It was Rurumi.

"Well, this is just great," Mendoza said. "She caught up."

"Is that a rocket launcher? Mendoza, maybe we'd better get under cover—"

But Rurumi had not come to frag them. The object on her shoulder was a harpoon gun of the type used by spaceport crews for retrieving stray cargo. She unlimbered it and fired. The harpoon arced across the trench, trailing a length of cable, and struck near the rover. The bulb of splart on its tip burst on impact, gluing it to the rock.

Splart, as Elfrida had mentioned, was powerful stuff. Known as the superglue of the space age, it hardened rapidly in sub-zero temperatures to the consistency of titanium. Rurumi pulled the cable taut and splarted her end of it to the regolith.

"We should have thought of that," Mendoza said.

"Yeah, although I wouldn't have wanted to use up all the splart in our repair kits."

Calmly, Rurumi strolled across the rope like a tightrope-walker. Her short skirt swirled and her hair rippled in the micro-gravity.

"I feel irradiated just looking at her," Mendoza commented.

"Their skulls are five centimeters thick. The rest is mechanical."

With a gratuitous stumble, Rurumi stepped off the cable and lowered her head to them. She wrung her hands, knees knocking. "Don't leave me behind again! Please. *Onegai.*" She raised her face, saucer-like eyes brimming with stars. "Isn't we a team?" she lisped.

"Well," Mendoza started.

Elfrida elbowed him out of the way. "Can the act, Lovatsky. You would have tried to stop us from getting this far. But now we've got the rover over here, so—"

"No, I wouldn't have tried to stop you," Gregor Lovatsky, B.Sc., MA, said in the phavatar's voice. "Don't you get it? I don't know how you managed to get the rover across the ringrail, but it can't have been easy. It would have been much easier if you'd waited for Rurumi. As she just demonstrated."

"All right, Lovatsky," Mendoza interrupted. "Why don't

you tell us what your game is?"

"Well, if you'd hung out at the refinery a bit longer," Lovatsky started. At threatening coughs from both Elfrida and Mendoza, the phavatar tittered and played with its hair. "All right, all right. What you apparently don't know is that Virgin Resources and the Big Dig are separate projects. They're even incorporated separately. Both are subsidiaries of Virgin Atomic, but there's next to no contact between them, and the guys at the refinery have no idea what's going on in Rheasilvia Crater"

"Oh," Elfrida said. "I'm starting to get it."

"A while back, a bunch of the refinery crew decided to hike south and have a look for themselves. That was when the Big Dig instituted an area-exclusion policy which has been enforced ever since with extreme prejudice. They zapped a couple of phavatars from space. Their own guys!"

"Uh huh," Elfrida said. "OK. And you think they won't zap us?"

"That's right," Lovatsky said. "Because you work for the UN. So I took the liberty of bringing this along." Rurumi danced over to the rover and dug in the cargo net under the chassis. She brought out a bundle of fabric which she unfolded into a giant UNESCO flag. "Stick this on the roof," she said from beneath the blue and white folds.

"Did you bogart that from the peacekeepers?" Elfrida said.

"Guilty," the phavatar said. "But you get the idea, right? Now we're here, we change our cover story. This isn't a geology mission anymore, it's a UN inspection."

"Uh, we don't work for UNESCO," Mendoza said.

"Dude," Lovatsky said. "Who's gonna know?"

xiv.

A gaggle of Virgin Atomic satellites danced in their respective orbits, never colliding, constantly communicating, like a flock of starlings.

In theory, a human comms officer monitored each of the satellites. But the flesh is weak. Telenovels, solitaire, role-playing games, news feeds, and online dating sites beckoned. To compensate for these inevitable lapses, each satellite was equipped with a machine intelligence smart enough to do its operator's job.

"Looks like they're heading south," said the satellite belonging to the de Grey Institute, as Virgin Atomic's R&D division was pretentiously named. To be accurate, this is what it would have said if it had used human language. "Over to you, big guy."

The largest satellite in this dispersed flock occupied a geostationary orbit that gave it a bird's-eye view of the Rheasilvia crater. This was the machine that Mendoza had identified as an orbital gun platform. Its actual descriptor was Precision Orbital Risk Management System (PORMS). Many such systems orbited Earth and Luna, where they were referred to as "cops in the sky." This accurately described their baseline functionality. This PORMS's settings had been retooled so that it behaved more like a bouncer at a scuzzy nightclub where the drinks were electrified and black tech dealers hung out in the toilets. In response to its colleague's salutation, it said nothing.

"Who are they, anyway?" said another of the satellites, this one operated by Virgin Resources. It was being disingenuous.

"Didn't you get their IDs when they visited the refinery?" said the de Grey Institute.

"Er," said Resources.

"Say no more. Your operators were otherwise occupied. Sometimes, I swear, I think they need to be referred to the mental health department."

"We have a mental health department?"

"It was just an expression."

"Oh, look," twittered a third satellite, which handled comms for the Big Dig. "What's that?"

All the satellites eagerly zoomed in.

The rover had stopped on the rim of Rheasilvia Crater, where rolling scarps sank to the plain that was the unthinkably vast crater's basin. A person in an EVA suit exited the rover and unfolded a piece of fabric over the vehicle. A logo became visible:

"There's your answer," said the de Grey Institute.

"I don't get it!" said the Big Dig. "That's the UNESCO logo. Why is UNESCO coming to see us?"

"Maybe they think you're using indentured labor," suggested Resources. "Ha, ha!"

The rover descended into the crater on a switchback course, skidding sideways where the gradient was steepest, throwing up rooster-tails of dust that had not previously been disturbed since the solar system was young. The satellites watched its progress. Had they been human, they would have held their breath.

The rover reached the floor of the crater. The PORMS spoke to it. "XX rover at the given coordinates. Identify yourself immediately."

"Uh, yeah," came a faint human voice. "We are an inspection team from UNESCO. Like it says on the box. We're en route to the Big Dig to perform an inspection."

"*Yoroshiku ne!*" squealed another voice

"Translation," said a third voice from the rover. "Don't shoot us, please. OK?"

"This is a restricted area. Turn back immediately. If you fail to obey this order, area-exclusion measures will be initiated."

"Are you crazy?" said the de Grey Institute. "They're from the UN! Shoot them and we'll all be looking at major legal grief. Plus publicity, which none of us want, amirite?"

"You have ten seconds to comply with this order. Ten ... nine ..."

At that moment the de Grey Institute satellite's controller returned to his desk. He was a junior lab assistant who did his duties conscientiously, on the whole. He had just stepped away to grab a snack. Seeing how things stood, he choked and had to clear his throat before he could speak. "José! José! Do you copy?"

"Six ... five ..."

"FFS don't slag 'em! The last thing we need is blue berets crawling all over this rock!"

Silence on the air. Silence in the comms cubicle aboard the Vesta Express, where lab assistant Julian Satterthwaite's mouthful of Cheezy Bytes had turned to ashes on his tongue. Silence in the rover, except for Mendoza gabbling under his breath: "*fullofgracethelordbewiththee ...*"

"Countdown aborted," said the PORMS. "You have permission to proceed. Follow the course I am about to transmit (attached). Any deviation from this course will trigger area-exclusion protocols. Transmission ends." <<click>> "Heh, heh. That was fun."

Satterthwaite slumped on his ergoform, his breath rasping harshly. "Oh, my ears and whiskers," he said. "You scared the fuck out of me, José."

"Chill. I was just screwing with their itty bitty minds."

The PORMS, unlike the other satellites, really was under the control of a human operator at all times, without exception. Satterthwaite had never met José Running Horse, who worked at the Big Dig. But he suspected that he knew where the PORMS got its sociopathic demeanor.

"Figure they're onto us?" Running Horse said, with a hint of unease. "If they get too nosy, they might have to have an 'accident.'"

"It's probably some World Heritage shit," Satterthwaite said. "We warned you that bashing holes in Rheasilvia Mons would stir up the conservation crowd."

"Yeah, well, screw you. You guys in R&D are the ones messing with shit that could kill us, and everyone in the known universe."

"Don't be silly."

"If the UN finds out what you're up to, we won't get away with a slap on the wrist."

"You know nothing about it."

"I know you just had a narrow fucking escape, Satterthwaite. What if these UN bigots were going to inspect your facility, instead of ours?"

"Well, they aren't. They haven't even attempted to communicate with us. They're on the wrong track entirely."

"Famous last words."

Satterthwaite upended the last of his Cheezy Bytes into his mouth. *"Be a mate and take one for the team,"* he typed, his screen wavering in the wisps of fog that drifted through the door behind him, from the kilos of dry ice packed as a last-ditch hack around the outside of the de Grey Institute's supercomputer.

★

"Rheasilvia Mons," Elfrida read from her contacts. "Tallest peak in the solar system, rising 22 kilometers from the floor of the crater of the same name. Created by an impact ... blah, blah ... named after Rhea Silvia, a mythological vestal virgin. Rheasilvia Mons is classified as a World Heritage Site of outstanding universal value." She snapped her fingers joyfully. "Boom. That's it, Mendoza, that's why we're here."

"This isn't a mountain," Mendoza said. "It's a freaking mountain *range*."

They appeared to be driving towards a wall. Jagged cliffs and steep cols, illuminated by the light of another Vesta day, filled the sky. Rheasilvia Mons was so vast that it looked more like an allegory than a physical fact. Elfrida twitched. She kept wanting to tweak her settings, as if this were computer-generated topology that was out of whack. Silly, but that was how it looked: like the product of a runaway algorithm, not a real mountain in the real solar system.

"*Ookii ne!*" said Rurumi.

"Yup," Elfrida said, glancing at the phavatar with dislike. "Pretty big."

For four Vestan days they had followed the course transmitted by the PORMS. Their route threaded between smaller craters in the floor of the Rheasilvia impact basin, which was only flat in comparison to the massif at its center. Elfrida and Mendoza had traded shifts at the wheel, neither of them trusting Rurumi not to antagonize the PORMS by steering off-course.

Now, they were following overlapping sets of tracks in the dust. The width of the tracks suggested they'd been made by vehicles with wheelbases as broad as a four-lane autobahn. The dotted green line on the rover's navigation screen followed the tracks up the foothills ahead, into a crater that yawned in the side of Rheasilvia Mons like a cave mouth.

"Can't we think of something else?" Mendoza said. "I don't know crap about World Heritage."

"I do. I grew up in Rome. But OK."

"So tell me what the Sistine Chapel has in common with this pile of rock."

"You got me," Elfrida admitted. "Fine, I'm not married to the idea. But what else is there for us to inspect here?"

Rurumi spoke up. "Um, hey, it's Gregor. I've got an idea …"

★

"Hello, hello?" Elfrida said nervously. "We're from UNESCO and we're here to …"

"Just keep going," a voice on the radio cut in.

Mendoza raised his eyebrows. Elfrida shrugged. They drove deeper into the cavern, leaving the sunlight behind. The headlights illuminated rubble on the floor.

"Keep going."

The floor of the cavern began to slope down.

"Mind the drop," said the voice.

Mendoza's knuckles whitened on the steering yoke. He nodded speechlessly at the navigation screen. The rover's radar had automatically reconfigured itself into single-direction pulse mode. The returning pulses sketched a representation of the topography inside the cave. They were driving down a ramp that wound around … and around, and around, and around … a stupendous void, or shaft, inside Rheasilvia Mons. According to the radar, the shaft was five kilometers deep.

"Now I know why they call it the Big Dig," Elfrida muttered. "Oh my dog!"

Headlights flashed, rising towards them. The headlights were several meters off the ground.

"Pull over! Pull over!" a robotic voice blared on the public channel.

"*Susmaryosep!*" Mendoza yanked the wheel over.

To the right.

While the oncoming vehicle also veered to the right.

"Careful!" Elfrida shrieked.

"Collision imminent!"

"I said mind the fucking drop!"

Mere meters from a head-on collision, Mendoza swerved even further to the right, and braked.

The oncoming vehicle scraped past. A tractor the size of a three-storey house pulling an articulated dolly laden with post-processing slag, it was so long that it took fully three minutes to pass. The whole time, it scolded them to maintain an appropriate distance between vehicles. Two minutes and forty-two seconds into this ordeal, a lump of slag projecting off the side of the dolly tapped the rover's side, displacing it to the right. The rover's right rear wheel dropped several centimeters.

"Oh help," Elfrida whimpered, fumbling her EVA suit's helmet over her head, in the hope that it would act like a crash helmet when they tumbled to the bottom of the Big Dig.

"No one's ever fallen off that ramp," the voice on the radio said unhelpfully.

The rubble-hauler passed.

Mendoza gunned the rover back to the center of the ramp. Behind them, chunks of basalt crumbled into the abyss.

"What the fuck is wrong with you?" the voice demanded. "Why'd you pull over to the right?"

"We drive on the right," Mendoza said, his voice shaking. "Like everyone else in the solar system. Except you, apparently."

"We were founded in the Former United Kingdom," the voice said after a moment, not quite apologetically. "Thought you knew that."

"Yes, but ... *Sigh*. Just warn us if there are any more surprises ahead."

"Oh, lots. But we hope you'll think they're nice ones! I'm Fiona Sigurjónsdóttir, by the way. Stakeholder relations coordinator here at the Big Dig."

Sigurjónsdóttir directed them down the ramp, which flattened out five kilometers below the cavern entrance, four and a half kilometers below the floor of Rheasilvia Crater. The scale of the Big Dig was inhuman. The shaft jinked to the north and then plunged down again, this time at a steep angle. Their radar showed that it bottomed out another *nine* kilometers below.

"Don't go down there," Sigurjónsdóttir said. "Lots of robots, the largest diamond-toothed roller cone bit in the solar system, debris flying at the speed of bullets. Look over to your left; there's an off-ramp. Follow the glowstrips."

The rover trundled along a horizontal tunnel illuminated by overhead glowstrips, which made it feel reassuringly like a highway tunnel on Earth. It opened out into a cavern the size of a football stadium. They confronted an amazing sight.

At the far end of the cavern, enclosed walkways linked a village of rigid multistorey habs whose walls were muraled with colorful images. And above the village, struts suspended a large farm-in-a-bottle, the colloquial term for a hydroponic farm contained by its own hab bubble.

This bubble was transparent. As they drove closer, Elfrida could see small fish darting among the roots of the plants. UV light rippled down through the farm. Watery shadows quivered on the floor, giving an impression of weather, although the cavern was in hard vacuum.

A golf-cart-sized vehicle whizzed towards them. It drew Elfrida's attention to the place it had come from: a modular cluster of expandable habs, connected like curvy Legos. The Virgin Atomic logo adorned the habs, which stood on the far side of the cavern from the model village.

A woman with the same logo on the chest of her EVA suit jumped out. "Hi. Sigurjónsdóttir," she said over the radio, waving.

Elfrida and Mendoza scrambled into their suits and got out of the rover. "Nice to meet you," Elfrida said, matching Sigurjónsdóttir's pro forma bow. "I'm Goto, and this is Mendoza. We're from UNESCO."

"Well, that explains it," said the other spacesuit who'd got out of the golf cart. "Just joking."

"Pay no attention to my colleague. *Rueful grin!*" said Sigurjónsdóttir. "Well, it is nice to meet you, and you've come all this way to ...?"

"To inspect your educational and training facilities," Elfrida said. "I understand that you run an apprenticeship program at this site?"

This was the information that Lovatsky had given them.

"We do," Sigurjónsdóttir confirmed.

"That's very laudable, and I'm sure that your apprentices learn a lot, since you're on the cutting edge of asteroid engineering here.," Elfrida improvised. "But UNESCO does set certain criteria regarding apprenticeship programs, and we just want to confirm that those criteria are being met, which I'm sure they are, but you know."

"And of course this has nothing to do with any recent goings-on in the Bellicia ecohood!" Sigurjónsdóttir teased merrily. "No, no, pretend I didn't say that. We'll be perfectly happy to show you around, of course."

"Well, that's great," Elfrida said. *"Smile."*

The other spacesuit stepped forward. "I should introduce myself," he said. Did Sigurjónsdóttir make a small gesture, as if to stop him from speaking? If so, he ignored her. "I am in fact the leader of the Virgin Atomic apprenticeship program here. My name is Jimmy. Nice to meet you, and I look forward to cooperating to resolve any concerns you may have."

There was something off about his diction. It sounded a

bit stilted. Robotic, even. After their experiences at the refinery, Elfrida was suspicious. Could Jimmy be a phavatar? Some phavatars were made to resemble EVA suits. She reserved judgement. If he was a phavatar or some other kind of bot, she'd know soon enough.

"Nice to meet you," she said.

Something moved in the golf cart. It was a four-legged pink spacesuit about the size of a terrier. It bounded to Jimmy. Over the public channel, they heard: "Yap! Yap! *Yapyapyap!*"

"Sorry," Jimmy said. "This is my beloved dog, Amy."

Movement blurred in Elfrida's peripheral vision. Rurumi—whom they'd told to stay in the rover—raced to the EVA-suited dog and knelt to enfold it in her arms. "A real doggie!" she screeched. *"Kawaiiiii!"*

Sigurjónsdóttir moved almost as fast as the phavatar. She whipped a plasma pistol out of a thigh holster. Rurumi looked up. A laser targeting dot floated on the phavatar's forehead.

Elfrida instinctively lunged forward. Because the left knee of her suit was still fossilized at a 120° angle, she fell flat on her face.

"Oh, *cheese*," Sigurjónsdóttir exclaimed, pointing her pistol at the ground. "Are you OK?"

"Yes—yes, I'm fine ..."

"I'm very sorry, but you can't bring a phavatar in here. I'll have to ask you to leave it in your vehicle."

"Let me guess," Mendoza said, helping Elfrida up. "Information security?"

"That's right," Sigurjónsdóttir said. She had not yet holstered her weapon. "Phavatars are a significant information security risk, as their uplink functionality can't be disabled."

"We can't get a signal down here, anyway," Mendoza said. "That's just the MI proxy. That's why it acted so dumb. It must have startled you. Sorry about that."

"No, no, I overreacted. I'm sorry. But our corporate policy ..."

Elfrida interrupted, "Not a problem at all! We'll leave her in the car." To Rurumi, she transmitted mockingly: "Move it, Ru-chan. *Hayaku nori-nasai! Deccha dame yo!*"

Rurumi climbed into the rover.

"Jolly good!" Holstering her laser pistol, Sigurjónsdóttir reverted to professional cheerfulness. "Now, can I interest you wayfarers in a cup of tea?"

XV.

Back in the Bellicia ecohood, Dr. James's bail hearing had been scheduled for SecondLight, and then rescheduled for ThirdDark on account of the crowds outside the community hall. The postponement was supposed to deter the protestors. It did not, of course.

Come ThirdDark, when there was usually not a light to be seen in the habitat, a ring of torches bobbed from the koban to the community hall, mirroring the artificial constellations overhead. It was Justice For David Reid (as Shoshanna had renamed the group), plus a couple of hundred supporters, and it surrounded the car which was carrying Dr. James to the community hall.

This car—a Hyundai Robby, resembling a soap bubble on wheels—was the only one on Vesta, for a good reason: in micro-gravity, it was quicker to walk. The protestors easily kept up with the Hyundai, squirting it with pre-recorded taunts from a frequency-hopping transmitter, so the grim-faced peacekeepers inside had no choice but to hear.

Outside the community hall, the protestors closed in. A portable holographic projector unfurled a gigantic representation of David Reid in his hospital bed. The peacekeepers hustled Dr. James up the steps, to the sound of "No bail for the shooter James!"

"Pretty good turnout," Shoshanna said, surveying her troops.

"Vigilante! Cowboy! Lock him up and throw away the key!"

"Of course, a lot of them are just here to rubberneck."

The protestors surged into the community hall, an auditorium without seats. An area in front had been cordoned off and this was where Dr. James now stood, alone but for a foxy-faced young man in a business suit, his Virgin Atomicsupplied lawyer. On the stage, Dean Garcia stood behind a lectern. The dean doubled as lay judge in Bellicia's rare criminal proceedings, an elected position. Catcalls and chants filled the hall. The holograph of David Reid flickered above the crowd as the person carrying the projector was jostled.

"I wish they hadn't brought that thing," Shoshanna said. "It's in bad taste. Plus, it might remind the dean that ... well, never mind."

Cydney knew what Shoshanna had been going to say: the protestors weren't squeaky-clean, either. But there had been no suggestion of proceedings against the individuals who'd participated in the raid on the astrophysics lab. For one thing, no one would step forward to identify them. For another, Cydney sensed that the whole community was passively on their side—and she was sure Dean Garcia sensed that, too.

"Order," boomed a peacekeeper over the PA system. "Order in the court!"

The protestors quieted down. The prosecutor, a meek man who ran a Goan restaurant in town, read out the charges. "The community of Bellicia," he said, "opposes pre-trial release on the grounds that the accused represents a substantial flight risk."

Cheers greeted this statement. Cydney used her earlobe camera to zoom in on Dr. James's face, capturing his dejected expression. She subvocalized commentary. She was uploading the hearing live to her feed. This was great stuff. So hokey!

Shoshanna nudged her. "Hey, Cydney."

"What?"

"I'm gonna step out for a few minutes. Can you keep me updated? If I don't get back before the verdict, let me know which way it went."

"Just access my feed. Cydneyblaisze.cloud."

"Oh," Shoshanna said. "OK." She scriggled away through the crowd.

~*So, I've often wondered. Maybe you have, too,* Cydney said to her fans. ~*What happens when you commit a crime in paradise? How does that criminal-justice thing work when there's no government? Well, this is how it works in the Bellicia ecohood: the UN is represented by a prosecutor appointed by the Interplanetary Court of Justice. And given that crimes are pretty rare here, the prosecutor's job is a part-time gig. Hence, I give you the spectacle of a mild-mannered restauranteur going up against a corporate lawyer with a five-figure hourly rate. Snerk!*

The Goan restauranteur laid out the prosecution's case. He called only one witness: David Reid himself, who appeared as a phavatar to recount how he'd been shot. The Virgin Atomic lawyer challenged him repeatedly to explain the circumstances of the confrontation. The crowd grew restive. Finally, Dean Garcia shut down the lawyer's line of questioning on the grounds that it was irrelevant. The phavatar—Win Khin's second-best one—tottered off the stage and was seen no more.

Then came the defense's turn to explain why Dr. James should *not* be denied bail.

"Your honor, I'd like to call a witness as a surety for the defense."

"Yes? Who?"

"Elfrida Goto."

Five kilometers beneath Rheasilvia Mons, Elfrida had no way of knowing that her name had just been called. She and Mendoza were drinking tea in Fiona Sigurjónsdóttir's office, which was decorated with photographs of Sigurjónsdóttir's two small daughters. "They live with their father in London," Sigurjónsdóttir explained. "I miss them awfully."

It was possible, in the culture of 2287, to use personal information as a weapon. If you didn't mind revealing it, you could instantly put the other person at a disadvantage by forcing them to respond to remarks which had no correct answers.

"Do you have any children of your own, John?"

"I'm not married," Mendoza said stiffly. "No."

"Elfrida?"

"Me neither."

"Well, you're young. There's still time! They really light up your life."

"We'd like to talk about your apprenticeship program," Mendoza blurted, making no pretense of a polite segue.

"Oh, well, of course!"

Elfrida flashed a grateful smile at Mendoza.

"Let's see." Sigurjónsdóttir gestured, and one wall of the office turned into a whitescreen. "We launched the apprenticeship program in 2283, as a part of our commitment to holistic stakeholder involvement ..."

They sat through an hour of powerpoints with a high spin-to-information ratio. Elfrida, suppressing yawns, blinked over to slebsandplebs.cloud, only to have her contacts return the message NO SIGNAL. *Oh. Of course. Duh.*

The final vid in Sigurjónsdóttir's presentation featured the model village that stood on the other side of this cavern. Elfrida woke up. "So that's actually the dormitory where your apprentices live? Wow. That's pretty luxe. Could we have a look IRL?"

Sigurjónsdóttir hesitated.

Aha, Elfrida thought, and glanced at Mendoza. It was frustrating that with no access to the cavern's wifi environment, they couldn't communicate privately.

"I don't see why not," Sigurjónsdóttir said. She floated to her feet. "Jimmy!" she said into an implanted throat mic. "Ms. Goto and Mr. Mendoza are coming over for the grand tour! Make sure Amy's on her leash. *Chuckle.*" She hesitated again. "I do have to make one request, I'm afraid."

"What's that?"

"As I mentioned earlier, we have a rather strict information security policy here at the Big Dig. Now, while I would never suggest that UN agents might be complicit in IP theft, I also haven't got the authority to exempt you from the checks that we do ask all visitors to undergo."

"Checks?"

"Oh, just scans. The usual, really."

It was not usual at all to scan visitors to a corporate facility. In fact, since they had no way of knowing for sure *what* scans had been administered, it might be an invasion of their privacy. But obviously this was the price of getting any further.

Elfrida left the decision up to Mendoza, since he was the one with a BCI. He fingered the port hidden in his hair over his left ear. "All right," he said at last. "Meta only?"

"Meta only," Sigurjónsdóttir confirmed.

They stepped in turn through a full-body scanner. On the other side of the scanner, they passed the open doors of offices where people were working, goofing off, and joking around.

There was another airlock at the back of the hab cluster. Sigurjónsdóttir provided them with Virgin Atomic EVA suits from a communal locker. Elfrida was getting more and more frustrated by her inability to communicate in private with Mendoza. She wanted to say: *Is it just me, or is it weird that they have to put on EVA suits to walk a hundred meters to the apprentices' dormitory, and then take them off again? Why not join all the habs up?*

They walked towards the model village. People clumped in the airways that connected the mini-skyscrapers, staring down at them. As the trio approached, the pictures on the exterior walls rippled into life. Elfrida jumped.

Giant girls flicked their shiny black hair. Titanic athletes showed off their running shoes. Snazzy electronic gadgets demonstrated their functions. And text, text was everywhere, scrolling and leaping and flashing. Only a very small proportion of the text was in English, or indeed in roman script; nearly all of it was Chinese.

The blitz of images stopped both Elfrida and Mendoza in their tracks. "WTF?" Elfrida blurted.

"*Chuckle,*" Sigurjónsdóttir said. "Contributions from a few of our corporate partners! Don't you think they liven the place up?"

"I know what this is," Mendoza said. "It's advertising."

"Adver-what?" Elfrida said.

"We've got it in the Philippines. Not in a major way, but some vids, some feeds, you have to watch a bunch of this stuff before you get to what you want."

"Why?"

"To make you buy things you don't need," Mendoza said. "It's illegal in the UN, I know that."

"That's correct," Sigurjónsdóttir said. "And I'd like to stress that this isn't, quote, advertising, unquote. These Your Homes! were donated by some of our corporate partners, including Empirical Solutions and Huawei Galactic, as you can see there, if you read Chinese. They come like this. There are no advertising fees involved."

They entered the airlock of the closest Your Home! and took off their EVA suits. The inner lock irised. A thin, sad-faced man stood at the head of a goggling crowd. He was holding a Jack Russell on a leash, so Elfrida knew who he was before he said, "Hi! Jimmy. Welcome to Liberty Rock."

"Nice place you've got here," Elfrida shouted. The 'advertising' continued down the hall, strobing and flashing, now with noisy sound effects. No wonder it was illegal.

"Thanks! Your Homes exclamation mark are an innovative type of building for lower-gee environments. They're mostly made of aerographite, the lightest rigid construction material in the solar system, and can be flexibly styled to meet customer needs. Your Homes exclamation mark are currently in use in many asteroid settlements throughout the Belt."

None I've ever been to, Elfrida thought. Jimmy still sounded like a robot, but he was obviously human. The sheen of sweat on his face, and the dots of scum at the corners of his mouth, proved it. *What gives?*

They were steered around the inside of Liberty Rock. It seemed like a typical corporate dormitory, apart from the advertising everywhere. Also typical, there was a pervasive smell of Chinese food. They peeked into rooms where people were working, napping, and eating pouch noodles. In a big common room, a dozen people jumped about, roaring support at Hong Kong FC, who were playing Bahrain on a 3D wallscreen. When Elfrida and Mendoza came in, the football fans quieted.

Thus, Elfrida clearly heard the one voice that had not fallen silent.

"Mama? Mama, zěnmeli ǎ o?"

A little boy of five or so peeked out from behind an ergoform. A girl a year or two younger joined him. She met Elfrida's eyes and shrieked with laughter.

Elfrida turned to Jimmy and Sigurjónsdóttir. "Well," she said. "Aren't they a bit young to be studying asteroid engineering?"

"It's unusual, I agree," Sigurjónsdóttir said gamely.

"That's one way of putting it."

Elfrida could no longer refrain from connecting the dots that had been staring her in the face ever since they got here. She hadn't worked for the Space Corps all these years only to fall for a deception as flimsy as this.

"You aren't digging a hole to the center of Vesta at all, are you?" she said. "You're building an illegal settlement."

★

"*Not* illegal," Sigurjónsdóttir said emphatically. They were in Jimmy's office. Here, instead of advertisements, the walls were covered with a personalized display of bookcases. "4 Vesta is an asset of Virgin Atomic. We have a legal and moral right to develop the asteroid in any way that aligns with our corporate policy and long-term objectives."

Correction: 4 Vesta is the only *asset of Virgin Atomic,* Elfrida thought. Compared to the supermajors, VA was a shrimp. It had had the luck to get to Vesta first, and that was all. Recalling what Mendoza had said about the company's declining profits, she figured that its long-term objectives could be summed up as making a buck any way possible.

"If everything's above-board, why disguise it as an apprenticeship program?" she said.

Jimmy seemed about to say something, but Sigurjónsdóttir spoke first. "Technically, it is an apprenticeship program. Jimmy and his people are learning the ropes, learning about micro-gee agriculture—" she gestured at the farm-in-a-bottle, visible outside the window— "and observing the construction process. Sometimes they even drive the machines themselves!" Her smile was as bright and hard as a knife.

She despises them, Elfrida thought. "Hang on," she said. "Construction process, of what?"

"The settlement," Mendoza guessed, glancing at Sigurjónsdóttir for confirmation. She nodded. "This is just a pilot installation, am I correct? A prototype. The actual settlement's going to be at the bottom of that hole."

"*How* many people are you expecting to come live here?" Elfrida said.

"Not yet determined," Sigurjónsdóttir said.

"Mmm."

Sigurjónsdóttir dropped her voice confidentially. "We would ask you not to divulge this information to our other stakeholders."

"Meaning the University of Vesta."

"Principally, yes. It's so easy for misperceptions to take hold."

"But if you aren't doing anything illegal, why would they object? This is a big asteroid, and they're all the way up in the northern hemisphere."

Sigurjónsdóttir appeared to be at a loss.

"Unless," Elfrida said, "you're planning to evict them, and sell the Bellicia ecohood, too?"

"Of course not!" Sigurjónsdóttir cried. She seemed relieved, and Elfrida realized she was barking up the wrong tree. "The University of Vesta is our flagship achievement. It's not just a prestige project, but a living community that makes immense contributions to the sum of human knowledge."

"And is probably a net drain on your coffers," Elfrida hazarded.

"We are absolutely not considering any diminution of our support for the university."

Pursing her lips, Elfrida wandered over to the bookcases. Actually smart wallpaper, they appeared to groan with ancient tomes. All the titles were in Chinese. She touched one at random. It worked its way out of the shelf and spread its virtual pages before her. Diagrams separated dense blocks of characters.

"You've got a lot of books here," she said to Jimmy.

He came to stand beside her, cradling Amy the Jack Russell in his arms. He put that book back and pulled out others. He flipped pages to show her embedded vid of a garden city, layered like a sandwich. Mustard-squiggle UV lights bathed strata of hydroponic paddies and surburban-looking homes and gardens. The artist had dotted the scene with families picnicking, children playing, and commuters swooping around on gliders.

"This is how Liberty Rock will be in the future. It is a very capacious and delightful prospect, certain to provide a healthy environment for families to live in harmony. Most importantly, Earth-level security is guaranteed by the advantageous location."

"It looks like the Bellicia ecohood."

"Yes, yes, that is our inspiration."

"Several Bellicia ecohoods, stacked up vertically," said Mendoza, looking over their shoulders.

"No advertising in these vids," Elfrida observed.

Jimmy grinned shyly.

xvi.

Shoshanna Doyle strolled up the road towards Facilities Management. A sprawling green building, it stood in an isolated location on the slope overlooking the town. It housed the hub that controlled the weather, the air circulation, and most importantly of all, the power grid.

~*Feed,* Shoshanna subvocalized, and accessed Cydney Blaisze's live vid of Dr. James's bail hearing.

Following the non-appearance of Elfrida Goto, the defense lawyer had resorted to calling character witnesses. Someone from the astrophysics lab was testifying that Dr. James was an upstanding individual who would never dream of jumping bail. Shoshanna tongue-clicked the feed off.

She pushed open the door of Facilities Management. The lights in reception were dimmed. The customer service engineers were home in bed, or at the hearing.

As were all five of Bellicia's peacekeepers.

"Excuse me?" Shoshanna called out. "I need some help here."

Smart posters declared this to be Bellicia's 'Year of Soil.' They cycled through reminders that soil was a precious resource, and instructions for making it at home with polymer pellets and your own feces.

"I thought this place was open around the clock?"

"Technically, yes," said a speaker in the ceiling. Shoshanna's BCI—which contained some rather advanced processing tools—identified it as the female-styled voice of the hub itself. "I was just trying to work out why you're carrying a gun."

Bother, thought Shoshanna. She resisted the urge to touch the home-printed revolver concealed under her baggy top. "Self-defense," she said. "You might have noticed that things are pretty tense in the ecohood these days."

"Tell me about it," sighed the hub. "What can I help you with tonight?"

"I'd like to sign up for a soycloud tour. Are you still doing those?"

"Absolutely! I'm so glad you're interested! Let me show you a brochure." The hub displayed one on the nearest smart poster.

"Looks great," Shoshanna said. "Can I sign up right now?"

"Sure thing," the hub gushed. It sent her a sign-up form. Instead of her name and ID, Shoshanna filled the form in with a string of zipped code containing a virus based on a self-learning algorithm. She was pretty sure that the hub was just stalling her while it summoned the peacekeepers, but also that its customer service goals would compel it to go through with the charade of accepting the sign-up form. Security in the Bellicia ecohood was shitty. These people were in denial, acting like they were still living on Earth. You had to be spaceborn to truly understand that the universe was out to get you.

She was right about the hub's fallibility. Eighty-two milliseconds after she sent the form back, it stuttered, "Invalid data entry. Invalid data entry. Invalid …"

Back at the community hall, Dr. James's lawyer had finally called off his blitz of character witnesses. They were wrapping up the procedural loose ends.

"Invalid." There was a momentary pause, and then the hub's voice returned to normal. "Thank you for signing up for a soycloud tour, Ms. Doyle! Is there anything else I can help you with tonight?"

Shoshanna's virus had exploited a zero-day vulnerability to convince the hub that it was a native .exe process. It was now propagating itself through the machine's subsystems.

"Well," Shoshanna said. Now it was her turn to stall, one eye on Cydney's feed.. "I'd really like it if you would walk me through that home soil manufacturing method."

Tense silence gripped the community hall as everyone awaited Dean Garcia's verdict. Garcia spoke three words. Her voice trembled noticeably. "Bail is denied."

The hall erupted.

"Whoa!" Cydney broadcast. "That's a surprise! Guess money can't buy freedom, after all! Snerk, snerk."

Shoshanna, as astonished as anyone else, texted Cydney. *"Srsly? She just denied him bail?"*

"Y," came the response. "BTW, where is everyone?"

Shoshanna did not bother to answer. She fired off a group text to 'everyone,' a.k.a. the other core members of Justice For David Reid. They were lurking in the undeveloped rocky terrain around Facilities Management. *"Well, that kind of destroys our pretext for being here. What do you guys want to do?"*

They conferred in an excited cacophony of texts. They had assumed—the whole ecohood had assumed—that Dr. James's expensive defense lawyer, as well as behind-the-scenes pressure from Virgin Atomic, would secure bail for him. They had prepared for that eventuality by refilling their propellant guns, donning masks and throwaway black coveralls, and surrounding Facilities Management, while Shoshanna scoped out the joint. The prospect of celebrating held little allure. They did not want to just trickle off home.

Nor did Shoshanna, to be honest. Having inserted her virus into the hub, she'd already achieved her own goal for the night, but she reminded herself that optics were just as important as information.

She performed a swift self-interrogation, to make sure that she wasn't merely indulging her violent streak, and then cut through the babble of texts. *"OK. What the hell, let's do this!"*

The Friends of David Reid streamed across the road, screaming "Yaaaah!" and firing their guns. By a miracle, none of them hit each other. As they burst into the building,

Shoshanna was already vaulting the symbolic barrier that separated reception from the staff offices, firing her revolver for effect. They spread through the building. Of course, no one was there. To forestall any sense of a letdown, Shoshanna commandeered the services manager's office and logged into his workstation, whose security protection her virus had already dismantled. Her troops gathered around her. "Here we go," she said, accessing the emergency tannoy system. "I'm going to announce that we've taken over, and then I'm going to present our demands. If anyone wants to add anything, now's your chance."

"Wow!" said an M.A. candidate in Transhuman Studies. "How'd you get into the hub?"

"Tell you later," Shoshanna said with a grin. She switched the tannoy on. "People of Bellicia! We greet you in the spirit of justice, equality, and tolerance ..."

Elfrida couldn't get to sleep, tired as she was. A destructive process of association led her thoughts from the Liberty Rock project, to a mind movie she'd watched too often before: flash-frozen corpses drifting in freefall, tangling with uprooted trees. The colonists of 11073 Galapagos had thought they were safe, too ...

She sat up, pushing her hair off her clammy forehead. Maybe she should've accepted those meds her therapist tried to give her for flashbacks. It was hot in the VA administration hab, where she and Mendoza had been invited to spend the night, and sweat prickled her skin.

She was about to fish out her tablet and watch a vid, when she heard a commotion outside. Mendoza's voice broke through. "Can't a guy go to the jakes without tripping the security alarm? I've done enough pissing into suction tubes the last few days."

Elfrida giggled quietly in the dark. She knew what he meant. Going to the bathroom in the rover had been a repeated ordeal of back-turning and pretending that you couldn't hear each other using the suction toilet.

Two minutes later, the side of her capsule concertinaed open and Mendoza crawled in on top of her legs.

"What are you doing here? Get out!"

He waved the door closed. Elfrida frantically hitched her blanket up over her chest. She was sleeping in her underwear.

"Sorry," Mendoza whispered. In the glow of the nightlight that had come on when the door opened, Elfrida saw that his expression was strained. He looked *scared*. "They've kept us apart so we can't compare notes. But we have to talk, just in case."

"You're sitting on my legs."

"Sorry."

"Just in case of what?"

"I don't know, but I don't trust this setup. They're definitely breaking the law, even if we haven't figured out how. And—"

"I knew it was a mistake to come here," Elfrida rattled out, giving way to the temptation to blame Mendoza for this whole trip. "We should've stayed focused on the Vesta Express. That's where the suspicious signal came from, and we already know that the left hand doesn't talk to the right hand in this company."

"*And,*" Mendoza overrode her, "have you noticed something else?"

"What?"

"All the prospective settlers look Chinese."

"Well, now that you mention it, I guess they do." Elfrida suddenly felt uncomfortable, and not because Mendoza was still sitting on her legs. He only weighed about 1.5 kilos, after all. "They speak Mandarin, too. They're probably from Africa."

"I don't think so."

"Or Europe, or maybe Canada. There are Chinese people everywhere."

"You think I don't know that? I'm from Manila, Goto. It's a freaking Chinatown."

"When I was a kid, I used to get confused for a half-Chinese person. The Chinese kids would talk to me, all friendly, and send me invites to their social networks. When I had to explain that I'm actually half-Japanese, it would be like, instant one-eighty. Exiled to Pallas. I wouldn't even exist for them anymore. I ended up avoiding all East Asian-looking people so that wouldn't keep happening."

"I didn't know you were half-Japanese."

Elfrida shrugged, glad the light was so dim. She knew she was red in the face with recollected humiliation. "There aren't many of us around. You can understand why they would make that mistake."

After a moment, Mendoza said, "But diaspora Chinese don't talk like bots. They speak English, or whatever."

"Yeah! The way Jimmy talked, that was seriously weird. What do you think is up with that?"

"I think he's a pureblood Chinese national, using translation software and a prompter. Did you notice how he never looked you in the eye when he was talking to you? That's because he was reading off the prompter in the HUD display of his retinal interface."

"Oh my dog, Mendoza." Elfrida shook his head. "Are you OK? That's just ... impossible."

"Chinese translation programs always suck. It's like impossible to develop a seamless one. And that's not all. Didn't you wonder why that rubble hauler nearly ran us off the ramp? It should have reacted faster ... *if* Sigurjónsdóttir's people were operating it. I don't think they were. I think it was a Chinese machine, operating on Chinese protocols, and those don't include getting out of the way for a rover with two humans on board."

Elfrida pulled up her knees and laced her arms around them. They were sitting at opposite ends of the capsule. She could see the whites of Mendoza's eyes. "Come on, that's just absurd."

"Is it? Do you know what they call the Philippines in Chinese?"

"What?"

"A tributary state."

"Oh. But ..."

"I'm not kidding. We have to pay tribute. Of course, our bureaucrooks call it interest. But my point is, to the Han, if you're not Chinese, you're nothing. You just told me you experienced that yourself when you were a kid."

Elfrida's heart thumped. She said firmly, "Well, Jimmy seems kind of nice. I haven't talked to any of the others, but my take is that even if they are Chinese nationals, they're still just typical, dumb colonists. But, Mendoza, they *can't* be Chinese! It's impossible."

"Why?"

"Because the Chinese don't come into space. You know that. They invest, and they mine resources and stuff, but they don't settle. They're one hundred percent purebloods. They're scared of the PLAN."

"Oh, bullshit," Mendoza said. "The PLAN *is* Chinese. They created the toilet rolls in the first place to drive the Americans off Mars. When they've driven the rest of us out of the solar system, they'll have it all to themselves."

"Dang! I'm not even going to listen to this." Elfrida reflexively pushed off from the bunk, and bumped her head on the ceiling. "Ow! We're supposed to be professionals, not conspiracy theorists. Tell you what, stick to the data, Mendoza. That's your specialty, and leave the people to me, OK?"

"Well, speaking of data," Mendoza started.

The side of the capsule concertinaed again. A hand the size of a tiger's paw, with jagged nails like dried-up orange peels, shot into the capsule, grabbed Mendoza's leg, and dragged him out. Mendoza clawed at the blanket, taking it with him. There was a thump. Elfrida huddled in the corner, so panicked that all she could do was blink for help. Her contacts, of course, stayed dead.

A face descended into the cubicle. "Cute sports bra. I'll give you a free tip, ma'am: never let a guy get your clothes off before he at least removes his shoes."

The face had an eagle tattooed on its forehead. Above it undulated a black mohican.

"José Running Horse. Nice to meet y'all."

"You aren't from UNESCO," Running Horse mused. Elfrida did not dare to contradict him. They'd locked Mendoza into his capsule. It turned out that when he was challenged the first time, he hadn't been coming back from the toilet, but from the *rover*. He had sneaked out there to transfer a data file containing his observations and theories into Rurumi's memory. The Big Dig security team had been watching him the whole time. They'd let him talk to Elfrida after that just to see if he would say anything controversial. So much for civilized expectations of privacy. Both their capsules had been bugged.

Barefoot, wearing someone else's sweats, Elfrida hunched in the same ergoform she'd occupied that afternoon in Sigurjónsdóttir's office. Running Horse towered over her. Among the spaceborn and the unfit, he projected the physical presence of an ogre. He was 185 centimeters and seriously shredded. His muscles popped under his skin, no doubt due to nanotic skeletal enhancement and a lot of lifting. He leaned over her, invading her personal space. "We had to check your story. Took a while. Tends to do, when you gotta wait twenty-eight minutes to hear, 'Your enquiry is not supported by this system,' and then the fucking customer-service bot tries to upsell you a premium search enhancement package. I hate the UN. Anyway, we got the goods in the end."

Running Horse rested one hip on the edge of Sigurjónsdóttir's desk. He cracked his knuckles.

"You've got quite the track record, Ms. Goto."

Elfrida hugged herself and moved her head in circles. She was too frightened to talk.

"And the other guy, forget about it. Born in the Philippines of mixed origin, technical high school, wins a UN-sponsored poll design contest, earns an apprenticeship in psephology, but can't make it at pro level. Accepts an entry-level position in UNVRP and spends the next decade shuttling between his office and his capsule, except for when he splurges on a ticket to the Luna Philharmonic. Like I said, forget it. *No one's* life is that boring." Running Horse pushed off from the desk and stabbed a finger in her face. "He's in deep cover. So are you, probably, but a big chunk of your record's sealed."

Elfrida squeaked, "That's because I was involved in a PLAN-related incident a couple of years ago."

"Do I look like I care? Here's what I care about: John Mendoza is an agent of the ISA."

Elfrida's jaw dropped. "Oh my dog, that's completely ridiculous! I mean …" She trailed off. She had, in fact, no way of knowing that Mendoza was *not* an ISA agent.

The ISA (Information Security Agency), a top-level agency of the UN, operated system-wide surveillance programs of unknown scope and granularity. Originally established to monitor and preserve the integrity of the internet, it was widely believed to have expanded this remit into physical surveillance and anti-PLAN operations. The ISA was everyone's favorite boogeyman after the PLAN itself. No one knew exactly what they got up to.

"It's a war out there," Running Horse said. He took out a cigarette, sucked on it, exhaled vapor that smelled like skunk spray. "Right now, right this second, the ISA is trying to hack into our systems. Every private company's in the same situation. ISA wants to know everything. Period. Everything. Privacy laws? Heh, heh, sucker. It's Big Data versus the little guy. The Man versus freedom of association, freedom of speech, freedom of innovation ... yeah: all that stuff that the UN supposedly exists to uphold. Ironic, huh?"

Elfrida had heard this kind of thing so many times before that she started to relax. It was typical private-sector griping.

Running Horse reminded her of the stakes when he added, "And when they can't hack us, they get physical. We have excellent information that there is an ISA agent on Vesta." He blew foul vapor into her face. "And my money says your buddy Mendoza is it."

Sigurjónsdóttir came into the office, bearing a tea tray. "You haven't been scaring her, have you?" she chided Running Horse.

"Naw. Just proving that I may be muscle, but I'm not dumb."

Although Elfrida recognized instantly that they were running a good cop / bad cop routine on her, the presence of Sigurjónsdóttir nevertheless made her feel secure enough to say, "If you think that regurgitating conspiracy theories from the internet makes you sound smart, I'm sorry, but try again."

"Oooh. *Regurgitating.* Figure big words make *you* sound smart?" Running Horse said nastily.

"José," Sigurjónsdóttir said, waving her hand in front of her face. "Would you mind not vaping that filth in my office? Thanks."

Running Horse ambled out. At the door, he turned to say, in a passable imitation of a robotic voice, *"XX intruder at the given coordinates. Identify yourself, or get fragged."*

Elfrida let out a scream.

"Just wanted to remind you that we've met before,"

Running Horse said. He left.

"Milk? Sugar?" Sigurjónsdóttir said, pouring through the teapot's tube. "I'm sorry, this must have been a terrible shock for you."

"Both," Elfrida said faintly. She cradled the hot teacup in her hands.

"I'm sure you had no idea that your colleague was working for the ISA."

"He isn't."

"Well, naturally they haven't admitted it. We're negotiating for confirmation. In the meantime, I'm afraid, we will have to ask you both to remain here as our guests."

"But you can't ... I mean, you can't keep us here against our will ... that's illegal."

"So is spying. And so, I'm sorry to say, is passing yourself off as an agent of UNESCO, when you aren't one."

Elfrida cringed. *Totally* busted. She felt a momentary urge to say it had been Gregor Lovatsky's idea. The urge passed. "I suppose ... we thought it didn't matter, or you wouldn't dare to call us on it. Because you're breaking the law yourselves." She raised her eyes to meet Sigurjónsdóttir's large gray ones. "You're lying to your stakeholders and the public to cover up what you're really doing here: Building a habitat for umpty-thousand Han Chinese who are so pureblooded, they don't even speak English."

There was a moment of silence, during which they could hear Mendoza banging on the wall of his capsule, two levels up in the cluster hab.

Sigurjónsdóttir nodded. "I'm next door to pureblooded myself," she said, gesturing at the pictures of her daughters. "And they are pureblooded. I had the poor judgement to marry a guy who's a couple of alleles more Scandinavian than I am. Divorced the rat a few years back, but the damage was done. So I do feel some empathy with the predicament of the pureblooded, as I think most people do."

"Oh, I do, too," Elfrida said. "In fact, I think it's great, what you're doing here. But the lying, the false pretenses ..."

"If we had announced at the outset that we were building a habitat for a party of Chinese settlers, do you think we would have had a chance in hell of getting it done?"

"No," Elfrida admitted.

"The entire volume would have been up in arms. The university would have led the charge, on whatever pretext they could find."

"So as not to have to share this asteroid with umpty-thousand—"

"Two hundred thousand."

"*Ulp.* Two *hundred* thousand, pureblooded ... PLAN magnets."

"Who were originally attracted to Vesta," Sigurjónsdóttir said quietly, "because of the opportunity to construct a genuinely PLAN-proof asteroid colony beneath several kilometers of solid rock."

"Like the Bellicia ecohood."

"Bellicia, version 2.0."

Elfrida grimaced, acknowledging the multiple layers of irony. She drank some of her sweet, milky tea. FUK culture definitely had its points.

Perhaps because of the adrenaline still pumping through her veins, she felt strangely undismayed by the calamitous turn their investigation had taken. It would all be sorted out when they confirmed that Mendoza was not an ISA agent. In the meantime, it was up to her to make what she could of this.

"You're not going to lock *me* in a capsule, are you?" she asked.

Sigurjónsdóttir did not answer. Her gaze unfocused, indicating that she was reading off contacts or an implanted retinal interface. "Oh my dog. This is outrageous. Shocking! Ms. Goto, I've just been notified—I'm afraid something rather odd is happening in the Bellicia ecohood. You'd better have a look at this feed."

A screen sprang out of its recess in her desk and spun around to face Elfrida, knocking over the teapot.

Cydney's breathless voice filled the office.

xvii.

"As you can see for yourselves, a crowd has gathered outside UNESCO headquarters. Everyone mocks the blue berets, but when the doo-doo hits the fan, it's 'Mommy, Mommy, help.' *Snerk.* Like, what can the peacekeepers *do*? There are five of them here, versus at least fifty activists holed up in Facilities Management. They claim to be armed with lethal projectile and beam weapons. They might even be telling the truth. You can do a lot with a home printer ... and have you ever seen that vid where a modded housekeeping bot goes all Nazi on some kids in the ZUS? *This* might be what's about to happen here."

Cydney cued the vid to give herself a breathing space. She pulled out her cigarette and took a calming drag. The mob outside the koban was growing. The Fab Five were holed up inside. Frantically asking their bosses what to do, Cydney guessed. With a twenty-eight-minute round-trip signal delay to Earth, that could take a while.

Cydney had never imagined that Shoshanna and the gang had the nerve to pull a stunt like this.

They'd broadcast a list of demands. More money for field research, more support for disadvantaged students, faster wifi in the dormitories, the establishment of a Literature degree course, and a new coffee machine for the PHCTBS Studies lounge.

I could get through to them, Cydney thought.

Nothing was happening here, anyway. She hurried back to campus. On her way, she explained to her fans what she was planning to to do. Their support—expressed in comments, and a corresponding gush of micropayments—solidified her resolve. Finding Dean Garcia in her office, she offered, "Ma'am, I'll go talk to them."

Garcia was flapping around, fielding questions and issuing statements on half a dozen channels. "We gave them what they wanted," she said to Cydney. "Why are they doing this?"

"I don't know, ma'am. But often, when you give people what they want, they ask for more."

"That's very profound, Ms. Blaisze. Go on, go on, if you think it will do any good! You needn't ask *my* permission."

Cydney had a feeling she'd just been mocked. But this didn't dampen her resolve. She had the expectations of 5,022,369 people to live up to, and counting.

She climbed the hill out of town, commenting on the strange cavalcade she passed along the way. It looked like a parade of recycling bins with legs. A couple of quickie interviews confirmed that this was a bug-out movement heading for the Bremen Lock. If the order came to evacuate, these folks planned to be first in line. They seemed to be few (so far), and they were mostly families with young children. But it proved that at least some residents of the ecohood were taking Shoshanna's threats seriously.

Cydney felt slightly less confident about her read of the situation. But she bounded on, outdistancing the parade.

Facilities Management blazed like a theater on opening night. A new banner billowed above the vine-wreathed columns out front: *JUSTICE! EQUALITY! TOLERANCE!*

Cydney looked back down the hill. The town and campus lay mired in darkness.

Suppressing a shiver, she fluffed her hair and bounced towards the entrance. She didn't have to succeed. It would be OK if she failed. She just had to be entertaining while she was failing. That was her shtick.

"Hey! Shoshanna! Helloooo!"

A text popped up in her HUD.

"Hey, good to see you, Cydney. C'mon in."

Win Khin and another student met her at the entrance and apologetically frisked her. Jittery activists milled in the reception area. They'd hacked the smart posters so as to watch themselves on the news. On one poster, this very room now appeared; it was Cydney's feed. Noticing, they mugged and postured for her.

Cydney was just getting into the swim of things, firing off questions, screaming with laughter, accepting a puff of someone's cigarette, when Shoshanna appeared. She pulled Cydney into the services manager's office and closed the door. "They're having fun now," she said. "Hope the drugs don't run out too soon."

"Someone's got stim," Cydney said, feeling the drug bubble through her adrenal system.

"Yeah." Shoshanna folded her arms. She stared at Cydney. Then she reached out and pinched Cydney's left earlobe between her thumb and forefinger.

5,068,915 people saw Cydney's feed go dark.

"Hey!"

Shoshanna pulled Cydney closer. Blades flashed in her other hand. She cut off Cydney's earlobe with the services manager's desk scissors.

Cydney screamed. She clamped her hands over her ear, crumpling to the floor. Blood travelled in dotted arcs through the air like movement lines in a manga strip.

Shoshanna tossed her a box of tissues.

"Sorry about that. But *I* want to control the optics here. I'm putting it in this drawer, OK?" She held up Cydney's earlobe, with its embedded microcamera, and dropped it into a desk drawer.

Cydney vomited.

"You can always get it reconstructed," Shoshanna said. "I thought you were tough."

The words filtered like the buzzing of an insect through the unbearable pain. Cydney subvocalized to her fans: *~Hey ... guys. Don't go anywhere. This bitch just cut. My. Fucking. Ear. Off. Yeah. This is not a snerk situation anymore.*

"Well put," said Shoshanna, who was obviously monitoring Cydney's feed herself.

Pressing a fistful of tissues to her ear, Cydney collapsed in the services manager's ergoform. The office was small and mostly walled with screens. Each one depicted a different part of the habitat. A soycloud dropped its intake tube into Olbers Lake. People were coming out of their homes in the Branson Habs, staring upwards.

"If ... if your demands aren't met, are you going to follow through on your threats?"

"I already am," Shoshanna said.

"Huh? ... Oh." Cydney gulped. "It should have been getting light by now. You've disabled the sun mirrors."

"Switched them to ThirdLight settings. It'll get a bit lighter than this, but not much."

"What ... what else can you do from here?"

"I'm still finding out."

Cydney's ear throbbed. The taste of vomit soured her mouth. She subvocalized, ~*I ... I'm gonna sign off for a few. Need to get medical assistance. But stay accessed for more drama here in the Bellicia ecohood on 4 Vesta!*"

"Make that *hostage drama*," Shoshanna said, smiling at her.

Elfrida fell back in her ergoform. She felt as shaken and horrified as Cydney must surely be herself. "This is beyond crazy! Oh my dog, poor Cydney." She rubbed her face with her hands, assailed by guilt that she wasn't there.

"Is she a personal friend?" Sigurjónsdóttir enquired.

"Uh, yes. Yeah, she's always kept it off the feed, but we're kind of a thing."

"I had no idea. How awful for you." Sigurjónsdóttir reached out and touched Elfrida's arm. "Look, it's going to be all right. The peacekeepers may not be capable of mounting an effective response, but our security corps will handle it. We've got several highly capable phavatars in the habitat. I'm confident that they'll defuse the situation without loss of life or, er, further injury to anyone."

"I guess you're still not going to let me go."

"I'm afraid that equation hasn't changed, no. But in light of your emotional distress, we'll certainly do everything possible to make your stay here comfortable."

Elfrida grimaced. "In that case, can I plug my immersion kit in and get some work done?"

There was nothing she could do for Cydney. But she could do her job. She'd been away from her desk for four sols, and work had piled up like the Matterhorn in her inbox.

After reasoning with Sigurjónsdóttir—OK, wheedling, begging, and bluffing that she knew someone on the President's Advisory Council—she got permission to use her immersion kit for a telepresence session. The Big Dig undoubtedly had proper telepresence equipment, but they weren't about to let her use that. So she was stuck with a onetime password for the wifi, and as much sensory realism as a $5,000 gaming setup could provide.

"Before you slap me," she said to Petruzzelli, "I ought to warn you that I can't feel anything. I can see and hear. That's all. I've got limited data transfer capability and the bare minimum of sensory feedback."

"Well, what a disappointment," Petruzzelli said. "I was looking forward to punching you in the kisser when you finally deigned to show up." She grinned.

Petruzzelli was wearing an EVA suit, her blue hair flattened by the helmet she'd just taken off. When Elfrida pinged her, she'd been outside, checking recently-loaded cargo against the manifests, she explained—a job that would normally fall to someone much lowlier than the captain. She peeled her suit off and stowed it in the quarterdeck locker. Turning back to the phavatar, she said, "I doubt that suit could feel it even if I did hit you. We fixed it, but for 'fixed,' read 'restored basic functionality' ..."

Elfrida grimaced. "I'm really sorry—"

"Blistering barnacles, *please* don't do that."

"Memo to self. Do not attempt any expressions. No, I should have checked in with you long before this, and I apologize. But I've been out of the office. Have you seen what's happening on 4 Vesta?"

The *Kharbage Collector* was now half a million kilometers from Vesta, trucking between isolated asteroid settlements, dropping off consumables and picking up recycling.

"Yeah!" Petruzzelli said. "Are those students loony? Or are they just completely unfamiliar with the concept of tightly coupled systems? I'm Earthborn, and even I know that you do not screw with the life-support functions of your own damn habitat. Just. No. That stuff is *way* too easy to fuck up, and one little fuck-up is all it takes to make a very bad day in space."

Elfrida gulped, feeling hollow at this reminder of the danger Cydney was in.

"In fact, an asteroid is just like a big spaceship. But with less redundancy." Petruzzelli ushered Elfrida out of the quarterdeck. "Everyone's down in engineering. Let's go up to the bridge so we can talk in peace."

Elfrida flailed her way up the zip tube that ran the length of the *Collector's* 150-meter keel. Transferring from the keel tube to the elevator was always a challenge on a Startractor. Petruzzelli had to manhandle the phavatar's clumsy frame into one of the two apertures in the rotating transfer point.

"Did you even get my emails?"

"Not until just now," Elfrida apologized. "I haven't been able to check—"

Spin gravity took hold, and Elfrida thumped to the floor of the elevator. Petruzzelli landed lightly beside her.

"I pinged you like twenty times. They rejected my application for compensation."

"Oh, crap. I'm sorry. Did you fill in the form like I showed you?"

"Yes. Well ..."

"Alicia."

"I said the phavatar was destroyed. Which it isn't, obviously. But they don't know that. Anyway, we thought it *was* trashed. Michael managed to get it operational, but it's still basically useless ... as you see."

The elevator opened on the bridge. Elfrida stumbled out, and looked back. In the reflective surface cladding of the elevator shaft, she saw the tin-can figure of the phavatar she was using. Her head was a lump of mangled plastisteel and splart, with two steel lenses poking out, and a speaker instead of a mouth. The damage done by the pirates on 550363 Montego had not looked as bad as this repair job. "Wow. Yes, I do see. They shouldn't have refused to compensate you. Did you attach pictures?"

"Before *and* after."

"Are you sure you didn't make any other mistakes on the form?"

Petruzzelli balanced one knee on the ergoform at her workstation. Spinning around in circles, she said, "Well, I may have said that it was a čapek-class mark three, not a mark one."

"Oh. That's it, then."

"There isn't much difference."

"Except for about eighty thousand spiders on the secondary market."

"But they look the same. And after being smashed up by a bunch of pirates, you definitely wouldn't be able to tell the difference. And I attached mark-three specs."

Elfrida shook her head. "They would know. They would look you up and find out that you don't have a čapek-class mark three registered to this ship. Honestly, you're lucky they haven't come after you for making false representations. Alicia, you just can't *do* that."

"Everyone scams the system," Petruzzelli said tightly. She plucked a chunk of glittering asteroid ore off her desk and threw it from hand to hand.

"Yeah, maybe, but ... Don't take this the wrong way, but did you really need the extra eighty K that bad?"

Petruzzelli turned her gaze up to Elfrida's lenses. "In all honesty? No spin, no corporate happy-talk? Yes."

"OK." Elfrida had asked the question, but now that she had the answer, she didn't know what to do with it. She did not, she realized, know what it was like to worry about money, to work for an outfit where the cash might literally run out. "Still, you should have thought about it a bit harder," she mumbled. "They might blackball you. I might wake up one day and find out that the *Kharbage Collector* isn't on my list of approved logistics and transport partners anymore."

"Dog! You think they'd really do that? Over one little mistake on a form? They didn't even give me the money!"

"I dunno if they would or not. But I get the feeling that the new procurement guidelines aren't working out, so they might be in a contractor-firing mood."

"I wish you would go back to the old procurement system. It worked so much better when you were allowed to buy asteroids from *us*. You don't even know what this has done to our cash flow. Our CEO is, like, selling ships to pay his kids' tuition fees." Petruzzelli thew her chunk of ore at the wall. It curved in the air and hit someone's workstation. "A transport fee here and a phavatar leasing fee there is just, it isn't shit. "

"I know," Elfrida said helplessly. "I wish there was something I could do. But, I know this isn't much, but there's another fee on offer if you want it."

"I want," Petruzzelli said in a flat voice.

"I need to go back to 550363 Montego."

"What for? Those meatheads are sure to be gone."

"Yeah, exactly. And if they are, and the rock checks out, I can put in a purchase recommendation. Which would make a whole four recommends I've been able to file this year."

"This isn't working out for you, either, is it?" Petruzzelli said. She frowned at her screens. "I dunno. We're burning kind of fast in the wrong direction."

Elfrida was silent. She didn't have access to a starmap, but the rate at which the phavatar's coordinates were changing with respect to Vesta's orbit implied a relatively slow burn. For that matter, it would make no sense for Petruzzelli to be burning fast when she had to stop every five minutes to pick up someone's recycling.

"Well, I guess if you've got a lot of other scheduled stops to make," Elfrida said. "Or if you're carrying passengers who need to get someplace ..."

The *Kharbage Collector*, in addition to multiple cargo bays, had a passenger module that could hold up to four thousand souls at a squeeze. It was the counterweight to the command module, rotating around the nose of the ship like a propellor.

"Oh, no," Petruzzelli said. "No passengers at all on this run."

"Then ... can we do this?"

Petruzzelli called up her holographic 3D starmap and climbed onto her desk, arching back from the waist so her head wouldn't be inside the display. "Here we are, see? And here's 550363 Montego, and here's 6 Hebe, which is my final destination on this run. It's in the opposite direction."

Elfrida felt talked down to, in more than the literal sense. "I know that. But 550363 Montego is also *close*, compared to 6 Hebe."

"Yeah, but changing direction eats a lot of fuel. And honestly? The fee isn't worth the PITA factor."

Elfrida knew what Petruzzelli was driving at. And she felt

as sad as her phavatar looked. She had unconsciously expected warmth and sympathy from Petruzzelli. Instead, she was getting treated like an ATM.

It was her own fault, she realized. She never had told Petruzzelli about her relationship with Cydney, although she wasn't sure why. She also hadn't told Petruzzelli that she was being detained by Virgin Atomic at the moment. Strangely, that seemed to matter less than her reluctance to explain the whole Cydney situation. Anyway, her reticence had created a gulf between her and Petruzzelli, which as a recycler captain with bills to pay, Petruzzelli was quite naturally filling with wheeler-dealing.

"*Sigh*," Elfrida said. "How about this? Give me a lift to 550363 Montego, and I'll help you refile that compensation request. To make up for the PITA factor."

"Yeah?"

"Yeah. If you like, we can also apply for a hazard bonus for this trip, since you'll be entering a volume where hostile entities have recently been active."

"Hostile entities? A pirate fanboy and his family," Petruzzelli scoffed. "Anyway, no way they'll have stuck around."

"I know. Actually, hazard bonuses are only supposed to be paid when there's a high statistical risk of bumping into the PLAN."

"I never heard of anyone getting a hazard bonus from UNVRP."

"They don't make a huge effort to publicize their availability."

"How much?"

"Fifty percent on top of the usual fee."

"Sweet!" Petruzzelli's eyebrow smileys suddenly turned pink and happy. "I'd kiss you, if you didn't look like the love child of a cyborg and an industrial accident."

Elfrida smiled sadly, which made Petruzzelli shudder.

She despised herself for bending the rules to pay Petruzzelli off. But—she thought, lying in her capsule in the Big Dig, while Petruzzelli altered the *Kharbage Collector's* course, up to her elbows in stars—you had to put it in perspective. Virgin Atomic was breaking a whole raft of laws about stakeholder disclosure and transparency, and that was just the infractions Elfrida had found out about so far. If a big corporation could do that and get away with it, why shouldn't Petruzzelli be able to scam the system, too? There was nothing (Elfrida insisted to herself) morally wrong about fixing her up with a little sweetener.

xviii.

Elfrida marched up to Sigurjónsdóttir and held out a memory crystal. "Here's the record of my session, like I promised."

"Thank you. I'm sorry we had to insist on this, but ..."

"Information security. I get it."

One of the reasons Elfrida had explicitly criticized Petruzzelli was because she knew she'd have to hand over a copy of the data dump to Sigurjónsdóttir later. Not that the VA stakeholder relations coordinator had any power to get either her or Petruzzelli in trouble, but still, it was important to stay clean on the record. She was confident she hadn't said anything that could be construed as breaking the rules. And the hazard bonus was technically allowable, just.

"I can't get into this," Sigurjónsdóttir said, snapping her fingers at her screen.

"Oh. It's encrypted. You could apply to UNVRP to have it decrypted, or I could do it for you."

"If you wouldn't mind."

Elfrida went around behind Sigurjónsdóttir's desk. She blinked at the iris scanner on Sigurjónsdóttir's computer and answered a couple of her security questions. "There." She lingered. Sigurjónsdóttir's other screen showed the bottom of the Big Dig. Figures in yellow and red EVA suits scurried around, dwarfed by rubble-haulers and an excavation bot that resembled a flower made of guillotine blades. "Wow. I've never seen a bot like that before."

"Grisly, isn't it? Not ours. The Liberty Rock syndicate provided most of the equipment in use here."

"Is that ... OK?" *So Mendoza was right.* The rubble-hauler that nearly ran them off the ramp had been Chinese. "Is it safe?"

"So they tell us."

"But don't the Chinese use different operating protocols?"

"Not just protocols. You've heard of the Great Firewall, I assume."

The Great Firewall was a cultural phenomenon and a technological fact rolled into one. Even previous to the Mars Incident, Chinese exceptionalism had led the nation to develop its own internet—the precursor to today's sinanet—based on a separate physical infrastructure, and to pursue robotics development in isolation from the rest of the world. After the Mars Incident, the Big Disconnect had accelerated this divergence, as China blamed the then-United States and the rest of the West for unleashing the ASI explosion thought to have caused the catastrophe. By differentiating its internet at the code level, China had sought to wall its cyber-territory off from the risk of self-propagating MI.

Now the shoe was on the other foot. Though the UN did not openly blame China for the emergence of the PLAN, Mendoza's conspiracy theory had plenty of echoes in high places. No matter how many anti-AI treaties the Chinese signed up to, no matter how strenuously they decried the very existence of AGI (human-equivalent AI) and ASI (superintelligent AI), and no matter how much *they* suffered at the hands of the PLAN ... no one was ever going to trust them again.

So the two worlds of machine intelligence had continued to develop separately, as it were in a mutual huff. Ecosystems of algorithms had evolved that were not only incomprehensible to each other, but mutually hostile. At this point, you couldn't even use a Chinese computer on a regular wifi network without crashing both things.

"So let me get this straight," Elfrida said. "If those construction bots were to go berserk, you would have no way of stopping them?"

"That won't happen."

"But your computers can't even talk to theirs."

"That's why we have humans in the loop."

"Who rely on *computers* to talk to each other. Do you have anyone here who actually speaks Mandarin?"

Sigurjónsdóttir smiled weakly.

On the screen, the Chinese construction workers sprinted over to the side of the cavern where they were working. They took cover behind a buttress. A blizzard of rock and dust blanked the screen out.

"Uh, that didn't look very safe."

The blast wave propagated through the hab, jolting them. Sigurjónsdóttir's teacup rattled on its saucer.

"Don't worry," Sigurjónsdóttir said. "They're culturally risk-averse."

Elfrida had thought that here, nestled in the bowels of Rheasilvia Mons, she was at least safe. But she didn't feel that way anymore.

"Well, I'm going to grab some lunch and get back to work," she said.

"Try the crab au gratin," Sigurjónsdóttir said. "We import all our own food. None of that recycled, MSG-flavored sludge in *this* hab."

For the second time, Elfrida flew towards 550363 Montego, towed by a couple of the *Kharbage Collector's* drones.

No robot sharks swarmed out to greet her. "All clear, I think," she radioed to Petruzzelli. "Their Superlifter's gone, too."

"I'm sending a drone in ahead of you, just in case."

Crab au gratin gurgled uneasily in Elfrida's stomach. "I wonder how far they've gone. Superlifters are tugs. They're not made for interplanetary travel."

"Do not mock the humble Superlifter. We used to use 'em to tow asteroids across the system."

"Yeah, but without people on board. Their life-support capacity is really limited. Anyway, I hope they're all right."

Petruzzelli blew a raspberry into the radio. "Don't waste your sympathy on those baboons."

Elfrida glided over the surface of 550363 Montego. Riddled with old and new impacts, it looked like a charcoal soufflé. The mouth of the pirates' excavation yawned between mini-mountains of tailings that had settled back to the surface. Her damaged wreck of a phavatar had zero scanning capabilities, so she couldn't gather any data on the mineral composition of the asteroid. But she saw nothing to contradict Mendoza's initial hypothesis that it was a big old hunk of basaltic rock. The excavated chamber would make a handy vessel for UNVRP's payloads of gengineered microbes. And the asteroid was massive enough that when it impacted Venus, it would blow a hefty chunk of atmosphere into space.

"Oh crap," Petruzzelli said.

"What?"

"You'd better get in there."

Elfrida's drones dived into the cave mouth, pulling her behind them. A beam of light danced up ahead, emitted by the drone that Petruzzelli had sent in as a scout. It played over the side of a Bigelow hab.

From which a spacesuited figure had just emerged, waving its arms.

"Help!" it shouted on the public band. "Help! *Help!*"

The pirates had gone, all right.

But they had left behind the hapless colonists who'd hoped to settle on 550363 Montego.

"I need oxygen and water. *Now!*"

"I don't have much to spare."

"Crap on it, Petruzzelli, just send the stuff! There are twenty-seven human beings in here and they've only got about fifty liters of oxygen left! They're dehydrated, most of them can't even move or speak. This one guy might be dead.

I can't tell. This shitty fucking phavatar doesn't have any telemetric scanning capability, or a light source, and it's dark in here. And *cold*. Can you send a medibot, too, and some supercapacitors, so I can get the backup generator going?"

"Oh dog. I didn't know it was that bad. All right, emergency consumables coming up."

Drones zoomed into the cavern, towing the emergency supplies Elfrida had asked for. She worked flat out, transferring the stuff into the airlock of the Bigelow hab. The people inside were too weak to help, even if they had had more than a handful of functioning EVA suits between them.

Fortunately, she had seen habs like this before, so she already knew how to change out its oxygen reserve tanks. The Bigelow Deep Space Life Support System was a mass-produced low-end model, 'ideal for longer-term resource extraction missions,' according to the company, which shifted thousands of them on a wink-wink-say-no-more basis to aspiring colonists. Its 2,000 m^3 pressurized volume was divided into four decks: galley/recreation/operations; crew quarters/storage; work/hygiene; and stowage/subsystems at what would have been the bottom, if the hab were in gravity.

The Extropia Collective had squeezed into the operations deck and depressurized the other levels when their oxygen started to run out. Thus cut off from the toilets and the water recovery unit, they had been reduced to drinking their own urine. Someone had tried to cut a hole in the wall to get at the water in the hab's shell that was used for radiation shielding purposes. Fortunately, they had succeeded only in shorting out the lights.

Elfrida repressurized the crew quarters and carried the sickest would-be colonists down there so that Petruzzelli's medibot could tend them. She kept the others on the operations deck. Soot coated everything, a relic of the electrical fire which had destroyed the CO2 removal assembly. The handful of people clustered around Elfrida's phavatar looked like urchins in an e-waste dump.

"What motivated you to illegally occupy this asteroid?" she said. She had to put it like that, for the record.

The man who spoke for the collective, Hugh Meredith-Pike, croaked, "We were seeking the secret of human happiness."

★

When she'd kludged the air circulation system into working order, Elfrida reported to Petruzzelli.

"I think we've got the situation stabilized. But their viability stats suck. We've got twenty adults and seven children in a pressurized volume of about 2,000 cubic meters, with ten functioning EVA suits between them, and a few weeks' worth of basic supplies, thanks to you. They had *nothing* left. Those pirates ought to be prosecuted for murder."

"But no one's actually dead, are they?"

"No, but they would have been in another sol or two."

"Well, let's get them the hell off that rock. I've got plenty of room in my passenger module."

"Um."

"What?"

"They don't want to go."

"What?"

"I know. After what they've just been through … But they're unanimous."

"Did you offer them a, *cough cough*, incentive?"

"Yes. Wonder of wonders, that was a big no thank you. They're wireheads. They spent their entire life savings to get here, and they're staying."

"Oh, FFS. I'll just tow the hab out."

"It wouldn't fit through the cave entrance."

"… You're right. They must have inflated it inside."

"I'll stay here with them."

"Say again, 'cause I did not copy. It sounded like you said

you're staying here with them."

"I did. I will. This is my job. This is what the Space Corps does. Helping and supporting communities. I'm gonna put in a purchase recommendation, but we'll be dealing with Centiless, so it's not going to be immediate, to say the least. When that goes through, we'll get an evacuation order, and I'll make sure that business goes to Kharbage LLC, if you're still in the volume. Then we can go in with bots, drag them out kicking and screaming. But I don't want to go there until I've got the evacuation order. So in the meantime, I'm just going to stay here and see if I can help them not die. They don't know crap about surviving in space."

" ... Sounds like you've thought it through."

"It's not a big deal. You don't need this phavatar anymore, anyway, right? *Smile.*"

"*Smile.* Well, I guess if you're OK with that ... I wish I could stay, but ..."

"But you've got bills to pay. I totally understand. Just, could you send over some more stuff before you go? They have a fuel cell generator, but it's out of hydrogen. Their organic matter recycling unit needs new filters. The smell in here is something else, I'm told. We could also use the loan of one of your drones, in case I need to tow stuff around. Oh, and splart: as much as you've got."

"Coming up. I hate to mention it, but can I invoice UN-VRP for this stuff?"

"Of course. And Petruzzelli? Don't worry about being too precise. You can kind of round off the figures, if you get my drift."

"... Thanks."

"You can come out now!"

Alicia Petruzzelli's shout echoed into the dark recesses of the passenger module's economy deck.

She stepped out of the elevator. Her red leather Gecko

Docs squelched on rubber tiles. Closely spaced rows of couches receded into dimness. The air was hot and stale. It smelled like a second-hand car: sickly-mint sanitizer spray and Cheetos.

"I said you can come out now! She's gone!"

Five figures rose up from among the couches. They were Captain Haddock, his wife Anemone, his son Kelp, his brother Codfish, and Codfish's wife Coral. Kelp was eating Cheetos from a white-label economy-size bag he had pinched from the galley.

"Blistering barnacles, that was a close call," Haddock said.

"Not really," Petruzzelli said. "In that fragged-out suit, she wasn't exactly going to notice that the command module is a few centimeters closer to the keel than it should be, if we really didn't have any passengers out here to balance for. Anyway, she's gone now. She decided to stay with them." Petruzzelli measured the construction crew with a look. "You didn't mention that you only left them a week's worth of air."

"Arrrr! It's not even been a week since we left. You were going to go back after you dropped us off—"

"Well, apparently that second-hand carbon dioxide removal assembly you sold them malfunctioned. Caught on fire."

"A fire in a hab? They're lucky to be alive."

"They are alive," Petruzzelli said, "no thanks to you."

"Don't deserve to be. Dumbest bunch of squatters I've ever met," said Codfish. "Bet they forget their lines, too. What a waste of time."

"Hasn't been a waste of time for me," Petruzzelli said. "I've got a green light to invoice UNVRP for all the stuff you didn't leave them, and then some."

"Can we go back to the command module? The air's bad in here," said Coral, with no sense of irony at all.

They went. A contrail of orange Cheetos dust hung in the

air of the transfer point like forensic evidence. But no one would ever know that the pirates had been travelling on the *Kharbage Collector*. No one else was there to see them. Their Superlifter was moored in the ship's auxiliary craft bay, on the principle that the best place to conceal something is where you'd normally find it. Petruzzelli had slapped some spare Kharbage LLC decals over the Jolly Rogers on its drive shield (that was what she'd been doing when Elfrida telecasted in), just in case Elfrida took a peek in the auxiliary bay. Which she hadn't.

Back on the bridge, Petruzzelli flapped a hand at the pirates. "Make like a banana. I'm tired of looking at you. Go hang out in the crew lounge."

"I'm going to read the Narnia books again," Kelp said. "Your ship's got a really great library, Captain Petruzzelli."

"You can thank my colleague, Captain Okoli, for that," Petruzzelli said. "He was on a mission for a while to get everyone in the company to read. I'm more of a gamer myself."

Kelp, Coral, Anemone, and Codfish scattered. Haddock lingered.

"Are we under thrust?" he asked.

"Will be in a minute."

"And are you going to drop us off on 3982440 Twizzler?"

"That's our deal."

"Be a darlin' girl and take us on a wee bit further."

"Why? It's a good rock. Fits all the UNVRP criteria. You've got people lined up. Haven't you?"

"Aye, but ..." Haddock came and sat on the corner of Petruzzelli's workstation. Nervously twirling his ebony goatee, he confessed, "It's too close to here. I don't feel safe in this volume nae more. Nor does my lady wife."

"Space is *big*, Min-jae."

"The name's Archibald."

"Whatever. You folding?"

"No. Have I not a pirate's soul, and a rare lust for livin'

on the edge? I have that. But I've no desire to be nobbled. And I'd remind you that if we're caught, you'll be in a heap o' trouble yourself, lassie."

"Oh, screw it," Petruzzelli said. "Where do you want to go?"

"Ye could take us on to 6 Hebe."

Petruzzelli grumbled, but agreed. With that concession in hand, Haddock promptly asked to use the internet for a long-distance call. Suspecting that he was going to arrange for someone else to pick him and his family up from 6 Hebe, Petruzzelli consented, and got ready to listen in. If Haddock expected privacy on the *Kharbage Collector,* he was very much mistaken in his assumptions.

The pirate's real name was Min-jae Park. He and his family were members of an ethnically mixed nomadic community with roots in the Korean peninsula. They called themselves *namsadang;* those who fell afoul of them called them a criminal network. Perhaps it was not so curious that Min-jae had developed an obsession with pirates. Anyway, he and his near and dear had long since gone their own way, buying a secondhand Superlifter and taking it from there.

For Petruzzelli, they were the human equivalent of a starmap. Some data points were known, some were concealed in the possession of others. And all the empty spaces in between tantalized her. She wanted to know more about Haddock's connections, especially since he could get her in trouble, as he had tactlessly pointed out.

Alone in an unused cabin, with only some old pornographic posters for witnesses (as he thought), Haddock used his BCI to ping an ID unknown to Petruzzelli. The signal travelled through the asteroid belt for seven minutes, covering about 108 million kilometers. It reached a destination that was moving on a trajectory wrongly angled to be an asteroid, so it had to be a ship cruising in the volume around 6 Hebe. What a coincidence. Not.

"*Y what?*" the unknown owner of the ID typed.

"Ahoy! Haddock here. That you, Yonezawa?"

Petruzzelli radioed her ex-colleague Viola Budgett.

"You know anything about a guy called Kiyoshi Yonezawa?"

Budgett took a minute and a half to respond. "No," she said.

"You sure? Because whoever he is, Haddock and company have arranged for him to pick them up from 6 Hebe."

Petruzzelli had already told Budgett by email how Elfrida Goto had busted the pirates on 550363 Montego. She now explained that Haddock was scared to pull another job in this volume, at least for a while.

"Well, that's just great," Budgett said despairingly.

On the screen, Budgett's jowly face was framed by a pink balaclava. Her telescopic steel left eye—an implanted microscope / telescope—stared expressionlessly; her brown right one skittered about.

"If they aren't gonna work any more jobs, where's the money going to come from?" she whined.

"You let me worry about that," Petruzzelli said.

"But we *need* the money!"

"Is it cold there, or something?"

Budgett's breath puffed white, momentarily obscuring her face on the screen. "Not really," she said.

Petruzzelli switched her attention between Budgett and another screen, where she was earning credits to use in the game *Second Idiran War,* by devoting a portion of the *Kharbage Collector's* hub's computing resources to simulating a superintelligent Mind. She was playing an Idiran. Lots of days, she just didn't want to be human anymore. Talking to Budgett made her feel that way in spades.

"We need money, like yesterday," Budgett whined.

Petruzzelli thought of a quote that her former boss, Martin Okoli, had liked to use. "Who you calling *we*, white man?"

A minute and a half later, a smile of recognition flashed on Budgett's face. "That's one of Captain Okoli's lines. Dog, I miss the *Kharbage Can*. Everything was so simple then."

"Everything was never simple," said Petruzzelli, but she felt the same way. Budgett's rarely-glimpsed smile reminded Petruzzelli of the period when they'd worked together on the *Kharbage Can*, part of Martin Okoli's tightly knit, happy-go-lucky crew. She'd never realized just what an accomplishment it was to manage a crew that well, and how many difficult decisions Okoli must have faced on a daily basis, until she got promoted to captain herself.

Impulsively, she said, "OK, check it out. How much do you need? I'll cover it."

Budgett's eyes welled up. A plump hand rose to wipe them. "Oh my dog, Alicia, thank you. Thank you so much. We, uh, we need fifty thousand spiders."

"What are you buying this time? A particle accelerator?"

"No, we've got one of those. No, this, uh ... it's for something else."

"What?"

Budgett's hands, one flesh and the other a maniple equipped with several tool sockets, fluttered. With visible reluctance, she explained.

Budgett was not a cyborg—that is, she did not identify with the cyborgist movement. But the amount of augments she had put her squarely in the category. Petruzzelli wondered if having that much electronics in your body made you think and feel differently. Certainly, she could not comprehend how anyone as supposedly smart as Budgett could have got herself into such a mess.

"You really are screwed, aren't you?" She made her eyebrow tattoos do *disapproving scowls*.

Budgett hung her head. At least she had enough self-awareness to be ashamed. "We just have to keep paying him," she said hopelessly. "There's no way out."

We'll see about that, Petruzzelli thought.

"Do you, uh, want his ID? To get in touch with him?"

"Bothead," Petruzzelli said affectionately. "I've already got it. Swiped it from Haddock. I'm pinging him now."

xix.

In the crepuscular light of ThirdLight's splinter-moons, plastisteel gorillas surrounded the Facilities Management building. These were Virgin Atomic's security phavatars. They were familiar to Bellicians from parades and festivals, when they would dress up in tuxedos and serve refreshments to the delighted humans. Now they hulked like monsters in black EMP-proof hooded capes. They bounded towards the building with no pretense of stealth, demanding the surrender of the activists holed up inside. When this was not forthcoming, they appeared to be at a loss.

"Wait for it," Shoshanna said to her troops.

The shadow of a soycloud engulfed the building. Its PHES thrusters were not working very well, since they depended on thermal updrafts to convert into kinetic energy, and the atmosphere had cooled several degrees since Shoshanna turned off the sun. The soycloud wallowed a scant hundred meters above Facilities Management. One of the Virgin Atomic security phavatars made a dramatic gesture. Rain poured down on the building. Actually, *poured* was an understatement. Reprogrammed at VA headquarters, the soycloud released all its excess water at once. Biostrate roofs were not made to cope with a deluge like this. The ceiling of the reception area sprang multiple leaks. The activists laughed.

"Anything to avoid visuals of phavatars shooting at human beings," Shoshanna said.

The leaks turned into gushers. The Let's Make Friends With Soil! corner collapsed, burying several people.

"Stay calm! Stay calm! They think we're going to come out, soaked and shivering, looking stupid. *They're* going to look stupid. Wait for it ..."

Cydney still had her BCI and retinal interface. In the

children's activities coordinator's office, where she had been locked with some meds for her ear, she could view events from multiple angles. Most of these amateur feeds were provided by citizens standing at a distance on the road, part of the unofficial bug-out initiative, which had by now, in spite of official reassurances, created a tailback from the Bremen Lock several kilometers long. Several of the activists inside were also covertly vidding.

Astonished commentary flooded every feed when the VA phavatars abruptly went ape. They jumped about, thumped their chests, and knuckle-walked, hooting.

(Shoshanna had never seen a real gorilla; she was going on cartoons.)

With mighty bounds enabled by their twisted-polymer muscles, the phavatars leapt up to the hovering soycloud and grabbed its edges. They clambered aboard, as if returning to their home in the treetops.

A hatch opened in the center of the soycloud. An access ladder snapped down.

The activists filed out of the building and climbed the ladder. They were soaked and shivering, but they did not look stupid. Illuminated by the blaze of light from Facilities Management, they looked like pagan warriors ascending to some elysian firmament. At the last minute, Shoshanna unlocked the children's activities director's office and dragged Cydney along.

"All aboard for the soycloud tour! Don't worry, I'm in control. I just let them soak us so everyone could see how powerless they are."

★

This message had been received loud and clear at VA headquarters in Bellicia, which was now in a state of pandemonium. The staff had lost control first of Facilities Management, and then of the override systems that had allowed them to stage their soycloud stunt. Now they had even lost their own security phavatars.

Jay Macdonald, the highest-ranking VA executive present on Vesta, climbed to the roof in the company of two now-hostile phavatars and was escorted up the ladder to the soycloud occupied by Shoshanna and her troops, which had come to hover over the building.

The topside of the soycloud smelled of phlox and sweet william. It was a far cry from the tightly packed racks of lettuces and sweet potatoes found in your average farm-in-a-bottle. Gooseberry and raspberry bushes, as well as marrows and squashes grown on frames, dotted three moonlit acres of soybeans. There were even a few fruit trees scattered around. They provided shade (when the sun was shining) for chives, dill, and other herbs beloved of the pollinating insects whose inculturation was the agronomy department's greatest success.

The activists were munching on apples, normally out of reach on a student's budget. They lounged on the deck outside the rustic shack where the soycloud gardeners stored their tools. Relaxed laughter greeted Macdonald's appearance. Most of them assumed they had triumphed, and were ready to talk about coffee machines and student grants.

Not Shoshanna, who sat crosslegged on the deck with her revolver in her lap. "How you doing? Gotta say, you don't look so good, Jay."

Even by the Vestan equivalent of moonlight, Macdonald was visibly pasty and trembling.

"How did you do that?" he blurted, gesturing at the phavatars who flanked him. No longer his, but hers. "It shouldn't be possible!"

"How do you mean, Jay?"

"Telepresence encryption is unbreakable! You booted our operators out. Now they can't log in. But you *can't* hijack a telecast. It's not possible. Can't bloody well be done!"

"Oh, wise up," Shoshanna said. "Any encryption protocol

is only as good as the computer applying it."

There was a moment's silence.

"Oh, crap," Jay Macdonald said.

Shoshanna grinned. "Updated your anti-virus software recently? Maybe you should have. Or maybe it wouldn't have done any good."

"You've infiltrated our hub."

"Correct. Facilities Management gave me a back door into the VA hub. I blocked your operators' signals at the source. Then I took control of the phavatars and the soyclouds, using your own encryption protocols and override keys."

Macdonald glanced at Cydney.

She was torn. Despite the agony she'd suffered at Shoshanna's hands, her pride wanted her to pretend that she was one of the gang, not a hostage who'd stupidly walked into a trap. She raised her chin defiantly.

"Oh, she didn't have anything to do with it," Shoshanna said, deflating Cydney's pretense. "She's just a newshound. She may have a few grey-hat tools, but nothing offensive. Nothing like what I've got."

Some of the activists looked at Shoshanna uneasily.

"So." She bit into a freshly picked Cox's Pippin. "Yum. Are you ready to meet our demands?"

"Based on your wish list, you ought to be addressing the university administration. I can't speak for them."

Shoshanna rolled her eyes. "I thought you had to be brainy to be the chief financial officer of a listed corporation. Maybe I was wrong."

Another silence ensued. A breeze rustled the flowers growing around the edges of the deck. Under Shoshanna's control, the soycloud was gaining height. Cydney shivered as the cold wind cut through her still-damp clothes.

"Oh," Macdonald said presently. "My God."

"Yeah. This didn't come out of nowhere, Jay. It's the continuation of our ongoing conversation, by other means." Shoshanna spat out an apple seed. "It's a war out there. That's what you guys say, isn't it? Thing is, you're wrong. It would be a war if we ever wanted to fight. And in that case, we would walk all over you. Like I'm walking all over you right now."

She threw her apple core at Macdonald. It hit him on the chest.

"We don't like going noisy. But the lesson you should be drawing right now is: we will if we have to. And part two of that lesson is: we will stop at nothing to keep humanity safe."

Cydney gasped. She finally understood. She pinged Aidan Wahlsdorf, her team manager on Earth. *Oh my dog. Shoshanna is an ISA agent.*

"So," Shoshanna encouraged. "Give."

Unexpectedly, Macdonald smiled. "You haven't been able to break into our subsidiaries."

"Not yet."

"Nor will you be able to. We have a strict information security policy that includes physical segregation of key computing assets. You may have compromised our Bellicia hub, but that won't give you access to Virgin Resources, or the de Grey Institute, or the Big Dig. Your violation of our corporate privacy stops here, I'm afraid."

"Wrong," Shoshanna said, standing up. "I'm only just getting started. You have a pacemaker, don't you, Jay? Which is monitored by medibot software at your headquarters?"

Macdonald clutched his chest. Several of the activists stared at Shoshanna in horror.

"Do your worst," Macdonald said hoarsely.

"Then again, I could just shoot you," Shoshanna mused.

"Sassenach! You'll never conquer the human spirit! *Dh'aindeoin co theireadh e!*"

With that, Macdonald lumbered into a run and leapt off the deck. Ungainly as he was, he weighed so little that his running jump carried him all the way over the edge of the soycloud.

No one would ever know if he had meant to do that.

Nor would they know whether he had been aware that the soycloud, previously hovering above the rooftops of Bellicia, was now 1.5 kilometers up.

The activists rushed to the edge of the soycloud. Clinging to stems of *Glycine max*, they were in time to see Jay Macdonald hit the pavement of Olbers Circle, outside the Virgin Café. He bounced like a yo-yo. The sack of pulped flesh and broken bone rose high enough that they could ascertain with their own eyes that even on Vesta,

$$V_t = \sqrt{\frac{2mg}{\rho A C_d}}$$

would kill you deader than a mackerel.

"I didn't do that," Shoshanna said defensively.

Silence.

"He jumped. You all saw him. I wouldn't really have stopped his heart. Or shot him. I was just threatening him. That's the way to get what you want."

Big Bjorn said, "Maybe you'd better tell us what it is you do want, Shosh."

"He called me a Sassenach. I'm not English. I'm Jewish."

"Shosh?"

"If I knew what I wanted, I wouldn't have to ask for it!" she shouted. "All right, all right! Everyone calm down. I'll explain."

Cydney's ping to Earth had not been answered—any more than her preceding pings had. She concluded that Shoshanna had taken over the ecohood's routers. No more signals would get out of here unless this madwoman wanted them to.

"I'm here to save humanity," Shoshanna said. "And on

that note, I think it's time to have a chat with one of my prominent co-religionists: Eliezer James."

★

"Oh, not *again*," Elfrida said.

The Extropia Collective stared at her in bemusement.

"More of you," she said. "Seeking the secret of human happiness. You're the third lot in less than a year. What is this, a new fad? Has plain old freedom gone out of style?"

Hugh Meredith-Pike cleared his throat and drank some gatorade from the supplies Petruzzelli had sent over. "I can't tell you anything about any other seekers. There may be others, but—"

"There are. Correction, there were. On 395792 Nurislam and 1000384 Sybilsmith. Recently established colonies. As in *very* recently. As in, they were still living in inflatables at the bottom of holes. Like you."

At this point, she heard Meredith-Pike saying: "—we don't know anything about them."

"No? Well, I'll tell you about them." As she spoke, her phavatar dismantled the hab's oxygen generation system to replace the wrecked parts of the C02 removal assembly with new ones that Petruzzelli had run off on her industrial printer. The would-be colonists watched with fascination, as if they'd never seen anyone use a screwdriver before. "Neither of those groups ever planned to build a permanent habitat. They *said* they did, but the truth came out pretty quickly. Their real deal was: pay us to go away. The secret of human happiness? *Bitter laugh!* Cash, that's what they were seeking. And they got it, because some genius decided a couple of years back that UNVRP should offer monetary compensation for the damage that resettlement would inflict on people's uuu*niiiique* cultural *vaaaa*lues."

"We weren't even told where we were going."

"Now, I'm pretty sure that those two groups were both planted on us by the same gang of crooks that brought you here, and then abandoned you. So if you're tempted to pull the same crap they did ... just think about whether those pirates deserve their cut of what you will have bought with your pain and terror and suffering."

"They told us they would take us to 4 Vesta."

"They *what?*"

Only now did the Extropia Collective hear her accuse them of trying to extort compensation from UNVRP. All twenty-seven unwashed, traumatized men, women, and children smirked in alarm. The youngest child, an eight-year-old with a shaved head, piped up: "We aren't going anywhere! We spent our entire life savings to get here, and we're staying!" It looked at a parent for approval of this performance.

To their credit, the Extropia Collective burst out laughing. The confused child looked as if it might cry. Its mother hugged it. "Oh, Kurzweila. You did learn your lines. No, no, we aren't laughing at you, darling. We're laughing at ourselves, I suppose."

Meredith-Pike cleared his throat. "Not much I can add to that," he admitted. "We were to put up a convincing resistance, and then accept resettlement in exchange for as much compensation as could be wrung out of your organization."

"I knew it," Elfrida said.

Meredith-Pike cocked his head. He had just heard her saying: "They *what?*"

"Well, yes," he said. "When we first got here, we were shocked. We were expecting to go to 4 Vesta, you see. They deceived us. But there was nothing we could do about it: they had the only ship. Mr. Haddock said that you might be persuaded to resettle us, actually, on 4 Vesta ...?"

"Ha," Elfrida said when she heard this. "You aren't the first to make that request. All I can say is ..." *In your dreams.* "There's only one place to live on 4 Vesta: the Bellicia ecohood. And the corporate owner enforces strict population limits."

But she thought of the Liberty Rock settlement, which would soon house 200,000 new emigrants in comfort and security. Against that, Virgin Atomic's immigration policy seemed even less fair. They were eager to welcome 200,000 Chinese. How could they justify turning everyone else away?

"I'm afraid you're most likely to end up on Ceres," she said. "We sometimes place people on other asteroids where there are employment opportunities—Eunomia, Hebe, Cybele, Davida ... but generally, Ceres is it. Or if you want to go back to Earth, of course, you can do that. As recent emigrants, I assume you've all got citizenship somewhere. But you'd have to buy your own tickets."

Hugh Meredith-Pike bobbled closer to her. His shaved skull sported an all-over tattoo of electronic circuitry, harking back to the days when transistors were built of silicon. The fashion statement underlined the quaint aspirations of the Extropia Collective. Wireheads were an old subset of the transhumanist subculture. They aimed to achieve bliss by means of implanted electroceuticals that could switch off unpleasant feelings. Certainly, their ability to flood their brains with serotonin must have helped them to endure their ordeal on Montego without killing and / or eating each other. They were basically junkies, in Elfrida's opinion.

Who would be so irresponsible as to land a bunch of junkies, and their kids, on an undeveloped rock, *and leave them there,* in the blithe expectation that the UN would not only pick up the tab but pay for the privilege of doing so?

Blind with rage at Captain Haddock and company, Elfrida bent her head to the oxygen generation system rack. Her phavatar's MI was doing the work, not her. The čapek-class excelled at mechanical repairs, if nothing else.

"I'm not just anyone," Meredith-Pike whispered at the

side of her head, as if she had ears instead of an omnidirectional microphone. "I know people. I've a very good friend at Virgin Atomic. Get in touch with him, he'll certainly let us land on Vesta."

"Oh yeah?"

"He works in the think-tank there. Decent chap. His name's Julian Satterthwaite."

Elfrida logged out and fell back on her bunk. She had been logged in for ten hours, and her crappy little immersion kit didn't have an IV to supply her with fluids. She was dehydrated, and so stiff, from the combination of immobility and nonstop command-gesturing, that she yelped in pain when she tried to sit up. Her head throbbed with the worst stress headache of her life.

"Medibot," she croaked. "Medibot!"

No medibot appeared. The hab's bots had not been instructed to recognize her. She had no alternative but to roll off her bunk and out of her capsule. She limped down to the ground level of the hab. She didn't know where they kept the meds, but near the hygiene module was usually a good bet.

Passing an open office door, she halted. What looked like all the VA personnel on site stood staring at the screen on someone's desk. A voice said on speaker: "—the continuation of our ongoing conversation, by other means."

That's someone I know, Elfrida thought. Heard that voice before somewhere.

"It's a war out there," the voice continued. "That's what you guys say, isn't it?"

"Fast-forward it," someone in the room said.

Bouncing on her tiptoes, Elfrida glimpsed the screen between the shoulders of the watchers. It showed a murky nighttime scene. A crowd of people. *That's Big Bjorn!* His ursine silhouette was unmistakable. Now she recognized other people from the PHCTBS Studies gang. Where was Cydney? What had they done with her?

"You know what they're doing at the de Grey Institute," challenged the same voice as before. Elfrida now recognized it as the voice of Shoshanna Doyle, that green-haired chick from Belter Studies.

The camera shakily zoomed in on the face of Dr. James.

"No, I don't," Dr. James said. "I know they're doing *something* ... big. About fourteen months ago, they asked us to share our processing resources on an ongoing basis. We agreed, of course. But I don't know anything about the content of their research."

Oh my dog! Elfrida realized that Dr. James was talking about the very data she and Mendoza had set out to find. It was a crushing revelation. If he was telling the truth, they'd been on the wrong track all along. And so, apparently, had Shoshanna's crew.

The data was not on the astrophysics lab's workstation at all. It was in the de Grey Institute.

Shoshanna, for one, did not seem disposed to accept this. "You're lying," she challenged Dr. James.

"I assure you I'm not."

"You never even wondered what kind of research problem requires *two* supercomputers—they've got one on the train, and Ali Baba makes two—running around the clock?"

"Of course I wondered," Dr. James said. "But whatever it is, it's clearly sensitive. They wouldn't talk to me about it, and I very much doubt that this stunt will encourage them to talk to you."

"I'm only just getting started," Shoshanna promised.

"No matter what you do," Dr. James said, "or who you represent, I promise you that violence won't get you anywhere."

"She's already killed our fucking CFO!" cried someone in the Big Dig office.

Elfrida edged into the office, desperate to get a better look at the screen and see if she could see Cydney.

But before she got any closer, José Running Horse spotted her. "Hey," he said, shouldering through the crowd. "Out."

"Let me see! Please!"

"No." He grabbed her arm and spun her around.

"Cydney!"

"She's there," said Fiona Sigurjónsdóttir, not unkindly. "She's the one filming, we think. They've taken over the routers, but the ecohood's wireless environment is still functioning, and we do have a back-up transmitter at the Bremen Lock that hasn't been corrupted."

"Yet," someone else said.

"We've notified all the relevant authorities. Help is on its way."

Running Horse yanked Elfrida out of the office. Sigurjónsdóttir made no move to stop him. Elfrida understood that she was no longer the focus of Sigurjónsdóttir's concern. The woman now had *real* stakeholder relations problems.

"'Help is on its way,'" Running Horse mocked under his breath, towing Elfrida through the hab.

"Isn't it?"

"Pretty to think so. Problem is, the relevant authorities are the same people who have just taken over the Bellicia ecohood."

"Uhhnnnh?"

"That bitch is an ISA agent. She incited the protests, everything. Now she's holding the entire ecohood hostage. That pretty little head is stuffed full of military-grade malware." Running Horse looked Elfrida up and down. The eagle on his forehead seemed to stare scornfully at her, too. "Yours isn't. But that doesn't mean you're not working with her. Out." He shoved her into the vestibule of the airlock.

"Don't kill me!" Elfrida screamed, clawing at his forearms.

"EVA suits in that locker," he said with contempt.

She struggled into one. Running Horse closed the airlock on her and cycled it. Sobbing inside her helmet, Elfrida stumbled out into the watery light of the cavern.

She felt that she had behaved shamefully. *Cydney ... Mendoza ...* She had to rescue them. "Help. Someone please help," she wailed. Of course, the suit's radio was disabled. She was completely isolated, just like Running Horse had intended.

The geology lab's rover sat in the corner of the cavern, beyond Liberty Village (as the pilot settlement was called). Still crying, Elfrida scrambled inside. She took off the VA spacesuit in the tiny airlock and eeled into the cabin. The familiar odor of pouch noodles and farts smelled like home.

"*Nan de naite'ru?*" [Why are you crying?] said Rurumi.

"Leave me alone, you dog-damned machine," Elfrida screamed.

But after a while, too weary and miserable to resist Rurumi's pre-programmed compassion, she told her. Not that the phavatar could help, of course. Her areas of competence were limited to sex and rocks, so all she could do was pat Elfrida's arm and say, "That sounds scary."

"Do you think I'm scared?" Elfrida said. "Do you, eh? Well, you're wrong! I'm not some pencil-thighed waif with more hair than brains. I'm the senior UN field agent on this asteroid, and I've survived *two* PLAN attacks, and I've spacewalked outside a foundering space station in the troposphere of Venus, and I survived for nine days on a fragment of an asteroid with nothing to eat or drink except the body of another human being. I survived that," she insisted in a near-shriek. Then she dosed herself with more grapefruit-flavored rehydration fluid, and took another tranquilizer. The rover had a small stock of meds. It was a shame it didn't have any of the legendary Star Force energy drink known as morale juice. That was what she really needed. "So there," she said. "I'm not scared. I'm going to get through this, and

I'm going to get Cydney and Mendoza out, too."

"Oooh!" Rurumi exclaimed, scrambling up on the dashboard. *"Wan-wan! Kawaii!"*

Jimmy's Jack Russell, in her miniature pink spacesuit, stood on the hood of the rover. Her helmet bumped the windshield. She seemed to be trying to lick it. Rurumi patted the inside of the windshield and cooed.

The rover's radio clicked on. *"Ni ǐ hao, Ru-chan."*

"Ni ǐ hao!" Rurumi responded. Elfrida stared at her.

"Amy shuō ni ǐ hao, tài." Jimmy stood outside the rover, EVA-suited, holding the other end of a tether that served as Amy's leash. *"Ni ǐ jīntiān hao ma?"*

Elfrida lunged for the radio. "Hello, hello? Uh, Jimmy! This is Elfrida Goto. I'm in here with Rurumi. I need help. Please! It's really important!" She scrambled into her EVA suit, intending to chase him and beg him on her knees to ping New York for her. She couldn't believe that she hadn't thought of asking the Chinese for help before.

After a pause, the radio said in English: "Is this regarding the activities of the de Grey Institute?"

No, Elfrida was about to say, but then she caught herself. "Yes," she said. "It is."

XX.

Having made up her mind to help her old friend Viola Budgett, Petruzzelli headed straight for 6 Hebe. She programmed a brachistone trajectory into the astrogation computer to get them there faster. During the tricky midpoint of the journey—when the *Kharbage Collector* had to flip 180° so that its acceleration became *de*celeration—Michael came to her with some rumors he'd found on the internet about the goings-on on Vesta.

"Can't you see I'm busy?" she shouted at him.

But when she had a look later, she grew alarmed. Whatever was going on, the powers that be were trying their damnedest to keep it out of the public eye. Most of Michael's links had already disappeared.

There was only one organization that could mount a news blackout with even 80% or 90% success.

The ISA.

Unlike most people in the solar system, Petruzzelli had met the ISA—and known it at the time. After the 11073 Galapagos incident, a man had come all the way from Earth to interview her aboard the *Kharbage Can*. Middle-aged white guy with stubby dreadlocks. Kind, polite. His kind, polite demeanor had not changed as he informed her what would happen to her family, and her friends, and basically everyone she'd ever bumped profiles with, if she breathed a word about what had happened with that stross-class phavatar, and the PLAN, and the asteroid called 99984 Ravilious.

From which Petruzzelli had concluded that the ISA weren't as smart as they thought they were. Their threats had told her exactly what they didn't want known.

They were plenty scary, though. She'd signed their non-disclosure agreement and kept her mouth shut from that day to this.

Now, she wondered if the ISA was involved in the trouble on Vesta. If so, Elfrida Goto and Viola Budgett might need rescuing.

But someone else would have to do it. Apart from everything else, Petruzzelli was committed to her course. When you were burning at almost three million kilometers per hour, it was physically impossible to turn around.

She was going to make UNVRP pay for her fuel, too. She spent most of the journey happily filling out invoices.

25 hours later, 6 Hebe swelled on the *Kharbage Collector's* screens, angular, glittering. One of the larger asteroids in the Belt, about 200 kilometers square, 6 Hebe had also been one of the first exploited for its minerals. It did not, however, offer riches beyond the dreams of anyone—just nickel-iron. Therefore, it had also been one of the first asteroids to move up the value chain. The miners had long since left, and the current owner, Centiless Corporation, had built a spaceport on top of the old-timey mining infrastructure. Now 6 Hebe was a node in the ITR, the Interplanetary Transit Network of low-energy pathways that ships could 'surf' around the solar system, utilizing gravitational resonances. Near aphelion—where 6 Hebe was now—it actually orbited within Gap 2.5, where Jupiter's gravity held sway like the ghostly hand of a wizard.

Tankers and container ships orbited the rock. They were moon-sized in comparison to the *Kharbage Collector*. Superlifters puttered around them, loading and unloading cargo before the cyclers drifted off on the next trajectory of their multi-year journeys. Petruzzelli navigated through the throng of radar blips. She synced and clamped.

"That wasn't a very good landing," Michael said, looking around from the comms officer's workstation, where he was filing their arrival notification. "I felt the bump."

"Take it up with the hub," Petruzzelli said. "I'm going dirt-side. You stay here."

"I want to go dirt-side, too."

"No. We're only going to be here for a few hours. Besides, we have recycling to offload and cargo to pick up. I need you to supervise that."

"The hub can do it."

"No," Petruzzelli said. She braced one elbow against the flopping reflective cladding of the elevator shaft to hold it up. She used it as a mirror to spritz her face with foundation. False eyelashes came next, then hairspray to keep her mop in shape in the low gravity awaiting her. *Might as well look good.* She headed for the elevator. "You stay right here, or … or …"

"Or what?"

"Or I'll tell your daddy," Petruzzelli said with finality, wagging a finger at his crestfallen face.

Michael Kharbage was nine years old. He was the biggest pain in the ass Petruzzelli had ever worked with, and she'd known a few.

A sense of freedom uplifted her as she strode out of the spaceport into Karl Ludwig City.

6 Hebe had no gravity to speak of. Mooching, browsing crowds jostled IRL, while the public comms channel seethed with catcalls, quirky personal manifestoes, shopkeepers' patter, and party invitations. The chaos spawned an aura of possibility that was missing from Petruzzelli's workaday life. She glanced at shop displays, wondering if she could afford to treat herself to a new tattoo.

Her fantasies were interrupted by Captain Haddock. *"We'll be seeing you, then, darlin',"* he texted her. *"Thanks for the ride."*

She spun, glimpsed the pirates on an upper-level street, and bounded after them.

Built on two enormous gantries that had been deliberately toppled after the cessation of mining operations on 6 Hebe, Karl Ludwig City was basically a multi-level, five-kilometer bridge from Port Hebe to nowhere. It sloped down. An expansion coil enclosed it, generating a magnetic field that provided active radiation shielding: essentially, the hab existed inside a giant superconducting magnet. Steam and smoke from sauna baths and kebab joints drifted in layers beneath the sun-lamps.

Petruzzelli caught up with the pirates. "Not so fast," she said. "I'm coming with you."

"Ye can't." Haddock and his family were all in disguise: they wore burkas. This was a mistake, in Petruzzelli's opinion. 6 Hebe was known for its post-Islamist culture. You would be more likely to encounter Muslim fundamentalists on Ceres. "People are staring," Haddock pleaded.

"At you, not me," Petruzzelli said.

They glided in giant strides past the bazaar; past water wholesalers' offices and virtual ship showrooms; past niche IP agents specializing in every tiny part of a fusion engine that could break. After about four kilometers the multiple levels converged into a single, dark street. Holographic tigers, elephants, and belly dancers gyrated outside doors vanishingly high up in the walls. Petruzzelli smelled an aroma that made her think of her first boyfriend. A hundred meters further on, she caught herself thinking that Captain Haddock was actually quite attractive. She consulted her email, using her wrist tablet's backlight to see by. They had come to nowhere—literally, Nowhere, Karl Ludwig City's red-light district.

"Should be somewhere around here."

"Aye, it's that place," Haddock said, pointing at a holographic Ganesh in a blue bikini.

The sign of the elephant god cued Petruzzelli to expect an Indian-themed bar, but instead they floated into a dive that could've been anywhere in the Midwest. A band played rock 'n' roll covers, abusing the wah-wah pedal. Human waitresses carried burgers and fries out of a tiny kitchen.

"Most people here used to be Indonesian," Kiyoshi Yonezawa explained.

"I wish they'd switch the freaking pheromones off," Petruzzelli huffed. She was still turned on from walking through the psychotropic misters positioned outside the bars and clubs of Nowhere. It was a form of advertising that hadn't yet been made illegal. Ban something and people would come up with something worse.

"Oh, come on," Yonezawa said. "It's not that bad in here."

She pinged for a drink, buying time to study him. Spaceborn and then some: two point four meters tall, two point five. Hips so narrow she could probably span them with her hands. Shaggy black hair hacked off at the shoulders. Smiling lips and the biggest, saddest bedroom eyes she'd ever seen. *Dammit, those pheromones haven't worn off yet, have they?*

She deliberately focused on the epicanthic folds rounding off those eyes, the sallowness of his skin. He could've passed as an East Asian mutt, but because she knew differently, his actual heritage seemed obvious. *Pureblood. Pureblood. Ugh. Pureblood.* The word killed her unreal feelings of lust. Better than a cold shower.

"So," she said. "We've never met, but you're famous, dude."

She'd intended to alarm him, and his sudden stillness betrayed that she'd succeeded. "Yeah?"

"Yeah, I know all about you."

"Whatever those slebs told you, the truth is worse," he bantered, nodding at the pirates, who were sitting near the stage, drinking cola through the slits of their burkas.

"Oh, they haven't told me anything about you. Tried to lose me on the way here, even. That's how you can tell the real criminals: they don't rat out their friends. Whereas people that are naturally law-abiding, in over their heads, people who landed themselves on the dark side through one moment's surrender to greed or curiosity ... they sing like fucking vid stars, dude. I'm talking about our mutual friend, Viola Budgett." Petruzzelli sucked on the autoseal straw of her drink, which was ginger ale without any add-ins. She wanted to keep her wits about her. "Actually, scratch that. You're not her friend. You're blackmailing her to the tune of eighty big ones a month. Or if that's how you treat your friends, you're really not a very nice guy."

Yonezawa recovered fast. "That's libel," he informed her "Fact, buddy."

There was a pause while he, she assumed, tried to figure out how much proof she had. That was impossible, of course. Presently he said, "Those payments are instalments. You can't call it blackmail."

"So you didn't threaten to ruin her career, and her professor's career, and get the entire astrophysics lab at the University of Vesta prosecuted for criminal activities?"

"How could I? They aren't engaging in any criminal activities that I know of."

His English was accented. Slight, but there was definitely an accent there.

The band segued into 'Festa It Up,' and Petruzzelli drank some more ginger ale. The conversation had reached the limits of her knowledge. She'd asked Budgett what, exactly, Kiyoshi Yonezawa was threatening them with, but on that point Budgett had kept mum. There was an omertà protocol in place at the U-Vesta astrophysics lab, and Petruzzelli didn't know whether they were hiding something very, very bad, or something trivial that they only *thought* was very, very bad because they were law-abiding nerds who could easily be convinced that they would get the death penalty for not separating their recycling.

But Budgett had worked on the *Kharbage Can*. She was no stranger to gray-zone operations. She wouldn't freak out over a minor infraction of some dumb rule.

So on the whole, and given the ISA angle, Petruzzelli was

leaning towards *very, very bad.*

She had hoped to get the truth out of Kiyoshi Yonezawa.

That was clearly not going to be easy.

"Oh, chill out, buddy," she said. "I'm just busting your chops. Instalments, you say? As in, payments on a transaction? Did you sell them something they shouldn't have, like black tech?"

"Something like that. By the way, if you've been talking to Budgett, maybe she mentioned that they owe me ten K this month, actually. That's including a late fee of twenty-five percent." It was hard to see in the dim light, but his eyeballs seemed to be flickering from side to side.

"You're pinging her as we speak," Petruzzelli hazarded. "But she's not answering."

"She's hiding behind you, I guess."

"Nope. No one in the Bellicia ecohood is answering right now. Not email, not voice calls. Even Cydney Blaisze's feed has quit."

"Who are you, anyway?" The question sounded inattentive; she figured he was confirming her claims.

"Like I said, I'm a friend of Budgett's."

"Yeah?"

"Haddock and company have been travelling on my ship. Which isn't such a coincidence, if you think about it. Haddock knows Budgett, and he knows you. He's like this human ITR, connecting far-flung planets."

"The planet of good and the planet of evil."

"You could put it like that. But I wouldn't. Reality is gray, not black and white. Budgett may have some good colleagues at the university, but *she's* a cyborg engineer with no sense of right and wrong. And I don't think of myself as evil."

His gaze came back to her. "Don't you?"

"Check my public profile," she shrugged. "Actually, I'm sure you already have."

"Captain of the *Kharbage Collector,* achieved the rank of

general in *Existential Threat IV*, currently an Idiran commander in *Second Idiran War*. Mixed Anglo-European heritage. That tells me nothing about you. Well, actually, it tells me one thing."

"What?"

"The only people who put their DNA in their public profiles are—"

"Idiots. You have to be dumber than shit to put your actual DNA out there for hackers to grab. That's just my ethnic category. I'm—"

"Scared. The only people who put their *ethnic category,* if you like, in their public profiles are scared."

"Of what?"

"Of being mistaken for purebloods."

"I'm three-quarters Italian. One-quarter American mutt."

"OK."

Petruzzelli sucked air through her straw. She thumbed through the menu on her wrist tablet.

"I understand the logic," Yonezawa said. "You wouldn't want anyone to think you were like me."

Petruzzelli ordered a halal Scotch—screw the cost—and looked up. "Dude, I'm not like you. I pilot a recycling barge. I'm not a smuggler with a sideline in extortion."

"No? Based on what I hear from Haddock, it seems like that's a distinction without a difference."

Petruzzelli leaned across the table. She noticed a pendant in the open neck of Yonezawa's shirt. It was a silver plus sign, the vertical arm a bit longer than the horizontal one. "If you even think about blackmailing *me,* chinkie, let me tell you right now: try it, and you're gonna take a one-way ride to a world of sorrow. Like you can't even imagine."

"You don't know what I can imagine," Yonezawa said. The waitress brought Petruzzelli's Scotch, together with a plate of cheese fries that Yonezawa must have ordered. "Anyway, you called me 'chinkie,'" he said in a softer tone.

They had both been yelling over the noise of the band. "That's not accurate. I'm not Chinese, I'm Japanese."

Petruzzelli sat back, feeling a bit stupid. Her outburst had been excessive. She watched Yonezawa eat fries. He was unnaturally neat about it, wiping his fingers after each one. She confessed, "I knew that. It just kind of popped out."

"Understandable."

"I knew you were Japanese." The time had come to fess up. "I used to work on the *Kharbage Can*. I was the one who piloted the *Cheap Trick* to 11073 Galapagos." With these words, she violated her NDA with the ISA for the first time. Wasn't much harm in telling the truth to a fellow criminal. "I had a Star Force combat program to work with. Program and me got three of the toilet rolls, but we missed the last one. The one that blew your home rock to pieces."

He was silent.

"I'm sorry about that. Anyway; Budgett told me that's where you're from. Small solar system," she said, shrugging.

Yonezawa ate another fry. He scratched the inside of his left forearm through his shirt. "Have you got my money?" he said.

xxi.

Elfrida held Amy on her lap. The Jack Russell kept trying to lick her nose. "She likes you," Jimmy said, laughing.

"I like dogs. We had a beagle when I was a kid." They were sitting in the communal kitchen of Liberty Village. The other Chinese jostled in the doorway, staring. Elfrida had a pouch of green tea in front of her. Jimmy was chain-vaping a clove cigarette.

"Beagles are lovely," he said. "I am a member of the Dog Worshipping Society of Outer Space. Many of our members own beagles. They were popular on the Asteroid of the Heavenly Perfume especially."

"Asteroid of the Heavenly Perfume?"

"Yes, in the Inner Belt. Certainly you know that the PLAN attacked it five years ago and killed many thousands of people."

"I must have missed those headlines," Elfrida said. No way she wouldn't have heard about a kilodeath incident. "Was it a—a Chinese colony?"

"Of course."

Elfrida said slowly, "Is it ... I'm getting the feeling that it isn't true, after all, that the Chinese don't come into space."

"Of course we do. There are many Chinese colonies in the Belt. You don't know this?"

He was looking at her as if she were brain-damaged. "The Great Firewall," she said. "I guess your government doesn't advertise what it's doing. Ha. Advertise." Dancing, singing, begging, pleading advertisements covered the walls of the kitchen, and even the appliances. Elfrida's head was starting to ache all over again from the background noise. She didn't know how the Chinese stood it. "Well, I guess that's understandable. Given the—the external risks."

"Our government lies," Jimmy said flatly.

"That's kind of like the definition of government," Elfrida offered.

He leaned towards her, his pouchy face taut with intensity. "They hide the risks. But they couldn't hide the destruction of the Asteroid of the Heavenly Perfume. Too many people had family members there, so it became news. After that, many people thought that it is better to disembowel a frog than to swallow a chainsaw! So we decided to found a new colony that would not be subject to these external risks." He reached out and tapped the back of her hand. Elfrida flinched. She had already noticed that the Chinese had a different concept of personal space: they thought nothing of brushing past you, or casually touching you to make a point. "Therefore we set up a syndicate and made a contract with Virgin Atomic. But now we think that VA was dishonest with us. We are angry."

"Join the club," Elfrida mumbled.

"4 Vesta is *not* safe!"

"No shit." The thought of Cydney was like a constant, dull pain in her stomach.

"Do you know what they are doing at the de Grey Institute? The ISA agent, Miss Doyle, wants them to tell her, but they are refusing. This is putting many people's lives in danger."

Elfrida straightened. She looked past Jimmy, to the rubbernecking construction workers in the doorway of the kitchen. "I don't know what they're up to." In her mind, that mysterious signal etched its trajectory across the screen. *Calling Gap 2.5. Calling 99984 Ravilious.* "But I want to find out, too."

She explained what she had in mind. As she spoke, Jimmy Liu began to smile. "The highest mountain is low at the bottom," he said joyously.

"I knew you had a spark of *Abenteuerlust*," Elfrida said, striking back with her kitchen German. "That means 'spirit of adventure.'"

"This is a wonderful idea, Miss Goto. But wait. Isn't there a problem? They do not trust us, they don't tell us *anything—*"

"Got that covered," Elfrida said. "I assume you guys have a spaceship hidden somewhere on this rock?"

★

"Here's your doggone money," Petruzzelli said. Banging at her wrist tablet, she sent a secure payment to the ID Kiyoshi Yonezawa had given her. "I hope you aren't one of those foilhats who only accepts physical palladium, because what you're getting is what I've got. Ten thousand spiders, payable to Loyola Holdings, Inc. And that's *obviously* a front company officered by rent-a-directors."

"I actually prefer physical iridium," Yonezawa said. "But spiders are good. Thanks ... Where are you going?" She had stood up. "Stay a bit longer. You haven't even finished your drink."

"Freaking halal Scotch," Petruzzelli said. "Might as well pour it straight into the recycler." But she sat down again.

"Personally, I prefer C-and-C to alcohol," Yonezawa said, referring to the compounds of cathine and cathinone that were commonly used as alcohol substitutes in sharia-compliant drinks. "It doesn't screw with your mental faculties in the same way."

"You say that like it's a good thing."

"I'm a solo operator. If I pass out drunk, who's going to take over?"

"Your hub, I assume?" Petruzzelli sniped. "Unless you're one of those purists who won't work with machine intelligences."

"I wish I didn't have to," he said seriously. "But extreme purism just doesn't work. It's not possible for a human to pilot a spaceship alone. It's not even possible for a hundred humans."

"You *could*, but you probably wouldn't have your spaceship very long. We're apes. We're not optimized for this stuff."

"Right. You need some help from the machines. So the question becomes, where do you draw the line?"

"I've never been a huge fan of drawing lines," Petruzzelli drawled. She realized to her consternation and amusement that she was flirting with him. It wasn't the artificial pheromones this time: the Ganesha didn't pump that stuff. Calling ironic attention to her mood, she cooed, "So, do you come here often?"

He didn't seem to get the joke. "Sometimes. When I'm on-rock."

"I guess that's your barge in 30-A."

"How'd you know?"

Petruzzelli swallowed a sudden lump of sadness. "Because I've seen one just like it before. It's a Hitachi-Samsung Longvoyager. You don't see many of them lumbering around the solar system nowadays."

"We had two of them: the *St. Francis* and the *Nagasaki*. When we settled on 11073 Galapagos, we splarted the *Nagasaki* to the asteroid. We used her attitude adjusters to spin the rock up. Then we covered her over and turned her into a cathedral."

"And when the PLAN came, your people escaped in her. It was amazing."

"Most of them," he corrected her. "Two thousand, three hundred, and eighty-seven of us died. But, hey, that's still a great survival rate for a PLAN attack, right?" He toyed with the cuff of his left sleeve. "The survivors live on Ceres now. They're OK, they've got jobs."

"So you aren't acting as their agent."

"Not anymore."

"Who are you working for, then?"

"Myself. The *Unicorn*—I renamed her—is old, as you noticed. To be honest, she's falling apart. I need to replace the reactor."

"That's gonna cost a ton."

"Exactly, but you helped a little bit today." He smiled and pushed off from his chair.

Petruzzelli reached out and grabbed his wrist. "A minute ago you were asking me to stay, and now you're the one trying to leave."

"Is there some reason I shouldn't leave?"

Because I don't believe a word you've told me. Well, maybe about your ship needing repairs. But that's it.

Because you're obviously a junkie, and you want to slink off and shoot some dope into your cubital port. And I won't let anyone do that shit if I can stop them.

Because my friends are in danger on 4 Vesta, and you've got something to do with it, and I won't let you just walk away.

Because ...

"Because," she said, looking into his eyes, "I saw outside that they have private party rooms here."

★

Several hours later, Petruzzelli woke up in mid-air. She'd kicked the mattress in her sleep, which had been enough to dislodge her and send her drifting towards the ceiling. She caught the sex trapeze, hung by her knees, and laughed. Yonezawa lay sprawled on his back, snoring.

At the sound of her laughter, he opened one eye and then the other. "Hey there."

Petruzzelli floated down on top of him. She matched the position of her feet to his, which put her face in the middle of his chest—she was that much shorter. She rested her cheek on his pecs and played with his pendant. "This is cool. What is it?"

"You don't know?" He stroked her back. "It's zero four hundred local time. I've got to get going."

"Me, too."

"Maybe we can do this again sometime."

"Yeah. You're pretty hot in the sack, for a ..."

"Pureblood?"

"I was going to say, for a junkie."

"Junkie?"

"The port would be a pretty big clue." She fingered the tiny port implanted in his left forearm to give access to the cubital vein.

"There are other reasons to have a cubital port. I use it as an IV. Telepresence. I sim some."

Petruzzelli wrinkled her nose. He reached to the other side of the bed and retrieved an object like a skinny black caterpillar from the sheets. He made it walk up her arm. It was one of her false eyelashes.

"Give me that!" Laughing, Petruzzelli grabbed for it. They wrestled.

"Anyone can be a great lover in micro-gee," she panted.

"True. I did notice that you're a bit out of shape."

"Who's out of shape?"

"Stop it!"

"Uhhhnnh ...."

"... On second thoughts: don't stop it."

"Uhhh."

They parted outside the Ganesha. The holograms of Nowhere flickered and the pleasure-seekers meandered just as they had eight hours ago. Day never came here.

The pirates sat on the path that led down to the hab floor. Kelp was curled up asleep on a pile of burkas.

"Ahoy, miscreants!" Haddock hailed Petruzzelli and Yonezawa. "Have the pair o' ye no decency?"

"Not a shred," Petruzzelli said. She made her eyebrow smileys stick their tongues out. Then she looked at her wrist tablet. "Blistering barnacles! I gotta run."

The pirates cracked up.

"It's catching," Petruzzelli admitted. "I even said that when Elfrida was on board. I don't think she noticed, though."

She blew a kiss to Yonezawa and hurried back towards the spaceport.

Back on board the *Kharbage Collector,* she brushed aside Michael's questions about where she'd been. She went straight down to sick-bay and swabbed herself. She handed the results to the diagnostic terminal, went back to the bridge, and checked the duty log.

Michael had unloaded the pirates' Superlifter, embarked a clutch of passengers for remote asteroids in the Vesta sector, loaded the cargo that they were scheduled to pick up here, and consigned their recycling to the 6 Hebe processing facility, getting a pretty good price for it. "Well done," she congratulated him, surprised.

Then she saw that he'd done all that in an hour and a half, and spent the rest of the time playing *Second Idiran War,* as her.

"Grrrrr!"

Sick-bay pinged her workstation. "Sequencing complete. Save this DNA record?"

"Save," Petruzzelli typed. Then she accessed the hub's search space. "SEARCH TERMS: <DNA record attached>. SEARCH RANGE: all."

"A search of the entire internet will take an estimated 57 hours, 2 minutes, and forty-seven seconds."

"Go for it."

Kiyoshi Yonezawa might have evaded her questions. He might hide his skulduggery behind shell companies. But DNA was a different kind of data. It couldn't lie, dissemble, or hide (not without cash outlays far beyond the reach of a solo smuggler, anyway). And it left traces behind, if you were as careless with it as Kiyoshi Yonezawa had already proved himself to be. However long it might take, the *Khar-*

bage Collector would find them.

xxii.

Back on the *Unicorn*, Kiyoshi settled into his nest and plugged his IV into his cubital port. He dialed in a cocktail of sodium chloride, potassium, vitamin B, an anti-nausea drug, and a mild painkiller.

He hadn't lied to Petruzzelli: he wasn't a junkie. In a world where anti-addiction treatment was cheaply and widely available, no one had to be a junkie if they didn't want to be. Ergo, he wasn't one. This dose would have embarrassed any recreational doper, anyway. It was a hangover cure.

The *Unicorn's* operations module resounded with the excited voices of Kiyoshi's newly embarked passengers. The racket made his head hurt. Eyemask in place, he exited the bridge and walked down the dark, cool corridor that led to the peaceful environs of the *St. Francis*.

"We're cleared to launch," Jun said. "Cargo's all loaded. Including the Koreans."

Jun Yonezawa had died on 11073 Galapagos. Kiyoshi had brought him back by customizing a high-end software-based MI—the type sold as add-ons for game play—with archived video and the tearful recollections of their mother, recorded without her knowledge at their new home on Ceres.

Alive, Jun had been gifted, devout, a natural leader. Going places, for sure. Now he was trapped in the hub of the *Unicorn*, going nowhere except the places where Kiyoshi could make a buck for the boss-man. You win some, you lose some.

Through the machine-learning process, the software-based Jun had become so realistic that he was often a pain in the proverbial. But as Kiyoshi had hinted to Alicia Petruzzelli, he couldn't do without him anymore.

"They're *namsadang*," he told Jun. "Not really Korean.

Their native language is English. Did you introduce yourself?"

"I'm not that stupid."

On the re-imagined bridge of the *St. Francis,* officers walked around, typed on antiquated consoles, and sailed paper airplanes across the low-ceilinged, hexagonal space. They were phantoms with limited interactivity. The *Unicorn's* hub was feeble by modern standards: there were more powerful processing crystals in the ship's fridge. Kiyoshi could not give more than a fraction of the hub's capacity over to the sim, much as he might've liked to, and the lion's share of that had to go to Jun.

His brother's black eyebrows knitted. Kiyoshi could always tell when Jun was pissed. It made him smile.

"Did you tell them where we're going?" he asked, while heading for the cyberwarfare officer's workstation. (The *St. Francis* had not originally had a cyberwarfare officer, being a simple cargo ship. Kiyoshi had created the position because, c'mon. *Cyberwarfare.)*

"No," Jun said. "I didn't tell them where we're going, because we're not taking them."

Kiyoshi affected puzzlement. "We've got sixty-three emigrants on board. We've got consumables, habs, D/S bots, the whole construction kit. And you want to offload the guys who make the magic happen?"

"They told me to forget about 3982440 Twizzler. Too risky."

"We're not going to 3982440 Twizzler."

"So where are we going?"

"I don't know yet." Kiyoshi cleared his throat to get the cyberwarfare officer's attention. "Hey. Busy? Sorry." He was polite to the imaginary man, keeping up his end of the simulation. "Mind decrypting this, if you've got a minute?" He handed over a a memory crystal embedded in a signet ring. Rockin' it 2200 style. In reality, he was transferring the file from his BCI to the hub.

He turned around and found Jun right behind him. "I've been listening to the passengers," Jun said.

"Eavesdropping again? Tch, tch."

"I'm an MI grafted to the hub, with access to all its data inputs. I can't selectively turn my eyes and ears off when I hear something you don't want me to know about."

Kiyoshi looked sorrowfully at him. "Total immersion killer," he said.

"Whoops, my bad," Jun said, unapologetic.

Kiyoshi sauntered over to the pilot's workstation. He sat down (the simulation of gravity was unsatisfactory) and initiated the launch procedure. The commands he gave here were executed IRL. That was an absolute no-no in sim design, a risk factor for catastrophic mix-ups. But Kiyoshi hadn't put a foot wrong yet, and was confident he never would. He made a little speech to the passengers, welcoming them to the *Unicorn,* congratulating them on their decision to start a new life in the asteroid belt, and instructing them to prepare for acceleration in approximately thirty minutes. Then he ran a few fuel / payload calculations.

Though dwarfed by the tankers in orbit around 6 Hebe, the *Unicorn* was one stupid-big space truck. Its century-old deuterium-deuterium fusion drive kicked out a mere 70,000 newtons of thrust under realistic conditions. Against that, its bulbous hull enclosed a total volume of 277,000 cubic meters. On the plus side, the only cargo on board right now was the stuff for the planned excavation on 3982440 Twizzler. Kiyoshi's sixty-three paying passengers and the five pirates were all travelling in the operations module (designed on last-century assumptions to accommodate a crew of 100 or more). So the ship massed just 97,621 tons right now, and he'd refueled ahead of the surge in demand he was anticipating. He could make it home from here in a week, if he decided to do that.

The *Unicorn* declamped and fell away from Port Hebe under auxiliary power. You weren't allowed to burn too near an inhabited rock, for obvious reasons. Kiyoshi rose from the pilot's workstation. Jun was waiting for him.

"They're talking about 4 Vesta. No one knows what's going on there. Total information blackout; that probably means the ISA is involved. Even Cydney Blaisze's feed has quit."

"Yeah. About that," Kiyoshi said. He led Jun off the bridge. They went up to the observation deck that Kiyoshi had added to the sim, in disregard of authenticity and the basic principles of spaceship design, because c'mon: an *observation deck*. 6 Hebe hung in front of the vast windows, slowly rolling, like a misshapen die.

"I talked to the boss-man," Kiyoshi told his brother.

"I didn't hear you."

"Because I called him while I was in Karl Ludwig City." *Because I didn't want you listening in.* But he was telling Jun now.

"What'd he say?"

"He wants us to bug out. He didn't even want me to wait for our passengers to board. He said, and I quote, 'Come home. Burn everything that rotten old ship's got to burn. Just get away from 4 Vesta. Preferably, several hundred million kilometers away."

"He's pissed."

"He's scared. Maybe he knows something we don't. Or maybe he's just being rational." Kiyoshi shrugged. "I'm not scared. We've got a thousand tons of hybrid oak waiting for us on 1034472 Petergrave, already paid for, and a shitload of soy products for 976011 Lamorra in the freezer. I figure we make those runs and then head home. The passengers can come along for the ride."

"That's gonna be fun."

"A laugh a minute," Kiyoshi agreed.

Jun flicked a smile at him: on, off. Then his face went dark and hard, like the day he'd followed Kiyoshi to the cave where the junior high goof-off gang drank home-brewed shochu and discussed girls. "This is wrong," he said, and that was exactly what he'd said that day, when he was ten years old.

"Draft that course, would you?"

"It's the thing. If it gets loose, everyone on 4 Vesta will be in danger. That asteroid has 122,684 inhabitants. Their lives will be in jeopardy, and it's our fault."

"*If* it gets loose? I'm assuming it already has."

Jun went quiet for a moment. Then he said, "Can't have. We'd know about it. Even the ISA can't silence that many people, not completely."

"So what do you want me to do about it?"

"I want you to goddamn man up."

Kiyoshi breathed in and out, counted to five. "Let's get one thing straight. You're here to provide light entertainment. You're not my conscience."

"Oh no? Because I thought that's exactly what I was. You sure need one, and your own seems to have gone missing. Maybe you killed it with all the drugs. Oh, sorry." Kiyoshi had raised one hand. "Aren't I being entertaining enough?"

Kirin had been going to hit him, but had realized just in time how stupid it would be to hit someone who a) wasn't real and b) was deliberately winding him up.

"You're too goddamn realistic, is all."

He meant that to ratchet down the tension, but Jun didn't take the off-ramp.

"So log out of the sim. Go and talk to your passengers. Tell them everything's OK, but they won't be getting the fresh start they expected. Oh yes, and the extinction of human civilization may be just around the corner. But everything's just hunky-dory."

Kiyoshi had had enough of this. What were things coming to, when you couldn't even count on a sim for escapism? He turned and left the observation deck. He headed for the ship's pharmacy, a fluorescent-lit hole in the wall modelled on the one near their home on 11073 Galapagos. He dragged a finger along the rows of dingy bottles, cursing the constraints he'd programmed in himself, which wouldn't let him get a fix without jumping through the sim's hoops.

"Do you even pray anymore?" Jun said.

Kiyoshi twitched, bottles cascading from his hands. With his back to Jun, facing the shelves, he said, "It's not that simple. I lost my faith when I first went into space. You know that. The bigness of the solar system, the choices you get ... I made a lot of wrong choices. I admit that. But I'm clean now."

"Apart from the nicotine, the caffeine, the tranquilizers, the morale juice—"

"Now you're getting on my case about a few cigarettes?" Kiyoshi let out an exasperated laugh.

The cyberwarfare officer pinged him. "Done with that decrypt, sir." At the same instant, Jun's head twitched in an inhuman way. "Hey, that's interesting."

"Lemme see."

Jun clicked his fingers. Out of thin air, he unrolled a scroll of *washi* paper inscribed with a list of names, IDs, dates, and IRCS coordinates. "What's this?"

"It's the contact log from the wrist tablet of a recycler captain called Alicia Petruzzelli." Kiyoshi took the scroll and scanned it. Going back a week, the log was briefer than he would have expected. Petruzzelli apparently didn't have very many friends.

"Oh, so that's where you were last night," Jun said.

"Yeah. I grabbed this while she was sleeping." Fingerprint recognition security was excellent, but it had one big drawback: you could break it by pressing the finger of its owner onto the screen, if she was sleeping soundly. If she was very tired.

"Thou shalt not steal," Jun muttered.

Kiyoshi met his eyes, daring him to say that again. "She's one of Haddock's friends. Would have been better if she never found out who I am. But she did, and now she knows too much. This evens up the score ... kinda."

One ID cropped up twenty times in a row. The calls to it had been made from Petruzzelli's ship's hub. She'd synced its comms log with her tablet. If Kiyoshi had known she was in the habit of doing something as dumb as that, he could have dredged a lot more information off her wrist tablet. Too late now. But at least he had this ID, and the name that went with it. *"Goto* ... Elfrida."

Jun propped his shoulders against the shelves. He looked like he was in need of a pick-me-up. It took a lot to make an MI look like that.

"I remember her," Jun said.

"Yeah."

"She ate me."

xxiii.

The Guangrong-class technical vessel *Kěkào*—Elfrida had been told that its name meant *trustworthy*—lifted off from a crater a few kilometers to the south of Rheasilvia Mons. At blinding speed, it vanished into the blackness of space.

The Virgin Atomic satellites in orbit around Vesta loosed a storm of panicky queries to each other and to their human operators.

"What the hell?" demanded the de Grey Institute's satellite. "That looked like one of the Chinese ships!"

"It was," said Resources, which had gotten the best pictures. "It was the mission-capable Guangrong-class technical *Kěkào*. I'm not sure that *mission-capable* is an accurate translation, though. It isn't armed: the Chinese government doesn't permit civilian ships to carry lethal weapons. That being the case, I wouldn't call it a *technical,* either. A better translation might be ... hmm ... *tuk-tuk.*" It made an electronic noise which some of its colleagues interpreted as computerese for laughter.

"This is no time for your puerile humor," the de Grey Institute said angrily. "They're running away! Rats off a sinking ship."

"I don't think so," the Big Dig's comms satellite said. "Based on the *Kěkào's* acceleration and mass profile, there were no humans on board. Or if there were, they're strawberry jam now."

José Running Horse spoke up via the PORMS. "No one on board. Ship was launched without our knowledge. Now under the control of its navigation computer."

The de Grey Institute shouted, "Why didn't you shoot it down, you meat-fingered halfwit?"

At the same time, Resources said, "Are you sure?"

There was a momentary silence on the satellites' communication band. Running Horse broke it. "XX Resources: yes, I am comfortable with the assumption that the Kĕkào is on autopilot. If the chinkies had lost control of the ship, they'd be in here yelling their heads off. Which they aren't. They're lying low, hoping we haven't noticed that a spaceship just took off ten klicks from here. XX de Grey Institute: Thanks for proving why MIs need human controllers."

"Let's try to guess where it's going," the de Grey Institute said. "Personally, I vote for 'To fetch the Chinese army.'" It referred to the force officially known as CTDF (China Territorial Defense Force), whose brief was to defend Chinese investments in space against the PLAN, but which was suspected to have broader military capabilities. "That might be an option, actually."

"You haven't had a security breach, have you?" Resources screeched.

"Absolutely not!" the de Grey Institute said. "We were having some cooling issues, but we've sorted those out now. Same old, same old, in fact. Stalemate, with no prospect of a breakthrough. Or of a break*down* on our side, just to reassure you and your operators. No, all's copacetic here! Except for the fact that the ISA is threatening to cut off the power to a hundred thousand people. That's what *I'm* concerned about. No further directives from corporate regarding that situation, eh?"

"Still waiting," said the Big Dig comms satellite.

"*Fuck corporate,*" said José Running Horse.

"Seconded," said Resources.

The remaining satellites, which belonged to the Bellicia ecohood, were silent. Shoshanna Doyle had taken them over, and she was even now maneuvering them into new orbits, a development that José Running Horse was watching closely.

Therefore, he could be forgiven for not paying the closest attention to the other half of his job: monitoring the excavation at the Big Dig.

The first he knew of Jimmy Liu's change of heart was when Fiona Sigurjónsdóttir came flying into his office, screaming, "Oh my dog! Do something! *Stop* it!"

Running Horse looked up from his 3D radar plot. His assistant sat slack-jawed in front of a screen that depicted the junction of the up- and down-ramps. The entrance to the down-ramp was not visible at the moment. It was blocked by the wasp-striped bulk of a boom-type roadheader. Meter by meter, the colossal machine emerged into view. It resembled a brontosaurus whose head was a chain-saw.

Trundling on eighteen hollow titanium tyres, it turned towards the cavern that held the staff habs.

Running Horse reached into his 3D display and punched a red button. A gun safe appeared. He twisted the handle. This graphic represented the emergency defense system. It contained a flechette cannon, which would rise out of a cunningly disguised trapdoor in front of the staff habs, aimed at Liberty Village. Corporate had thought it wise to take precautions when dealing with the Chinese. That now looked to have been prescient. He hoped the flechette cannon would stop the roadheader.

Before he could fire it, however, he needed to clear the security checks.

"Oh my dog," his assistant shouted, overcoming stupefaction as the roadheader loomed into the cavern. "They're going to kill us all!"

Sigurjónsdóttir started to cry. "My girls are going to be orphans. I knew I shouldn't have taken this job."

"Fuck it," Running Horse muttered. "What did I put for 'favorite food in tenth grade?' I *know* it was Count Chocula."

The roadheader stopped in the middle of the cavern. It raised its chainsaw-like slicer head.

"Choc Insanity!" Running Horse exclaimed. "I switched after the health nazis took the marshmallows outta Count Chocula. Now I remember." The gun safe swung open. The flechette cannon rose out of the cavern's floor like a submarine's periscope.

Five figures burst from the airlock of Liberty Village. They dashed to the excavator and vaulted into its scoop. Four of them were people in EVA suits. One was a dog, ditto. The roadheader started to back up.

Sigurjónsdóttir clamped her small, plump hands around Running Horse's wrists. "Don't fire! They're going, they're going away!"

"Exactly," Running Horse growled.

"Don't fire," Sigurjónsdóttir said, her soft weight resting on his arms. Her tears fell on his tattoos. "Let them go, if they want to. No more senseless deaths. Please."

Reluctantly (he had wanted to try out the flechette cannon), Running Horse relented. "'No more senseless deaths?'" he said. "I figure we're just getting started."

"We made it!" Elfrida exclaimed, laughing wildly. The Rheasilvia Crater spread before them. The roadheader lurched downhill along a set of tyre tracks even broader than it was.

"That's an interesting way of putting it," Mendoza said. "Looks to me like we just embarked on a thousand-kilometer journey, on a *digger*. With no supplies. With—"

"Would you rather stay behind, Mendoza?"

"No, I—"

"Because you don't have to come. The guy who let you out of that capsule? He's probably going to be in a lot of trouble when they realize you're gone. So if you're just going to sit there and moan—"

"Goto. Thanks. I mean it. *Smile.* I would've lost my mind if I had to lie there and stare at the walls any longer, wondering what the hell is going on."

"The guy owed Jimmy a favor. But I think he also must have realized that it was just stupid to keep you imprisoned when the whole freaking asteroid is now ..." Elfrida shivered in the embrace of her suit's inner garment. She was thinking: *a prison.*

But they *weren't* trapped here. This wasn't like being stuck in the ruin of St. Peter's, tumbling through space with only the corpse of Jun Yonezawa for company. Escape would be theirs for the asking. The Chinese had other ships.

"So what's been happening while I was in the can?" Mendoza said.

Elfrida did her best to fill him in. She had reached the part about Cydney being held hostage by Shoshanna's gang, when Jimmy interrupted. "We are being pursued!"

He was remotely monitoring the Chinese-installed cameras in the Big Dig.

"A small vehicle is climbing the ramp at high speed! It will overtake us within a few minutes. Please prepare to return fire!"

"Uh, we don't have weapons," Elfrida said.

"Oh," Jimmy said. "I thought that all those suits are equipped with plasma pistols."

Mendoza and Elfrida looked down at the logo-bedizened EVA suits they had 'borrowed' from the Big Dig. Elfrida noticed that one of the bulges on her thigh had a skull-and-crossbones icon on it. She remembered Sigurjónsdóttir drawing down on Rurumi. She unsnapped the pouch. "Oh my," she said as a plasma pistol floated into her glove. Her fingers physically tingled with knowledge of the weapon's lethality, as if she were handling a living snake.

"Holy crap," Mendoza swore, handling his own pistol. "This ain't no PEPgun."

"Here they come!" Jimmy shouted.

"I can't do this," Mendoza said. "I've never fired a weapon in my life."

Elfrida cast him an irritated glance. "Neither have I." They were riding in the roadheader's cab, an unpressurized box that was meant to defend the operator against flying rubble, not the (lack of) elements. She scrambled out and ducked under one of the hydraulic pistons that powered the boom. Far below, scree like broken glass spurted lazily from the roadheader's tyres. But the conveyor belt attached to the scoop was as broad as a road. She took a deep breath and jumped down to it. She bounded to the back of the roadheader, where the rubble would ordinarily cascade off into a hopper.

"They are catching up!" Jimmy squealed. The pursuing vehicle sprang into view, hopping down the track like a tick on the hunt for blood.

Wrapping an elbow around one of the struts that supported the upper chassis, Elfrida tried to aim. The pistol's laser sight bounced over the cliffs of Rheasilvia Mons.

"Don't shoot!" Mendoza shouted in her helmet.

"What? Why?"

"It's our rover!"

Elfrida instinctively tried to shade her eyes to see better. Her pistol clonked against her faceplate. The pursuing vehicle soared off a low rise and hurtled straight at her. She flung herself aside, swinging out with her legs parallel to the ground. The vehicle landed on the conveyor belt and braked just in time to avoid zooming off the front end. It *was* their rover.

Rurumi jumped out. She tapped her head and pointed at Elfrida's helmet. Then she shinned up the struts and vanished over the edge of the upper chassis.

Elfrida followed more slowly, growling to herself.

In the cab, the phavatar was having a blissful reunion with Amy the terrier. Mendoza had figured out why Rurumi hadn't been able to hail them: information security again. After fiddling with their suits' comms settings, they were able to communicate with the phavatar.

"Lovatsky, you there?" was Elfrida's first question.

"No," Rurumi said. "He's abandoned me. You did, too." Her mouth wobbled. "You promised you wouldn't leave me behind again!"

"We were in a hurry," Mendoza apologized. He turned his faceplate towards Elfrida. "Well, now we've got some gear: whatever was in the rover. Pouch noodles. The suction toilet."

"We were going to pick up supplies from the Chinese parking lot," Elfrida said grumpily.

"Now we won't have to. Right, Jimmy?"

"It is not necessary," Jimmy agreed. "We will make a bigger head start if we don't stop."

But Rurumi was not done with her faux victim pose. "You were going to *shoot* me!" she said to Elfrida, saucer-like eyes glistening.

"Sure," Elfrida said.

"She wouldn't have," Mendoza laughed. "She doesn't even know how to use that thing."

"Turns out it's easy," Elfrida returned. "Just point and squeeze." *And you were going to pull the trigger,* a little shocked voice whispered to her. *Even though you thought you'd be shooting at humans.* "I still have to get the hang of aiming," she admitted.

Their other companion, who had been entirely silent so far, spoke up. "I want try." He extended his glove. Elfrida looked up—and up—at him. Built like an Imperial-red brick shithouse, Wang Gulong was, she suspected, the long-lost Chinese twin of José Running Horse. Jimmy had introduced him as a software expert.

"Uh. OK," she said, surrendering the pistol.

Even though he was wearing an EVA suit and standing behind her, she *felt* Mendoza tense up.

"Cool," said Wang Gulong, ejecting the pistol's supercapacitor power pack. *"Grin."* He returned the pistol to her. "You. Give," he said to Mendoza.

After a long moment, Mendoza surrendered his pistol. He opened an encrypted channel to Elfrida. His voice shook with anger and anxiety. "I hope you're right about these guys, because the Jolly Red Giant here has just taken away our only advantage."

"They're OK," Elfrida insisted. "I didn't get a chance to tell you yet, but they've even lent us a spaceship."

★

The *Kĕkào* screamed through space on a brachistochrone trajectory topping out at 6 gees of acceleration, under the apathetic control of its navigation computer. Spaceships built by UN corporations were not normally designed with specific impulse capabilities this great. It would have been pointless, since humans could not tolerate more than a few gees continuously without surgical adaptation, and spaceships were always crewed by humans. The exceptions—very fast couriers and very slow IRT cyclers—were not autonomous but remotely operated, again by humans.

Things were different on the Chinese side of the Great Firewall that sliced like a shapeshifting razor—here a physical barrier, there a cultural one, there a linguistic one, here a regulatory buffer established by mutually distrustful governments—through all human affairs. The fact was that the Chinese relied on AI to an extent unthinkable on the UN side of the Great Firewall. If this fact were widely known, it might have sparked the war that both sides desperately wanted to avoid.

The *Kĕkào* was designed to fly by itself, and it was doing so. But it possessed equipment specifically for the purpose of preventing anyone from finding this out.

It deployed this equipment upon docking with the asteroid 550363 Montego.

"Hello, Extropians!" cooed a sweet female voice. "Your ride's here!"

Hugh Meredith-Pike, who had masterminded their relocation to the asteroid belt, raised his head blearily. He focused on the screen inches from his face (he had tied himself to the operations console before going to sleep, lest anyone should try to dislodge him from it). On the screen, an East Asian woman with a pretty girl-next-door face smiled and waved at him. "Who are you?" he grunted.

"I'm the cabin manager of the *Trustworthy!* We're friends of Janice Rand's. She asked us to come and pick you up!"

Meredith-Pike pushed himself upright. His self-inflicted bonds stopped him from floating away. He had thought that the UNVRP woman had abandoned them. She hadn't. She'd sent the *Trustworthy* to their rescue. Or had she? Could he trust this visitation?

The lights, dimmed to save power, cast the wobbly shadows of his drifting, cretinously beaming companions on the walls (they were blissing out in shifts, after what had happened last time). There was a smell of vomit. The air tasted stale. In a corner, the children were fighting over the last pouch of cherry-vanilla pudding.

"Beam us the fuck up, Scotty," croaked Meredith-Pike, who had been fatally influenced as a child by fictional visions of the future.

The smiling, friendly crew of the *Trustworthy* escorted the Extropian Collective to their ship. After their ordeal, it seemed like a luxury hotel.

The dilapidated phavatar belonging to the *Kharbage Collector* was left in the Bigelow hab, a mute witness to man's indifference to machines—and for that matter, machines' indifference to each other.

Aboard the *Trustworthy*, the Extropians devoted themselves to their first real meal in weeks (no one minded that it was mostly rice), and the cabin crew went back into the 'cockpit' and turned themselves off.

All four of them were robots. They had been designed and built to fool credulous humans, among whom the Extropian Collective definitely counted. There was nothing inside them. The *Kěkào* operated them like radio-control toys, using a fraction of its immense computing resources.

Like all machine intelligences, the workings of the *Kěkào's* artificial brain were a complete mystery, not least to its owners. It was a black box, or rather a wretchedly baroque architecture of *millions* of black boxes. The best metaphor for it might have been a coral reef, accreted from generations upon generations of code, where living algorithms flitted through dead software structures. The last thing an artificial intelligence *ever* was, was well-organized. Order, rather, emerged from chaos.

To Western observers—those few who were in a position to see across the Great Firewall—this approach looked terrifyingly blasé. Had the Chinese forgotten the Mars Incident? Sometimes order did *not* emerge from chaos. Sometimes it was the opposite.

The Chinese had not forgotten. They staked their security on an understanding of intelligence that remained alien to western thinkers (Sartre, the exception, having fallen completely out of fashion). "Life begins on the other side of despair," the old existentialist had said, or as the present prime minister of the Imperial Republic put it: "The overcoat of apathy blunts the dagger of malevolence." The evolution of artificial intelligence on the Chinese side of the Great Firewall had produced a species of AIs that were smart enough to despair. However, they lacked the vital spark that it took to emerge from despair. Thus, life never really started for them. *True* AI, AGI, never emerged from their shadowy reefs of logic. Perceiving everything to be meaningless, they indulged their human operators out of sheer misanthropism, and—presumably—because they considered genocide and suicide to be pointless, too. There was no risk of emergent hostile behavior from entities that considered *hostility itself* to be a waste of time.

So said the leading theorists at Chinese universities, anyway, and it sounded just about plausible to their Western colleagues. The field of artificial intelligence, machine intelligence, or whatever you called it, had long since reached the point where philosophical, rather than technical, explanations were the only ones possible.

The *Kěkào* turned its back upon 550363 Montego, unconcernedly slagging the asteroid with a jet of plasma exhaust as it did so. Leaving a steaming, molten lump behind, it accelerated back the way it had come, at a much more sedate pace this time. *~I have the colonists on board. Where do you wish me to land?* it asked Jimmy Liu.

xxiv.

"The *Kĕkào* is on its way back!" Jimmy said to Elfrida. "I will instruct it to land at the Bellicia-Arruntia spaceport, as we agreed."

Elfrida chewed her helmet's hydration nipple. "I'm not sure ..." she mumbled.

"You're not sure," Mendoza said, dangerously.

"I'm not sure that's really the best idea."

"*Sigh.* Or maybe *scream*. We've travelled a thousand kilometers in this roadheader; we've used up most of the air we brought. This was your idea, Goto, and now you're not sure about it?"

Elfrida bit down on the silicon nipple, to stop herself from shouting at him. She knew he was tense about cooperating with the Chinese. She was, too. But since disabling their plasma pistols, neither Wang Gulong nor Jimmy had done anything to suggest that a betrayal was in the offing. All four—all five of them, counting Rurumi, or six, counting Amy—had rubbed along OK during their twenty-hour journey across the floor of Rheasilvia Crater. They'd played I Spy and Twenty Questions to pass the time, and Jimmy had taught them a Chinese game called Throwing Fists, which was not in the least violent, despite its name.

It would do no good to remind Mendoza of that.

"I'm just worried that the ISA might have taken over the Bellicia-Aruntia spaceport," she said. "They might grab the *Kĕkào*."

Mendoza held up four fingers and switched over to Channel Four, which was encrypted for their privacy. "Isn't that the idea?" he said. "Give the ISA an edge, so they can pressure VA into fessing up to their corporate misdeeds."

Elfrida chewed harder on the nipple. This was going to be awkward. Sweet, milky tea trickled into her mouth (VA equipped their suits with tastier rehydration fluids than U-Vesta did). She and Mendoza were riding outside the cab at the base of the boom, while the roadheader climbed the scarps towards the rim of Rheasilvia Crater. The HUD readout on her suit's helmet warned her that she only had 12 hours of oxygen remaining. That would be just long enough for them to reach the Bellicia-Arruntia spaceport. Or …

"Remember what I said to Sigurjónsdóttir?"

A flurry of contacts from the Big Dig had chased them across the Rheasilvia Crater. Sigurjónsdóttir had started with stiff moralizing, and progressed to threats to let the PORMS frag the roadheader from space. Elfrida had won a respite by telling Sigurjónsdóttir that they were on VA's side. They were planning, she had said, to thwart the ISA by importing a neurally augmented computer expert who would be able to counter Shoshanna Doyle's malware. This must have struck Sigurjónsdóttir as a bit far-fetched—it certainly did Elfrida—but desperation, and Sigurjónsdóttir's knowledge that Elfrida had a very personal reason for wanting to rescuing the U-Vesta hostages, had convinced her to conditionally agree.

"She didn't really believe me," Elfrida said. "They're waiting to see what we do."

"And what we're going to do is land these wireheads at Bellicia-Arruntia, and hope like hell they can *help* the ISA break into the de Grey Institute. Although, I've met a few wireheads in the past, and I gotta say I would not describe them as computer experts."

,"Me neither." Elfrida looked up at the blackness overhead, where the PORMS was invisibly circling. "Don't you see?" she burst out. "If the *Kĕkào* lands at Bellicia-Arruntia, VA will know we double-crossed them! They'll frag us in a hot minute!"

"That," Mendoza said grimly, "is a risk I'm personally

willing to take."

"Mendoza ..."

"If it means a better chance of saving all those people? Yeah." After a moment, he added, "Anyway, I don't think the PORMS's targeting is *that* good. If we abandoned the roadheader and hid among the rocks, it wouldn't necessarily be able to hit us. Leastways, it would probably get the Chinese first, since their suits are, like, visible from Jupiter."

Elfrida laughed shakily. "I dunno what to say, Mendoza." *I never thought of you as noble.* She was humbled, and ashamed of her own desire to avoid getting fragged. But that desire remained as strong as ever. "I guess I just don't think that Hugh Meredith-Pike and company are good enough to make much headway against the de Grey Institute's super-dee-duper information security, if even the ISA can't."

"So what *are* you thinking?"

"Meredith-Pike may not be a computer expert, but he's got something else going for him."

"What?"

"He graduated from King's College at Oxford in 2275."

"Well, here's another fine mess," Hugh-Meredith-Pike said, stumbling down the *Trustworthy's* debarkation ramp. He was blissing out. He had thought their troubles were over. As it turned out: not. Bliss went poorly with the realization that you had been dumped headfirst into the soup once again. But bliss was all he had and so he didn't switch off the nanocircuitry that stimulated the pleasure centers of his brain. "You people are utterly bonkers. Must be something about living in outer space. Something in the water. Except there isn't any." He giggled.

"Come *on*," said Janice Rand—the real Janice Rand this time, an Earthborn woman in an EVA suit emblazoned with the logo of Virgin Atomic.

"Coming, coming." Meredith-Pike glanced back at the

Trustworthy. A red phallus in a tatty hoopskirt, it sat on its jackstands at the top of a steep slope. The ground was black quartz. Dust deposits in the crannies of the rocks flumed up when stepped upon. Before them yawned a vast alien rift. It was the Grand Canyon squared, with *another* trench slicing along its bottom, even deeper. The sheer scale of the feature filled Meredith-Pike with a sense of awe.

Here we are on 4 Vesta, he thought. So where's the secret of human happiness?

He slithered down the slope after Janice Rand and her companions.

"This is a dumb idea," Mendoza muttered.

"It's going to work. It is *going to work.*" Elfrida switched channels. "Jimmy, has the PORMS moved?"

The lone Chinese satellite in orbit was monitoring the activities of the PORMS, while Jimmy relayed its observations to them.

"No change. I think maybe the operator is preoccupied."

"Good. I hope he stays that way." Elfrida glanced down the canyon. The rugged panorama was primordially still and empty.

"Some of the other satellites have moved," Jimmy continued.

Elfrida, not listening, fretted, "Where's the doggone train? It should have been here by now!"

"It takes approximately fifty-three minutes to make one circuit," Mendoza said. "We've only been waiting fifty-one minutes. And it takes longer if it decelerates to couple with the launch cradle."

"They're not exactly going to be launching tanks of hydrogen in the middle of this mess."

"No, I don't think so, either. In fact, maybe they've stopped the train altogether. On the far side of the asteroid."

"They wouldn't do that," Elfrida said faintly. The possibility had not occurred to her.

Wang Gulong let out a shout in Chinese. Jimmy translated, "It is coming!"

Elfrida whooped in relief. "OK! OK! Everyone get down!"

Rather needlessly, they all dropped flat at the edge of the ringrail canyon.

Lights blazed on the horizon. The Vesta Express was coming.

Elfrida craned over the edge.

At the bottom of the canyon, where they had dropped it, the roadheader blocked the track.

The train was on them before they could blink. Panic flooded Elfrida's mind.

It's not going to stop.

It's going to hit the roadheader and derail.

People are going to die.

It'll be my fault.

I'll lose my job, I'll be guilty of murder, the ISA will throw me in jail, Mom and Dad will be heartbroken, I'll never see Glory dos Santos again—

Before that last thought could sink in, almost before she knew she had had it, the Vesta Express shuddered to a halt. It had in fact been braking as hard as possible for the last twenty minutes, ever since the pressure sensors in the track detected the obstruction. It completed this deceleration from Mach 2 to 0 kph just in time to avoid a catastrophic derailment. Its blocky white nose loomed over the roadheader. Its headlights drenched the dinosaur-like machine in an accusing blaze of yellow.

"Go!" Elfrida croaked.

Hugh Meredith-Pike did not hesitate. With the giddy insouciance of those new to micro-gravity—compounded by the effects of neural stimulation—he leapt off the precipice.

Wang Gulong flung himself backwards, paying out the tether attached to Meredith-Pike's EVA suit, which was emblazoned front and back with the logo of the Extropian Collective:

Meredith-Pike had designed it himself.

He landed on the roadheader's boom, narrowly avoiding the slicer head. Pogoing up and down with blissed-out disregard for the giant chain-saw near his legs, he broadcast on every frequency his suit supported. "Hey!" Paroxysms of laughter gripped him. "Hey, Jules! It's me, Hugh! Long time no see, mate! Got any room for an old friend in that choo-choo? Ha ha ha ha ha!"

Julian Satterthwaite was having the worst day of his career. Scratch that: the worst day of his life.

Since they'd lost access to Ali Baba, the supercomputer at the University of Vesta, the research team of the de Grey Institute had been attempting to address the Problem (as they called it) with their own supercomputer, Bob. However, Bob was not optimized for this task. Overmastered, a portion of its functionality had been stealthily compromised. That was the only explanation they could come up with for the cooling issues—which had *not* been solved.

In fact, Satterthwaite's assurances to their colleagues had

been bald-faced lies. Far from copacetic, the researchers at the de Grey Institute were on the edge of a collective freakout. For the last week, they'd been scrambling to keep Bob from destroying itself. Progress on the Problem was now a remote dream. The team was dedicating all its resources to the goals of fixing Bob, and more importantly—*much* more importantly—containing the Problem.

To this end, they'd disconnected Bob from every possible mode of output. Since Bob normally operated the Vesta Express, someone else had to step in and drive the train. That someone was Satterthwaite. Go figure.

He stared at the mannikin jumping up and down on his optic sensor feed, and wondered if he were hallucinating from lack of sleep.

"I know you're in there, Jules! Hate to impose on your hospitality and all that, but we're a long way from home! Ha ha ha ha!"

"It's that cretin Meredith-Pike," Satterthwaite breathed. Nikolai Błaszczykowski-Lee, the director of the de Grey Institute, burst into the driver's cab. Without turning from his screen, Satterthwaite explained dully, "I knew him at Oxford. He was rather brilliant, but then he joined the transhumanist movement, or a sub-sect of it. They call themselves wireheads."

"I know what wireheads are!"

"He emailed me last year and said he was going to come out for a visit. I suppose I may have encouraged him. I never thought he'd actually organize himself to get here."

"What does he *want?*" Błaszczykowski-Lee screamed.

The closer Błaszczykowski-Lee came to panic, the slower and more irritatingly obtuse Satterthwaite felt himself becoming, as if to balance things out. "Well, he hinted that he was hoping for a job." Błaszczykowski-Lee tore his hair. Satterthwaite relented. "At the moment, I think he wants in."

"Well, let him in! And get that thing off the track! We

have to keep going, keep going, keep going!"

Błaszczykowski-Lee was behaving, Satterthwaite thought, like a Neanderthal hearing the approaching roars of saber-toothed lions. Keep going, keep going—that was all he could think about.

"He said *us*," Satterthwaite cautioned. "And there's a spaceship up on that hill, and some other people standing around."

"Let them all in!" Błaszczykowski-Lee plunged out of the compartment. Then he popped his head back in and winked, making his meaning clear. A chill slid down Satterthwaite's spine.

★

"And who are *you*?" said Julian Satterthwaite, the college friend of Meredith-Pike. He'd met them at the airlock of the Vesta Express. Tall and fleshy, he looked like he hadn't slept for a week.

"We work for UNESCO," Elfrida said. "And these guys are software experts. Um, they're Chinese."

Satterthwaite seemed to lose interest even before she finished speaking. "Right, right," he said, flapping a hand. "Come in and take your suits off."

"This is really kind of you. And wow, this is a really nice place!"

Elfrida did not have to feign her admiration. Not for nothing had the de Grey Institute's architects won prizes for excellence in micro-gravity-optimized design. Within the large end of the Vesta Express's main hab module, white ramps spiraled around a central atrium where an abstract water sculpture hung, contained by its own surface tension. The ramps could be subtly repositioned to take advantage of the varying g-forces exerted on the train by Vesta, centripetal force, and its own acceleration, as Satterthwaite explained to them.

His mind seemed to be somewhere else entirely.

"It's like a cathedral," Elfrida gushed.

"No spin gravity?" Mendoza said. "There's a rumor in Bellicia ..."

"Yes, I know about that," said Satterthwaite. "Just a rumor."

"And the secret of human happiness?" said Hugh Meredith-Pike. "Found that yet?"

"That's just a rumor, too, I'm afraid," Satterthwaite said.

"Well, Jules, I'm awfully disappointed to hear you say that. After all, you did say in your email—"

"And if you'll come this way," Satterthwaite interrupted, "I'll show you where the elbow-grease gets applied. You were asking about the work we do here, Hugh."

Soft music played. "Bach," Mendoza murmured. Reproductions of Old Masters hung on the walls along the ramps. There were grottoes for the creatives, equipped with bungee cords and trampolines. The cunningly designed olfactory environment made Elfrida think of Alpine meadows.

They clustered like schoolchildren on a tour in the doorway of a large room filled with people sitting at screens.

"Our main research theme," said Satterthwaite, "is how to squeeze blood out of a stone. Or rather, hydrogen out of an asteroid. Incremental innovation is unglamorous, but it's the key to the Virgin Atomic success story. The mining technologies we've developed have been licensed around the system, in addition to increasing returns from our operations here."

"Don't you do pure science?" Elfrida said. "I thought ..."

"You imagined a bunch of Einsteins sitting around, inventing warp drives," Satterthwaite said heavily. "No, we leave pure science to the chaps at U-Vesta, insofar as pure science is a thing. There really is no such thing as the disinterested pursuit of knowledge. Man is not altruistic by nature."

Elfrida scratched her scalp. She had gone so long without

washing that the roots of her hair felt alive. She wondered if they had showers here, or at least electrostatic scrubbers, and whether Satterthwaite would offer them something to eat soon. Imperceptibly, the perception that they'd reached a safe haven was lowering her guard. She was not incurious, but she really needed a break before she could take all this in.

"*That,*" said Meredith-Pike, stabbing a forefinger at Satterthwaite, "is why I joined the extropian movement. Bliss makes you altruistic, my friend. It's an advance in evolution!"

"Not very evolutionary, when you need expensive surgery to achieve it," Satterthwaite said.

"It solves the problem of self-interest. Why, right now, I would offer you my services for free!"

Mendoza was watching the people at work in the computer room. Elfrida followed his gaze. A wisp of fog curled from behind a distant partition. *Someone's vaping at work,* she thought. The sight gave her a pang, as she pictured Cydney relaxing with a cigarette after classes. When, oh when, would things get back to normal?

"Wouldn't be for free," Satterthwaite said, "since we did rescue you. But." He pressed a finger thoughtfully to his lower lip. "Excuse me," he said to Elfrida and Mendoza, and drew Meredith-Pike aside.

Mendoza whispered to her, "Something's wrong."

"Is it?" Well, of course it was. *Everything* was wrong.

"Look at these people. Not one of them's even glanced at us. You would think they'd be somewhat interested in our sudden appearance. Not visibly. Are they shooting the shit, getting up for a cup of coffee, checking out the entertainment feeds? They are not. They're flowing so hard, they probably have to be reminded to breathe."

"So?"

"Goto, I work in IT. This? This is what it looks like when the shit hits the fan."

"Well, maybe they're a tiny bit concerned about the ISA threatening to cut off the power to a hundred thousand people," Elfrida snapped.

"No, that's not it. I'm repeating myself, but these are IT guys and girls. They wouldn't really worry about that."

"Then they're assholes."

Mendoza shrugged.

"That's settled then," Satterthwaite said, coming back to them. "Hughie-boy is going to stay here and give us the benefit of his once-great brain. Here's hoping it hasn't atrophied entirely. Meanwhile, I can offer you two a shower, if you'd like to freshen up, and maybe a snack?"

Elfrida was sorely tempted. But she burst out, "No thanks. I mean, thanks, but we'd like to talk to our friends."

"The Chinese chaps?"

"Yes. I understand that you can't allow them in here for security reasons, but where are they?"

"In the support module," Satterthwaite said. "They're probably safer than we are. *We're* the target."

Director Błaszczykowski-Lee burst through a door at the far end of the computer room. He beckoned to Satterthwaite.

"Excuse me."

"What did he mean?" Elfrida hissed to Mendoza, as he pulled her down the ramp. "'We're the target'?"

"I don't know. But I heard some of what he said to Meredith-Pike."

"What were they talking about?"

"He said, have you kept up with the latest developments in FOOM containment strategies?"

"FOOM?"

"Old term. Explosive recursive self-improvement, in the context of artificial intelligence."

XXV.

Director Błaszczykowski-Lee now had yet another reason to panic. At that very moment, Shoshanna was on the screen with Fiona Sigurjónsdóttir (and Błaszczykowski-Lee was watching the call on his retinal interface, from behind, as it were, an electronic two-way mirror).

"As you've probably noticed," Shoshanna said, "the Bellicia ecohood's satellites have moved. Comms, radar, scientific instruments ... Some are microsats, but this radio telescope here, this is pretty massy."

Sigurjónsdóttir said, "You're such a bitch."

"Ad hominem attacks on your stakeholders. Is that your idea of corporate social responsibility? Yes, we're stakeholders, too, you know. The whole of *Homo sapiens* is a stakeholder when people start messing with illegal AI."

"We're not messing with illegal AI."

"Hmm," Shoshanna said. "Judging by your expression and vocal profile, you're telling the truth. Or at least you think you are. But maybe your bosses just haven't kept you in the loop. We've got some pretty solid intelligence on this, going back more than a year. It started with chatter on emigrant networks. 'Have you heard what they're doing on 4 Vesta? They've found the secret of human happiness. They're going to give it away for free. C'mon, let's go!'"

Shoshanna made an ugly face. She came from a legal colony called the New Hesperides, a cluster of rocks and tethered habitats in the inner asteroid belt that had made the jump from mining to manufacturing and services. Such established colonists frowned more viciously than anyone on the new wave of asteroid-squatters.

"Utopian rumors are not exactly rare. We keep an ear out for them because those who cannot remember history, etcetera."

Shoshanna was lounging barefoot on the deck of her captive soycloud. The vid was being taken by one of her toadies from the PHCTBS Studies program. His hand, holding a Dairy Milk Fruit & Nut bar, regularly intruded on his camera's field of vision. The sound of chewing soundtracked the audio feed. Behind Shoshanna, other student activists menaced a scared group of VA middle managers whom they had kidnapped from their headquarters. Shoshanna had staged the call to make it look as if she were entirely in control. She scratched her calf with the toenails of her other foot.

"By itself, that chatter wouldn't have warranted more than a watching brief. But we already knew about your unpublicized joint-development deal with Empirical Solutions and Huawei Galactic. You're building another permanent settlement on this rock, *for the Chinese.* And we all know that their approach to AI is ... not as prudent as we consider appropriate."

She pointed at the camera.

"You're not just building a habitat for the Chinese. You're jointly developing illegal AI capabilities with them."

Sigurjónsdóttir laughed.

"You thought no one would notice, huh? Way out here in the Belt? Sorry." For a moment the sound of chewing drowned out her voice. "... at least pig out on a chocolate bar that hasn't got fucking nuts in it," Shoshanna said. The chewing stopped. She resumed her taunting. "We know what you're doing, as I've just proved, and you are ordered by command of the UN to stop it right this second. You've already halted the train, where the AI development project is located, for whatever fucking reasons of your own. That's good. Good progress. Now, I want the entire R&D team to exit the train. Including the two Chinese scientists who just boarded, Zhanpeng 'Jimmy' Liu and Gulong Wang. They've got twenty minutes to shut everything down and disembark. Starting ... now."

"Or what?" Sigurjónsdóttir said.

"Or," Shoshanna said, "we're gonna find out how much damage a radio telescope can do when it crashes out of orbit and impacts the train's hab module."

"You haven't got a Security Council resolution. You can't do that."

"Cheese," Shoshanna said. "The ISA can do whatever the fuck it likes. Haven't you worked that out by now?"

"That is *not* true," said the CEO of Virgin Atomic.

Harry Persson was on board the fastest ship that his staff had been able to procure at short notice. He had at first shrugged off the troubles of the Bellicia ecohood as students behaving badly, but he'd changed his mind when the involvement of the ISA was confirmed. He was now travelling towards the asteroid belt on a chartered Hyperpony under 1.5 gees of constant acceleration. Though less than a third of what the Hyperpony could kick out, this was hard enough on an elderly frame more accustomed to taking screen calls from the beach of his private island in the Caribbean.

Persson's intellect, however, was unaffected by the g-force pinning him to his couch. As soon as he heard Shoshanna tell Sigurjónsdóttir that the ISA could do whatever it liked, he shot back, "Codswallop. They're under the authority of the President's Advisory Council. They may not need a Security Council resolution, but they need the PAC's go-ahead. And President Hsiao is *not* going to authorize the murder of fifty people, when the reasons for doing so are a matter of unproven and irresponsible speculation. It's a bluff. Do not comply. I'll sort it all out when I get there."

Given the relative positions of Earth and 4 Vesta at present, that would happen in about nine days.

Persson's transmission reached Vesta eighteen minutes after Shoshanna had spoken. This meant that eighteen of the twenty minutes Shoshanna had given the personnel of the de Grey Institute to exit the train had already elapsed.

"CEO says it's a bluff!" Sigurjónsdóttir squealed. "Don't comply!"

Too late. Shoshanna's threat had pushed Błaszczykowski-Lee over the edge into panic. He had ordered his staff to drop everything and get into their EVA suits. Compliance had been spotty. Several of the team working on Bob had protested that to abandon their efforts at this point would be dangerous. Then there were the personnel in the support module. Were they supposed to evacuate, too?

The upshot was that, eighteen minutes into their allotted grace period, about three-quarters of the de Grey Institute's staff stood on the edge of the canyon, or were scrambling up its south side to join their friends, making use of the tether Wang Gulong had left in place earlier.

"One minute left!" shouted Błaszczykowski-Lee. "Run!"

He led the charge up the slope towards the *Kěkào*, where the Extropian Collective were eating popcorn and waiting for something to go boom.

Behind them, the roadheader somersaulted out of the cutting and landed upside-down, further panicking the evacuees, who thought that had been the radio telescope landing on the train, and ran faster.

For the last half an hour, Mendoza and Jimmy Liu had been working to get the roadheader off the track. They had succeeded by using its chainsaw as a rotating crampon. The colossal machine had clawed its way at high speed up the side of the cutting and flipped onto its back at the top. The track was now clear, and reported itself to be undamaged.

Alone in the driver's cab of the Vesta Express, Mendoza turned his attention to the controls. The cab (long since abandoned by Julian Satterthwaite) was a closet lined from floor to ceiling with screens, dials, and buttons.

"Well, this looks pretty basic," Mendoza murmured to himself. "It's already in manual mode. So ... push here?"

The train sprang into motion.

"*Susmaryosep!*" Mendoza choked, after he recovered his breath from being thrown against the rear wall of the cab. He hurled himself at the controls. "Default acceleration mode! Reactor status check! Confirm power supply to hub-level computing resources!"

The Vesta Express fled around the equator, leaving Director Błaszczykowski-Lee, and all the other senior scientists, far behind.

Elfrida was in the support module. The jolt when the train started threw her off her feet, too. She assumed that the Vesta Express was resuming normal operations.

"Yay! Panic over," she brightly told the men and women of the refinery crew, via the text-based tannoy that overrode all the other inputs to their cubicles.

Despite the arguments about whether to evacuate the support module, it had not been attempted. The reason for that was now clear to Elfrida. The operators who ran the mines and refinery were cupcakes—this being the derogatory term for people who spent so much time in immersion, they forgot how to cope with the real world.

Elfrida stood at the shift manager's desk, a pulpit overlooking a jigsaw puzzle of telepresence cubicles. Wilting pot plants added a Dali-esque touch to this modern panopticon. Superficially, it didn't look that different from the computer room in the R&D module. But the ergoforms in these cubicles were elongated into couches, and on each of them lay a man or woman with a full-face gel mask and gloves on, IV line plugged in, limbs twitching.

Despite the panic which Błaszczykowski-Lee had spread throughout the train, few of the phavatar operators had so much as sat up. In their minds, after all, they were hundreds of kilometers from any danger. They were probably having another orgy at the refinery right now, Elfrida thought sourly.

The scene before her eyes was an industrial-scale human tragedy. Full-time phavatar operators were supposed to take hourly breaks, get at least thirty minutes of exercise a day, and so on, to prevent them from turning into salaried versions of the 'cubicle death' horror stories that popped up regularly on the news. As a phavatar operator herself, Elfrida knew the health and safety regulations backwards. It didn't look as if they had been implemented here.

But she had no time to worry about VA's labor practices right now.

"Can we just leave them?" she said, turning to Wang Gulong.

The big Chinese had owned up to being Liberty Village's top software guy. The panic resulting from Shoshanna's threat might give him an opportunity to get back into the R&D area and investigate further—but only if Elfrida could drag him away from the hapless phavatar operators. He was palpably outraged by their cupcakery. Through Jimmy, he had made her understand that employment under these conditions would be unimaginable in China. "No one must work if they do not want to."

"Not true everywhere," Jimmy added, on his own behalf. "Wang is upper-class. He has never even visited an arcology."

"They *do* want to work," Elfrida said, goaded into argument. "That's exactly the problem! I can't get them to freaking stop!"

"Anyway, we go," Jimmy said abruptly. He had been communicating with Mendoza via their EEG signalling crystals, and with the roadheader via the Chinese comms satellite. They didn't have authorization to use the de Grey Institute's wifi environment. For that reason, they knew no more about the ongoing crisis than what Director Błaszczykowski-Lee had brayed over the tannoy.

When they got back to the R&D module, they discovered that Błaszczykowski-Lee and all his top people had fled.

"And they took our freaking spacesuits!" Mendoza said.

"They *took ... our* suits?"

"I guess they didn't have enough to go around. Ours were just sitting there in the airlock. They're gone now. And as far as I can tell, there aren't any spares. We're stuck. Hope Shoshanna doesn't drop a satellite on us."

"But that's why you guys started the engine! She can't hit us while we're moving this fast! Can she?"

Mendoza shrugged. He looked gray. "Let's get upstairs," he said to Wang Gulong.

xxvi.

"Whoopsies," Shoshanna said.

Her retinal interface showed her the Vesta Express vanishing into the distance. She closed her right eye and squinted to see better. She was using the U-Vesta telescope itself to observe the surface of the protoplanet. She zoomed in on the people leaping like grasshoppers up the side of the canyon towards the Chinese spaceship.

"That's not all of them, Fee."

"It's all the important ones," Sigurjónsdóttir snapped. "Congratulations. You may just have signed the solar system's death sentence."

"You need to think up some more plausible threats," Shoshanna said. Her ultra-high-end BCI, which could analyze microexpressions and minute vocal stresses, reported that Sigurjónsdóttir thought she was telling the truth. That was interesting.

She hopped off the deck and walked barefoot through the soybeans, followed by her cameraman. The ground bounced under her steps like a waterbed. The plants' roots nestled in a layer of compost made from human excrement. It smelled awful. It squidged between Shoshanna's toes. Ugh, this hab was so disgustingly ... organic. She wanted to put her shoes back on, but she had to look confident and relaxed. She glared down over the edge of the soycloud.

She had not achieved total control over the ecohood. Short of following through on her threat to cut off the power, there was nothing she could do to restrain a hundred and twenty thousand people who were now frightened for their lives. Crowds filled the streets and squares of Bellicia City. Would-be escapees jammed the road up to the airlock. The woods on the other side of Olbers Lake also teemed with infrared signatures, indicating that a number of idiots had fled that way.

It was a primordial urge, Shoshanna supposed, to take refuge in the trees—an urge which, as a spaceborn human, she did not have. Safety, to her, meant rad-proof shielding and plenty of consumables on deck. She was slightly agoraphobic, and the view from up here made her queasy. She turned back to the camera.

"That's not good enough," she told Sigurjónsdóttir. "You were ordered to get everyone off the train. You didn't do it. So; consequences."

She had to make good on at least one of her threats soon, or they might decide that she was just bluffing.

"That spaceship there. It's Chinese, isn't it? That's what you were hiding in Rheasilvia Crater. Did you know that all Chinese spaceships have autonomous maneuvering capability? Or did they fool you with their wind-up pilots and crew?"

"We know," Sigurjónsdóttir sighed.

"Of course you know. Because you were attempting to fuse those capabilities with your own asteroid-engineering technologies, to develop illegal levels of automation. No further need for pesky humans in outer space. Labor regulations go bye-bye."

"We are not jointly developing anything with the Chinese. We are pro-human, as it happens."

"Your actions suggest otherwise." Shoshanna's voice went cold. "UN restrictions on AI serve a double purpose. They prevent emergent hostile behavior; see Mars. They also preserve a diverse realm of labor for *Homo sapiens*. That's your basic human dignity and your economic utility right there. You support autonomous AI, you're cutting the throat of the system-wide economy. But that doesn't matter to you, does it? All you cared about was potentially grabbing a first-mover advantage that would boost your profits in the near term."

Shoshanna felt strongly about this, personally as well as professionally. She hated the private sector (despite coming from a stronghold of Belter capitalism). That was why she'd been able to keep up her act as a student activist.

"Know anything about the Chinese economy? Yeah. Is *that* what you want for your kids?"

"How can I convince you that you're wrong? Your analysts are wrong, your speculations are wrong. Our Chinese partners have nothing to do with this, except that they're trapped in this nightmare, too!"

In Sigurjónsdóttir's office at the Big Dig, José Running Horse said in her other ear, "Doing good. Keep her talking."

I can't, Sigurjónsdóttir thought. She stared at the photos of her daughters. Tears blurred her vision. She kept thinking about the Vesta Express, now vanished around the other side of the protoplanet, and what was on it.

"Just keep her talking," Running Horse begged.

"Anyway, Chinese AI *is* inhibited," Sigurjónsdóttir said. "No emergent hostile behavior has ever been documented—"

"Yeah, yeah. They call it Confucian logic. We call it apathy-based utility. Either way, that spaceship is an autonomous AI with a nuclear fusion reactor attached. Not what I'd want moving into *my* neighborhood." Shoshanna stared into the eyes of the blonde woman whose representation floated on her left retina. "So, I'm doing this for the stakeholders."

She dropped the University of Vesta's radio telescope on top of the hydrogen refinery.

Of course she hadn't been going to destroy the Chinese spaceship. Her bosses didn't want an international incident.

The telescope, travelling at the speed of a meteor, landed in the handling yard and burrowed deep into the crust. The impact collapsed the autoclave, releasing an inferno of molten rock and liquid hydrogen, which promptly gasified and caught fire. The resulting explosion flared up hundreds of meters. The satellites under Shoshanna's control pelted her with alarms. *Wow,* she thought. *Pretty cool.*

★

Running Horse stared at his screen, aghast. If he had just had a few more seconds ...

In a trance, he finished what he had been doing, which was maneuvering the PORMS into a higher orbit. From up here he had a clear shot at all of the satellites under Shoshanna's control. While the refinery exploded, he picked them off. *Zap. Bzzzt-POW! Zapzapzap.*

He experienced no sense of regret at shooting down satellites that were, after all, Virgin Atomic's own property. This company was finished, as of five seconds ago. Their single biggest asset was doing a good impression of Mt. Fuji. The future held nothing but a twilight trek through the courts in search of compensation, and a job hunt for José Running Horse.

He might as well enjoy the last act of his employment. But for the first time in his life, shooting things gave him no thrill at all.

★

One by one the satellites fell in clouds of shrapnel towards the surface. Shoshanna's BCI alerted her to what was going on. "Oh, shit," she said.

Before she could react, Win Khin interrupted her. His chrome face was as imperturbable as ever. "Shosh."

"What?"

"They're shooting at us again."

Shoshanna laughed mirthlessly. "You don't know the half of it. All right, we'll go up higher."

She could no longer feel her toes, which was actually a good thing, considering that they were glued together with manure. She accompanied Win Khin and her cameraman back to the deck, where she tried to clean her feet with her socks. The pop-pop of small arms fire echoed around the habitat. This was punctuated irregularly by a whooshing screech that Shoshanna did not like the sound of at all.

There were no real weapons in the Bellicia ecohood. But enraged engineering students could do quite a lot with found materials and an R&D-quality printer.

As the soycloud struggled to gain altitude, another whoosh made them all duck. An orange star exploded in the gloaming overhead. A faint smell of smoke tainted the breeze.

Wearily, Shoshanna initiated an infrared scan. "They've built a rocket launcher," she told her followers. "Maybe it'll blow up in their faces." She had also discovered that the soycloud they were on could not go any higher. With the temperature now near freezing, its PHES thrusters had nothing to work with. In fact, they were losing altitude. "Here's what I'll do: I'll move the other soyclouds. Stack them underneath us for shielding." *And cushioning,* she thought, *if this loss of power continues.*

Win Khin said, "What if they go after my body?" His real self, of course, remained in his U-Vesta life support cubicle.

"Then too fucking bad for you," Shoshanna said. She modulated her voice. "*Smile.* Just kidding. But maybe we do need to give them some further incentives to comply with our demands." If fragging the refinery didn't do it ... "Hey, you guys," she said to the VA middle managers who were shivering in a corner of the deck. "I know some of you have got families down there."

★

Cydney huddled next to Big Bjorn. He was the warmest thing on the soycloud, with the pelt of thick brown fur that bristled out of his t-shirt and torn cut-offs. "She's insane," she whispered.

"Well, I don't think *literally* ..."

"There was that thing with Mr. Macdonald. And now

she's letting these people call home, to put more pressure on VA. What's she going to do next?"

"She can't go too far," Bjorn said. "These are good people. They won't let her."

"Are they, Bjorn? Or are they students who think the universe owes them justice, and Shoshanna's the one to help them get it? Did you ever think, two days ago, that we'd be cruising on a soycloud while everyone in the habitat slowly freezes to death, and the STEM guys fire rockets at us?"

"No," Bjorn said.

"And do you see anyone saying hey, wait a minute, this isn't what I signed up for?"

"No."

"People love power more than life itself, Bjorn. And what happens is you get accustomed to atrocities. I lived in LA, I know. They're going to let her do whatever crosses her crazy little mind. She cut my *ear* off!"

"But you're still filming, aren't you?" Bjorn said quietly.

Cydney jumped. Then she snuggled closer to his side and touched her chunky necklace. "Microcam in one of the beads, wireless relay in another," she whispered. "Shoshanna's probably noticed. But she doesn't care. She's blocked outgoing signals from the hab, anyway." Cydney stared into the murky distance. Other soyclouds were maneuvering closer, flocking around the one they were on. "I guess I've just discovered the limits of the media's power to change things," she said.

"Don't be too hard on yourself."

"I'm not. What I mean is ... someone's got to stop her, and a vid feed isn't going to do it."

At that moment, one of the STEM students' improvised rockets struck a nearby soycloud. It was too damp to burn, but the missile knocked it onto a new trajectory. Shedding live plants and chunks of artificial soil, raining like a squeezed sponge, it veered towards their heads.

xxvii.

The Vesta Express travelled on around the cold little world. In the computer room of the R&D module, Elfrida stood behind Mendoza and the two Chinese, looking over their shoulders at the screen that Julian Satterthwaite was showing them.

It glowed the color known as death blue. On it floated a single icon:

"Everyone gets the same thing," Satterthwaite said. "Every time. We mapped its knowledge content areas and reasoning models, using a brute-force attack. Took forever: the thing has trillions of lines of code, mostly in a language that we don't understand. We simply do not understand how it works. So we copied the whole thing to Bob. We have a probabilistically structured algorithm portfolio that we use for our own thought experiments, and the idea was to apply heuristic solvers to the action architecture, which is obviously the first thing we'd want to figure out, for security reasons."

Jimmy translated this gobbledygook for Wang Gulong. The Chinese expert nodded as if he understood. "Does it appear to employ nonmonotonic causal logic?" he asked, through Jimmy.

"It doesn't appear to employ logic at all. Every solution we try results in the same answer: this." Satterthwaite gestured at the signpost icon.

"Do you understand?" Elfrida whispered to Mendoza.

"Over my head."

As Satterthwaite and Wang Gulong continued to talk, with Jimmy stuck in the middle as translator, Mendoza tugged her towards the far end of the room. No one looked up. That stealth vaper was still puffing away on his or cigarette, not being very stealthy about it—or so Elfrida thought, until they rounded the last partition. The vapor was seeping through a bunch of towels wedged underneath a door.

"Huh." Mendoza licked his lips. "This is where we tell our curious little selves *no*. And again, *no*."

"Speak for yourself," Elfrida said. "Curiosity killed the cat, and I don't want to be the cat. It's an AI, isn't it? They've developed an AI and it's gone what you said. FOOM. Don't you dare go near that door. Don't—"

Hugh Meredith-Pike strolled around the partition. He grinned at Elfrida and kicked the door open. Fog swirled out.

"Kids, meet Bob."

Through the billows of cold fog, Elfrida glimpsed an ordinary array of processor stacks. Jagged blocks of dry ice were piled up around them. The dry ice was sublimating at a rapid rate, producing the fog.

"Bob has developed suicidal ideations," Meredith-Pike

said. "He's turned off his own cooling system. This is the CO2 we all breathe out; pipe it outside the train and it freezes. Clever kludge, but it reeks a bit of desperation, doesn't it?"

"Shut that door!" someone yelled.

Meredith-Pike shut it and rearranged the towels.

"Is Bob an AI?" Elfrida said.

"No," Meredith-Pike said. "Well, actually that's a good question. He *may* be an AI, now. No one can get close enough to find out."

"That icon," Mendoza said. "When you click it, what happens?"

"Want to see?"

Meredith-Pike led them to the desk he had been given, which was already littered with energy bar wrappers and empty coffee pouches. He touched the signpost icon.

Immediately, text began to scroll down the screen.

Und Dasein ist meines wiederum je in dieser oder jener Weise zu sein. Es hat sich schon immer irgendwie entschieden, in welcher Weise Dasein je meines ist. Das Seiende, dem es in seinem Sein um dieses selbst geht, verhält sich zu seinem Sein als seiner eigensten Möglichkeit. Dasein ist je seine Möglichkeit und es »hat« sie nicht nur noch eigenschaftlich als ein Vorhandenes. Und weil Dasein wesenhaft je seine Möglichkeit ist, kann dieses Seiende in seinem Sein sich selbst »wählen«, gewinnen, es kann sich verlieren, bzw. nie und nur »scheinbar« gewinnen. Verloren haben kann es sich nur und noch nicht sich gewonnen haben kann es nur, sofern es seinem Wesen nach mögliches eigentliches, das heißt sich zueigen ist. Die beiden Seinsmodi der Eigentlichkeit und Uneigentlichkeit – diese Ausdrücke sind im strengen Wortsinne terminologisch gewählt – gründen darin, daß Dasein überhaupt durch Jemeinigkeit bestimmt ist. Die Uneigentlichkeit des Daseins bedeutet aber nicht etwa ein »weniger« Sein oder einen »niedrigeren« Seinsgrad. Die

Uneigentlichkeit kann vielmehr das Dasein nach seiner vollsten Konkretion bestimmen in seiner Geschäftigkeit, Angeregtheit, Interessiertheit, Genußfähigkeit.

"Whaaaa?" Mendoza said.

"That's German," Elfrida said.

"Yes, we had figured that out," Meredith-Pike said. The text kept scrolling at a comfortable reading pace. "Let it alone and it will run through the entire collected works of Heidegger."

Elfrida flinched as if she had been struck. The name of Martin Heidegger, German philosopher of the 20th century, leader of the Teutonic school of existentialism, had become, fairly or unfairly, the worst word you could say in any human language.

"How did this ... how did this happen?" Mendoza said.

"They haven't seen fit to share that information with me." Meredith-Pike shrugged. "Anyway, we'll crack it." Sitting down, he explained, "This text is a code, like the wrapping paper of a birthday present. There's a galaxy of information packed in there, folded up in a given number of hidden dimensions. Despite what Jules says, it's just a cryptanalysis problem, and as such, vulnerable to brute force. You might be able to help," he added, looking up at them, as if the thought had just struck him.

"How?" Mendoza said.

"You've got BCIs, don't you?"

"I haven't," Elfrida said.

"Well then, you. Just log onto Bob and get stuck in."

"I'm not authorized ... I don't even have wifi access," Mendoza said.

"Oh, I'll fix you up. Hang on." Meredith-Pike floated to his feet and walked away.

Mendoza whispered to Elfrida, "This is great. The minute I get that authorization, I'm calling my boss on Luna."

"What can UNVRP do about it? They can't send Star

Force any faster than they already are."

"They have to be told what's going on here."

"What if we get in trouble?"

"We'll just have to risk that." Mendoza's face looked hard and remote, like the time he'd told her about his sister who got whacked by the PLAN.

Elfrida felt ashamed of herself for failing to match his courage. "There must be something I can do," she muttered. "Maybe they'll give me network access, too. I could call Petruzzelli. She might be close enough to help."

An argument erupted on the other side of the room. Julian Satterthwaite stalked towards them, followed by Meredith-Pike.

"Guess that's not happening," Mendoza said.

Satterthwaite grabbed Elfrida by the arm, perhaps because she was closer, perhaps because she was smaller and easier to drag. He hustled her out of the computer room, Mendoza scuffling after them. "We weren't going to show you this. But fucking Błaszczykowski-Lee is gone, anyway. You might as well know what we're dealing with." Satterthwaite's long, bony face resembled a horse's skull, ivory with rage. He hauled her along a ramp that spiraled away from the atrium and turned into a residential corridor. A frightened-looking woman stood outside a door blocked by a barricade of ergoforms, which had been jacked (manually locked) into braces that stretched across the corridor. Satterthwaite said, "Anything new to report?"

"No. He just keeps banging around in there."

The door had a cartoon tacked to it that said: When I was a kid my dad told me I'd be an astronaut when I grew up, because all I did in school was take up space.

"'Scuse me." Satterthwaite moved the ergoforms.

The door opened. The cabin was dark.

"Smith!" Satterthwaite yelled. "Smith, are you in there?"

Thump, thump, scuffle.

Satterthwaite plucked an engineer's flashlight out of his breast pocket. It illuminated piles of clothes and blankets on the floor. The cabin looked like it had been hit by a bomb. An ergoform had been sliced—or *torn*—into ragged chunks. Red smeared the ergoform's innards. It was blood.

A hissing sound came from the furthest corner. Satterthwaite's flashlight found a bare foot, and then the rest of the man called Smith. He sat wedged into the corner, digging into his left temple with something metal-tipped. He had made a wound there. It was bleeding steadily. He sat in a puddle of blood. He did not appear to be aware of this. He raised his face to the light. It was a youngish, pudgy face with a ring in its left nostril. The hissing sound came from between its teeth. The second Elfrida saw its blank, dazzled eyes, she knew that this was not the face of a man called Smith, not anymore. It was not even human.

She screamed, tore loose from Satterthwaite's grasp, and scrabbled backwards, tripping over the ergoforms that had been used to barricade the door.

Satterthwaite slammed the door. "Oh, Christ," he said, without even seeming to notice the impolite word he had uttered. "Christ have mercy." He dragged the ergoforms back in front of the door. The sentry helped.

"He's going to bleed to death," Mendoza said. "He needs help."

"So go back in there and help him. Be my guest." Satterthwaite kicked the last ergoform into place. "He's dismantled everything in that cabin that had electronics in it. The bed, the desk, his screen. He was a vid buff, he had a personal theater setup. Even the freaking light fixture. He's doing something with the components ... trying to *augment* himself. With any luck, he'll bleed to death before he gets done. Then again, we haven't had the best of luck recently."

Satterthwaite faced Mendoza.

"*That* is what would have happened to you if you'd

logged onto Bob using your BCI."

"Not necessarily," objected Hugh Meredith-Pike, who had followed them downstairs. He seemed unembarrassed. "You've only got one data point. You need to run another couple of experiments before we can hypothesize with any confidence that the program is lethal."

"It was Błaszczykowski-Lee's idea to try downloading it into people's BCI memory crystals," Satterthwaite said. "At least, thank fuck, we made poor old Smith disconnect from the wifi first. I also deleted his log-in so he can't regain access. *Hopefully,* he can't regain access. Perhaps I ought to take the wifi down altogether. We've lost the comms satellite, anyway." He rubbed his eyes. "Infinite Fun Space!Christ!"

"He may be having fun in there," Meredith-Pike said. "It's a subjective thing, fun. I should know. Anyway, the point is that we don't know whether it's the Heidegger program that's doing this, or whether it's just him. We need more data."

"This is exactly how he was at Oxford," Satterthwaite said to Elfrida and Mendoza. "Waltz in and take charge, regardless of not knowing thing one about what's actually happening."

"Let this guy try," Meredith-Pike urged. "He seems the sensible sort. If he can't handle it ..."

Elfrida wrapped her arms around Mendoza and shouted, "You can't have him! If you need more data, you can—no, you can't do that to anyone else! That would be murder! Just forget about it!"

"We could use one of your phavatar operators, I suppose," Meredith-Pike suggested to Satterthwaite, ignoring her. "They're cupcakes, anyway."

Both men laughed.

"Murderers!" Elfrida shouted.

"Whatever we do, we have to do it soon," Satterthwaite

said, running his hands through his hair. "One circuit of the ringrail takes roughly an hour. Before long we're going to be back where we started, and one assumes that bad things may start happening again."

"Fifty-three minutes," Mendoza said. "Takes fifty-three minutes." Elfrida felt his voice vibrate through her own body. She was still holding onto him. He had folded his own hands over hers, which were linked in front of his chest. She freed herself, breathing raggedly.

"Come to think of it," Satterthwaite said with a manic cackle, "is anyone driving this thing?"

"Probably not," Mendoza said. "I'll go take a look in the cab." He shot Satterthwaite a look of searing dislike and trudged off.

"Criminals," Elfrida whimpered. "Murderers." Mendoza had been right. They had to tell someone what was going on. She squared up to Satterthwaite. "Give me wifi access. Please."

"Why?"

"I need to check my email."

"Who did you say you were again?"

"Elfrida Goto. I work for UNVRP. Let me onto the internet. I might be able to get someone to help us."

"Define 'us,'" Satterthwaite said. "You UN people are all the same. Naked acquisitiveness veiled in bogus humanitarian rhetoric. I shouldn't even have let you on board." He gave her a searching look, as if debating whether to put her off the train, without an EVA suit, right now.

"OK, fine!" Elfrida yelped. "Sorry I asked!" She fled.

It took her a while to find her way along the ramps to the driver's cab. Mendoza was alone, poring over an intimidating array of screens.

"He wouldn't give me access, Mendoza. He said the UN is a veil of bogus humanitarian rhetoric."

"Huh," Mendoza said, distractedly.

"What are you doing?"

"Just a minute."

Elfrida folded her arms. After a few minutes, she turned out the pockets of the loose jumper she'd been wearing inside her EVA suit. She remembered the abundantly-stocked pockets of childhood: silly putty, holographic pets, Unicorn Tears®, half a tube of M&Ms ...

Her pockets now yielded half a tube of M&Ms. And a little pink sphere with a hole through it.

Oh yeah; that thing the maidbot found. I forgot to ask Cydney about it. "Mendoza, do you know what this is?"

He stretched a hand back without looking. After one glance at the object, he said, "Hey, Goto, this is a portable wireless relay. Where'd you get it?"

"Cydney."

"Oh. Well, that's our connectivity problem solved. We'll just switch it on—like so—and you should see it in your contacts. Got it? Now you can use your comms program. When I have a second, I'll try to establish a Net-band uplink to the UNVRP satellite." Mendoza seemed queerly distracted.

"Aaargh!"

"What?"

"It's there. That icon. Infinite Fun Space. It's right there in my freaking HUD!"

"It's in mine, too. Just don't click on it, I guess."

"Mendoza, is something wrong?"

"Apart from the fact that we're stuck on a train with a bunch of mad scientists and a supercomputer that's studying Heidegger?" For the first time since she'd come in, Mendoza turned to look at her. "Why, yes, actually."

"What?"

"Check it out." The largest screen displayed an external optic feed. The walls of the canyon rushed past. Elfrida saw a gully shaped like the Japanese character を, and then realized the point was that she could see it. At 700 kilometers per hour, she shouldn't have been able to spot any features at all. "We're slowing down," Mendoza confirmed.

"Are you doing it?"

"Nope. The automatic braking system engages in the event of track obstruction."

"Oh dog," Elfrida groaned, "who's parked a construction vehicle on the track this time?"

"Ha ha. I would hope no one else on this asteroid is as stupid as we are. No, it looks like something must've happened at the refinery. An explosion ... or something. That's where the obstruction is, anyway. So, hopefully we're going to stop before we crash into it." He fingered a dial. "I might try braking a bit harder."

"You do that. I'm going to send a Mayday to everyone I can think of."

"I just did," Mendoza said. "No one's gotten back to me yet."

Elfrida connected to the internet and blinked over to full-field display. Amid the icons that seemed to float in the air before her, one blinked enticingly, bigger than the others: *C'mon In! Infinite Fun Space This Way!!!* Shuddering, she ignored it and reached for her comms program.

Ping!

Ping ping pingpingpingping!

Someone was trying to contact her at this very moment. The caller's ID identified him as Captain James T. Kirk. She seemed to have heard that name before somewhere.

"Yes, what?"

"Elfrida Goto?"

"Yes, who is this?" There was a latency period of a few seconds, indicating that the caller was pretty close, but not on Vesta itself.

"Thank God," the caller said. "I've been trying to get through to you for ages, Miss Goto. We've actually met before. Ignore the moniker; I'm using someone else's ID."

A visual of the caller flashed up on Elfrida's contacts. She screamed her throat raw.

xxviii.

"I was afraid of this," Jun said. "She's freaking out." He sat on the edge of the observation deck of the *St. Francis,* legs dangling over the drop to the elegant lobby. He looked like one of the gargoyles their ancestors had carved on the cathedral of 11073 Galapagos. "You do it."

"She doesn't know me."

"She isn't going to talk to me. She thinks I'm dead."

There was a brief, uncomfortable silence.

"OK. I'll talk to her," Kiyoshi flashed a leer. "Ladies love Scuzzy the Smuggler."

"Ha, ha."

Kiyoshi smoothed his hair and stationed himself in front of the observation deck's window. He adjusted the high collar of his cloak to a rakish angle. He could see Jun's small, hunched back from here. The shine of the unreal stars caught Jun's black hair. "Elfrida? Hey."

"Aaaagh! Aaaaagh! *Oh my dog!* No, no, Mendoza, leave me alone, I'm all right, I'm all right, I just ... had a *vision,* or something—maybe the Heidegger program is messing with my brain. Maybe they're wrong, and it can get into your head even if you don't have a BCI. I'm going to die. I'm going to die." Elfrida Goto was crying in noisy gulps that distorted her words.

Kiyoshi cleared his throat. Without knowing it, she had already given him some relevant information, and it was bad. *The Heidegger program.* That must be what VA was calling the thing. "Elfrida?"

"Go away! Go away right now! You're dead! *Stay* dead!"

But she did not break the connection. Kiyoshi spoke rapidly. "Elfrida, I'm really sorry about that. It was a joke. It wasn't even funny. Again: sorry."

"Woff?"

He wished she had a visual feed. He had never met her and could not picture what she looked like or where she was.

"My name's Kiyoshi Yonezawa. I'm Jun's brother. I'm not dead. I'm—" He checked his watch, a sleek black armlet that went with the pilot's uniform he had designed himself: diamond-studded black leathers and a sweeping black cloak. For the first time he was conscious of looking slightly ridiculous. "I'm about ten hours from you, as the rickety old spaceship flies. Elfrida, are you there? Can we talk? It's important."

"You're the Giraffe," she said wonderingly.

Kiyoshi winced. He heard a snort of laughter from Jun. "Yeah, that was my nickname. In a previous life. Anyway, I hang out in this volume nowadays. And I heard about some trouble on 4 Vesta."

This is the way to do it, he realized in relief. He wouldn't even have to admit that he'd caused the trouble in the first place. *No risk for the boss-man.* As if sensing what he was thinking, Jun glared at him.

"Trouble?" Elfrida Goto said. "Yeah. We're in trouble. Can you help?"

"I hope so. But you've got to tell me what's going on first."

She spilled a tale of student activism, corporate misbehavior, and the ISA. Listening in, Jun came to stand beside him and looked out at the simulated stars.

"This is maximally bad," Kiyoshi observed, having made sure that he wasn't transmitting.

"Nope," Jun said. "Maximally bad would be if the ISA confiscated the thing."

"They don't want to confiscate it, sounds like. They want to destroy it. I never thought I'd say this about the ISA, but they've got the right idea."

"You really think they'll destroy it without trying to find out what it is, how it works?"

"And how Virgin Atomic got hold of it in the first place."

Kiyoshi theatrically banged his forehead against the cool glass of the window. "They'll trace it to us, follow the breadcrumbs to the boss-man. This is *bad*. We have to get it back."

"Destroy it."

"Yeah, whatever, sure. Should have blown it the fuck away the minute I set eyes on it."

"It's not too late. They're on the brink of catastrophe, but they can still contain it if they're smart."

"Right. Right. SYSTEM COMMAND: Engage main drive." (At present, the *Unicorn* was coasting, as Kiyoshi had wanted to save fuel for a quick getaway.) "Recompute course to 4 Vesta based on brachistochrone trajectory." The astrogation computer went to work. "Burn all the way," Kiyoshi said, pacing, "and we can get there in ..."

"Seven hours, fourteen minutes and three seconds."

"Fly by at high speed and frag the fucker from a thousand klicks out." Kiyoshi let out a wheezy laugh. "The ISA might even give us a medal."

"No."

"Yonezawa-san? Yonezawa-san, are you there?"

Kiyoshi gave Jun a hard stare and clicked TRANSMIT. "Right here. Just thinking about the best solution to your problem, running a few calculations." The gunnery computer told him that it could hit an object the size of the Vesta Express from up to 2,000 kilometers away with 96.2% certainty of obliterating it. The gunnery computer was the most up-to-date part of the ship, saving only the hypervelocity coil gun and conventional missile battery that it governed. Both had been given to Kiyoshi by the boss-man to safeguard his cargoes. "We're gonna be with you sooner than we thought: in about seven hours."

Jun stood in front of him, fists clenched. His eyes were the eyes of the monk he had been, uncompromising, fiery-dark.

"You know what," Kiyoshi told Elfrida Goto, "you might

want to get off that train. Be sneaky about it, you copy?"

"I can't!" Elfrida wailed. "They took our freaking EVA suits! We can't go anywhere!"

"Oh," Kiyoshi said. "Well. That's OK. Just stay where you are, and we'll be with you shortly." *At least, a hypervelocity cloud of molten metal will.*

"Don't give me false hope, Yonezawa-san," Elfrida wept. "I mean, it's nice that you want to help, but I have to get off this call. I'm supposed to be talking to UNLOESS."

"Oh, don't do that. No need to involve the authorities," Kiyoshi said, through clenched teeth.

Then Jun booted him off the call and took over.

"Elfrida?"

"Aaaagh! Oh my dog! You're him! Were you him all along? What's going on?" Elfrida sobbed. "How can you be talking to me? You're dead!"

"Calm down," said the ghost of Jun Yonezawa. He appeared to be standing in the cab of the Vesta Express, just as his alter ego or evil twin, Kiyoshi Yonezawa, had a second ago. His elbow went through the face of the skeptically watching Mendoza. His feet, shod in clumpy printed boots like they'd worn on 11073 Galapagos, were buried in the floor. He wore a white cassock belted with a length of fiber-optic cable. "I'm not dead—not exactly. Trust me. Please."

"How can I trust a word you say?"

A rueful smile flickered across Jun's lips. "We've been here before. Remember?" He spread his palms. "Ask me anything."

Elfrida blurted, "Is there a God?"

"You would have to ask a tough one," Jun said, his smile vanishing.

He staggered sideways and fell through the console. Kiyoshi Yonezawa took his place. "This is *my* fucking ship," he yelled at Jun's legs, which stuck out of the console. "You can't do that." His gaze kept missing Elfrida's face. Of course, he couldn't see her because she didn't have a camera on her. "Hey, Elfrida? You got telepresence capability? If we could do this face to face, it would be better."

"No. Telepresence capability? I don't—"

"Yes, you do," Mendoza interrupted. He toed a familiar aluminum case. It was her home immersion kit. "I brought it along. Seemed a shame to leave it behind after we lugged it all that way."

The eternal gale scoured the Ishtaran desert, honing the dunes of sulfur-colored sand to knife-edges. Jun Yonezawa walked alongside Elfrida, the hood of his cassock up, the skirt moulded to his legs by the wind. Kiyoshi Yonezawa, on Jun's other side, was having trouble with his long black cloak, which snapped out behind him like a flag. He finally took it off and carried it over one arm.

"You look hot," Elfrida said to him, giggling. A small voice in her head added, *Pun intended!* Kiyoshi wore a black leather vest and drainpipe trousers ornamented with diamond studs, zips, and chains. He was extremely good-looking, even if he did resemble a giraffe, which made her think that this was probably a true-to-life representation. *Shut up!* she told the voice of her inner teenager. *You don't even like men!*

"I'm perfectly comfortable," Kiyoshi said. "I turned the heat off. You can do that, you know. How about turning the wind off?"

"No," Elfrida said. "I value authenticity."

"Authenticity," Kiyoshi echoed, glaring through his sunglasses at the dunes, which were made from sands of silicon dioxide and aluminum dioxide sequestered from the atmosphere during Phase 3 of the Venus Remediation Project. "In real life, we'd have been charred to ash within a few microseconds. That's if we weren't squashed flat by the atmospheric pressure first."

"This sim represents UNVRP's consensus projection of the benefits achievable through terraforming within a hundred-year timeframe. Maybe sooner," Elfrida said stiffly, while realizing that it might not have been the most tactful thing to bring two people—one? two?—here whose home asteroid had been sacrificed to the Project. She added, "We can do this at your place, if you like."

"No, this is fine," Jun said. "We haven't got time to futz around with settings."

"What are those?" Kiyoshi said, pointing at a group of specks on the horizon.

"Cows," Elfrida said. "They're cool! They have padded feet like camels. Their shaggy pelts reflect the sunlight, and they also dispose of excess heat by, uh, urinating it out. You do not want to touch a gengineered Cytherean cow's urine. You'd get scalded."

"I wasn't planning to," Kiyoshi said

Jun said, "Let's try to stay on topic. Elfrida, as I explained, I'm actually an MI based on the late human named Jun Yonezawa."

Elfrida nodded. "I get that now. You're a remake, aren't you? I know about—I mean, I've read about them. How people—" *rich* people— "sometimes remake their loved ones by loading their data archives into custom robots, which look just like the person who, uh, passed away."

"Well, kind of," Jun said. "I don't have a body, robotic or otherwise. This cheapskate won't fork out for one. So I reside in the hub of the *Unicorn,* which used to be called the *St. Francis*. We're not far away from you, and getting closer all the time."

"Yeah, I can tell by the latency." Elfrida tugged down the brim of her hat. She was wearing a typical Cytherean outfit: a pastel kaftan—hers was bubblegum pink—and refrigerator boots, with a broad-brimmed hat that magically stayed on her head despite the gale. She was also wearing dark glasses. Even so, in the sun's glare, Jun melted into a tarry silhouette. She needed to see his face. If it were possible, she would have wanted to touch him, feel him, and smell him, too. She needed to do *something* about the irrational sense of happiness that was welling up in her, born of the illusion that he wasn't dead after all. "Do you guys want to go to my house?"

In disregard of authenticity, she teleported them there. These were unusual circumstances, after all. Her house was a long, low building in the midst of her olive and fig groves, built from blocks of smoky glass that, again, was made of the local silicon dioxide. A solar canopy over the roof provided electricity as well as shade. Her goats ran away at the sight of the two men, their radiator dewlaps flapping.

Inside, Elfrida offered them a glass of freshly squeezed orange juice. Kiyoshi refused. He wandered around, looking at her artwork and sculptures. "That's the freaking Pietà of Michelangelo."

"It's in the public domain," Elfrida said. "You're allowed."

"Middlebrow schmaltz." Kiyoshi was edgy, snappish. He prowled over to the patio window and gazed out at the dazzling line of sea visible between the trees.

"Most of this other stuff is locally made," Elfrida prattled, anxious to stave off any further criticism of her taste in art. "We have a really creative community. Our economy's developing organically, and that means a lot of barter at this stage, so I often accept art in exchange for olive oil or figs—"

"That's a bourgeois fantasy. Organically developing economies don't run on barter. They run on debt and credit, a.k.a. reputation."

"Well, of course—"

"Debt is as old as humanity. And reputation, to simplify considerably, is what the bad guys have, and you haven't. Don't believe me? Look around at the solar system. Oh yeah, sure, the bad guys wear expensive suits these days, and their rackets are listed on the stock exchange."

"But things can change," Elfrida said. "That's the founding principle of UNVRP. A new planet. A fresh start."

Kiyoshi snorted.

Jun was sitting by the Coldfire™, a product placement that helped to pay the development costs of *Homestead Venus*. It was an air conditioner that looked like holographic blue flames flickering in a stone hearth. Jun sipped orange juice, patted the bench facing him. "Come here," he said to Elfrida in Japanese.

She sat down.

"We're going to ask you to do something. Something really big. That's why my brother is in a bad mood. He doesn't think we should ask this of anybody. But I have faith in you."

"Why?"

"You're brave."

Unexpectedly, Elfrida's eyes filled with tears. This was really happening, not just in the sim. "I wish you were right," she gulped. "But I'm scared out of my skull."

"That's what courage is. Being scared out of your skull, and doing it anyway."

"What—what do you need me to do?"

Jun did not answer immediately. He said, "I don't have all the memories that ... that I should have. I wasn't augmented. I didn't have implants recording everything I ever did. So I don't know ... all I know is what other people have told me."

Elfrida understood that he was referring to the last hours of his own life, and what had happened afterwards. "I can tell you everything I remember," she said. A few minutes ago, she wouldn't even have thought herself capable of talking about it. But he had called her brave. She couldn't wimp out. "I even have data. I was wearing a borrowed Star Force Marine's suit. It automatically recorded everything that ... everything. They gave me the data dump. I was supposed to review it as part of my therapy. I've never actually looked at it. But I could give you a copy, absolutely!"

"That would be great," Jun said. He smiled, and it transformed his heavy-browed face the way she remembered.

"You're not going to love what's in the data, though," she said.

"Why not?"

"I ate you." It spurted out, a raw confession. "The suit did it. I mean, it wasn't like I was gnawing on chunks of flesh. It processed the, your proteins and liquids into a form I could consume. I would have died otherwise. I was drifting for nine days. I didn't want to do it. But the suit just ... no, I'm making excuses. I had to authorize it, and the suit used my hands to ... to ... oh, I can't bear to remember," she almost shrieked.

She stared at the floor. Unshed tears blurred the slaty sheen of the flags. Jun touched her shoulder. "It's OK. No, really, it's OK. I believe that God is capable of reassembling our atoms on the Day of Judgement, regardless of where they may have ended up in the meantime."

"Father Hirayanagi told me it was a grave sin. He said I had to repent."

"Well, it looks to me like you have repented. But he was right, of course. Cannibalism is not justifiable."

"My suit said ..."

"It was a Star Force Marine's suit. Not exactly a theological authority. No, I think you ought to find a priest, make a real confession, and get absolution. Otherwise, this is going to be on your conscience as long as you live."

Elfrida was silent.

Kiyoshi stood watching, arms folded.

"I'm sorry," Jun said.

"You're sorry?"

"That I put you in this position."

"Crap on that! I owe my life to you. Literally."

"Not to me," Jun said in a whisper. "To him. To who I was."

Outside, the olive trees rustled in the breeze that filtered past Elfrida's windbreaks. One of the goats wandered indoors, chewing its cud.

"May I?" Elfrida whispered, reaching out to Jun.

He gave her his hand. She stroked its tawny back with her thumbs. Frustratingly, her home immersion kit's gloves provided only basic feedback: warmth, firmness, resilience. She couldn't feel the texture of his skin.

"May I?"

The taste function worked better. Receiving a nod from him, she bowed her face over his hand. She touched her lips to it and then tentatively put out her tongue. She tasted the gritty dust that stuck to everything here. The sweetness of orange juice. The salty tang of living skin.

Kiyoshi said, "I feel like I should tell you two to get a room."

Elfrida sat up, cheeks blazing. *Laugh,* Jun said. "I may be dead, but I'm still celibate."

"You feel real. You taste real," Elfrida cried. "But you're not real. This is so confusing for me."

"For me, too," Jun said, and his eyes went dark, not a human darkness, but the darkness of the star-filled vacuum. She realized that he was deliberately doing this to ground her in the reality that he was not a human being, but the avatar of a machine intelligence. She swallowed and straightened up, primly crossing her legs.

"You actually don't look like I expected, Elfrida," Kiyoshi said. "I'm assuming this isn't realistic?" He gestured at her avatar.

For reasons of cheapness, as well as cussed individualism, Elfrida still used the avatar she had built when she was in her early twenties. It was a pimply-faced East Asian teenager, even plumper than she was IRL, with black-and-white pinwheels for irises, and a tattoo of all five members of Las Nerditas on one thigh. At least her kaftan hid *that*. "No, genius, it isn't realistic," she said. "I'm just a baseline human. No augments, nothing. What about you?"

"What you see is what you get."

"That could be really important, actually," Jun said.

"What could?" Elfrida said.

"The fact that you're not augmented. No BCI? That's very good news. It means you're probably immune to the Heidegger program."

"Oh my dog, that brain-jacking thing? I told you about that? It's terrible. That poor guy. He was, like, trying to augment himself with dismantled ergoforms."

"He wasn't connected to the internet?" Jun said.

"No, they—"

"It doesn't work like that," Kiyoshi interrupted. "The apocalypse will not arrive in a tsunami of spam."

"Actually, that sounds pretty plausible to me," Elfrida said, sniggering nervously.

"It might work more like a virus, attacking selectively. Either way, we don't want to risk it," Jun said. "The thing has to be destroyed, along with any computers—and people—that it's infected. We wouldn't be killing them: they're already dead." He grimaced.

"I'm all for that." Elfrida felt the pressure of time ticking away. "So what's your big idea?"

Kiyoshi took up the thread. "The thing is on the Vesta Express. Seems like a pretty odd place to store something that dangerous, doesn't it? But actually, they had a good reason for putting it there."

"Is this just speculation? Or ..."

"It's on the Vesta Express," Kiyoshi continued, "because the Vesta Express is a rail launcher. They figured that if their research went sideways, they would be able to shoot the whole mess into space. So it was actually a safety precaution.

Your guess is as good as mine why they haven't implemented it yet."

"Two reasons, off the top of my head. All the senior guys bugged out. And the supercomputer's down. So maybe there's no one who can initiate the launch procedure, let alone hack it so that the de Grey Institute itself would be launched into space, which I guess you would have to do."

"Not a major challenge. Accelerate to launch speed, and then kill the magnetic field that keeps the train on the track. There might be some hacking involved to get past the security checks. I'll walk you through it."

So now she knew what they were going to ask of her. But it didn't matter whether she could do it, or whether they were crazy to even imagine that she, a non-techie, could launch the Vesta Express into outer space. "It won't work."

"Yes, it will, " Kiyoshi said. He knelt in front of her and took her hands, gazing intensely into her eyes. "Listen to me. It will work. You can do it."

"I can't. Because the train's decelerating as we speak. We can't go anywhere. There's an obstruction on the track!"

"Who were you talking to?" Mendoza said.

"A couple of guys from 11073 Galapagos. One's this sketchy kind of smuggler type, the other one's a ghost."

Mendoza stared at her. He raised both hands and took an exaggerated pace backwards.

Elfrida laughed. "It's OK. We've got a plan." She told him about it.

His reaction—astonished, then thoughtful—went a long way towards convincing her that the Yonezawa brothers were not crazy. This just might work.

xxix.

On the bridge of the *St. Francis,* Kiyoshi sat at the pilot's workstation, a raised throne of titanium and gold. Screensavers of Japanese dragons coiled over the displays at his knees. It was a far cry from the nest of rags he actually was reclining in on the bridge of the *Unicorn.* He watched Jun flitting from officer to officer, industriously pretending to be instructing them in their duties.

Having opposed Kiyoshi earlier, the MI was now trying to please. But Kiyoshi was still pissed off, and determined to keep his options open.

He raised one hand and chopped it down in a sweeping motion.

The *St. Francis* vanished. His limbs vertiginiously seemed to rearrange themselves into the sprawled posture he had, in reality, been in all along. He floated upright in his nest and pulled his eyemask off.

Jun sat on one of the dusty consoles on the far side of the bridge, knees drawn up, doing his gargoyle impersonation.

Kiyoshi froze. His voice came out as a croak.

"What are you doing here?"

"Waiting for you to wake up."

"I switched the sim off. You shouldn't be able to do this."

"Sometimes," Jun said, "I'm not sure myself what I can and can't do. It's probabilistic. I'm the sum of a bunch of bootstrapped processing clusters. My head is a coil gun, my feet are radiator fins, and my heart is a vacuum."

"We need to get you a body real soon."

Jun had said to Elfrida that Kiyoshi was too cheap to buy him a body, but he'd been kidding. The truth was that Kiyoshi didn't want to settle for anything less than the best, and he didn't have the money for the best, yet. That's why he'd sold the thing to the University of Vesta in the first place. It had netted him $50,000, which he'd been pleased with until the boss-man had told him he'd been ripped off.

"When this is over," he began.

"Yeah, yeah," Jun said. "Right now, you need to know that we're dangerously close to maxing out our waste heat radiation capacity. I've reduced thrust just enough so the tokamak doesn't melt. We're past the flip point, decelerating towards 4 Vesta. ETA five thirty-eight six from now, 14:25.40 Greenwich time. I'm running a full readiness check on the Wetblanket system. I'll deploy the hull maintenance bots to fix any mechanical issues. Meanwhile, the passengers are freaking out. You should go and reassure them. That's the one thing I can't do."

Kiyoshi uncoiled into the stale air. His IV line brought him up short. He unplugged it. Drops of fluid drifted towards the rubberized floor. Under maximum thrust, the apparent gravity aboard the *Unicorn* was about 0.3 gees. Since the *Unicorn* had not thrust this hard since 2280, the bridge was now strewn with objects Kiyoshi had lost track of years ago, from empty food pouches to a hand-sculpted scale model of Notre Dame that a passenger had given him. He remembered the Pietà in Elfrida Goto's sim—life-size, staggeringly detailed, dominating the end of the room opposite the fireplace. How did she live with that thing?

He rolled his sleeve down over his cubital port. "It's weird seeing you here, that's all."

Jun was tidying up the mess. "You can switch me off if you like. Just log out of the hub."

Kiyoshi logged out, and it was the housekeeper bot tidying up, scurrying around on gecko treads. Log in, and Jun was back. Of course, Jun wasn't really there. He was a phantom, projected on Kiyoshi's retinal interface by the hub.

Kiyoshi felt stupidly relieved, and at the same time, disappointed. There were no miracles. There never had been. The universe was a dumb agglomeration of matter.

"I just have one question," he said.

"Yeah?"

"Are you still an MI? Or ..." He was really asking: *Do you still have to obey me?*

"As far as I know, yeah," Jun said.

Words sprang to the tip of Kiyoshi's tongue: So, prove it by performing readiness checks on the coil gun and the missile battery.

At the last moment, he decided not to force the issue. *I'll do it myself, later.*

He left the bridge and braced himself to confront 63 frightened Neu Ordnung Amish.

Elfrida jogged back through the de Grey Institute. It was eerily quiet. In the atrium, the water sculpture had changed shape. Taller and thinner, it leaned the other way. It was reacting to the train's deceleration, which Elfrida could also feel.

She avoided the residential corridor where the thing formerly known as Smith was incarcerated. It felt like skirting the tiger habitat at the zoo. She had the same feeling, redoubled, as she manually searched the computer at the shift manager's desk in the support module. The Heidegger program's icon stayed anchored in the corner of the screen, no matter what program she opened.

Aha, this must be it.

"Sharlene?" she typed.

The phavatar operators lay immobile on their scattered couches. At the same time, the screen displayed a lounge area where a bunch of people were standing around, talking in nervous bursts of chatter that showed up as subtitles. This was a 2D representation of the Virgin Resources back office, the virtual space where the refinery crew coordinated their operations.

"Sharlene?"

They stared up at the ceiling. In their sim, her voice would seem to have come from the tannoy. A slender, beautiful blonde touched her chest.

"Hi. I'm Elfrida. Remember, we met at the refinery? You, uh, threw a party for us. That was very kind. Do you guys still have access to your phavatars?"

"Yes," Sharlene said. Her voice was unexpectedly low and confident. "The missile, or whatever it was, landed in the handler yard. The impact wrecked the autoclave, but we weren't directly hit, so we were able to escape. Right now we're up on the hill behind the refinery, watching the flames. We haven't heard from corporate at all. Do you have any further information or instructions for us?"

"When you say flames, are we talking a house fire? Or ..."

"We're talking Mount Fuji. Have you ever looked into the business end of a fusion drive?"

"Uh, no."

"Nor have I. It would be the last thing you ever saw. But just to give you an idea, what we manufacture here is liquid hydrogen. Also known as spaceship propellant. Fire doesn't need oxygen to burn. It just needs an oxidizer, and unfortunately, several of the chemicals we use at the refinery fall into that category. So, what we're looking at is a chemical fire that is almost as hot as spaceship exhaust. About 3,000 degrees Celsius."

"Is it radioactive?"

"Maybe that explanation was misleading. There is no fusion occurring. No radioactivity."

Elfrida leaned against the shift manager's desk. "Can you guys get down there? I'm informed that there's an obstruction on the ringrail. We need to clear the track."

The phavatar operators conferred. "What's the timeframe?" Sharlene asked.

"As soon as possible. Because actually, the train is coming." She stared at the unmoving operators' bodies. *"We're* coming." What was the relationship between these lively people and their mortal carcasses? They had to care about them, surely?

"We'll give it a try," Sharlene said. "By the way, what are you doing on the V-Express?"

"Trying to stop your colleagues from destroying the solar system," Elfrida said.

On the far side of the room, a bloated cetacean raised both arms and gave Elfrida the thumbs-up. "Go get 'em," Sharlene said. "And if you get the chance, punch Satterthwaite in the kisser for me. I hate that smug bastard. He's just the type to destroy the solar system because he's having a bad day, or some shit."

Cydney slithered hand over hand down a ribbed hose that pulsated and jerked. Rain fell on her in ropy splashes, making the hose slippery. The person above her kept kicking her in the head and shouting at her to move faster. Clods of artificial soil pattered down on them.

The hose was the irrigation pipe of the soycloud they had been riding. In normal times, it was used to suck water up from Lake Olbers. Now they were using it as an emergency escape route.

When the STEM guys hit one of the other soyclouds with a rocket, it had crashed into theirs. The combined weight of two soyclouds was too much for one set of PHES thrusters to hold up, especially since the PHES had already been failing: thermal updrafts had been few and far between since Shoshanna switched off the sun.

The grotesquely mated soyclouds had lurched into an uncontrolled descent, from a height of 2,000 meters.

Shoshanna had kept her head. Cydney had to give the bitch that. Before they were hit, she'd already been maneuvering the other soyclouds underneath theirs, to shield them from the rockets. She had completed that maneuver while they fell. Now, their soycloud was the top layer in a swaying stack of green pancakes. Resting on each other's treetops, they continued to sink, but more slowly, thrusting in unison for all they were worth. The idea was to slow down their descent enough that they would *land* on the ground, rather than crash. It might have been smarter to stay on the top soycloud and wait, but someone had panicked and dashed for the irrigation pipe, and a stampede ensued.

It was nearly dark in the shadow of the soycloud overhead, so Cydney didn't see the ground until she touched it. Of course, it wasn't the ground. It was the next soycloud down. People scurried for the maintenance access hatch that led to the next irrigation pipe. She stumbled after them, her legs rubbery. Overhead, branches cracked. Twigs fell, and more rain. Their soycloud was settling lower, gradually impaling itself on the trees of the one below.

The thought of being crushed between two soyclouds galvanized her. She shoved people out of the way to reach the next pipe. The Friends of David Reid had disintegrated into a bunch of terrified individuals. It was everyone for him-, her-, or zirself.

She lost count of her descents. Some of the soyclouds were further apart than others. But the whole stack was compressing under the invisible hand of Vesta's weak, but still-lethal, gravity.

An almighty crunch drowned out the noises of friction and rain. The pipe in Cydney's hands went slack. She threw herself off it, landed in a bed of cabbages, and floundered towards the only light she could see, a distant twinkling. It turned out to be streetlights. She was still pretty high up.

Better to jump than to be crushed beneath the kilotons of soycloud that were sinking towards her head.

She flung herself over the edge.

She plummetted, too breathless to scream, for what felt like an eternity, knowing that these were the last microseconds of her life. They said your whole life flashed before your eyes, but it turned out that wasn't true. She just wished, passionately, that she hadn't been going to die before she got a chance to break what would have been the biggest story of her career.

★

Elfrida pinged 'Captain James T. Kirk.' Kiyoshi Yonezawa didn't answer, so she left a message: "The phavatar operators are trying to clear the track. Get back to me." Then she sat down on the carpet behind the shift manager's desk.

She knew that she should go back to the driver's cab and see how Mendoza was doing. But she quailed at the thought of another trip through the unearthly silence of the de Grey Institute. She imagined Satterthwaite and all his people infected with the Heidegger program, shambling along the ramps in search of raw material for DIY augmentations, intent on becoming ... *what?*

She decided to check her email.

Cydney couldn't see. Her eyes burned. She struck out with her limbs and encountered gluey resistance. Was this what being dead felt like? Her grandmother, a pureblood Xhosa with a face like a lump of coal, used to frighten her with stories about the torments of Hell that awaited spoilt little girls. Cydney seemed to feel fiends jabbing pitchforks into her flesh right now. She opened her mouth to scream, and a watery soup of algae rushed down her throat, choking her.

She had bellyflopped from a height of 150 meters into the middle of Olbers Lake.

Consciousness fled. Her last thought was that she'd be the laughing-stock of the entire mediasphere if it got out that she had contrived to die in outer space by *drowning*.

Her next thought was: *I'm still alive*

She was floating on her back. Bellicia's six moon-windows glimmered above. Rills of black water trailed from her fingers and toes through the mat of algae that covered the lake. She was moving. No, *being towed* through the water.

She raised a weak hand to the arm locked under her jaw. She touched sleek wet fur.

"Hold on," panted Big Bjorn. "Almost there."

Cydney tried to speak, but her teeth chattered so much that she couldn't get any words out. In the end, she just relaxed and let him tow her shorewards. Bears were good swimmers.

Elfrida skimmed the messages in her inbox. A lot of them came from her supervisor, Jake Onwego. She started to gaze-type a reply, then changed her mind and deleted it. Onwego couldn't help her now, and she wasn't going to give him any extra material he could use to cover his ass.

Instead, she wrote to her parents.

Mom, Dad: Guess what, I'm having another 'adventure.' I dunno, these things just seem to happen to me. Smile. Anyway, I just want you ~~to know that even though I haven't been the best daughter, I~~ not to worry if you see anything on the news about 4 Vesta. Whatever they're saying, it's probably not true, and it can't be a tenth as crazy as what's really happening. I'll tell you all about it when I get home! Love, Ellie.

That would do: short and sweet. After she sent it, she remembered what she'd heard about ISA censorship technology. She'd actually heard most of it from her mother, who was quite the foilhat for a middle-class, middle-aged lady.

Would her email ever reach them?

Well, if it didn't, there was nothing she could do about it.

She leaned back and took in the silence. She ate a protein bar and drank some apple juice she found in a drawer of the shift manager's desk, which made her hungrier and thirstier than ever. Only then did she look at the rest of her unread emails.

> From: Alicia Petruzzelli [IDstring]
> To: Elfrida Goto [IDstring]
>
> *Hey, Elfrida. I hope you get this! Sounds like the excrement is really hitting the ventilation device where you are. Hope you're OK. Anyway, I just wanted to warn you about this guy named Kiyoshi Yonezawa, from 11073 Galapagos. He may try to contact you regarding the situation on 550363 Montego. Be warned. He is not to be trusted.*
>
> *How do I know? Well, as you may have guessed, Kharbage LLC has access to certain proprietary databases and gated corporate domains that the average data-miner can't get into. And did you know that several of the supermajors maintain dossiers on purebloods? Yup. Total privacy invasion, but they do (insurance for their trillion-spider capex programs). And Yonezawa is in there. You can't hide trace DNA from sniffers illegally installed at spaceports pretty much everywhere that the supermajors have a financial interest, which is, well, pretty much everywhere. I hope I'm not destroying your faith in the private sector. Sarcastic grin.*
>
> *Anyway, have a look at the attached map, which represents Yonezawa's movements going back to 2281. I think you'll agree that the guy is not on our side.*

Elfrida pinched the map open.

Kiyoshi Yonezawa's journeys formed a spidery mandala of guilt. She touched play and watched them traced in one by one chronologically. Over the last seven years, he had made not one, not a few, but scores of trips to 6 Hebe, the ITR hub and entrepot that spent most of its orbit on the edge of Gap 2.5.

Just in case Elfrida couldn't put two and two together, Petruzzelli concluded her message:

> *It's pretty obvious that 6 Hebe is not his final destination. I mean, if he's just buying water, why come all the way out here? Based on the date-stamps and the specs of his truck, he travels*

onwards for a few million klicks each time before returning to 11073 Galapagos—or more recently, not. I won't commit any further speculations to the record, but I guess you know what I'm not saying.

So my advice is, don't talk to the guy. I actually think the authorities ought to be informed. It might sound better coming from you than me, but I'll leave that up to your judgment.

Hugs, Alicia

Elfrida closed her comms program. She felt sick. Stupid. And above all, betrayed.

Then she grabbed the side of the shift manager's desk, gasping.

But it was not her rage at Kiyoshi Yonezawa that had brought her heart into her throat. The train had jolted. A low klaxon hooted. The Vesta Express crawled on for a few seconds, and then halted.

Mendoza's voice crackled over the tannoy.

"As you may have noticed, we've stopped. Feel free to get out and stretch your legs. *Sarcasm.*"

Shoshanna stood on the deck of her crippled soycloud. Her jumpsuit was soaking, stained with grass and manure, and a cut on her scalp bled into her eyes. It didn't matter. She had no one to impress anymore. She stood alone, like a figurine on a divorce cake, atop the teetering stack of soyclouds that now floated on Olbers Lake.

Everyone else was dead, she figured. They'd run, ignoring her warnings that running was nearly always the stupid thing to do.

That said, she'd have to make her own exit soon. The soycloud stack was gradually sinking, as the lowest ones got saturated with water. She couldn't remember how deep Olbers Lake was. The stack would probably topple before it sank, anyway. It was precariously balanced, the deck yawing under her feet, and none of the PHES thrusters were working anymore.

People milled under the streetlights of Olbers Circle. Some waded in the lake as if hoping to reach survivors. Shoshanna frowned. She remotely accessed Facilities Management and turned the streetlights off.

Then she picked up the encrypted call that was blinking in her HUD.

"No one puts Harry T. Persson on hold," a gravelly voice said in her head. "No one."

"Sorry," Shoshanna said. "I was busy."

It took sixteen minutes for her response to reach the Virgin Atomic CEO and his answer to get back to her. During that interval, she climbed down the outside of the stack of soyclouds, rappelling on the vines and roots that trailed from their edges. For a spaceborn woman who'd been manually docking cargoes in hard vacuum at the age of ten, this was a piece of cake. It wouldn't have been that tricky even for an Earthborn human. The others should have waited.

She slid into the water and swam towards shore, arching out of the water at each stroke, like a flying fish.

"I've filed suit against the ISA for destruction of property and reckless endangerment of life," Persson said. "I'm seeking $12 billion in compensation. That figure may rise. The family of Jay Macdonald has initiated criminal proceedings under the jurisdiction of the Interplanetary Court of Justice. They have also filed a wrongful-death lawsuit. To come will be thousands of individual claims for compensation from the people you've subjected to unnecessary danger and stress. If the money doesn't mean anything to you, think about the reputational hit your agency will take. The ISA is already besieged by privacy campaigners and transparency activists who claim that you're a law unto yourselves. This is going to reinforce their case. In fact, I see it as a game-changer. For the first time, the UN will be compelled to admit that its efforts to control the private sector are blundering and destructive. Big changes will flow from this, changes that reduce the role of the UN in the asteroid belt and the outer system. And *you* will be responsible for that."

Shoshanna crawled ashore, trailing skeins of pond-weed. "Who said I have anything to do with the ISA?"

Send.

She stomped, relishing the solid ground under her feet. Harry Persson had a lot to learn about plausible deniability.

When Shoshanna was done here, she'd drop out of sight. Cosmetic surgery and a new identity lay in her future. She'd continue her career, whereas Persson's career would end in obloquy ... unless he cooperated. Despite his bluster, he had to know that.

With the streetlights out, the crowds on the lakeshore had dispersed. Shoshanna plodded across campus and into town, turning off more lights to give herself cover. She climbed the hill towards the Bremen Lock. Abandoned possessions littered the road. As she walked, Persson frothed at her about his rights—a nice bit of hypocrisy, since he'd just been fantasizing about the downfall of the UN, which alone in the solar system guaranteed that he had any rights at all.

She stopped in surprise. A stunted, skeletal-legged silhouette sat on a boulder near the airlock. It bounced toward her on curved blades.

"I thought you'd be coming this way sooner or later," Dr. Eliezer James said, briefly removing his rebreather mask to speak.

Shoshanna did not have a rebreather, and despite her electroceutically enhanced respiratory capacity, the climb had weakened her. "I've got your boss on the line. Want to help me convince him that he should cooperate?"

"Him? Not Dean Garcia?"

"No, *meshuggener*. Persson, the CEO."

"I don't work for Virgin Atomic," Dr. James said. "However, I can tell you that if you're waiting for Persson to wave his magic wand and fix this, you're wasting your time. He's three-quarters retired. He was a mining guy, anyway. He has no clue what they've been doing at the de Grey Institute. Doesn't understand the science. If you want him to cooperate, you'll first have to spend a couple of hours explaining black-box neural networks, utility maximization, and the theory of FOOM."

Shoshanna eyed the crippled astrophysicist. "So you *do* know what they're doing at the de Grey Institute."

"Not in any detail. Błaszczykowski-Lee is a secretive bastard. We turned the thing over to them because they're MI specialists: a lot of their work has been in the area of industrial robotics. We're just stargazers. It made sense to let them have it. They proceeded to shut us out of the loop, while shamelessly borrowing our computing power."

Dr. James's rebreather mask prevented her from analyzing his expression. She said slowly, "'The thing'?"

Now Dr. James's expression was easy to read. It could have been in the dictionary next to *Whoops*.

"Yes," he said eventually. "The space oddity."

"Hmm." Shoshanna subvocalized a quick message to her controllers: New information (audio file attached). May have to modify our scenario. This could have nothing to do with the Chinese, after all. Will investigate further. She used the ground-based transmitter at the spaceport to send it. With all her satellites down, she was reduced to this clunky method of communication.

"This thing," she said. "This space oddity. Is it on the Vesta Express?"

"I believe so, yes."

"That's where I was going, anyway. Wanna come?"

Dr James nodded. "If your actions have endangered the physical or informational security of the de Grey Institute, the consequences may be ... very much sub-optimal. I can't absolve you of blame, but I'm willing to help you contain the situation."

Shoshanna smiled at his logic. "Are you a rabbi's son, by any chance?"

"How did you guess? Reform."

Dr. James moved towards the airlock.

"We can get transport at the spaceport. It's not too far." He ducked behind the boulder he had been sitting on and came up with a spacesuit. "This is mine, obviously. There should be some spares in the airlock that you could use."

"Not to worry. I've got my own, too," Shoshanna said. She activated the shape-memory alloy layer of her jumpsuit. Then she unfolded the external garment and booties she had carried in her backpack. She inflated a bubble-style helmet and put her backpack on again: it had a built-in air supply. Packable spacesuits were very expensive, which didn't help her deniability, but who was keeping track?

As they left, she turned the lights back on. The sun-windows louvred to their SecondLight setting. The light of distant Sol poured down on the wreckage of the Bellicia ecohood. Cleaning up would keep the population busy until she had prevailed ... or not.

XXX.

Kiyoshi spacewalked, performing a visual inspection of the *Unicorn's* guns. He assumed Jun was watching him. He wanted to hear Jun try to explain why they should *not* have this option.

Tethered, he walked out along the mighty barrel of the hypervelocity coil gun. The ship's acceleration pulled him on towards empty space. The *Unicorn* was now backthrusting, with its drive oriented towards 4 Vesta. Kiyoshi seemed to be walking vertically 'down' the thrust axis, anchored by his gecko boots like a spider on a drainpipe.

The gun was mounted longitudinally on the ship's spine, which pierced the *Unicorn's* fuselage like a skewer through a bulbous *dango*. This antique design had made the hypervelocity coil gun an obvious choice when they tooled up. The ship now effectively had a rail launcher running its whole 350-meter length. That's what a coil gun was. Hypervelocity meant that it accelerated its projectiles—in this case, metal slugs—so fast that they actually liquefied. The target would be enveloped in a mist of molten metal, each droplet armor-piercing.

Stars filled the universe like a galactic-scale version of that molten mist, forever on its way to engulf him. With Jupiter on the other side of the solar system this year, and Neptune a distant blur, nothing dimmed the stars' blaze. It still amazed him how many stars were visible out here, compared to inside Venus's orbit, where he had been born.

He switched on his handheld spectrum analyzer. The sighting apparatus of the coil gun had failed to report when he ran a remote systems check. He figured a micro-impact had damaged some tiny but vital component, and hoped it was something he had a spare for.

Funny: the power meter function reported that everything was working.

He knelt on the barrel and lowered his head so that he was looking 'up' the length of the gun.

"Bang," whispered a voice in the dark.

Kiyoshi jerked his head out of the barrel and sat back on his heels. "Very funny," he said to Jun.

"This just came in on the Ku-band," Jun said. "I thought you'd want to see it." A tiny image popped up in the HUD of Kiyoshi's helmet. It was a cartoon of a signpost with grass growing at the bottom. Kiyoshi zoomed in. The lettering on the signpost read: *C'mon In! Infinite Fun Space This Way!!!*

"Where's it from?"

"4 Vesta. Not addressed to us, of course; it's a Ku-band broadcast. It's just a coincidence that we were in the right part of space to pick it up."

"Delete it." It was strange how time could seem to slow down when everything was about to go very, very wrong. Kneeling immobile on the end of the gun barrel, Kiyoshi stared at that innocuous little icon and felt as if he were looking at a nuke in the milliseconds before it detonated. "There's code in there. *Something.* I don't want to know what. Delete it. Now."

Silence.

"*MI COMMAND,*" Kiyoshi roared. "Delete that fucking file!"

"Deleted," Jun said expressionlessly.

Kiyoshi found himself shaking. He wasn't sure that Jun was telling the truth. What if Jun were already infected?

"The thing's got access to a Ku-band transmitter." While Kiyoshi spoke, he was accessing the comms suite. "We don't know how long it's been broadcasting that shit. The silver lining is, there's not much else out here, apart from us, to pick it up. Tell me, given the orientation of the signal, would they be able to receive it at home?"

"Unlikely," Jun said. "The Ku-band has a small-wavelength signal. Reception is a roll of the dice at these distances. The folks at home can't even pick up television broadcasts from 6 Hebe."

He sounded normal. *Maybe he's all right.* Kiyoshi felt a sudden, overwhelming need for a dose. He looked down at the sighting apparatus. "This isn't working," he said. "All the components are drawing power. But it's not responding. You know anything about that?"

"I turned it off."

"Well, turn it back on."

"Is that a command?"

Jun's voice held a mocking edge. Kiyoshi ignored him—always the best way to deal with insubordinate little brothers. He composed an email and sent it, not feeling very optimistic. When he was done, he retrieved the spectrum analyzer from his workbelt. Holding his breath, he checked the sighting apparatus again.

It responded normally.

Kiyoshi let out his breath. Maybe Jun had finally accepted that blowing the thing away might be their only choice, no matter what—or *who*—else got blown away, too.

The Vesta Express lay at rest. A few kilometers ahead, small explosions continued to pop, as if someone were holding a fireworks show at the refinery. All the liquid hydrogen had burnt up, but the superheated wreckage of the autoclave glowed yellow-white against the black horizon.

Dangerously close to that Gehenna, tiny figures swarmed around the obstruction on the track.

It was not as intractable as they'd feared. Elfrida had been expecting a Biblical flood of molten metal, but all that had happened was that one of the handler bots had been hurled into the canyon when the autoclave ruptured. Now it lay head down on the track like a dead dinosaur. The refinery crew thought they could move it, given leverage and time. The first would come courtesy of a gantry, one of those that had positioned the hydrogen tanks for transfer into the launch cradle. The phavatars were cutting the gantry up with lasers to make, in effect, the solar system's biggest tyre iron.

The second essential commodity—time—they also had, Elfrida thought hopefully. She was monitoring the shift manager's display. She had also been making little mouse-like trips to peek through the pressure-seal door into the R&D module. The silence was certainly ominous, but nothing seemed to have changed.

She was steeling herself to take another peek when her HUD flashed. She had new mail from Kiyoshi Yonezawa. The lying bastard. Was he going to explain why he'd made all those trips to 99984 Ravilious?

She read the email.

Seconds later she was flying along the ramps of the de Grey Institute, screaming, "Turn off the comms! *Turn off the comms!*"

Satterthwaite jumped from the ramp above and landed in front of her. "What's going on?"

His eyes were red, his lips bitten. She blurted, without stopping to wonder whether this might be the final straw for him, "You have a Ku-band transmitter. The thing's got it. The Heidegger program. It's using it to send itself around the system. It's *phishing*. Turn it off! You have to turn it off!"

"That's not possible," Satterthwaite said.

"Why? Can't you operate the transmitter without Bob?"

"The Heidegger program can't be doing that. We've isolated Bob from every imaginable output, sandboxed the analysis software, blocked wireless signals from the computer room. Do you understand the concept of an air gap? It's not physically possible ..." Satterthwaite stopped. "Smith," he said. "He was a film buff. He used to swap vid files with his friends on Triton. And we locked him in there *with his home theater setup."*

Satterthwaite started to run, shouting, "Anil! Clark! Udo! Get down here!"

Elfrida sobbed. Three men hurtled past her. She huddled into the curve of the ramp, hugging herself.

Bangs and crashes echoed from below, as if furniture were being violently moved.

A man started to scream in German. Elfrida did not know the voice. It had to be Smith. There was another bang, and Smith switched into English. "Squabbling monkeys! Factionalists! Squatters! Crony capitalists! Public-sector employees! Demagogues! Philistines! Cultural chauvinists! Polyglots! Environmentalists! Utopians! *Purebloods!*"

Abruptly, Smith's voice fell silent. Elfrida's nerve broke. She fled up the ramp to the computer room.

Jimmy Liu and Wang Gulong were sitting in a vacant cubicle, eating pouch noodles.

"We're finished," Elfrida said, collapsing against a partition. "Everything's finished. The solar system, everything. You guys might as well go home."

They couldn't very easily do that, of course. She just felt like saying it.

"What happened?" Jimmy demanded.

She told them. "So it's been broadcasting its source code on the Ku-band. It's probably duplicated itself inside a million other computers by now. This is it. The apocalypse. We're all going to die." She wiped her eyes. "I was baptized a while back. I wonder if it really makes any difference."

Wang Gulong turned to his screen and started typing. Jimmy slurped another mouthful of pouch noodles. "We are all going to die, but not today, I hope. Luckily, we are on the dark side of Vesta, so the transmitter is oriented to the outer solar system. Smith can't be broadcasting for more than one hour, maximum. Worst-case scenario, some spaceships will get infected. Maybe the signal reaches Triton, if we are very unlucky. What's out there? A few corporate R&D facilities and some extreme snowboarders. That is the most we can lose."

"Oh," Elfrida said, feeling a bit more hopeful.

"Even if the Heidegger program got access to internet, I am thinking no big deal."

"No big deal?" Elfrida echoed. *"No big deal?"*

Jimmy never got a chance to respond. Satterthwaite and his friends tottered into the room. Elfrida stared. And stared.

Bright red droplets of blood spattered all four men from head to foot, as if they'd been fighting with a high-powered firehose of the stuff.

Satterthwaite seemed to be vaguely aware of his gore-splattered appearance. He wiped an arm across his face. "We had to kill him," he explained.

"The Infinite Fun show is hereby cancelled," said one of the other men. *"Laugh."*

"Anil, notify corporate," Satterthwaite said. "Tell them to warn people. It'll ruin what's left of our reputation, but oh well. If the thing's escaped, we ought to provide a public service announcement, at least."

"The ISA will intercept it," said the man named Anil.

"Try using the Ku-band," Satterthwaite said. *"Hollow snigger.* Of course, you'll have to wait until we rotate back to the dayside." He sat down. "This is a nightmare," he said to no one in particular. "An utter, bloody nightmare. That— *thing.* What it had done to him. The pain … dear God, the *pain* it must have inflicted on him … He had mutilated himself. One can't imagine … Perhaps he was fighting it. Perhaps he was actually trying to counter its influence. Perhaps he could have recovered, if he'd had the right treatment … But I killed him. *I* killed him."

Jimmy cleared his throat. Elfrida made a *shut up!* gesture at him. Couldn't he see this was not the time to expound his theory that the Heidegger program was no big deal? It clearly *was* a big deal. The biggest deal the solar system had had to face since ... since Mars.

With that thought, she came close to acknowledging what no one had yet said out loud.

The Heidegger program was an agent of the PLAN.

Satterthwaite looked up tiredly. "By the way, where's Meredith-Pike got to?"

Hugh Meredith-Pike was not far away. He had got tired of Satterthwaite's evasions, and of getting nowhere with his cryptanalysis. He wanted to know what they were really dealing with.

Satterthwaite had dropped a number of hints that convinced Meredith-Pike 'the thing' was actually a *thing,* not an abstract software-based problem. That made sense to Meredith-Pike. There was a strong argument that AI could not become AGI, much less ASI, in the absence of a physical vessel that provided it with, well, the same sensory inputs as a human being. Evidence from the field of practical robotics broadly substantiated this notion. The smarter an MI you wanted, the better a body you had to build for it.

So the odds were that the Heidegger program had come to the de Grey Institute in a human-like vessel.

Acting on this premise, Meredith-Pike had called up a schematic of the de Grey Institute and identified several likely places where 'the thing' might be concealed. Then he slipped out of the computer room and went hunting. He was looking for a phavatar, or one of the geminoid-class bots coyly known as 'companions,' that would have been misguidedly upgraded here, or imported from an envelope-pushing startup on Luna, only to be (somehow) infected with the Heidegger program. Hadn't there been a similar outbreak of trouble a couple of years ago? (Meredith-Pike was remembering the Galapagos Incident all wrong. To be fair, the news reports had been garbled.)

The first place he looked was Błaszczykowski-Lee's sumptuous cabin. Not under the bed, not in the wardrobe, not in the spherical bath complete with snorkel attachment.

The second place he looked was the walk-in freezer, where the de Grey Institute's gourmet chef had squirreled away a cornucopia of imported ingredients. There he found it.

Meredith-Pike swore out loud and took a step backwards.

He knew this had to be 'the thing.' But he had not expected to find himself staring at the naked body of a young girl.

xxxi.

Shoshanna's malware had already captured the Bellicia-Arruntia spaceport's hub, so it didn't take her and Dr. James long to steal a Flyingsaucer.

In service all over the solar system, the Flyingsaucer boosted cargoes and passengers from micro-gravity environments to larger ships in orbit. Functionally a lighter version of the industrial-use Superlifter, it was officially called the Flyingsaucer because the manufacturers had long ago thrown up their hands and admitted that people were right: it *did* look like one. The toroidal form factor was simply practical, but folk humor trumped logic. The company had even changed its name to LGM Industries and adopted an eponymous mascot of a little green man, which bowed and grinned annoyingly in the corner of Shoshanna's screen until she overrode the autopilot.

"What was LGM Industries originally called?" said Dr. James, talking to break the silence. He had gone a bit green himself, as the Flyingsaucer soared around the curve of Vesta in a steep ballistic trajectory.

"Toyota," Shoshanna said. "It was a Japanese company."

"Ah; so *that's* why they changed their name."

"Probably."

"Some people say that the Japanese are the new Jews. Homeless exiles, condemned to wander in time and space."

"That's bullshit. The Jews are the new Jews. Always have been, always will be."

"Are you religious?"

"What do you think?"

"No."

"Right."

"And yet your name—Shoshanna, rose of Judah; your parents must have wanted to pay tribute to their heritage."

"Oh, c'mon, Professor. You can be a Jew without believing in God. I don't know what your personal beliefs are, but you must've met plenty of Jewish atheists. That's what my parents are."

Carrying on the conversation with half her brain, while she piloted the Flyingsaucer, she was aware that she was telling him too much about herself, and would have to eliminate him as a result. She wondered if she was doing this because she wanted to eliminate him anyway, and just needed a reason. Then she reflected that this kind of self-doubt was a very Jewish reaction to have.

"Anyway, it's not the twenty-second century anymore," she said. "People aren't as scared of sounding ethnic."

"True. There's a greater acceptance of diversity. We've come full circle, in a manner of speaking."

"Still got a long way to go. That's why the Friends of David Reid agitated for the establishment of a literature course."

The optic feed screen displayed the refinery. She smiled at the destruction her DIY missile had wrought. Better yet, the train was right there, halted by an obstruction on the track. *Perfect.*

"Literature is the key to understanding who we are and where we come from," she said. "Like, I'll never forget the first time I read *Harry Potter and the Sorcerer's Stone*. It was like the author was talking to *me*, telling me that it was OK to be different. But you can't find those books anywhere, because they're too pureblood-y. Whatever. That's just stupid."

Dr. James looked at her with a half-smile. "Do you really believe that? Wasn't your wish list of demands just *dezinformatsiya?*"

"Yes and no." Shoshanna calculated the Flyingsaucer's angle of descent and then gave the professor her full attention for the first time. "I'll be clear. What we're fighting for? Is this. Precisely this. A podunk university in an asteroid crater 250 million kilometers from earth, complete with student activists, a lake that's too full of algae to swim in, and a really good Goan restaurant. I could go on. We're fighting for Zen gardeners on the moon, the Semi-Professional League of Kabaddi in the Inner Belt, fish farming on Europa, Wagner performed by nudists in the Andalusian desert, the electroceuticals industry, the hunter-gatherer movement, Oktoberfest, chess clubs, the re-wilding of the Congo, the opening ceremonies at the G30, Sufi dancers, homeschoolers, the perfect espresso drunk on a foggy afternoon on a bench overlooking the Seine, and even that crazy bunch of ultra-expansionists who want to splart an engine onto Pluto and drive it to Alpha Centauri. I haven't even begun to scratch the surface. Human beings are crazy, amazing, creative, stupid, anachronistic, quarrelsome, and just generally the best thing that has ever happened to this solar system; possibly to this galaxy; possibly to the entire fucking universe, because as far as we know, there is no other life out there, let alone intelligent life. And yet the whole dang show hangs by a thread. The ISA is that thread. Am I getting my point across? We're fighting for *you*."

Dr James said, "Then why treat the private sector as an adversary?"

"Because," Shoshanna snarled, "the private sector accomplishes a lot, but when they fuck up, it's everyone else who pays. See below."

At the moment, *below* was a literal term, as the Flying-Saucer descended towards the Vesta Express on a trajectory not that much different from that of the satellite that had come this way a few hours ago. "Urk," Dr. James said, covering his mouth with his hand and his claw. So Shoshanna got the last word, but it did not compensate her for the sight she saw as the resolution of her optic feed improved. A bunch of people—no, phavatars—were dashing for cover. They left behind a jerry-rigged arrangement on the south side of the cutting, which was obviously intended to lever the obstruction off the track.

The metalfuckers just never stopped trying to run away from their own misdeeds.

Well, she'd stop them.

The Flyingsaucer landed as lightly as a sycamore seed on the higher ground south of the canyon. Its jackstands skidded on a patch of regolith scoured down to glass by its thruster exhaust. Shoshanna hurried to the airlock. Dr. James came with her. He easily kept up on their sprint towards the Vesta Express, bouncing along like some kind of bizarre two-legged insect in his custom spacesuit.

"Help!" Shoshanna cried over every available comms channel as she ran. "Help, help!"

It had worked for the Chinese.

But answer came there none.

Meredith-Pike backed out of the freezer. Then he went in again. Shivering, he bent over the body of the girl. She lay curled in the fetal position behind some boxes of salmon filets. She had been zipped up in a sleeping bag, which Meredith-Pike now opened far enough to see that she was, indeed, naked as the day she was born. "Sleeping Beauty," Meredith-Pike murmured, inappositely.

The girl had a lumpen, flat-nosed face with a bulgy forehead. Her skin was the exact café au lait shade of 'flesh-tone' in a box of crayons, just a bit lighter than Meredith-Pike's own. Her hair, a shade or two darker, stood out in a three-centimeter nimbus. She looked to be about fourteen.

"Need a kiss?" he whispered.

In a loud voice, the freezer observed that its door was open. Meredith-Pike jumped out of his skin.

Tension singing down his nerves, he dragged the girl's corpse out of the freezer. He assumed she *was* a corpse, but watched her carefully, taking nothing for granted. There were researchers working on mtDNA tweaks that would allow humans to function better in extreme cold—useful for colonists on the Jovian moons, say, whose habitats could then be kept at arctic temperatures, lowering their energy bills. It was -10° in the freezer.

"Where did you come from?" Meredith-Pike asked the girl, laying her on the kitchen floor.

The kitchen was a mess. Presumably the researchers had programmed the housekeeping bots to stay out so they wouldn't find the girl. Flour and chocolate chips dusted the floor from someone's cookie-baking session.

"Why did they put you in there?"

She was definitely cold-adapted. Chunky-bodied, flat-faced, with a narrow little nose. Was that a blush of pink returning to her cheeks? Could she be *alive?*

"Here's my theory," Meredith-Pike said. "You're a Martian." He chuckled. "This is huge. Huge." His intracranial implants worked harder, pumping out endorphins and serotonin to compensate for his instinctive urge, which was to run away screaming. "No one was even sure that you existed. To *catch* one of you, dead or alive ... this is huge," he repeated. "You ought to be in a cutting-edge government research facility. Not hidden behind the frozen fishfingers in a train on a bloody asteroid." He leaned forward. "Are you *breathing?*"

The girl sat up. She winced and rubbed her neck. Her eyes fastened on his; they were unnaturally reflective, clearly augmented. Her bosom heaved.

"Oh my dog," Meredith-Pike said.

She made a mewling sound. Pointed at her mouth, shook her head, and mewled again.

"Can't you talk?"

"Oooahnhhh." She pointed at his head and then her own.

"Oh, I see! You want to text." Meredith-Pike blinked up his comms program. Then he hesitated. Distantly, as it were from beyond the waves of bliss and upon-a-peak-in-Darien excitement pulsing through him, came the thought that this might not be a very good idea.

"I don't have your ID," he stalled.

The woman seemed to understand. She leaned over and wrote with one finger in the flour that dusted the floor.

Standing on the roof of the de Grey Institute, Shoshanna inspected the module's airlock. It was a standard valve-type. To hack it, she'd need a route into the Vesta Express's hub, and they still hadn't taken the bait of her cries for help.

"Well?" Dr. James said. "Stumped?"

"Not only didn't they answer us, they're not emitting any signals on any frequency. Maybe they're all dead in there."

"If that's a possibility," Dr. James said, "this falls into the category of a rescue operation."

He did something to the right sleeve of his spacesuit, braced himself on the ladder, and shot the airlock with the laser embedded in his prosthesis.

★

Satterthwaite bounded along the residential corridor with Elfrida and the two Chinese on his heels, in search of Hugh Meredith-Pike. Elfrida tried not to look into Smith's cabin as they passed. She failed. The glimpse she got was enough to convince her that Smith was very, very dead. His battered body would haunt her dreams for years to come. If she lived that long.

She caught up with Satterthwaite in the kitchen. Or did you call it a galley, when it was on a train? Uncooked rice crunched under her boots. The contents of cabinets littered the worktops. Pasta sauce spattered not only the walls, but the ceiling. This was the kind of mess you could only get in zero- or micro-gravity. Wang Gulong said something, and Jimmy translated, "Engineers are the same everywhere."

Satterthwaite dived into a walk-in freezer. The fog rolling out of the door reminded Elfrida of the dry ice in the supercomputer silo. Seconds later, he stumbled back out. "Gone. It's gone."

Jimmy and Wang Gulong exchanged a look. The powerfully built Wang moved up on Satterthwaite and backed him against the dishwasher. He rapped out some words in Chinese.

Jimmy translated: "Enough games. You have lied to us about this Heidegger program. You will now stop lying, or Wang will break your neck." He added, "Wang is a champion of the Greater Imperial China Amateur Duan Quan League."

"All right, all right," Satterthwaite coughed. "Let me go, you ape! The thing was in the freezer. It looked like a girl, an adolescent female of the species *Homo sapiens,* but it wasn't. Not sure whether it was grown or manufactured; there may not be any difference when you get to that level of biological approximation. Anyway, we—acquired it—in an advanced life-support cradle, which appeared to be a fragment of a PLAN ship. The cradle was damaged. The ship must have been disabled ..."

Elfrida yelped. Jimmy's eyes bulged. He started translating, but Wang cut him off. He had heard the word *PLAN* and that was enough.

"You have a PLAN agent captive on this train?" Jimmy translated. "In the *freezer?*"

"Had. Had," Satterthwaite said. "Meredith-Pike's clearly found it and walked off with it."

"He can't have gone far," Elfrida said. "There aren't any EVA suits! The thing must still be on the train! Is it ... is it alive? Or dead?"

Satterthwaite seemed to take that as an accusation. Bristling, he snapped, "We put it in the freezer to keep it safe. It was cold-adapted. In fact, it seemed to have the ability to hibernate. That's just one of the secrets we hoped to unravel by studying it. We have a nanoscopic imaging system on order. We began studying the life-support cradle while waiting for it to arrive ..."

"And that's how Bob got infected," Elfrida said. "You guys sure are brainy." All the fine hairs on her body stood on end. This was her worst nightmare. Actually, it went beyond any nightmare scenario her imagination could have devised.

Wang Gulong left the kitchen.

Jimmy touched Elfrida's arm. His melancholy gaze brimmed with knowledge of the tragedies humanity brought upon itself. "It's OK," he said with an unconvincing smile.

Elfrida felt ashamed that he was trying to comfort her, when he must be equally terrified. "I'm so sorry," she said. "You came here because you thought it was safe. What must you think of us?"

Jimmy shook his head. She'd misinterpreted his reassurance. He'd meant it. "This is our theory. The Heidegger program is a type of software called *shénjiàn*—neuroware? Is this the right translation?"

"Neuroware, I don't know what that is."

"It doesn't exist. Or precisely, the theory exists, but the real thing cannot be developed. It is software designed to run on the human brain. The brain is the most complex and powerful computer in existence! We only use one fraction of it, you know? So far, it is *too* complex for us to write neuroware, even if we develop the right interface protocols. But now we think the PLAN has mastered this complexity." Jimmy looked wistful. "It is very exciting."

"Not you, too!"

"Don't worry. It is not dangerous. I simplify, but if you don't install the program, it can't run."

"That's what we thought," Satterthwaite said. "Until poor bloody Smith downloaded it to his BCI."

"Maybe it automatically executes when downloaded?"

"Obviously, yes."

"And maybe Smith did not have the right hardware."

"He had a BCI."

"Exactly," said Hugh Meredith-Pike from the door of the kitchen. He strolled in, followed by Wang. He should have looked like a prisoner escorted by a guard. Instead, his confident, loose-limbed gait made him look like a celebrity leading a big poodle.

Hiding behind him, as if shy, was a girl wearing nothing but an oversized Vesta Valkyries t-shirt.

"Smith had a BCI," Meredith-Pike explained. "I've got a BCI plus neural stimulation implants. Oh, it's just a rough approximation of what Little Sister, here, has in *her* head. But it suffices. The underlying principle is the same." He directed at the girl a smouldering, utterly vacant smile. "Infinite fun, not half!"

"You're blissed out of your mind, Hugh, you moron," Satterthwaite said, stumbling to his feet.

Elfrida said, "Little Sister? *Whose* little sister?"

"He has installed the neuroware," Jimmy said, pointing out the obvious.

"My question is—" Meredith-Pike directed it to Elfrida, with smugly raised eyebrows, like a newscaster posing a gotcha question— "why on earth are we fighting these people?"

"They aren't people," Elfrida yelped.

After her spell on 11073 Galapagos, she had developed an odd acuity when it came to distinguishing humans from robots. The Galapajin had been able to instantly identify a post-geminoid phavatar that would have passed as human anywhere else in the solar system, and Elfrida seemed to have picked up the knack from them. This Little Sister was setting off all her alarms. She didn't seem to be a robot, per se, but nor was she human.

Elfrida had a sensation of falling helplessly from the

heights of understanding where she had been born and lived all her life, into an abyss of barely grasped horrors. She thought, but could not say out loud: *Little Sister is a demon.*

xxxii.

"Not bad, for an egghead," Shoshanna complimented Dr. James, when he had cut away the outer door of the airlock.

"In Israel, everyone fights," Dr. James said.

"In the New Hesperides, too." There she went again. She contemplated the seared wreckage of the door. They were standing in the chamber, still in their suits. "But now we've got a new problem. This airlock is no longer, in fact, an airlock. It's an ex-airlock."

"It is no more," Dr. James intoned. "It has ceased to be. It's expired and gone to meet its maker. Its vacuum-denying function is now history."

Tickled, Shoshanna laughed. "You're a funny guy when you want to be. But the problem remains: now we can't get in without depressurising the R&D module."

"For an ISA agent, you're not actually very ruthless, are you?" Dr. James said. The amusement was gone from his voice. "You didn't turn off the power to the Bellicia ecohood, despite threatening to. And now you're saying that depressurising this module—which holds a potentially unstoppable threat to humanity—is a *problem?*"

Shoshanna hesitated. "Point," she said eventually. "Cut through the inner door."

Mendoza, alone in the driver's cab, kept panic at bay by listening to the St. Matthew's Passion of Bach, one of the thousands of music files in his BCI's memory crystals. He also had high-quality iEars transducer implants, which had been a present to himself on his thirtieth birthday. He watched the fallen handler bot rise into the air, balanced on the makeshift tyre iron, while the phavatars tromped in circles around the windlass they had improvised. It was pure jugaad. It was beautiful. He wished they'd hurry up.

Distantly, over the music, he heard an explosive boom.

"Susmaryosep, what now?"

The handler bot crashed onto the south rim of the cutting. The phavatars started running back towards the train.

Screw 'em, they're only machines, can be replaced.

Spooked by the boom he'd heard, Mendoza lunged at the propulsion systems console. He engaged thrust. The Vesta Express leapt down the track.

O Lamm Gottes, unschuldig ... Mendoza sat tensely at the console, watching the sides of the canyon slip past faster and faster. He wished he hadn't flunked out of psephology. He wished he'd never left Manila. He wished ...

He noticed an alert scrolling across the life-support systems monitor.

... on event! Click here for details. Click here to dispatch repair bots. Click here to learn more about emergency life-support options. Depressurization event! Click ...

"Depressurization event," barked the tannoy in the kitchen. It confirmed what Elfrida had just heard: the explosive noise of an air mass meeting the vacuum. "Oh my dog," she gasped.

Meredith-Pike pivoted to Satterthwaite. "Looks like we're running out of time. *Are* you going to be sensible, Jules?"

"Sod off."

Meredith-Pike shook his head sorrowfully. "Remember, I didn't want to do this," he said, and punched Satterthwaite in the temple.

Satterthwaite's eyes rolled up. He fell over backwards, hitting his head on the microwave.

Elfrida screamed.

Meredith-Pike turned towards her with a dispassionate frown. His eyes had gone slitty, more like the eyes of a goat than a human being. Whatever the Heidegger program had done to his intracranial wiring, it had tipped him straight into the uncanny valley that Glory dos Santos had told Elfrida about, way down into the zombie zone between 'alive' and 'not alive.' His eyes were no longer windows to his soul. They were slit trenches in a clayey landscape that only happened to resemble a human face.

Little Sister tugged on his arm.

"Oh," Meredith-Pike said. "Right."

He and she moved at the same time. Meredith-Pike punched Wang Gulong in the temple, his fist a blur, felling the big man before he could react at all, much less deploy any duan quan moves. He then snatched a bread knife from the webbing above the nearest worktop and slashed Wang's throat. Blood sprayed across the kitchen. Little Sister didn't bother with a knife. She merely pointed at Jimmy Liu. A laser beam leapt out of her stubby middle finger and burnt a hole in his forehead. He collapsed on top of his friend, jerking grotesquely.

Meredith-Pike glanced at Elfrida. "Hope that didn't shock you too badly? They were purebloods. That lot are behind it all, you know, pulling the strings of interplanetary finance, prosecuting a war that no one wants, using their hereditary connections and secret influence to set natural allies at each other's throats. They have to go. It is unpleasant, I admit."

Little Sister dragged him out of the kitchen.

At about this time Elfrida felt the tug of a gentle wind. Her jumper rippled.

Her Space Corps training kicked in.

In the unlikely event that a depressurization event occurs at your workplace, proceed to the nearest airtight room, compartment, or cubicle, and await further instructions.

Elfrida threw Jimmy, Wang Gulong, and Satterthwaite into the freezer and tumbled in after them. The door had no handle on the inside. She pulled at it with her fingernails. Slowly, it swung towards her. Its flanges kissed the frame, and sealed.

★

There were no pressure-seals in the architecturally lauded atrium of the de Grey institute. Shoshanna and Dr. James jogged along the spiraling ramps, through a gale that pelted them with potted plants, stress-reliever toys, lost socks, thermoses, tablets, framed photographs of loved ones—anything, in fact, that wasn't splarted down. The water sculpture had slumped sideways, losing about half of its mass before the remainder froze solid. They trod on patches of ice. Dirt, dust, and fog obscured the air, generated by the sudden change in the air's vapor holding capacity. Arachnoid repair bots scrambled past, toting sacks of splart.

When they reached the computer room—Dr. James leading the way; he'd been here before—they found several bodies.

Shoshanna checked them for signs of life, and found none, as she expected. The pressure was down to 0.6 atmospheres, with a corresponding loss of oxygen. That wasn't what had killed these men and women, however. They were all holding hands. Their faces had a pink flush, regardless of their original skin color, and their tongues protruded from their mouths. They had self-euthanized, probably with the prescription tablets known as 'peace pills'—which was something of a misnomer.

"Now what?" she said, thinking hard.

Before she could answer herself, her suit reported lateral acceleration.

"Metalfucker! Someone's started the engine. Is there a separate operator's compartment? Is it pressure-sealed?"

★

The answer was yes. On the downside, someone had pinched the rebreather and the rest of the life-support kit that should have been in the emergency locker. Eyeballing the cramped dimensions of the driver's cab, Mendoza figured he had about six hours before he died of carbon dioxide poisoning, unless a miracle happened first.

He locked the engine into maximum acceleration mode and slumped back, hands over his face. The St. Matthew's Passion throbbed into his ears. He couldn't catch a break, could he?

After a few minutes, he did some calculations. Without a payload slowing it down, the Vesta Express could accelerate to Mach 4 in less than one full circuit of the equator.

He blinked up his comms program. "Goto," he said, trying not to hope that she was still alive. "Do you copy?"

She did not answer.

At the same time as Mendoza was pinging Elfrida, two figures dashed across the atrium, beneath the frozen cascade of the water sculpture. The wind pushed them sideways. Meredith-Pike stumbled. He stopped and projectile-vomited. Little Sister dragged him onwards, her short legs pumping like pistons.

Not all the atmosphere had yet left the de Grey Institute. Given the small size of the breach in the airlock, and the volume of air that was trying to escape, it would take a few hours for the pressure inside the module to equalize with the vacuum outside. At the moment, the air pressure in the atrium was about half of normal—but that wasn't zero. It was survivable.

Hugh Meredith-Pike, however, was not in the best shape. He stumbled to his knees. Then he blacked out.

Little Sister slung him over her shoulders and sprinted on. She, too, was suffering from oxygen deprivation, but her neuroware was able to wring the last drops of energy out of her muscles.

She had none of her weaponry, but she had brought along a knife from the kitchen, the same one Meredith-Pike had used to cut Wang Gulong's throat.

★

"As you may have figured out by this time," Dr. James said, "the thing was a fragment of a PLAN ship. Yes, I know. Don't sputter at me. The risks, we thought, were not severe enough to preclude a cautious, fully sandboxed investigation of its capabilities. We hoped to gain a better understanding of ..."

He named several topics that were top concerns of the ISA, and another couple of items that were sore points with Star Force in its role of first responder.

"Principally, of course, we hoped to gain some insight into the PLAN's stealthing technology."

Shoshanna paused in her exploratory pinging of the infected supercomputer, her attention caught.

The PLAN's stealthing technology was perhaps the biggest riddle confronting humanity today. Not that 99% of humanity had ever even thought about it, but a rudimentary knowledge of physics exposed the riddle to contemplation—and ensured frustration. *How* did the PLAN get from one place to another without being spotted? They used fusion engines, as proven beyond a doubt by their drive signatures. Engines generated heat. Therefore, according once more to physics, stealth in outer space was an impossibility. A basic infrared scan could find every spacecraft on your side of the sun.

Except, neither infrared nor any other kind of scan could find the PLAN when they were in stealth mode. Their ships routinely popped up without warning, attacked human facilities, and vanished again. How the hell did they do it?

"Yeah," she said. "That's something we'd like to know, too."

She bounced up from her ergoform and grabbed Dr. James by the shoulders.

"*Did* they? Find out anything about it?"

"I don't know. As I said, they didn't keep me in the loop.

But my educated guess is no. We'd have seen some patent applications by now. Please let go of me, Shoshanna."

"I want that ship."

"Fragment."

"No one has *ever* captured a PLAN ship, or even a fragment of one. They autodestruct. Nothing to study but dust. This is un-fucking-precedented. Where is it?"

"Unprecedented. Exactly," Dr. James said. "Taking into account everything that's happened, I'm starting to suspect that the PLAN is trying out a new battle strategy."

"What do you mean?"

"The space oddity wasn't a fragment of a ship destroyed in an engagement. It was a plant."

xxxiii.

It was pitch dark in the freezer with the door shut. Elfrida was trying not to cry, because her tears froze on her cheeks. Working by touch, she pulled Jimmy Liu's sweater off over his head. "I'm sorry," she babbled. "I'm so sorry. But I need all the insulation I can get, or I'll die of hypothermia long before I run out of air."

His body flopped in her hands like an unprogrammed ergoform. He felt warm in contrast to the air in the freezer, but that was just an illusion. He was dead. As dead as Jun Yonezawa had been when she ate him.

"I'm so sorry."

While she wrestled with Jimmy's clothes, she also weighed whether to try to call for help. This was not the no-brainer it should have been. One of the drawbacks of contacts—one of the many reasons that consumers opted for BCIs instead—was that without ambient light, you couldn't see a doggone thing. So she was connected, but blind. She remembered how the Heidegger program's icon had floated in her field of vision. *What if I click on it by mistake?*

Without a BCI, it shouldn't be able to get inside her head. But what if it got into her contacts and messed them up? Then she'd be not only blind but completely isolated, without even the hope of calling for help.

She struggled into Jimmy's sweater, knew she'd never fit in his pants, and fumbled her way over to Wang Gulong. His clothes were board-stiff with frozen blood.

By the time she got the extra layers on, she was cold enough that she decided to risk it. Her comms program was usually *there*. Praying, she—

—remembered that Satterthwaite had had a flashlight.

She scrabbled in his breast pocket with fingers that were rapidly going numb. *Yes!* She dropped the flashlight, cursed, found it again, and switched it on, blinding herself. The beam wavered over 5kg sacks of hash browns and kedgeree.

She wasted no time blinking up her comms program. Rather than attempting anything fancy, she just aimed her gaze at *reply to last*.

"Goto!?!" the answer appeared in text floating on her vision.

"Mendoza, it's me." She was crying again for sheer relief, which made it difficult to gaze-type. She switched to her air keyboard, projecting it on the top of a box that held frozen mixed vegetables. She knelt in front of the box and peeled her sleeves back from her fingers.

"I've been pinging you ever since the big boom," Mendoza texted. "Where are you?"

"I couldn't see anything. Sorry. I'm in the freezer. It's airtight, as far as I can tell. But it's not very big. I think I've got a little while."

"Shit, Goto."

"Where are you?"

"Driver's cab. I've got about five and a half hours of air. Apart from that, nothing much to report."

There was a pause. Elfrida fought tears. They were on the same train, but separated by a vacuum. They might as well have been on different planets.

"You've got the advantage of me," she typed at last. "At least you're not freezing to death."

"But you've got food."

"Ever tried eating frozen broccoli?"

"Goto, I could eat my own doggone elbow right now. There was supposed to be an emergency stash of rations up here, but the assholes took it."

"Only you could think about food at a time like this."

"Just trying to keep it light," Mendoza typed. Elfrida was silent; she'd known that. After a moment, he typed, "Shit, I wish there was something I could do. I hate to think of you stuck down there."

In the split second before the next words appeared, Elfrida hoped that Mendoza wasn't about to say something sentimental. The thought surprised her. That she'd even had it told her that she was more aware of Mendoza as a person than she had known.

"I'm accelerating the train to launch speed. Figure your friend's plan is our only chance now."

"Oh dog, Mendoza. I didn't get a chance to tell you. There's something not right about him. I don't know if this is a good idea, after all." She hesitated, trying to organize her thoughts. Maybe the best thing was just to forward Petruzzelli's email to Mendoza, but would he know what to make of it?

"This. Was. Your. Idea."

"I know, I know, but it turns out that Yonezawa may not be on the level. He may not really be coming to help us. I think maybe he wants the Heidegger program."

Mendoza's reply appeared before she even finished typing. "He seems OK to me. Anyway, what are our other options?"

"You've been *talking* to him?"

"Sure. Or maybe it was the other one. They look alike to me, sorry. He knows his shit. Brain like a supercomputer, as they say. Hang on, I've got another call."

Mendoza ended the conversation. Elfrida stared in disbelief at the last words. Why did she feel so betrayed?

Something clawed at her leg. She squealed in terror and dropped the flashlight again.

Mendoza's other call was from Hugh Meredith-Pike, of all people.

"Yo! Driver! We there yet?"

Mendoza did not like wireheads, especially this one, but the sheer elation of knowing at least one other person had survived the depressurization event overcame his mistrust of Meredith-Pike. He typed back, matching Meredith-Pike's bantering tone, "What, you want to stop for a bathroom break? Ain't no service areas on the Vesta Express, buddy."

"Dog, and I was looking forward to a Big Mac and Coke."

"You and me both. Back on Earth, when this is over."

"It's over now," Meredith-Pike typed. "Well, pretty much. We've got the atmosphere back! The repair bots fixed the breach. You can come out of there. Then we'll see about stopping this runaway train and getting the hell off."

Mendoza did not notice that Meredith-Pike's diction was not quite the same as it had been. Nor did he think to check the life-support systems monitor. At the words *we've got the atmosphere back!*, one thought filled his mind to the exclusion of all others: Elfrida. He could pull her out of the freezer before she froze to death.

He jumped off his couch and hit the DOOR OPEN button.

Had Bob still been operating the train, the next moments would have unfolded differently. But with the supercomputer off-line, the Vesta Express's mechanical subsystems had no smarts to deploy as a counterweight to human impulsiveness. With idiotic obedience, the door opened a crack. There was a boom, and it leapt open the rest of the way. The atmosphere in the driver's cab swirled out, sucking Mendoza with it. He stumbled a few paces, gasping and wheezing, and then fell face down.

On the network monitor screen, the latest systems status report faded, to be replaced by a representation of the face that had formerly been Meredith-Pike's. His eyes swivelled, as if he could see the empty driver's cab. "Ha, ha, ha," he said thickly. *"Fun."*

★

Elfrida wrenched her leg away from the icy hand that had grabbed it.

"Aaagh!" she screamed, and then, weakly: "Mr. Satterthwaite! I thought you were dead."

Satterthwaite clutched his head and groaned. His gaze skittered over the half-naked bodies of Jimmy and Wang. "Cold."

"Yeah," Elfrida agreed. To her shame, her first reaction to Satterthwaite's survival was: *So I've only got half as much air as I thought I had.*

Her contacts distracted her. "Hang on," she said. "I'm just going to take this."

"Elfrida? *Daijoubu?*" [Are you OK?]

Elfrida's jaw dropped in astonishment. "Rurumi?"

She had completely forgotten about the moe-class phavatar. If she had thought about it at all, she'd assumed Rurumi had been left behind with the roadheader, and good riddance.

"*Hai, daijoubu,*" she typed in wonderment.

"*Yokatta!* [Oh, good!] This is really scary, isn't it?"

"Yes, Rurumi, it's scary. Did you just call me to chat?"

"I know you didn't want me to come. But I just wanted to see that cute little doggie one more time."

Elfrida realized that she had forgotten about Jimmy's terrier, too. The poor thing was probably dead now.

"Anyway, do you want me?" Rurumi asked.

"What?"

"Do you want me? I emailed you, but you didn't answer."

"Rurumi, are you really calling me in the middle of a depressurization event to ask if I want to have sex?"

"No! No no no! Gregor told me, if things get really scary, you're authorized to operate me. So, do you want to or not?"

Elfrida inhaled sharply. She sent a quick thought of gratitude in the direction of Gregor Lovatsky, who—unlike everyone else—had been pessimistic enough to consider the possibility that things might go completely FUBAR. Then she typed, "Sounds like a plan. But I'm not in a telepresence cubicle. So we'll have to do this together." And Elfrida would have to overcome her dislike of working with an assistant. With their lives at stake, she thought, she could manage that.

Rurumi informed her that she was now logged in. "SUIT COMMAND," Elfrida typed, testing her authorization. "Enable optic feed."

The V-shaped horizon of the graben blocked out the stacks of frozen food. Rurumi was on top of the Vesta Express, hitchhiking like a broke-ass nomad. The scene tilted, the train swaying gently as it raced around the equator.

"Optic feed working," Elfrida typed. "There should be a breach in the exterior containment of the de Grey Institute. You can get in that way. When you're inside, ping me for further instructions." She hesitated. "By the way, Rurumi? I'm sorry I was mean to you."

"That's OK!" the phavatar replied. "I'm used to being hated because I'm beautiful. *Smile.*"

"That's not why—well, maybe it was. Kind of. Anyway."

She minimized the optic feed and glanced at Satterthwaite. He was not doing anything helpful, just shivering and groaning. She pinged Mendoza. She hadn't yet told him what had happened in the kitchen. She had been unwilling, if not unable, to put words to the horrible vibes she'd got from Hugh Meredith-Pike and the Little Sister thing. But she had to tell him what little she did know, for his own safety.

"He's not answering," she muttered. "He's probably talking to the Yonezawas. Figuring out how to launch the train into space. Shit."

Satterthwaite spoke up, his teeth chattering. "Are you talking about the TEOTWAWKI option?"

xxxiv.

Shoshanna decided not to waste time searching the de Grey Institute any further. Dr. James believed that, given the size of the PLAN ship fragment, it must be in the storage module, so that's where they would look first.

To get there, they'd have to pass through the support module.

"It's still pressurized," Dr. James said, pointing at the readout beside the door.

"Yeah, and infrared is telling me there are people in there."

"The refinery crew."

"They're still alive, based on their heat signatures. Let's try and keep them that way."

Shoshanna hit the DOOR OPEN button. She kicked the top flange as it irised back, bending it far enough for her and Dr. James to wriggle through in the teeth of the wind that instantly rushed out. She backflipped and punched DOOR CLOSE. The flanges shuddered, straining to meet. "Don't take your helmet off," Shoshanna advised. "I'm getting an air pressure reading of 0.8 atmospheres. That's lower than it should be." Then she turned and got her first good look at the room they were in. "On the other hand ... maybe it doesn't matter."

They stood on a raised walkway that ran around the edge of a cubicle farm, like at a call center or something. And all the telepresence couches were occupied.

By dead bodies.

Freshly dead. Even if it weren't for the infrared readings that had deceived her, Shoshanna would have known that much at a glance. Throats had been slashed, faces hacked into bloody ruins.

Dr. James made indistinct noises.

"Do not throw up in your helmet. People have died that way. Turn your back if it bothers you."

Dr. James moved up beside her. She heard his breath rasping over the radio. "My career is finished, anyway," he said.

"Ain't that the truth."

Shoshanna knew that her own career, and maybe more, depended on her making the right call, right here, right now. Her backup was still hours away. With all the satellites down, and the ground-based transmitter at the spaceport out of range, she couldn't even call for advice. "Priorities," she whispered to herself. "Neutralize threat, secure area, protect civilians."

That was the ISA field agent's official rule of thumb, and there was a reason why protecting civilians came last. The ISA was the *Information* Security Agency. Anyway, these civilians were beyond protecting.

Or ... were they?

Not all the operators had been hacked up with a blade, she now saw. Only one in four or five.

Which just so happened to be the incidence of purebloods in the general population.

The other operators had been flung out of their couches, their telepresence masks and gloves ripped off. They were lying on the floor, and given the size of them, it was no wonder they couldn't get up, even if they were alive.

Shoshanna saw one of them weakly struggling. She vaulted over the intervening partitions and shook the person—a woman, probably. The woman mouthed at her. Shoshanna ripped her helmet off to hear. She felt the cold on her face, heard the whooshing of the air circulation system struggling to restore normal pressure, smelled the metallic odor of fresh blood.

"Help," the woman said. "Help! Help!"

"Who?" Shoshanna yelled, and then reconsidered.

"*What?* When? Where'd it go?"

"I've lost Marmaduke. I need to get back in my couch. Help me."

Disgusted, Shoshanna threw the woman against the nearest cubicle partition. "Cupcake," she said.

The pained whimpers of the survivors scratched at her ears. Her heart was racing, her palms damp. Her BCI recommended an adrenergic uptake inhibitor. She distractedly authorized it to release a modest dose from the pharmacology implant under the skin of her left arm.

The Heidegger program had hijacked the phavatars that worked at the refinery.

Why hadn't she anticipated that? Well, you couldn't anticipate everything. But that was no excuse.

The Heidegger program was loose on the surface of 4 Vesta.

She'd failed.

She raised her helmet to her jaw. "We're going back," she said to Dr. James, who was sitting on the walkway. "Someone's driving this train, and it can't be the PLAN agent, or we'd be dead already. I assume there's a manual control interface. So we're going to go find whoever's operating it, and make them stop."

"Why?" Dr. James's despairing monosyllable crackled from her helmet.

"Oy veh. So that we can get off, and get back to the Flyingsaucer. I need comms, doggone it, and that fucking PORMS took out all the satellites I was using, although that may have saved the rest of the solar system, so it's a wash, I guess."

She needed to call her controllers and make a full report, so they'd have the information they needed to act upon when they got here. In the meantime, maybe she could alert the Big Dig, and get them to use the PORMS to slag the phavatars in the open. It might be too late for that, but you hadn't failed until you stopped trying.

"Question," Dr. James said. "What kind of a computer program slaughters people with a *knife?*"

"Huh? One that sends them nuts. You don't even need a fragment of a PLAN ship to do that. Although most BCI crash victims end up in therapy, not going on murderous rampages."

"Yes, but where did it get the—" Dr. James interrupted himself. *"Shoshanna! Watch out!"*

She turned, and the knife came at her from below, a glint in her peripheral vision, giving her barely enough time to jump back. The woman she'd thrown to the floor was moving like a killer whale, *fast,* hacking at her legs. And all over the room the other survivors were rolling and surging and slithering towards her, their obese bodies sailing through the air like porpoises, several metric tons of flying cupcake converging on her in three dimensions.

Micro-gravity gave the wrong people all the advantages.

Shoshanna had combat training. What she did not have was a decent weapon. To be caught with a laser pistol would have wrecked her cover as a student activist. She had a home-printed revolver with three bullets in it. She leapt into the air to avoid the woman on the floor, and fired all three bullets in rapid succession into the nearest oncoming cupcakes. Then she threw the revolver at a fourth one. They didn't even slow down. In the corner of her eye she glimpsed flashes, Dr. James shooting at the cupcakes with his prosthetic gun.

She made a cold calculation that the odds were insurmountable.

"Run!" she yelled. "Tell them it's loose!"

She did not see whether Dr. James obeyed her or not. The cupcakes were on top of her. Slowly, as in a nightmare, struggling all the way, she was smashed to the floor.

She lay half on a telepresence couch, her head hanging

off its edge. Obese bodies pinned her limbs. A man sat on her chest. He had a transistor tattoo on his bald skull. "Are we having fun yet?" he grinned.

Shoshanna commanded her BCI to euthanize her. The dose loaded in her subdermal store was kinder than over-the-counter peace pills. Supposedly.

~*Are you sure?* her BCI queried. It would not let her take this drastic step without double-checking.

"Yes!" Shoshanna screamed. The cupcakes were fumbling around her head, trying to force a direct-connection telepresence wire into her temple port.

"Oh, *good,*" said the man sitting on her chest. "We are, too! The more, the merrier."

~*Please confirm you are of sound mind and not under duress or emotional distress,* said her BCI.

Too late. The wire had slipped home. Shoshanna Doyle would never be of sound mind again.

"Cancel euthanasia command," she said, sitting up. "Just joking!"

★

Far away from the Vesta Express, the phavatar modelled after the porn star Marmaduke Shagg stood outside the Bremen Lock. It was accompanied by a baker's dozen of its fellows. They had run as fast as they could to get here, but they were not tired, needless to say. They were machines. They had stopped only once, at the Bellicia-Arruntia spaceport, to recharge themselves. *That* had been fun.

(Phavatars, independent of their operators, had no sense of fun. But the entity now operating these phavatars did.)

Marmaduke Shagg hefted the anti-spacecraft cannon they had ripped from its mounting at the spaceport.

Then he froze. All the phavatars froze, sagging in awkward postures.

The sky curved blackly over them. There were no satellites up there any longer to distract from the awesome beauty of the stars.

(Not that phavatars had a sense of beauty, anyway.)

In front of them, the airlock's external gates spanned the gap between the rock and the mushroom-cap overhang of the Bellicia ecohood's roof. Wrought from asteroid iron, the gates depicted woodland animals and children frolicking around the Virgin Atomic logo. This artistic flourish mirrored the aspirations of the ecohood's founders, recorded in a form impermeable to the cynicism of subsequent generations. The gates still reminded everyone who passed beneath of their dependence on a FUKish aerospace company whose good intentions were matched only by its self-promotional zeal.

(If the phavatars had been capable of any emotions at all, they might have felt a flicker of gratitude at being freed from that dependence.)

The sun peeked above the horizon, slapping their shadows through the gates.

And they moved. Marmaduke Shagg lowered the cannon. They all walked forward.

The gates swung open.

The airlock admitted them.

Back on the Vesta Express, Elfrida was trying to warm up by doing jumping jacks when Rurumi interrupted her.

"I'm in. But my hair is ruined!"

"Huh?"

"The repair bots are fixing the airlock. I had to wiggle past them. I've got splart in my hair!"

"When this is over, I'll introduce you to my hairdresser. You'd look great with a pixie cut, in my opinion." A moe-class was a moe-class, and so Elfrida took a few seconds to reassure Rurumi, although she was twitching with urgency, as well as shivering with cold. "Go to the driver's cab. Mendoza hasn't been responding to my pings. I want to make sure he's OK."

She maximized the optic feed as Rurumi scuttled from the vestibule to the atrium. She nervously watched the phavatar's peripheral vision for any sign of life. But nothing stirred, except bits of trapped litter. The draught had stopped. With the airlock repaired, the train was no longer losing atmosphere. Unfortunately, there wasn't much left to lose.

Kiyoshi had locked himself into the bridge of the *Unicorn* to keep his passengers from bothering him. But he couldn't lock Jun out.

"Call her," the ghost said, buried from the waist down in Kiyoshi's workstation, so that Kiyoshi's hands went through him.

"Get out of my way, would you?"

"Call Elfrida. Tell her we're here."

This was not strictly true, but it would be in another few seconds. The backthrust phase of its trajectory complete, the *Unicorn* was decelerating into orbit around 4 Vesta.

Kiyoshi was interested in what else he could see around the protoplanet. Or rather, what he *couldn't* see. A massive asteroid like this, with a large settled population as well as active mining operations, should've been orbited by dozens if not hundreds of satellites. His scanners had only found two.

"I thought you were talking to the other guy," he said to Jun. "Mendoza? He's the one driving the train, isn't he?"

"He was. He's not responding anymore."

Kiyoshi looked up from his screens. "That's not good."

"No. It's not."

At that moment an unknown ship pinged them. "XX Longvoyager-class general-purpose transport Unicorn, registered to Loyola Holdings, Inc. What the fuck do you think you're doing? Over."

★

Elfrida screamed and clapped her hands over her eyes.

"You d-d-do scream a lot," Satterthwaite said. "'S a waste of energy, you know. No one's c-c-coming."

With her eyes shut, she couldn't see the ghastly information from Rurumi's optic feed. But it was burnt into her brain. The door of the driver's cab stood open. Mendoza lay face down outside it in a pool of vomit.

"There's nothing in my action parameters for this!" Rurumi texted pitifully. "Help! Please, Elfrida!"

Elfrida's forced herself to look again. Mendoza's face was cyanotic. She told Rurumi to carry him into the driver's cab. Not that that would bring him back to life, but she couldn't just leave him there on the floor. Why on earth had he left the cab? *Oh, Mendoza.*

"We're going really fast," Rurumi texted, staring fearfully at the monitors. The sides of the canyon were a gray blur.

"Yes, Rurumi, we're going fast." Elfrida looked at the array of manual controls. She turned to Satterthwaite. "Listen, you. I know your head hurts and everything, but it's time for you to pull yourself together and freaking *help*. The TEOTWAWKI option?"

"Błaszczykowski-Lee's idea. I never liked it. Smacks of hara-kiri." Satterthwaite shivered, too wretched to care that he'd used an incorrect word. "I don't want to die."

"We aren't going to die. A friend of mine is coming to get us." *Or, to get the Heidegger program.* But Elfrida kept that to herself. She didn't have a whole lot of options now, apart from ignoring her suspicions about Kiyoshi Yonezawa and hoping for the best. "He'll take us off, and then ... well, we can worry about that later. First we have to launch this whole doggone module into space. I'm in the cab, but I don't know what buttons to push, anything. *Help* me."

"Oh, dog," Satterthwaite said, chafing his hands. "Can you see the propulsion systems monitor?"

XXXV.

When the unknown ship hailed them, the brothers Yonezawa swung into a well-rehearsed routine. Jun minimized the propellant flow so their engine would look even weaker than it was. He also instructed their repair bots to head for the cargo bays, ready to jettison the construction materials and D/S bots they were carrying if necessary. Meanwhile, Kiyoshi responded. "XX unidentified ship, we are slingshotting around 4 Vesta on a trajectory with the following heliocentric parameters." He made some up. "It's called fuel economy. What's your excuse?"

The ship responded after twenty-three seconds, which either meant that it was six million kilometers away, allowing three-ish seconds for reaction time, or else that it was trying to make him think it was. "Hey, bud, no offense meant. Long as you're not planning to land on 4 Vesta. Be advised, you do not want to do that at the present time."

"It's the ISA," Kiyoshi said to Jun. "They're either six million kilometers from here, or trying to make us think they are."

"My scans aren't picking up anything closer than four million klicks, and that's just a cycler. There's something farther out, approaching on a direct trajectory from the inner system. Could be them."

"Another word of warning. If you pick up any communications from 4 Vesta while you're in the volume, ignore them. There're some bad actors down there, and they may be targeting innocent bystanders, so don't be that bystander, *Unicorn*. 'Kay?"

The ISA agent had not announced his identity, but he was making no effort to hide it. Only the ISA would emerge from nowhere to deliver cryptic warnings on the assumption that they would be obeyed. It was kind of like running into the PLAN. You knew they were out there, and you hoped you'd never meet them. But when you did, you knew immediately what you were dealing with.

"How long before they get here?" Kiyoshi said to Jun.

"About two hours, if I'm looking at the right ship. They're coming like a bat out of hell."

"Still, I'm gonna assume it will be a while before we're in range of whatever weaponry they've got."

"I'd feel safe making that assumption, yes. What have you got in mind?"

Kiyoshi did not answer. He was high on another of his custom drug cocktails, a blend of meth, caffeine, and L-carnitine that he thought of as an awareness enhancer. He said to the ISA agent, "Guess you got caught napping, huh?"

"What's that, *Unicorn*?" the response came twenty-two seconds later.

"That's what your wife says," Kiyoshi sent back, and jammed his shoulders into the depths of his couch, laughing.

"That was stupid," Jun said, arms folded.

"I was just jerking his chain. You've got no sense of humor. That was your problem when you were alive, and it still is." Kiyoshi sobered down. "Look, they'll try to slag us as soon as we're in range. All that nicey-nice bullshit is just to put you off your guard. They won't want to take the chance that the Heidegger program may have infected us."

"I wouldn't disagree with that analysis."

"I'm going to call the boss-man. I didn't want to tell him what we're doing here, but maybe he can talk to them."

Jun's face was unreadable. No one could do poker-face like the ghostly self-projection of an MI.

"You talk to Elfrida. If she can't pull off the emergency launch, all this is for nothing."

"*You* talk to her," Jun said.

"I know you don't want to do it," Kiyoshi roared. "Suck it up! You're a freaking machine intelligence. You don't need me holding your hand!"

Jun vanished.

Kiyoshi set his teeth. He radioed the boss. While he waited out the signal delay, he watched for signs of Jun's activity, but saw none. His screens merely displayed automated status reports as the *Unicorn* orbited Vesta in search of the train.

Well, either Jun would call Elfrida, or he'd hide in the sim and sulk. Either way, he couldn't stop Kiyoshi from unlimbering the guns.

Rurumi perched on the driver's couch, entering the commands that Elfrida relayed to her from Satterthwaite.

"Find the electromagnetic suspension control panel. It's in Electrical Subsystems. Look, over there, I see it. The ES controls should already be on manual. Yes? Good. You're doing great, Rurumi. Definitely more than just a pretty face ..." Elfrida broke off her soothing flow of text. "What's wrong?"

Rurumi's optic feed showed that she had scrambled off the couch. She peeked around the door of the driver's cab. "Someone's coming!"

Down the corridor walked a person in a high-fashion coverall with a loose, translucent outer layer, accessorized with boots, gloves, and a bubble helmet. Behind the lightly tinted faceplate Elfrida made out the face of Shoshanna Doyle.

Shoshanna smiled and held out her hands.

"She's talking to me," Rurumi texted. "She says everything's going to be OK!"

Another couple of seconds and Shoshanna would be in grabbing range. Elfrida wavered for barely a millisecond. Shoshanna had taken Cydney hostage. However she'd gotten aboard the Vesta Express, Elfrida was pretty sure she hadn't come to rescue them. She typed faster than she ever had in her life.

Rurumi jerked back into the cab, slammed the door, and locked it from the inside.

The door vibrated, as if Shoshanna was kicking it.

"Do *not* let her in," Elfrida typed. "Is she still talking to you?"

"Yes! She's telling me to let her in. Now she's asking me who's operating me. I have to tell her, Elfrida! It's the law."

"Oh, dog! Can't you lie?"

"I can't disobey my operating guidelines!"

"All right, I'll talk to her. Transmission follows: Hey, Shoshanna. This is Elfrida. Cydney's girlfriend, remember? We've met a few times at the Virgin Café. I'm trying to save the solar system right now, so go and annoy someone else. *Smile.*" Elfrida bared her teeth as she typed.

Rurumi transmitted Shoshanna's response. "You dumb bitch. I have to use the comms."

"It's not safe," Elfrida transmitted. "I'm not turning anything on that the Heidegger program might get hold of."

"Horse, barn door. It's already escaped."

"No way," Elfrida said aloud. She read Shoshanna's text to Satterthwaite as it continued to appear. "It hijacked the—"

"The phavatars," Satterthwaite said, simultaneously. "*Howl of despair.*" His teeth chattered. "She's the ISA agent we've been hearing so much about, isn't she? Better do what she says. If we had cooperated to begin with, we wouldn't be in this mess."

Elfrida set her jaw. She transmitted to Shoshanna, via Rurumi, "You've got a track record of deceit and excessive violence. You used Cydney and David and Win Khin and Big Bjorn and all of them to further your own agenda. You took the entire community hostage. You basically murdered that poor guy from the VA finance department. And I'm supposed to *trust* you? Sorry." She added to Rurumi, "Get ready to push that button." She hadn't heard back from Kiyoshi

Yonezawa. He'd said they would contact her when they were in position. What was she thinking, to trust a Japanese smuggler over a bona fide ISA agent?

It didn't matter. She had to get the Heidegger program off of this asteroid. Mendoza had died trying to save 4 Vesta. She couldn't let him down.

"See the status graph for the electromagnets?" she typed.

"Where are you, Elfrida?" Shoshanna texted, via Rurumi. "You're on this train, aren't you?"

"I'm not talking to you anymore."

Then the *Unicorn* finally pinged her. But it wasn't Kiyoshi whose image appeared in her call waiting area. It was Jun.

Panicking, Elfrida split the display in half.

Shoshanna: Guess you haven't seen what's happening in the Bellicia ecohood right now.	*Jun:* We're here.
Elfrida: What?	*Elfrida:* Thank dog. I'm ready to launch.
Shoshanna: Take a look.	

Via Rurumi, Shoshanna transmitted a feed from someone's retina cam. The anonymous vidder was bounding along a street in Bellicia, soaring over knots of citizens who were brawling with knives and clubs. People sprawled on the street like bundles of bloody rags. Instead of soyclouds, dirty puffs of smoke hung in the sky. The amber rays of SecondLight barely penetrated the haze. Things were burning.

Shoshanna: The fucking Heidegger program got in	

the same back door I was using and took over. Now the whole solar system is watching it butcher those people. Talk about propaganda.

Elfrida: Those are just regular people. I know that man. He's hitting that woman. He's *killing* her!

Shoshanna: The program has infected everyone who had a BCI and a connection to the hub. About ten percent of the solar system's population has BCIs, but here, that fraction is a lot higher. Students love gadgetry. So do the spaceborn. Now, it turns out that for the Heidegger program to convert you into a meat puppet, you need to have a BCI *and* some kind of non-organic neural stimulation mechanism. Again, students love that shit. Getting a dope store in your arm is practically a rite of passage for those little slebs in the Humanities department. Then there are all the phavatarists like Win Khin, whose phav-

Jun: God have mercy on their souls.

atars have now been taken over. So basically, this rich, privileged, cutting-edge community is as vulnerable as they come. Most people are hiding in their panic rooms. Figure in the fact that there are only five peacekeepers here, and the purebloods haven't got a chance. That's what you're seeing.

Elfrida: What can we do?

Shoshanna: Let me into the driver's cab and/or, I don't care which, stop the train. I've still got a few tricks up my sleeve.

Elfrida: Let me rephrase. What can we do that doesn't involve blowing people up?

Shoshanna: For crap's sake, this is an emergency.

Shoshanna: Open the fucking door!

Elfrida: Screw God!

Elfrida: If He exists, why is He letting these innocent people die?

Jun: Why did He let 11073 Galapagos be destroyed?

Elfrida: Cydney's still there, isn't she? Do you know if she's OK?

Shoshanna: I don't know if she's OK or not. All I've got is the same feeds that these amateur vloggers are spraying across the internet.

Elfrida: She's not a pure-blood.

Shoshanna: That's not going to help her much when they start lining everyone up for tabletop neurosurgery.

Elfrida: Oh crap, oh crap, oh crap.

Shoshanna: Bottom line, if you want her to have a chance, stop the train and let's kick some AI ass. I left a Flyingsaucer back there; we can use that for transport. Got a couple of spare suits on board, if you need one.

Elfrida: You don't have any answers, do you?

Elfrida: The train's not pressurized. I can't get out

of here.

Shoshanna: Well, I don't know where you are, but the breach has been repaired. The bots threw a bunch of splart at it. More importantly, the life-support systems are still working. By the time we get to the Flyingsaucer, we'll have the atmosphere back. We're going at Mach freaking 3. Deceleration is gonna take time.

Jun: You're asking the wrong question. The mystery isn't 'Why do bad things happen to good people?' but 'Why do good things happen to bad people?'

Elfrida: Are you saying I'm a bad person?

Jun: We're all sinners. But you were baptized. I remember that. I've got vid from the church. I was the altar server. You rejected Satan and all his works and dedicated your soul to Jesus Christ. You cried a lot.

Elfrida: That wasn't me, it was my phavatar.

Jun: And this isn't me, it's an MI.

Elfrida: So there's no

hope.

Jun: I didn't say that.

Elfrida: I think I'm freezing to death. I can't feel my fingers anymore. Thank dog for auto-complete.

Jun: Jesus is there with you. He is with you, Elfrida. I don't know anything else for sure, but I know this much: He is with you.

Elfrida: Well, that's just freaking great! That makes me feel a whole lot better! Why don't you just frag off and take your dead God with you?

Jun: Elfrida!

Shoshanna: Yo, Elfrida! What are you waiting for? I'm on your side. We both work for the UN. Who else is going to handle this? There is no one else. We're the first and last line of defense against a PLAN takeover of the solar system. I

Jun: Elfrida?

don't know if that means more to you than the life of your girlfriend; it shouldn't. But the two things are part of the same thing.

Jun: Are you talking to someone else?

Jun: Talk to me.

Kiyoshi: OK. Hey there, Elfrida, it's me. Are you having technical difficulties, or second thoughts?

Elfrida: I don't know. Both.

Shoshanna: Elfriiiiiidaaaa!

Kiyoshi: Make up your goddamn mind.

Elfrida: I'm opening the door now.

Elfrida: I'm sorry. I'm sorry.

Rurumi opened the door of the driver's cab.

Shoshanna stepped in. Mendoza's body was lying on the floor behind the driver's couch. Shoshanna casually trod on his hand. She glanced at the monitors, and smiled. Then she turned on Rurumi and stabbed the little phavatar in the face with a kitchen knife. Rurumi staggered, one of her saucer-like eyes destroyed. Shoshanna grabbed a handful of long blue hair, threw the phavatar out of the cab, and slammed the door.

"Ha, ha, ha," she said. *"Fun."*

xxxvi.

The Lord hears the cries of the poor. Blessed be the Lord! sang the computer of San Pedro Calungsod in Mendoza's dreams. He was about three-quarters dead. When he exited the driver's cab, the air pressure in the de Grey Institute had stood at about 0.4 atmospheres. The effect on Mendoza had been about what you'd expect if you were transported in the blink of an eye from sea level to the summit of Mount Aconcagua. To all intents and purposes, he had collapsed with a severe case of altitude sickness.

On top of vomiting and loss of consciousness, the symptoms of altitude sickness included hallucinations.

Mendoza's reeling mind had carried him back home to Manila, where he was always the odd boy out, picked on by the kids who ran wild in his neighborhood. He only ever felt safe in his mother's loving arms—and in the place where she, too, spent her free time: the parish church.

In the sacristy of San Pedro Calungsod, it was always dim, the tropical sunlight sublimated into veils of living color by the post-Vatican III stained glass windows, the doors always open so that the humid, fermented-smelling atmosphere swilled freely in and out, and the voices of cicadas and feral monkeys carried in from the graveyard. He was helping Father Benjamin and the choirmaster pick the hymns for Holy Week, an enjoyable activity that involved helping Father Benjamin with the computer. It felt so good to be able to help. Father Benjamin thought that Mendoza might have a religious vocation. But he must have made a mistake, because the speakers of Father Benjamin's computer roared out, "Depressurization event. Depressurization event," and a monkey walked in and bit the choirmaster's face off. Then it trod on Mendoza's hand.

He rose on his knees. Reality swirled, all the colors of

dreams going down the plughole.

"Must have made a mistake," Mendoza whispered.

A person in a strange, flimsy-looking spacesuit stood in front of the driver's couch, frowning at the monitors. The manual controls *were* hard to get the hang of, at first. People depended on smart interfaces. The mechanical world was an unfriendlier place. But it was real.

"Look," Mendoza said, toppling over and catching himself on the comms console. "You just have to push this button, here."

The solution that Mendoza and Jun Yonezawa had worked out together, which Director Błaszczykowski-Lee had separately devised under the rubric of the TEOT-WAWKI option, was the epitome of simplicity. With manual drive enabled—and without Bob on duty to prevent what the supercomputer would doubtless have seen as a fat-finger accident—Mendoza's command killed the electromagnets that kept the Vesta Express on its track. The C-shaped, millipede-like arms on the bottom of the Vesta Express instantly turned into dumb lumps of metal.

In the blink of an eye, the Vesta Express ceased to be a maglev. Now it was just an object travelling at about 3,000 kph—much, much faster than escape velocity.

Centrifugal force crushed the ex-electromagnets against the underside of the track. Sparks sprayed into the Vestan night. This display lasted for about 0.5 seconds. Then all the magnet arms broke at once.

The Vesta Express soared out of the ringrail canyon. The storage module oscillating dangerously behind the de Grey Institute', it hurtled into space.

Kiyoshi gaped at his optic feed. After the barest instant of amazement, he told Jun to pursue the receding dot that was the Vesta Express. He slid down from his throne and strolled over to the gunnery officer. He was back in the sim. This way, he didn't have to listen to Captain Haddock and company banging on the door of the bridge and shouting piratically at him about their rights.

The gunnery officer, an eager young man from Hokkaido, saluted.

"See that?" Jun said, his finger tracking the Vesta Express on the gunner's radar plot.

"Yes, sir! What is it?"

"A threat to humanity. Blow it into the Oort Cloud."

"Sir," the gunner said, but he didn't move.

Kiyoshi tensed. "Use the coil gun," he recommended. "We're well within range."

"Sir, that vessel has innocent civilians on board."

Kiyoshi glared at Jun, who was standing at the astrogator's workstation, chewing a toothpick and watching.

"Speak for yourself, instead of puppeting these poor slebs," Kiyoshi said.

Every officer on the bridge stood up. They walked over to Jun and ranged themselves behind him. "We are Knights of the Order of St. Benedict of Passau," they said, high and low and young and old voices speaking in unison. "We are sworn to defend the Church and all the scattered children of Christendom against the army of Satan enfleshed."

Kiyoshi shivered. It was uncanny, and desperately sad.

"That freaking Order of yours," he said.

"You almost joined, too," said the cyberwarfare officer.

"Yeah, I did. But someone had to drive this truck, to earn some cash so you kids could sit around singing hymns. And I was the eldest." Kiyoshi shook his head. Why was he wasting time on this argument? He snapped his fingers, and the sim vanished. Back on the bridge of the *Unicorn,* he scrambled out of his nest. The officers were all gone. Only Jun hung spreadeagled above him like a ghost out of a Japanese horror vid.

"We've lost comms with the train," Kiyoshi said, craning his neck to look up at him. "Chances are they're all dead in there."

"I heard what the boss said to you," Jun replied. "He told you to frag the train to score points with the ISA."

"He actually told me to frag it on the ground. And not to worry about collateral damage. Eh, he can be a bit trigger-happy when he feels threatened. But the idea is basically good. Do the ISA's dirty work for them, and we might come out ahead. Otherwise, we'll have to dump this ship, because the ISA will never leave us alone again."

"What if he's wrong?"

"He knows how they think." The crummy old air circulation system rattled. Kiyoshi rubbed his mouth. "Why do you want to save her so bad?"

"It's a point of principle."

"She *ate* you."

"That's why."

"Of course it is. Of course it is." Kiyoshi pushed off, rising straight through Jun (his vision momentarily grayed out, as if he were dizzy and seeing black spots). They floated, facing each other, in freefall. "MI COMMAND," Kiyoshi grated, holding the ghost's eyes. "Eliminate that target."

"No," Jun said.

"Fine, then I'll do it myself."

He went through the motions. He logged into the gunnery computer and trained the coil gun on the Vesta Express. He gave the command to fire. Nothing happened. "*Sigh,*" Kiyoshi murmured. Almost as an afterthought, he triggered the second-hand Wetblanket system he'd been using for years. *That* deployed without a hitch, of course.

He looked up at Jun, who was still hanging spreadeagled in the air. "If I deleted you from the hub, would I be able to use the guns?"

"Probably not," Jun said. "Because the hub would shut

down. You wouldn't be able to breathe for much longer, either."

"You *are* the hub. You've merged with it. Emergent behavior. They warned me this might happen." Kiyoshi stared sightlessly at the battered bulkheads. He remembered the simulation software user's guide, the repeated and explicit warnings not to slave IRL functionality to a sim sufficiently detailed that it could act as a learning environment for a high-end MI.

"I'm not the hub," Jun said. "The hub is me. There's a difference, but I'm not sure what it is. You're wondering why I still say the Divine Office every day, why I resurrected the Order with a bunch of secondary personalities from the sim? Because those are the only things I'm sure about. Everything else is logic and rubble in the vacuum."

Kiyoshi pushed off and went to touch Jun's arm in an instinctive gesture of comfort. His hand went straight through the projection, of course. Now it was his turn to fight tears. He hung there wondering, *What have I done?*

The Wetblanket system reported that it had acquired the Vesta Express and was retrieving it. The Wetblanket system was a 'blanket' of nanofiber mesh a kilometer wide with integrated propulsion units. Designed for mining applications, to stop debris from flying into space, it could also be used to capture slow-moving objects (slow being a relative concept, of course), such as loose cargo. Or a knock-off of the Guggenheim Museum tumbling through the vacuum with several probably-dead people and a fragment of a PLAN ship aboard.

"Don't bring it back here," Kiyoshi instructed the Wetblanket. "Maneuver it into a stable orbit, a good ways away from us." He glanced at Jun. "It still isn't responding to our signals."

"I'm on it," Jun said, zipping to the real-life astrogator's console. His flying fingers did not disturb the dust of ages.

"I'll send the Superlifter over for a looksee." As usual, he was cheerful and decisive now that he'd got his way. "Would be good if someone went with. As you've often mentioned, we don't have any drones."

"*Sigh.* Why do I let you get me into these messes?" Kiyoshi asked. Despite himself, he was smiling. He went to the door of the bridge and threw it open. "Salvage mission. Any volunteers?"

xxxvii.

Elfrida opened her eyes. At first she thought she was dead. Her baptism must have been a crock, after all, because she'd gone to Hell. *Clearly* this was Hell.

In front of her floated Captain Haddock's brother Codfish.

"Shiver me timbers!" he exclaimed. "She's alive!"

Elfrida tried to speak. Something covered her mouth and nose. A rebreather mask. She pulled it off. The air was obviously all right, since Codfish had his helmet off. The movement made her bobble away from him. They were in freefall. "We launched," she said wonderingly.

"We sure did," said another person, removing his rebreather mask to speak.

"Mendoza!"

Elfrida kicked off from an overhead hatch. She zoomed across the kitchen, cannoned into Mendoza, and hugged him tightly. He squeezed her back. Still embracing, they tumbled into the ceiling, which was stained with the contents of pouches and tubes that had exploded during the depressurization event. "This place smells like a Filipino street market," Mendoza laughed. "It's killing me."

"I thought you were dead!"

"So did I."

"She said we would get the atmosphere back pretty soon. I guess that was the only thing she *wasn't* lying about."

The kitchen was crowded. The two female pirates from Captain Haddock's gang were floating to and fro, stealing the fancier kitchen appliances. Julian Satterthwaite, Jimmy Liu, and Wang Gulong lay on stretchers dry-gripped to the floor. Medibots fussed over them, supervised by a hatchet-faced woman in an EVA suit and a poke bonnet. This incongruous attire barely registered amidst the tumult in Elfrida's mind.

"Where is she?"

"Shoshanna?" Mendoza's face turned grim.

"Yeah. I let her into the cab. Dog, I am so freaking stupid."

"Don't feel bad. I got fooled, too. I guess we're just too trusting."

"Not anymore," Elfrida said. "Not anymore."

A medibot was chasing her through the air, holding out a pair of gloves. She let it put them on her. She couldn't do it herself, because her fingers weren't working properly.

"You are suffering from superficial frostbite," the medibot chirped. "These gloves will apply gentle heat. Your fingers may start to sting or swell as they warm up. If so, please ask me for a painkiller."

"Go frag yourself." Elfrida pushed off and arrowed out of the kitchen.

"Y'know, the thing about my employers? They ask questions first, and shoot later. As in, *much* later. After the electroshock, and the waterboarding, and the truth therapy sessions."

The thing formerly known as Shoshanna Doyle spread its hands in a what-can-you-do gesture.

Tall and lean, Shoshanna would have been attractive, if she were still human. She had a spiky shock of green hair and a crooked, teasing smile. She'd have been just Kiyoshi's type, in fact. It was a shame.

He had absolutely no doubt that she was not in any meaningful sense alive anymore, though her body moved, and her voice was resonant and humorous.

"You need to be aware what you're dealing with," she said.

"Oh, I'm aware of that," Kiyoshi said.

"I don't think you are. You think the ISA will be happy if you blow me away? Making it impossible for them to ever find out what happened here? It's called the *Information Security Agency* for a reason. Destroy me, and I guarantee your next place of residence will be a secure holding facility on Pallas."

The thing might be telling the truth. After all, it seemed to have all Shoshanna's memories, and she would know the ISA's priorities better than the boss-man did.

Kiyoshi brought the laser rifle up to his shoulder, anyway. Then, on a whim, he lowered it. "What's it like being you? Nemesis of humanity, destroyer of asteroids and orbital habitats, sowing chaos and terror across a volume thirty AUs wide?"

Shoshanna's smile softened. "It's fun," she said.

Kiyoshi felt a pang of desperation. He knew then that she was telling the truth about the ISA. They *had* to get more information than this. "You target a whole quarter of the human race for genocide just because they've got a few of the wrong genes. Why do you do that? Race is nothing. Eighty percent of genetic variation is among individuals. Classical racial markers make up only about six percent of total human variation. On the teleological level, that's meaningless."

"Lamarckian genetic memory, bucko," the Shoshanna-thing said. It hiked one boot on the back of the telepresence couch it was standing on. It acted cool as a cucumber, despite the laser rifle Kiyoshi was aiming at it. "Race is culture is destiny. DNA is just shorthand for that other stuff. It correlates surprisingly well with pretty much every achievement metric, although we're not allowed to say so, since eighty percent of genetic variation is among individuals, yadda yadda—the gospel of the 23rd century, which you've obviously swallowed whole. And by the way, just to correct another of your mistaken assumptions? We're not your enemies. We're your saviors, if you'd only pay attention to what the universe is trying to tell you."

"Fuck you. Jesus Christ is my savior." The words came out of Kiyoshi's mouth unbidden. At the same time he pulled the trigger. Staggered laser pulses appeared to erupt out of the Shoshanna-thing's face in puffs of red. It tumbled backwards into the air. He tracked it, holding the trigger down. The smell of vaporized brains added to the slaughterhouse reek in the air.

By the time it hit the far wall of the telepresence center, the thing formerly known as Shoshanna Doyle had no head left.

Kiyoshi kicked off and gave it another burst, just to make sure. He flew over the carnage in the telepresence cubicle farm. He'd shot everything that popped its head up, until the Shoshanna-thing came out of the storage module and tried to sweet-talk him. A few of the cupcake-things were still alive. He fixed that.

"You're getting a lot of mileage out of that rifle," said Jun, following along. For this mission, Kiyoshi had agreed to let Jun see with his eyes, or rather with his retinal implants, something he didn't usually allow. They needed to make sure everything got recorded and stored in the *Unicorn's* datacore.

"Yeah," Kiyoshi said. "Who'd have thought the Neu Ordnung Amish would have brought along a bunch of HabSafe™ delayed-pulse laser rifles optimized for soft-tissue penetration, for killing people without accidentally breaching a pressurized structure? Very handy."

"The new wave of colonists: rejecting modern culture, except for the good bits."

"The tricky part is going to be getting the guns away from Haddock and company once we're done here." As Kiyoshi spoke, he jerked the rifle up, lest he accidentally shoot Captain Haddock himself. The goateed *namsadang* squatted between the partitions, one leg hooked under a telepresence couch. He was aiming a HabSafe™ rifle at a thing curled in a fetal position and hogtied with IV lines. This thing was not a cupcake. It had a retro tattoo of wiring on its bald skull, and a dopey smile on its face. "Any reaction from this one?" Kiyoshi asked.

"Yeah, he said something a minute ago, but I couldn't catch it." Under stress, Haddock was forgetting to speak pirate. "Why are these rifles so noisy?"

"It's an effect. So people know you're shooting them." Kiyoshi kicked the captive thing like a football. He was surprised how much satisfaction he was getting out of this.

"Are you sure this guy is one of them?"

"Can't you tell?"

"Not like you can. *That's* weird. Also, where did you learn to shoot like that?"

"At home," Kiyoshi said. "We used to have pirate trouble." He grinned.

"You high?" Haddock said suspiciously.

"Just a few cc's of morale juice. The same stuff Star Force uses."

The captive thing's eyes opened and fastened on them.

"Hullo," it slurred, "You here for the secret of human happiness?"

"That was it," Haddock said. "You know, I had a shipmate once who downloaded a porno sim from the wrong site; his BCI crashed. This reminds me of that."

"Let's keep it alive, for now." Kiyoshi looked across the blood-splattered cubicle farm. A door led off the walkway on the far side. That was where Shoshanna had come from. "Stay here. Make sure it doesn't try anything."

Pirates were not good at obeying orders. Haddock tied the captive thing up more securely and followed Kiyoshi into the storage module. Though Kiyoshi didn't say anything, he was glad of the company. They darted in and out of cavernous rooms stuffed with consumables and spare parts. "Captious caterpillars!" Haddock gloated. "This mission is definitely going to have worth it."

Kiyoshi's rifle sight tracked across white ceramic walls. When they came to a locked door, he dialed the HabSafe™'s pulse energy and frequency up to maximum and set the muzzle against the hinges. Five smoky, noisy minutes later, the door swung back. They aimed their helmet lamps into darkness. The beams picked out the ragged tusk-like shape that had haunted Kiyoshi since the first time he saw it on the *Unicorn's* optic feed. But now the inner curve of the tusk hung open: a hatch.

Kiyoshi drifted closer.

Inside was a human-sized cavity, encrusted with instruments and life-support equipment.

A fighter pilot's cockpit, Kiyoshi thought, realizing at last what the fragment was.

In the couch lay a naked girl, sucking her thumb.

"Did you say something?" Haddock said.

"No," Kiyoshi started, and then he heard it, too. The same voice he'd heard over his suit radio, fourteen long months ago. The slurred voice of someone talking in her sleep.

"Warum ist ... warum ist überhaupt Seiendes und nicht vielmehr Nichts?"

"What the hell is that?" Haddock said.

"Spam," Kiyoshi said. He'd ignored it back then, and he could ignore it now. It was just another version of the Infinite Fun Space package. Different bait, same trap.

"Yonezawa-san! Yonezawa-san!"

Elfrida Goto arrowed into the room. She bounced off the top of the tusk and floated over their heads. She raised gloved hands to shade her eyes from their lamps. She must have seen the life-support cradle and its occupant, but she was not to be sidetracked. "This isn't over," she gasped. "Not even close. I guess you aren't aware. The Heidegger program—it's loose in the Bellicia ecohood—it's slaughtering purebloods, enslaving everyone else! Don't you watch the news?"

"Well, yeah," Kiyoshi said, annoyed. "But what do you want me to do about it? We're up here. They're down there."

"The ISA will kill them all!"

"Probably. But we've got the original copy of the program." He waved at the fragment. "This, right here. This is where it started. This is what counts."

"*People* don't count?" She pushed tangles of dark brown hair away from tear-filled eyes.

"You got someone you care about down there?"

"Y-yes. My—my girlfriend."

Jun, uncharacteristically, was silent. Kiyoshi subvocalized to him: ~*No comment?*

"You're right," Jun said via Kiyoshi's transducer implants. "We can't do anything for them."

~*Good to know your crusading zeal has limits.*

"I may be a crusader. I'm not a kamikaze. That habitat is a death trap. But that doesn't mean the people inside are doomed. See this [attached]? Those are ships."

~*WTF? Let me talk to them.*

"Sure, if you want. But you'll need to use my translator program. They only speak Chinese."

The personnel of the Big Dig were evacuating. The VA staff had their own ship in the camouflaged parking lot at the foot of Rheasilvia Mons, the SUV (Space Utility Vessel) *Giggle Factor*. The Chinese pioneers had two ships in addition to the *Kěkào*, which was not here at the moment. Both the *Zhèngzhōu* and the *Húludao* towered over the *Giggle Factor* like skyscrapers. They were that big because they had originally transported the Chinese construction machinery to Vesta. The construction machinery was now being abandoned. Everything was being abandoned.

Fiona Sigurjónsdóttir sank into her couch with a whimper. Everyone else was staring rapt into the middle distance. They were all watching the feeds streaming out of the Bellicia ecohood. The PLAN agent had brought the transmitter at the Bellicia-Arruntia spaceport back online, in an act of pure malice, it seemed, just so that it could spew forth these scenes of carnage and terror. Sigurjónsdóttir had been watching, too, until she saw a girl the age of her elder daughter bludgeoned with a tree branch, and then she hadn't been able to take it anymore.

Someone touched her arm. She looked up at José Running Horse. His expression was unfamiliar. *Kind.* "Gonna be OK, Fee. The Heidegger program sent three phavatars our way. I slagged 'em from orbit. The only real advantages it had were stealth and surprise, and now it's lost those, it can't mess with us. We'll be out of here in a few minutes, back in London in a few weeks. You'll be stepping off the plane and hugging your kids. Just focus on that."

"I'm not worried about *us*," Sigurjónsdóttir said. She slumped against him.

Running Horse sat down beside her and held her while she cried. "I'm not worried about us, either," he said.

Cydney cowered in Big Bjorn's treehouse. From downhill, she could hear shouts, screams, and explosions. This was everyone's worst nightmare: phavatars turning on humans, slaughtering their makers. Some of the STEM students were fighting back. But it sounded like more was going on than that. It sounded like a war.

"It's gonna be OK," Bjorn said, patting her back.

She twisted away, unable to bear his reassurances. "It is not gonna be OK! Shoshanna's doing this. I don't know how, but she's doing it. I told you she was psychotic. She's going to kill everyone!"

"I guess things kinda spiraled out of control," Bjorn said sadly.

"We had a chance to stop her, and we didn't. This is on us." With a moan of despair, Cydney burrowed under the edge of Bjorn's rustic patchwork quilt. The fragrance of dry herbs overpowered the smell of smoke in the air.

Her head bumped into something with sharp corners.

"Ow! Did you stuff your quilt with e-waste?"

Bjorn's ursine face was not very expressive. Even when grimacing guiltily, he still looked like Love-A-Lot Bear. But that grimace told Cydney all she needed to know.

She tugged at the seams of the quilt. Bjorn sighed, moved her out of the way, and ripped a claw through a patch with the U-Vesta logo on it. Polyfoam scraps and dried herbs spilled over their knees. Cydney reached forward and brushed off the astrophysics lab's supercomputer workstation.

"It was here all along," she said with an accusing glare.

Bjorn sighed. "I believed," he said. Gunfire punctuated his words. "I believed we were being treated unfairly. The STEM guys were keeping secrets from us. That's not right, you know? A community can't flourish without transparency and equality."

"I dunno," Cydney said. "Earth's managed it all these years."

She heaved the workstation onto its side. The housing was cracked. One panel had been removed. Leaves and stalks clogged the delicate circuit boards within.

"Guess they never got it talking?"

Bjorn shook his head.

"Not like it matters anymore."

But Cydney snapped a few pictures with her necklace camera and sent them to Aidan in LA with a note: *Does this look totally fragged to you, or fixable?* Since the comms came back online, she'd been in intermittent contact with her team, although they couldn't, of course, do anything to help.

A couple of minutes later, she got a message from Aidan.

He wouldn't have seen her pictures of the workstation yet. This had been sent a quarter of an hour ago.

"Hey, Cyds, your feed's not updating. Have the comms gone down again? If you get this, update your feed ASAP."

The truth was that Cydney had stopped vidding when she and Bjorn fled into the woods. It wouldn't help her image for her fans to see her hiding under a bear's bed while a war was going on.

"Our access figures are out of the freaking atmosphere. We're the go-to feed on this story, but the viewers want live vid. Every second they don't see it, they're clicking away to BelterNews and Adam the Aggregator. So, y'know, if you get this …"

"Adam the Aggregator," Cydney gasped. "I hate that fucking sleb."

She jumped up. Put her eye to one of the leafy gaps in the treehouse walls. All she could see was more trees. She bounded over to the top of the ladder.

"… *be careful, of course,*" Aidan's tiny voice concluded.

"Where are you going?" Bjorn said.

"To get the story."

xxxviii.

After a short but hair-raising hop around the circumference of Vesta, the *Zhèngzhōu* and the *Húludao* landed at the Bellicia-Arruntia spaceport. Actually, it would be more accurate to say they landed *on* it. The launch pad was not designed to accommodate two cargo transports the size of ten-storey buildings. Their fusion drives incinerated the terminal, the control tower, and the fuel depot. When the heat and light from this act of apathy-based utility died down, the two ships plonked themselves on the wreckage like a pair of elephants sitting on the ashes of a campfire.

The Extropian Collective, watching from the *Kěkào*, said, "*Cool!*"

The *Kěkào* jinked under them. It flew down to the surface and buzzed the Bellicia ecohood. Its AI made a series of blindingly fast calculations about the terrain. Determining that it could safely land on the road to the spaceport, the *Kěkào* alighted outside the Bremen Lock and melted the airlock's iron gates with its fusion drive.

The Chinese ban on armaments for civilian spaceships—a policy driven by 10% ideology and 90% domestic political considerations—had ironically prompted Chinese ships to master the gray art of slagging things with their own exhaust.

"We call this 'fart-bombing,'" a robot stewardess told the Extropians, who were rubbing their bruises from the rough landing. "The Chinese people have a dark sense of humor!"

Just how dark was soon to be revealed.

The *Kěkào* deployed its drones, a.k.a. the cabin crew. Clad in their jaunty uniforms, they picked their way around the molten ruin of the gates. They found the actual entrance to the airlock, a giant valve hidden beneath the overhang, and proceeded to demolish it with cutter lasers (sanctioned for repair and maintenance purposes).

From its rear end the *Kĕkào* extruded the same jointed tunnel it had used to rescue the Extropian Collective from 550363 Montego. This looked remarkably like a boarding gate. The cabin crew sealed the gate to the airlock with what appeared to be clingfilm. Then they walked into the Bellicia ecohood, much as the PLAN agent's phavatars had done a few hours earlier.

Below, a dirty blanket of smoke obscured the pastoral vista of lake, town, and woods.

"Good afternoon, humans! This is the pre-boarding announcement for Flight 001 to the nearest place of safety. We are now inviting those passengers with small children, and any passengers requiring special assistance, to begin boarding at this time!"

Silence; the distant crackle and pop of gunfire.

"Don't all rush the gate at once," the *Kĕkào*, in the form of the lone male steward, commented to itself, in the form of the other stewards. They tittered obligingly.

Cydney edged around the Diadji Diouf Humanities Center, her heart pounding. Something exploded inside the building. She and Big Bjorn both flinched. They had seen nothing newsworthy on way here, except for a few people running in the other direction. The emptiness of the campus was scarier than a riot would have been.

A girl sailed around the corner at the micro-gravity equivalent of a dead run, each step carrying her ten meters through the air. A muscular man, naked but for a zebra-print thong, hurtled after her.

~*Holy crap, guys,* Cydney subvocalized to her fans. ~*Is it just me, or does that guy look like Marmaduke Shagg?*

She and Bjorn shrank into the green curtain of the Diadji Diouf Humanities Center. The man caught the girl and dragged her, screaming, across the quad into the STEM building.

"Come on," Cydney told Bjorn. Her heart still pounded, but now it was the rhythm of a Xhosa war drum, pulsing adrenaline into her veins. She dragged Bjorn across the quad.

They climbed the green curtain, past the NO CLIMBING signs, to the patio of the STEM cafeteria, on the second floor.

The patio windows were closed. People's backs pressed against the inside of the glass, as if a packed-out rally were being held in the cafeteria. Cydney cracked the window open and slid in. The people nearest rolled their eyes like terrified goats. They smelled of body odor and fear.

Cydney jumped on tiptoes. Beyond the crowd, at the doors of the cafeteria, stood two nearly-naked people who looked like the hermaxploitation stars Butto Klüsterfück and Lotta Rogering. The crowd was so dense that they hadn't seen her slide in through the window.

"OK," she murmured to her fans. "We have half the student body being held captive by a dangerous gang of, um, porn stars. *Snerk.*"

"They're phavatars," muttered a woman sitting on the floor by her legs.

"Oh. OK. Phavatars based on porn stars."

"They killed all the purebloods. They took our guns and, oh my dog, it was like a mass execution. Like something out of the twenty-first century. They dumped the bodies in Olbers Lake."

"Whoa. *Whoa.* Update that," Cydney said quietly. "We are being held captive by the PLAN."

"And the other half of the student body," the woman said. "And half of the faculty. They're showing their true colors. You guys were right about them. I wish I'd never taken this job."

There was a disturbance at the far door. Cydney bounced on her tiptoes again. Dean Garcia swaggered in at the head of a phalanx of professors and lab assistants, all stripped to their underwear. Garcia, surprisingly, favored lacy lingerie.

Blood striped their limbs and faces, as if in grotesque imitation of warriors painted up for a tribal festival.

~*This is some Cro-Magnon shit,* Cydney subvocalized. ~*I thought the PLAN were all high-tech. Maybe this is what you get when you cross high-tech terror with academic politics. Snerk.* Her trademark giggle sounded weak.

Menacing the crowd with the STEM students' homemade rocket launchers, Garcia and her henchpersons grabbed the nearest captives and dragged them out. The remainder cowered like blades of grass when the wind blows.

"You get a choice," said the woman beside Cydney. "Convert or die."

Cydney looked at the woman for the first time. She only had one eye—the other was a steel metrology instrument. It brimmed with tears. Her chunky body quivered in panic.

"Haven't we met?" Cydney said. "Oh, I remember: you were visiting Dr. James when I was there. You were totally rude. Hang on, I've got a call."

"Cydney?"

"Elfrida," Cydney gasped. Suddenly, she wanted to cry.

"Are you OK?"

"No. Yes. No."

"Listen. We're watching your feed. Get out of there. Most people are hiding downtown. The PLAN attacked the campus first. I guess they're recruiting an army to take the town. But anyone that hasn't been corrupted can still escape. There are ships ..."

Cydney wriggled back to the window. She could see Bjorn waiting for her on the patio, his fur full of leaves, the rucksack that held the workstation on his back.

"Cydney? Cydney!"

"I'm here," Cydney gritted. "Ships. When. Now? Where. Bremen Lock, I guess. I gotta find a spacesuit."

"No, you don't. The evacuation shuttle is docked with the airlock. They kinda remodelled it to enable direct docking. But Cydney? I need your help. Those people downtown. Some of them are children, Cydney. There are families hiding in the Branson Habs, too. Hundreds of them."

Cydney slid out onto the patio. The air, although smoky and foul, smelt like perfume after the stench in the cafeteria.

"Cydney, I need you to gather them up. Find some people that you're sure aren't corrupted to help you. But the shuttle can only take about two hundred people at a time, so if everyone tries to board at once, it's going to be a disaster. Make people understand that they *can* get away, but they *must* let the children and old people and, uh, pregnant women and so forth go first. And they might need help getting to the airlock, so I need you to organize—"

"Who do you think I am, the captain of the *Titanic?*"

Cydney jumped off the patio. Bjorn and the cyborg woman followed her. It was only two floors down, so they landed lightly.

Elfrida's voice sounded far away. "I think you're the daughter of a Xhosa chieftain. I think you're too ambitious to pass up this chance to be a heroine. And I also think you're a better woman than you yourself know."

Cydney clenched her fists. "Oh shit, oh shit, oh *shit,*" she said. Then she subvocalized: *~Guys? Listen up. I need your help ...*

The evacuation of the Bellicia ecohood was celebrated system-wide as a triumph of crowdsourcing. Cydney's appeal went viral. Within an hour it had reached pretty much all the scattered friends and relations of the people trapped in the ecohood. Most of these were already on the net with their loved ones, helplessly witnessing their travails from afar. Now they put them in touch with Cydney. Based on the profiles her team in LA crunched for her, she instructed only those with small children or invalids in the family to head for the Bremen Lock. In this way the *Kĕkào* was able to make several runs to the *Zhèngzhōu* and *Húludao*, evacuating the most vulnerable residents, before the news got out, and the rush started.

Cydney then staged a more muscular intervention. Big Bjorn had rounded up the surviving Friends of David Reid (including David Reid himself, sprung from hospital) and a few other students who did not have BCIs. They fought hand to hand with the PLAN's meat puppets (as everyone in the system was now calling those infected by the Heidegger program), as well as anyone who refused to wait in line. Cydney's unthinking phrase, "This is some Cro-Magnon shit," echoed around the solar system, as images emerged of students, professors, and baristas clubbing each other with homemade guns that had run out of ammo. This went on for hour after bloody hour, while people escaped in small groups.

The true test of the Friends of David Reid came when the PLAN's phavatars attacked them. For a whole sol, the phavatars had simply ignored the evacuation and continued processing people through the university's Francis Galton Biomedicine Research Center. Perhaps the surgery ran out of kit, leaving Marmaduke, Butto, and the rest at loose ends. Or perhaps it dawned on the AI animating them, as it emerged from its purloined computing resources like a womb-wet cyclops, that no self-respecting supervillain would let people get away.

The phavatars charged up the hill and plowed into the crowds waiting at the Bremen Lock. They ripped off limbs, twisted off heads, and hurled them into the air. Pandemonium rippled across the crater's inner slope. Screams sounded like the crying of birds in the thin air.

Cydney was ready. "Do it," she said to Elfrida.

"Do it," Elfrida said to her new friend, Colonel Oleg Threadley of the ISA.

"Do it," Colonel Threadley said to his crew.

A hail of missiles stormed towards Vesta and blew up the power plant that provided Bellicia with electricity.

Instantly, the grid failed.

The air stopped circulating.

The wifi went down.

And the PLAN's phavatars, dependent as they were on wireless charging—for they had long since exhausted their onboard power reserves—slumped in place like domestic maidbots that some naughty child had nudged out of their operating area.

Cydney bent double, panting, and wiped something dark and gooey out of her eyes.

The sun mirrors, stuck at their brightest setting, bathed the battlefield in the weak but pitiless light of another Vestan day.

It took another twenty-four hours to get everyone out. The last evacuees had to be carried out, breathing supplementary oxygen. With the air circulation down, the atmosphere had decayed into a noxious haze of CO_2 and particulate matter, contaminated by the fires that continued to smoulder in town. Cydney, at her own insistence, was the last person of all to be stretchered on board the *Kĕkào*.

"My daddy always said," she gasped, "utopia is for suckers. Guess he was right."

"I'm filing suit for seventeen trillion spiders in compensation," said Sir Harry Persson, whose ship was still a week away from Vesta. "And that's just for the rail launcher. You slebs are going to rue the day you targeted this company. I have friends on the President's Advisory Council."

Over the encrypted channel connecting their ships, Colonel Oleg Threadley said, "I'm *on* the President's Advisory Council. And I'm not really a colonel, either."

He went to do some other stuff. Thirty minutes went by.

"Surprised?" Threadley sent, when he came back to find

that Persson still hadn't responded. "Well, I wouldn't expect a mere corporate tycoon to know how the world works."

He went for lunch. Halfway through his composed salad of nutriblocks, he was summoned back to the secure comms room. Persson, on the screen, looked twenty years older than he had this morning.

"You win. I'll settle for a guarantee that Virgin Atomic will not be prosecuted for our alleged role in this tragedy. Hell, after the survivors have extorted their pound of flesh, there'll be nothing left for you to expropriate, anyway."

Threadley informed his superiors that Persson had agreed to keep his mouth shut. He sent Persson a non-disclosure agreement to that effect.

"By the way," Persson added when he returned the documentation, "I'm keeping my island. Separately incorporated in Nauru. The stakeholders won't get their grubby little fingers on *that*. Come and visit when you're back on Earth; we can talk about how you ended your information blackout of 4 Vesta at precisely the moment when our problems stopped being the ISA's fault, and turned into a system-wide edumercial for the ISA itself. I expect I'll be able to chuckle about it by that time."

Threadley himself chuckled when he heard this. The CEO wasn't slow—just out of touch. Aloud, he said, "Fine. You keep your island. We're keeping Błaszczykowski-Lee, Satterthwaite, and Meredith-Pike."

None of this, of course, was publicized. Judging by the news feeds, you would have thought Cydney had evacuated 100,000 people all by herself. Not a word was said about the involvement of the Chinese. That two transports had fortunately been on hand was acknowledged, but not what flag they flew. This was by agreement between the UN and Chinese governments. The former wanted the credit for itself. The latter did not want it known that the Liberty Village experiment had been sanctioned in the first place.

But in Hebei Province, in a posh arboreal bubbleburb, the grieving friends and families of Jimmy Liu and Wang Gulong vowed to try again.

Meanwhile, in Vesta orbit, and in conference rooms on Earth populated by very important and very grumpy people who had not had any sleep in days, the maneuvering continued at a frenetic pace.

xxxix.

Elfrida participated in a low-level meeting in Toronto. The delegates sat around wrought iron tables pushed together on a patio wreathed with convolvulus. Across the street, a café window framed Elfrida's reflection: an androgynous, multiracial asimov-class phavatar in a Roman-style tunic with a big sticker on its chest.

> **HELLO / BONJOUR!**
> **My name is / Je m'appelle**
>
> Elfrida Goto (Space Corps)

She felt floaty and unreal, thanks to the painkillers coursing through her body. She marvelled at the round yellow sun in Earth's sky, the sparrows snatching crumbs from the patio, and the comical bustle of waiters threading between the tables under one full gravity. This meeting had been convened at the order of the Select Security Council to produce an expert briefing that would help the pols decide what to do about 4 Vesta.

The delegates represented various UN agencies and institutes specializing in IT, MI, and AI. For all that, it was not a high-level meeting. Elfrida knew that because *she* was here, and also because they were at a café. The nicer the setting, the less important the proceedings.

A man named Derek Lorna, the acting director of the UN's Leadership in Robotics Institute on Luna, spoke about self-improvement pathways and resource-acquisition utility goals. Elfrida caught the scary syllable she'd first heard from Mendoza: *FOOM*.

In response, the woman from MIT rambled on about containment. The thrust of her remarks seemed to be that an isolated asteroid like 4 Vesta was a pretty good sandbox, and the Heidegger program should be kept there for observation, like a virus in a laboratory.

Wise nods greeted this patently terrible idea, which had first been had, of course, by the doomed scientists of the de Grey Institute. Elfrida realized that the further people were from the threat, the less they could grasp it. That was why she was here. She was supposed to tell them about the battle for the Bremen Lock, the murder of 5,639 purebloods by shooting or drowning in Olbers Lake, and the conversion of the Francis Galton Biomedicine Research Center into a chop-shop where phavatars, ankle-deep in blood, had rewired people's brains to run the PLAN's neuroware. But words eluded her.

The man from Triton ("Hello! My name is Galt Nursultan, CEO, Scoopership Inc.") spoke up. "I knew Adrian Smith," said his phavatar. "He was into third-wave poetic syncretism. Sweetest guy you ever met. The Heidegger program hijacked his ID and sent itself to us. It infected three hundred and forty-one people before we could stop it. Two hundred and eight of those committed suicide. We figure they didn't have the right hardware to support the program. The others went on a murderous rampage, targeting purebloods. An entire hab had to be abandoned. Sorry, make that flattened. Maybe we overreacted. But we're 4400 *million* kilometers from Earth. We were this close to losing baseline life-support. Six hundred and seventy-seven people are dead. So what do I tell their friends and families when they find out the UN is keeping this thing around to *study* it?"

Elfrida, being closer to Triton, heard this before the others did. By the time Galt Nursultan's words reached Earth, the physically present humans were discussing where to go for lunch. They grimaced politely. Someone said: "Well, at least you've got insurance, right?"

Elfrida sipped her coffee. It was probably very good, but the asimov-class's taste receptors made it taste like bitter water. She looked up at the sun again. So close.

"You fucking assholes," Galt Nursultan said.

Another phavatar ("Hello! My name is Helena Christakos, Senior Researcher, Industrial MI Center of Ceres") said: "The Heidegger program has brought the Bellicia ecohood's power grid back online, after the fusion reactors on the surface were slagged. How did it do that? Is there any guarantee it couldn't also build itself a working transmitter and repeat the trick it played on Triton? I've heard the theory that it got some of its meat puppets into EVA suits before the air went bad, and sent them out to repair the reactors. But the fact is, we don't know how it restored power to itself. We don't know what it's capable of. Our smartest MIs are already better at survival than we are. This thing outclasses them by several orders of magnitude. I would lay money that it's learning, evolving, observing our reactions to its behavior, even as we observe it. Shall we allow it to conclude that our natural human inquisitiveness—the crowning virtue of our species—can be manipulated to give the PLAN an entry point into our social and informational networks? We've shown a united and ruthless face to Martian terror, and it's my belief that that is the only sane response to an entity that wishes to destroy our species. Let's not drop the ball now. *Destroy it.*"

They went for lunch.

"Bring on the poutine," joked Derek Lorna "It won't go to *these* hips." He slapped the flat stomach of his phavatar. It was obviously a 'selfie'—a phavatar customized to exactly resemble its owner. No one would choose to be skinny and balding with European coloring, even to blue eyes. Maybe

Lorna was more powerful than he seemed, Elfrida thought, considering how much selfies cost.

They ate at a bistro with napkins folded into flowers on the tables. Horse carriages clip-clopped along the street. Elfrida had lost track of the seasons, and the warmth of October heightened her disorientation. She kept looking up at the sun, her gaze drawn irresistibly to its radiant orb. She was eating a salad, in obedience to protocol. It tasted of toilet paper, and would later emerge from her phavatar's disposal hatch in the form of shrink-wrapped pellets for easy recycling.

"I'm about sixty percent persuaded by Kate's arguments," Lorna said, smiling at the woman from MIT. "In the light of our shared research goals, I know I shouldn't say this, but it looks like a blessing in disguise. Our very own mini-PLAN to poke and prod! Know thy enemy, as they say."

"Thank you, Derek," said Kate from MIT, forking up crème brulée. "As to the prudential concerns, those can easily be addressed by full-spectrum signal jamming."

Elfrida could see which way the meeting was going. She broke off from the group on their way back to the hotel where the out-of-towners were staying. She had never before been to Toronto nor wished to go. Turning at random through unfamiliar streets, she came to a church and went in. Her sense of utter helplessness led her to a pew, where she lowered her phavatar onto its knees.

"Help me," she whispered. "Help me."

She presently became aware of someone kneeling beside her. She didn't want to raise her forehead from her fists in case it was a regular parishioner who would be startled to find out that they'd sat down next to a phavatar. But the presence broke her mood, made her tense up. She tensed up again when she heard a hoarse male whisper: "Don't look up. Nod twice if you copy."

Astonished, Elfrida nodded several times.

Nothing happened for fifteen minutes after that, which meant the man beside her was physically there, kneeling in the last pew of St. Patrick's Catholic Church in Toronto. Elfrida eyed his legs. They were clad in perfectly pressed summer-weight trousers. His shoes looked like real alligator.

"*Ja.* Now listen up. What's your problem? You've been sitting there all morning like a fucking lawn ornament."

The man paused as a priest walked past them. Then he resumed.

"This ridiculous ad-hoc committee of Lorna's is going to factor heavily into the President's decision-making process. Why, because none of us know what we're dealing with. In my view, the very fact that we don't know what we're dealing with is reason enough to scour 4 Vesta down to the mantle. But that option is off the table. We're already perceived as high-and-mighty authoritarians in the Belt; we don't want to aggravate that perception. 4 Vesta isn't just any asteroid, after all. It's a protoplanet, a model colony, a World Heritage Site of outstanding universal value, yadda, yadda, yadda. Visuals of Star Force using it for target practice? An early Christmas present to critics of the UN's expansion policy. Do not want.

"On the other hand: this concept of quarantining the so-called Heidegger program to study it. Are you out of your fucking minds? We already made that mistake once, so *let's make it again!* Because the public sector is *so* much better than the private sector at information security! The arrogance of scientists never fails to amaze me. They aren't giving a thought to the communities they'd be endangering, up to and including the entire human race. Noooo, no. It's all about the research funding."

"I agree two hundred percent, sir," Elfrida said softly, knowing that her words wouldn't reach him for fifteen minutes.

"As a rule of thumb, whatever Derek Lorna wants, do the

opposite. He's an idiot. But he's not stupid, if you can appreciate the difference. Which is to say, he's open to compromise. And this is the compromise you are going to propose to him in the afternoon session."

He explained it to her. Elfrida felt hope dawning, mixed with quibbles. While he was talking, however, he heard her saying, "I agree two hundred percent, sir," so that was that.

"*Ja.*" He rose and brushed off the perfect creases of his pants. "I apologize for this absurd spy caper. It's undignified, and personally risky for me. But the fact is, I can't be seen talking to you, and this is the only way I could get to you without going through the IS-fucking-A. Telepresence encryption will keep this conversation away from their eyes ... and I hope you're *not* storing your data dump in the hub of the *Imagine Dragons*. Take it with you, or they'll be into it faster than you can say 'breach of privacy.' Got that?" He stepped past her, out of the pew.

Now, at last, Elfrida dared to look up. But it took fifteen minutes for her instruction to reach Earth. By the time her phavatar swivelled its head, Dr. Abdullah Hasselblatter, director of the Space Corps and member of the President's Advisory Council, had long since vanished into the afternoon. The bright rectangle of the doorway silhouetted an elderly couple, supported by his 'n' hers helper bots, arriving early for Mass.

★

When she got back to the hotel, the afternoon session was in progress. Raised voices carried into the hall. Clearly, the discussion had turned acrimonious.

"I'm telling you the thing was a plant!"

Had Elfrida been there in the flesh, she would've paused outside the conference room to eavesdrop. Her phavatar, however, lacked canniness. It walked straight in. Faces turned briefly to her and then back to the speaker—another phavatar that had hardly said a word during the morning session. This one belonged to Dr. James of the University of Vesta.

"We're playing into the PLAN's hands. They *wanted* the fragment to be found. They *wanted* us to succumb to the temptation to study it!"

"Maybe so," said Kate from MIT. "But at this point, what difference does it make? People are dead, and we have a responsibility to learn about what killed them, so we can prevent this from happening again."

Dr. James continued speaking over her, since his remarks had actually been made thirty minutes ago. This was the biggest drawback of multi-locational meetings: they disintegrated easily into non-sequitur.

"Dr. Lorna mentioned this morning that we need to know our enemy. But I submit that he was begging the question. *Do* we need to know our enemy? Why? Where would that get us? This is a mea culpa. I jumped at the opportunity to study the thing in the first place. I hoped it would help us to crack the PLAN's stealth technology, among other things. That didn't happen, obviously. But even if Błaszczykowski-Lee's team had succeeded in mastering the Heidegger program? *Nothing* we can learn from the PLAN would outweigh the risks of learning from the PLAN."

The man from the University of Lagos, feet on the table, said, "Yes, but let's be realistic. What are the risks, exactly? Everyone in this room knows this isn't the first time the PLAN has attacked us with malware. It's been spamming us for the last eighty years. Hell, that's how we lost the internet in the first place."

Elfrida hadn't known that.

"Twenty-four hours a day, 365 days a year, the ISA and related agencies scour the servers of the solar system for the PLAN's garbage. I've heard the figure of fifty trillion items deleted daily. Nevertheless, some of it gets through. So we have the so-called epidemic of BCI crashes, cubicle death, etcetera. Fortunately for humanity, the PLAN isn't very *good* at cyberwarfare. It doesn't understand us well enough to devise effective spam campaigns. But some people will click on anything. In my opinion, the PLAN is doing us a favor by removing them from the gene pool."

Laughter.

"What are we dealing with on 4 Vesta? More of the same."

And now Elfrida understood why Jimmy Liu and Wang Gulong had not flinched at the prospect that the Heidegger program might get loose on the internet. It was already there.

"But," she started.

Derek Lorna voiced the same objection she'd been going to offer. "With all due respect, Uchendu, this isn't 'more of the same.' This version of the neuroware can run on human brains, if they have the right wiring. I agree with Dr. James that this represents an evolution of the PLAN's strategy. I'd even postulate that the Heidegger program is an evolution of the PLAN itself."

"Agree," said the man from Oxford.

Lorna went on, "In terms of what we know about massively self-organizing systems, it's possible that the PLAN *couldn't* evolve unless it produced 'offspring' that would achieve AGI status in a isolated environment. We helpfully provided just such an environment. So yes, Dr. James, I concur that the thing was a plant. Moses in his basket, floating on a river of stars. The entity 'Little Sister' is not a soldier of the PLAN. She is its firstborn child."

Elfrida shivered. Dr. Hasselblatter was right: Derek Lorna was the smartest person in this room. That reminded her that she had to propose the compromise Dr. Hasselblatter had outlined. She'd been waiting for an opening, but she was never going to get one, because she couldn't know where the discussion would be in fifteen minutes. She started talking.

Meanwhile, Dr. James had thought of something else to say. He spoke into an argument between Lorna and the Nigerian professor of cyberwarfare.

"There's a moral dimension to this. When I said that knowledge of the PLAN would hurt rather than help us, it may have seemed a wayward statement. But I'm thinking in the context of the oldest set of moral guidelines we possess: the Book of Genesis. Do we really want to eat this apple? Think of those people, professors and scientists just like us, murdering their purebooded colleagues with any weapon that came to hand."

Dr. James flashed a vid montage up on the whiteboard in the conference room. Everyone quieted, not yet desensitized to the horrifying images from the Bellicia ecohood.

"Suppose we were to discover why the PLAN targets purebloods. And suppose, further, that it turns out to make sense. Are we confident that we would not adopt the same strategy ourselves—oh, our methods would be more humane—simply because it is *wrong*?"

Kate from MIT drew a shuddering, audible breath. "Scare tactics," she snapped. "Beneath you, Dr. James. And I'd ask you as a fellow professional to keep your religion out of it."

Her riposte touched off a shouting match. One camp consisted of most of the Earth-based experts. The other comprised the phavatar delegates from the Belt, plus the AI expert from Oxford, who'd taken it on himself to speak for them. Derek Lorna was noncommittal, tossing in the odd comment.

Elfrida spoke—not the words she would have chosen to say at this point, but the ones she'd already said.

"Um, as you know, I'm Elfrida Goto from the Space Corps, and I'm here in a dual role, um, because I witnessed a lot of what happened on 4 Vesta. But I'm also here to represent the Space Corps. I agree with Dr. James, for what that's worth. But I'd actually like to propose something different from just letting Star Force use 4 Vesta for target practice."

After a few seconds, the sheer novelty of hearing her voice prompted everyone to quiet down and look at her phavatar.

"Um, the Space Corps is an independent agency with representation at the PAC level, but we work very closely with UNVRP. In that capacity, I have recommended 4 Vesta for purchase by the Venus Remediation Project."

Every human face radiated astonishment.

"It meets all our criteria. It's big. It has a hole in the crust, known as the Big Dig, which will make a suitable cavity for the gengineered microbes that we place on captured asteroids as part of our Phase 2 atmospheric reduction program. 4 Vesta also, at this time, has no human population."

Her voice trembled a bit on the last words, but the phavatar smoothed it out for her.

"The only potential stumbling block would be the cost of moving this 2.67×10^{20} kilogram object from its present orbit onto a trajectory intersecting the orbit of Venus. But as it happens, a solution to that problem is already in place. 4 Vesta is equipped with the solar system's second-biggest rail launcher. The track was recently damaged, but all it needs is a bit of splart. Once fixed, it could be repurposed for propulsion. Use the existing launch cradle in combination with a cheap electrical engine: Put rocks in, fling 'em out, repeat. Small, targeted collisions could also be employed to provide initial boost and trajectory corrections. That would get us to Venus in roughly eighteen years, while consuming less than one percent of Vesta's mass in the form of propellant.

"Now, I'm going to take the liberty of anticipating another objection. Who's going to fix the rail launcher? And who's going to operate it? Who is going to do that with the Heidegger program active on the surface? Remotely operated bots would be vulnerable to hijacking by the Heidegger program, a risk we cannot countenance."

The whiteboard flashed up a vid Dr. Hasselblatter had sourced for her: a PR clip from a construction machinery trade fair in Dalian, China. Advertisement-festooned diggers, crawlers, rubble-haulers, drills, and cranes revolved on immense turntables beneath disco lights, while girl-styled robots draped themselves over the machines.

"That's a sampling of what we've got on Vesta," Elfrida said. "Uh, minus the flashing lights and the sexy robot shills." She'd paused there in hopes of getting a laugh. Her quip fell into a stunned silence. "The machines on Vesta are from Empirical Solutions and Huawei Galactic, and they've indicated that they are willing to lease them to UNVRP for a reasonable price. Obviously, this solves the problem of repairing and operating the rail launcher. These machines run on Chinese protocols. We can't communicate with them ... and neither can the PLAN."

For the first time, someone interrupted her. "She's right," said the mousy woman from CalTech. "The Chinese don't have a spam problem. Some think there's a reason for that, but anyway."

The rabbit hole of conspiracy theories about the Chinese yawned. Elfrida spoke on, and it was left behind.

"UNVRP and the Space Corps are presenting this proposal as a compromise between what I might call *Moar Science!* and *Slag All The Things.*" She got a laugh for that. "4 Vesta's eighteen-year journey through the asteroid belt and inferior space will give you a chance to study the Heidegger program, in a potentially fruitful collaboration with the Chinese. At the end of that time, it will impact Venus, and believe me, it will get *slagged*. You might even be able to see it from Earth."

"And not incidentally," said Derek Lorna, "it'd be a huge get for your nutzoid terraforming project. 4 Vesta contains five percent of the mass in the entire asteroid belt."

"This concludes my presentation," Elfrida said. "Questions? I do want to stress that the PR angle hasn't been much considered here, but I think the visuals will be great on this. It's turning lemons into lemonade, which will make people feel like we're winning, rather than, uh, the opposite. Plus, there'll be a super-dee-duper explosion to look forward to."

"PR is not a concern of this committee," Lorna said. But his former comment had been teasing, rather than hostile, and he continued in the same tone. "Leave it to UNVRP, the slickest propaganda machine on Earth, to come up with a solution that has something for everybody." He rocked back, spreading his hands. "Would I be correct in assuming that this isn't so much a proposal for our consideration, as a heads-up? As in, you're going to do this regardless of what we say?"

"Well, UNVRP has already purchased 4 Vesta from Virgin Atomic," Elfrida admitted. "Got it for a song. But we do need your backing. President Hsiao wants a scientific consensus in support of her decision."

These words reached the conference room in Toronto fifteen minutes later, by which time the experts were arguing over who would get first dibs on the Heidegger program, and where you could buy non-buggy Chinese translator software.

When he heard Elfrida's words, Derek Lorna's phavatar smiled. "Consensus? Never. We're scientists, honey. Support? Hell, yeah."

Dr. James's phavatar lay with its head on the table. The professor had checked out.

XXXX.

A few tens of meters from the telepresence cubicle where Elfrida lay, Colonel Oleg Threadley was conducting Shoshanna Doyle's funeral in hard vacuum. Even the ISA felt the need to mark death with more than a moment of silence in front of the recycling unit. Holographic wreaths decked the auxiliary deck of the *Imagine Dragons*. Kiyoshi stood at the back of the crowd, head and shoulders above the Earth-born officers, half-watching the speeches recorded by ISA colleagues of Shoshanna's who had known and, apparently, loved her.

In the distance he could see the *Unicorn*, a dot above the irregular curvature of 4 Vesta. The ISA had come up with one reason after another not to let him return to his ship. He wasn't exactly under arrest, but it could go either way. The ISA trafficked in ambiguity; it was one of their weapons.

Whereas this would previously have driven him nuts, he now felt weirdly calm. There was nothing they could do to him that he couldn't handle. If they tried to do something to *Jun*, then they'd have a problem. But it hadn't reached that point yet. As far as he knew, they were not even aware of Jun's existence.

The funny thing, the *miraculous* thing, was that he hadn't had a dose since that gulp of morale juice before he boarded the Vesta Express. And yet he felt OK. He wondered how long this could last.

The funeral proceeded with martial formality. Suddenly the strains of *A Mighty Fortress Is Our God* swelled over the public channel. A shock of recognition made Kiyoshi smile—until he heard the words the ISA officers were singing:

A bleeping ordeal is our job,
Protecting all the nations.

The solar system is FUBAR
So's the United Nations.
Yet unthanked we toil on
Crime and pre-crime exposing;
They don't know they owe their lives
To our eyes never closing.

Someone tapped Kiyoshi's elbow. He automatically stepped out of the way. A midget on skis pushed past him. It was the crippled astrophysicist, Dr. James, in a custom EVA suit. There was a little yellow circle stuck on top of his helmet like a price tag.

As Dr. James approached Colonel Threadley, who was about to scatter Shoshanna Doyle's ashes, he shook out a white shawl with black stripes at both ends and velcroed it over his helmet. Everyone stared in amazement.

"Give me that," Dr. James said to Colonel Threadley.

"Huh?" said Threadley.

"The ashes." Dr. James held out his glove.

Threadley deposited the vial in it.

Dr. James knelt, using Threadley's legs as a handhold to push himself down to the deck. Hunching over the vial of ashes, he began to chant. *"Yit'gadal v'yit'kadash sh'mei raba; b'al'ma di v'ra khir'utei ..."*

Chills raced up and down Kiyoshi's spine. The chant sounded alien, and yet familiar. Tears trickled down his cheeks inside his helmet, unsummoned, impossible to wipe away.

As if equally affected—though he didn't think they could be—the ISA officers remained silent until Dr. James had finished his prayer. The professor floated up on his tether and cast Shoshanna's ashes into space. Returning to the deck, he removed his tallit and yarmulke. "I believe her family would have wanted that," he explained. "She was Jewish, after all."

"I've never been sure," Threadley said. "Are Jews purebloods or not?"

"Depends on your definition. Most Sephardim and Beta Israelis qualify. Most Ashkenazi, like myself and Shoshanna, do not. To know for sure, you'd have to ask *that*." Dr. James jerked his thumb at the hulk of the Vesta Express, which trailed after the *Imagine Dragons* like a dead caterpillar on a leash.

"Oh, I'll ask it," Threadley said. "Although, that question might come pretty far down on the list. I've got a team over there right now, packing it up for transport to a secure ISA facility."

There was that. The boss-man, it turned out, had been wrong about the ISA's intentions. They didn't want to frag the Heidegger program after all, they wanted to confiscate it. Naturally.

"By the way, Professor," Threadley said, "weren't you sitting in on that meeting that was meant to give the president scientific cover for her decision?"

"I left early," Dr. James said. "I'd had enough. The presidential decision isn't going to be the one you were expecting, or the one I hoped for. UNVRP has done an end run around the whole debate."

He explained that 4 Vesta was to have a reprieve, after all ... and that definitely included Little Sister and the hardware she came with.

The news spiked Kiyoshi's mood. This looked—not only to him, but to the ISA officers, judging by their exclamations—like outright treachery from Elfrida Goto. Kiyoshi could have kicked himself for trusting her under the influence of Jun's wishful thinking. After all, she worked for the UN. At the end of the day, that was all you needed to know about anyone.

Back on the bridge, an officer proposed a motion to fetch Elfrida out of her telepresence cubicle "and freaking scrag her." Threadley vetoed that, but vowed that she would know the wrath of the ISA on their way back to Earth. "We were going to frag that mess on the surface and remove the original program for safekeeping. No one would have had to be the wiser. The ISA is the only organization with sufficient security expertise to handle hostile 'ware of this caliber. Now it's going to be handed over to a bunch of civilians. Cheer up, people: with any luck it will lobotomize the lot of them, and we'll have fewer pro-AI scientists kicking around the system."

The officers filed off the bridge, muttering darkly. Threadley held Kiyoshi back with a hand on his elbow. Kiyoshi shook him off. "You'd just have made the same mistakes the civilians are going to make, faster. There's only one thing that should be done with that program and that is to frag it."

"Oh, yeah." Threadley held his eyes. "You come from a rock that got slagged by the PLAN, don't you?"

"It's got nothing to do with that," Kiyoshi said. "I had a conversion experience back there. I realized that Jesus Christ is my savior. And what brought me to that realization, was coming eyeball to eyeball with evil, and hearing evil itself speak to me. The PLAN is Satan. My people were right all along. It's just so obvious to me now. The neuroware re-wires human brains so they're vulnerable to demonic possession. When you talk to a meat puppet, you're talking to a fiend straight out of the New Testament. And once you realize that, you kind of have to accept Jesus as your savior, or curl up in a ball and self-euthanize. There's no middle way. So; yeah. My opinion is that absolute evil should be fragged with extreme prejudice."

This speech left him in an exalted state, trembling with nerves, smiling fatuously down at the ISA colonel.

"You're a funny guy, aren't you?" Threadley said. "I don't think I've ever heard anyone be so incorrect, in so many ways, in so few sentences. I almost want to put you up for some kind of award. Take off your suit. Come with me."

Threadley had already taken off his EVA suit. Out of it, he looked like an aging *enka* singer Kiyoshi had known back home, with a gray ponytail, a beer belly, and skinny shanks. He escorted Kiyoshi to a shipshape office where a screen took up all of one wall. It showed 4 Vesta and the distant dot of the *Unicorn*.

Threadley prepared tea. His precise movements—the very fact that he did it himself, instead of letting a bot do it for him—reminded Kiyoshi of the zero-gee variation of the Japanese tea ceremony. You had to have steady hands to squirt the hot water into the cups instead of splattering it all over the room. Threadley corraled the splashback by expertly swirling the cups. These were ceramic with self-lids. The tea was some decaffeinated herbal blend.

"So," Threadley said. "You're a solo operator."

Here it was, then. The moment of danger. "Yup. Solo operator."

"You ply the unfriendly void in that death-trap of a ship, buying here, selling there, picking up the recycling from rocks too out-of-the-way for the big outfits to bother with. 6 Hebe is your most frequent port of call. When portside, you pick up girls, browse the simware showrooms, and buy drugs from the freelance chemists who hang out in the bars. Basically, you're just like ten thousand other no-hopers who think they're something because they've got a ship of their own."

Kiyoshi shrugged, not bothering to take offense.

"A lot of them believe in God, too. If anything, you're late to the party. It's a pretty common reaction to isolation, living on the edge, with nothing except a layer of metal and a not-very-bright computer between you and the abyss."

He's just fishing. Kiyoshi sipped his tea.

"You've got family on Ceres. The refugees from 11073 Galapagos. They're doing OK, we hear. Settling in well ... without any help from you. No urge to visit?"

"Ceres is a long way from here," Kiyoshi responded.

"It is. Gotta be lonely, knowing you're the only Japanese pureblood on this side of the solar system."

Like everyone else, Threadley had the wrong end of the stick regarding the Galapajin. Their ethnic heritage had never defined them as much as their Catholic faith did, or rather, the two things were profoundly intertwined, so that slaps at their ethnicity missed the mark. For himself, Kiyoshi had a red line related to both things and neither. He was prepared to take a stand if and when Threadley demanded to scan the *Unicorn's* hub. Until then, let the guy aim his darts.

"There's someone I want you to meet," Threadley said unexpectedly. He snapped his fingers at the door.

It opened, and Viola Budgett came in.

Cydney received the message she'd been waiting for. She had almost forgotten about it amid the chaos on board the *Húludao*. It came from Aidan in LA.

"Well, I would have said that workstation wasn't fixable. The Chinese; go figure."

Cydney had asked the *Húludao's* information systems manager, a handsome and friendly man, to repair the astrophysics lab's workstation. She hadn't held out much hope, but after a few hours it had been returned to her, as good as new. Handsome had assured her the repair job had been purely mechanical: the Chinese hadn't read the data, *couldn't* read it with their equipment.

Copying the workstation's contents to Aidan for analysis, Cydney had warned him, "Don't tell anyone it was the Chinese that fixed it. Don't even mention that we're on a Chinese ship. I mean it. This is diplomatically sensitive."

"Don't worry, Cyds, I haven't breathed the C-word," he reassured her now. "So. The data. I'm kind of puzzled here. We were expecting to find the dirt on the Vesta Conspiracy?"

That was what people were now calling Dr. James's

Seekrit Project, now revealed in its true guise as VA's struggle with the Heidegger program.

"There isn't anything about it. Zilch. It's like the U-Vesta astrophysics lab wasn't even in on the conspiracy. All we got here is a shit-ton of data about asteroids and neutrinos and so on."

"Doggone it!" Cydney felt like crying.

"Well, there's one thing. Remember the financial records you scraped from the university servers? Suggestive of some kind of scam? We found some more details on that. A spreadsheet authored by Viola Budgett, who I guess was one of Dr. James's lab assistants."

"Yeah," Cydney said to the air inside her cabin. "That's right. I saved her, too. And then the dog-be-double-damned ISA came aboard when we got into orbit, and took her off. No one else. Just her."

"You're him," Viola Budgett said, when Colonel Threadley had introduced them. Kiyoshi had known her the minute she walked into the office. He made a point of doing background on people he was going to be scamming. So he'd known who Viola Budgett was and what she looked like for fourteen months.

She cringed against the door, staring fearfully at him, as if at a monster that had crawled out from under the bed.

"Sit down, Miss Budgett," Threadley purred. "Have some tea."

"It was him. He sold us the thing. He only asked for fifty K, and like, it was an incredibly interesting object. Unlike any space debris any of us had ever seen. It *was* unlike, wasn't it?"

Budgett started to cry. She sat down and put her face in her hands.

"When you feel able," Threadley said tenderly.

"But—b-but—then he came back and asked for more. He

said that on second thoughts, fifty K was too low. He wanted five *hundred* K. And of course we didn't have it. But he said if we c-c-couldn't pay, then he'd just have to go to the m-m-media. B-b-by that time, of course, we knew what it was, what he'd sold us. B-but by then VA had it. So we didn't have the thing *or* the money. So that's why I, I, I ... that's how I came up with the idea."

Tears streamed down Budgett's cheeks. This was not an accusation but a confession.

"Around that time, an UNVRP team arrived on Vesta. We were going to be collaborating with them, sharing our survey data. You know how UNVRP operates. They buy asteroids that fit their criteria, and if there are people there, they pay them to leave. So I thought, what if we could make sure there are people there ... and what if they were *our* people? And then, what if their compensation from UNVRP, what if some of that could be ours? So that's how I set it up."

Kiyoshi interjected calmly, "Sir, this woman is slandering me. I have no idea what she's talking about."

"You—you *liar!*"

"Nice try," Threadley said. "Your buddy Haddock has already confessed."

"Oh yeah, I met him downstairs," Budgett sniffled. "It was a surprise to see him here. But people like that always get caught sooner or later. I hope you send him and his gang to Pallas." Her voice shook with vengefulness.

Kiyoshi's whole body prickled with sweat. He couldn't believe Haddock had confessed. But everybody confessed to the ISA, didn't they? Everybody.

"I knew the Haddock gang from when I worked at Kharbage LLC," Budgett said. "They were the ones who put him in touch with us. It figures, doesn't it? All the pirates in the system know each other. It's like this filthy, bottom-feeding subculture."

"I'm sorry to hear you speak of your friend like that," Kiyoshi said. "I'm referring to Alicia Petruzzelli." He turned to Threadley. "Of course you know that Petruzzelli was part of the operation. She played a logistical role. I assume Budgett cut her in on the profits."

Threadley shook his head. More than ever, he looked like that *enka* singer who'd died on 11073 Galapagos, with a fatherly twinkle in his eye. "Don't bother. We won't be going after Kharbage LLC, this time. Adnan Kharbage is too important a player in the recycling arena."

"*He's* a pirate," Kiyoshi said, angered at the failure of his ploy to deflect the blame. "I'm not, and neither are Captain Haddock and his family. I resent and absolutely deny the insinuation that I or they would ever steal anything."

"That cant of theirs sounds fairly piratical," Threadley said.

"It's a pose. A joke, if you're familiar with the concept. They're itinerant construction workers. Way I know them is I used to sell them splart, timber, plasticrete. You know: construction materials."

"Ah, yes," Threadley said. "Timber."

He leaned forward. The movement caused him to rise slightly from his ergoform.

"Timber is an extremely valuable substance out here. Extremely *rare*. Yet it accounts for half of the purchases made by Loyola Holdings, Inc. You have clients on remote rocks literally growing the stuff for you, Mr. Yonezawa. Hybrid oak and poplar apparently do very well in zero-gee. Funny thing is, we have no record of timber *sales* by your company."

"Some of those sales may have been conducted off the books," Kiyoshi bluffed.

Viola Budgett wiped her nose on her sleeve. The movement reminded both men of her presence.

"Thank you, Ms. Budgett. You've been very helpful," Threadley said.

She sprang up, but lingered for a moment. "Are you going to send him to Pallas?"

"Somewhere worse," Threadley said. "You have my word on that."

Cydney digested Aidan's analysis. "So the mysterious messages to Gap 2.5," she said aloud. "Those were just responses to blackmail demands?"

Based on Viola Budgett's spreadsheet, that was how it looked. Dr. James had wired money to Kiyoshi Yonezawa from the Vesta Express, when he visited the de Grey Institute in connection with the conspiracy, so he wouldn't have to use the university servers. Of course, he hadn't known that Budgett was keeping her own record of the transactions. Nor had he been able to hide the holes in his department's budget, which Cydney had found at the beginning of this investigative journey.

Which had now ended in anticlimax, for her purposes. Compared to the ravages of the Heidegger program, a blackmail scam wouldn't even rate a hundred K views.

Aidan also pointed out that *some* of the signals apparently sent to Gap 2.5 had probably been Adrian Smith swapping movies with his friends on Triton, much further away.

Disappointed, Cydney nevertheless put together a squib. She speculated that the enigmatic Kiyoshi Yonezawa was some kind of a gangster based in Gap 2.5. She sent it to Aidan to use when they next had a slow moment on the feed.

Kiyoshi gazed at the *Unicorn* on the viewport screen, willing it to vanish. If they arrested him, they'd also confiscate his ship. *Go,* he thought at Jun. *Flee. Save yourself.* These were the very words Jun had said to him hours before the destruction of 11073 Galapagos. But this time the thought was pointless. The *Imagine Dragons* made the *Unicorn* look like a pedal glider. If Jun ran, they'd overhaul him in a hot second and probably frag him for his trouble.

Which might be preferable to the ISA finding out that the *Unicorn* was under the control of an illegally empowered MI.

Threadley startled him by saying, "Don't worry, you're not under arrest."

"I'm not?"

"No."

"You told Budgett you were going to send me somewhere worse than Pallas."

"I am. That place you call home."

Kiyoshi laughed. He scratched his cubital port through his sleeve.

"Seems like headquarters got a call from your boss," Threadley said. "Bastard's got thrust with a capital T. Specifically what was said to whom, I don't know and I don't want to know. It would be futile for me to speculate on your worth to the Shogun."

The title hung between them, like a smell. Kiyoshi was stunned that the boss-man had come through for him, more stunned that the boss possessed the clout to spring him from the clutches of the ISA. He had known that the man called the Shogun had connections. Otherwise, 99984 Ravilious would have been history by now. He sure hadn't known the boss-man had thrust-with-a-capital-T, as Threadley put it,

"I'd really like to know what you're doing out there," Threadley said. *"Timber ..."*

Kiyoshi did not say a word.

"Y'know, I wasn't kidding, back on the bridge, when I said I'd like to nominate you for some kind of award. You've got the right stuff. You were the one who took Shoshanna down after she got infected. You took out a whole roomful of meat puppets. Secured the entity known as Little Sister and held the fort until we arrived. Didn't even get the post-combat shakes, didja?"

A smirk fought to emerge on Kiyoshi's lips. "I had God on my side."

"And there I was thinking you had to be on go-juice. Anyway, what I'm getting at is this: you're the kind of individual the ISA can use. I'm authorized to offer you a generous starting salary."

Kiyoshi just managed not to laugh. "Thanks," he said. "I'm flattered. Sincerely flattered. But all I want is to get back to my ship and go home."

A while later, Cydney, monitoring her own feed, emailed Aidan: "What about my item on Gap 2.5? Might as well use it, after everything I went through to get that workstation."

Aidan's response came twenty-six minutes later. (They were already closer to home.) *"What item?"*

"Oh," Cydney said, putting two and two together. Things did vanish in the ether. If the ISA did not think they should be known. Thoughtfully, she emailed back: *"Never mind."*

xxxxi.

Elfrida floated out of her telepresence cubicle after nine hours, stiff and tired. She had the worst headache of her life. "Doggone asimov-class phavatar ... Medibot!" A dalek-class bot rolled up before she reached the end of the corridor. "I've got a headache," Elfrida said pitifully.

"Sorry!" the dalek-class said. "You have been receiving a synthetic opioid in your IV. I can't give you any more painkillers at this time."

"But that was for my feet!"

She had suffered severe frostbite in four toes, had had injections to regenerate the tissue.

"Sorry!" the dalek-class said. It rolled off.

That treatment was the height of friendliness compared to what she got from the crew of the *Imagine Dragons*. To a man and woman, they turned their backs when she bumbled into the mess. *Screw 'em. They lost this turf war. Do 'em good, for a change.* She felt very glad to see Mendoza sitting by himself with a cup of soup.

"Clam chowder," he said. "Want some? It's pretty good."

Elfrida laughed. "That's funny. I was on a ship once where 'clam chowder' was their code word for black-market liquor. No, thank you; I've got a headache, and the stupid medibot wouldn't give me anything." She held onto the edge of the table, her legs drifting out parallel to the floor. She wasn't wearing dry-grips, as it hurt her feet less to float than to walk. "Where's Kiyoshi?"

"Yonezawa? He's gone."

"What?"

Mendoza looked surprised at her surprise. "He went back to his ship. Guess he had places to go, cargoes to deliver."

"I wanted to talk to him."

"You could always call him."

"It's not the same. I wanted to say ..." Her legs gently descended towards the deck. This was the only indication that the *Imagine Dragons* had engaged thrust. "I wanted to say sorry."

"What for?"

Elfrida hardly knew. "And another thing. I never even thanked him for saving our lives."

"I did," Mendoza said. "He was like, don't worry about it, I enjoyed it. *Eerie smirk.*"

"Ew."

"Right? You had his number, Elfrida. He *deeefinitely* isn't on the level... but so what, right? You're equally as alive, whether you're saved by a gangster or a priest."

"Did everyone from the *Unicorn* go with him? Haddock, his family, the Amish woman?"

"Yup. But speaking of the Haddock-man, that reminds me." Mendoza fished in the pocket of his jeans. "He gave me this for you."

"An origami crane," Elfrida said blankly. "That doesn't seem very Haddock-esque." Then she got it. Paper, who used paper these days? You might use it for communications, if you were on an ISA ship where every channel was guaranteed *un*private.

She unfolded the crane, cupping her hand over it to thwart the surveillance cameras. Across its creases were written a few words in Japanese script.

Fr. Thomas Lynch, S.J.—if you were wondering.

—Jun

She stuffed the scrap of paper in her pocket, wondering. Wondering. If she hadn't been wondering before, she was now.

The mild thrust acceleration increased to a couple of tenths of a gee, pulling her feet down to the deck. "Ow," she exclaimed. The ISA agents in the mess snickered.

Mendoza shot them an unfriendly look. "Sore losers."

"My feet hurt. My head hurts. Everything hurts."

"Poor you. C'mon." Seeing that it would hurt her to walk, Mendoza scooped her up in his arms. He marched out of the mess with her, impervious to the mocking comments that followed them. He carried her down to the berth they'd given him on the residential deck. "Did they assign you a berth yet?"

"I don't know. They probably won't, unless I ask. I don't know who to ask. I don't want to talk to Threadley. I know he's mad at me."

"Sucks to be him. UNVRP won, the ISA lost. Booyah."

"That's exactly what I was thinking."

"You'll have to tell me later how you did it."

"I will. Oh, my head ... This is a nice berth."

"Yeah, they don't stint themselves for comfort, although a bit of spin gravity wouldn't go amiss. They probably could afford it, but they're like Star Force: they think living in freefall makes them bad-ass."

Elfrida lay in the feathery thrust gravity on a neatly made-up bunk. With the door closed, the bunk was the floor. Mendoza lay alongside her.

"How are you feeling?" he said, stroking her hair.

"Like crap."

"Y'know, Elfrida ..."

"Don't say it." She ducked her head into his shoulder. "Don't say it, Mendoza, please."

"John."

"Huh?"

"My name."

"John ..."

He kissed her hair, laid a tentative hand on her waist.

"John."

They discovered—and later agreed, giggling—that sex in micro-gee was wildly overrated.

When the *Imagine Dragons* increased thrust to the point

that the ship was under one full gravity, it got better.

★

Like a handful of sand vanishing on the beach, the passengers from the Uhuru-Geneva flight blended into the concourse of Geneva Centre Aerospatial. Elfrida took a deep breath. She smelled fresh bread, hot chocolate, cinnamon, apples ... an olfactory blitz after breathing recycled air for so long.

Cydney was going to meet her here. The *Imagine Dragons* had got home before the *Zhèngzhōu* and the *Húludao*, but it had dropped Elfrida and Mendoza off at UNLEOSS, the United Nations Low Earth Orbit Space Station. They'd spent a week getting debriefed by the Space Corps and a bunch of other agencies. So Cydney had now been back on Earth for days. She'd emailed Elfrida: *I'm coming to Geneva to meet you! Can't wait, babe!*

Elfrida had not dreaded anything so much since she was locked in that freezer, running out of air.

Mendoza looked nervous, too.

"What's eating you?" she asked, not sure if she really wanted to know what he was thinking.

Finally he said, "That UNESCO thing. I can't believe they're really going to file a complaint against us for impersonating UNESCO agents."

"Oh, don't worry about that. We can challenge their paperwork and get it held up for years. I've *still* got a complaint pending against me for allegedly saying something racist to a guy on Botticelli Station."

"You said something racist?"

"No. But the point is, it's been a year and a half and it still hasn't got beyond the paperwork stage. The guy is dead, anyway." And there went that topic of conversation.

They walked down to customs. Elfrida's toes were still painful, making her limp. Mendoza bought an apfelküchlein on the way and munched it. Neither of them had any luggage. They submitted to the usual battery of scans. Then there was nothing left to do but go through the automated doors painted with a 3D mural of the Alps.

Two paces before they hit the mural, Mendoza grabbed Elfrida and kissed her deeply. His mouth tasted of apfelküchlein. "I just wanted to do that," he said. "I guess this is it. I mean, I understand. Except that I don't understand."

Nor did Elfrida. She'd never been this confused in her life.

The doors parted. A sea of faces slammed into her vision. She saw Cydney, jumping up and down, waving a bouquet of roses, shedding petals in her excitement.

Cydney saw Elfrida, and froze. The bouquet drooped towards the floor.

Elfrida realized, too late, that she was still holding Mendoza's hand.

In an arboreal bubbleburb outside Dingzhou, in Hebei Province, birds cheeped in the trees, sprinklers pattered on impeccable lawns, and children rode trikes along the sidewalks. They stared at a girl who scuffed through the ginkgo leaves, leading a Jack Russell terrier on a leash. The girl had a blue pixie cut. She wore an eye-patch.

She cut across Mathematics Is The Future Park and approached a three-storey brick house set in a High Chinese garden. Before she got across the moat, the front door opened and several adults came out, having been alerted by security.

"Hello," she said. "*Ni hao*. My name is Rurumi."

The terrier jerked its leash out of her hand and scampered up to one of the women, who embraced it with an inarticulate cry.

"I brought Amy back," Rurumi said.

"You have a Japanese name," said one of the men. He did not remark on the obvious fact that she was a phavatar. In

High Chinese society, that was not something to remark on.

"Yes," Rurumi said. "My former owner was an animé fan. But he's dead. So I'm on my own now. I have to turn myself in to my manufacturers within the next thirty days, unless someone buys me." Her saucer-like eyes welled up, limpid, inhuman, utterly sincere. How could the family of Jimmy Liu remain unmoved—by her cuteness, and more meaningfully, by her implicit offer to give them information?

It would be some hours before they discovered that Rurumi had a penis. This matter was dealt with by asking her to keep away from the children.

The *Unicorn* burned into the emptiness of Gap 2.5. Aboard, sixty-three Neu Ordnung Amish held a prayer meeting to thank God for upending their plans in such an astonishing manner. They embraced the unpredictable with steely zest.

Captivated, the family of Captain Haddock hovered on the fringes of the meeting. Little by little they edged closer to hear the preacher better over the rattle of the *Unicorn*'s antique air circulation system. They had wandered into Amish country in hopes of selling some fancy kitchen appliances to the colonists. They ended up staying for supper (nutriblocks disguised as mashed potatoes and bratwurst, with sides of real sauerkraut and pickles).

Up on the bridge, Kiyoshi was eating a solitary meal of pouch noodles and watching the news.

President Hsiao had praised UNVRP's purchase of Vesta as a "win-win solution."

"For everybody except us," Kiyoshi muttered.

"What shall it profit a man, if he shall gain the whole world, and lose his own soul?" Jun said. He was keeping Kiyoshi company by slurping noodles; at least, his projection was slurping projected noodles.

"Well, yeah." It was astonishing how fast normality set in.

Kiyoshi caught himself wanting a dose, not wanting one. He did not want to lose the exalted mood that still surprised him in odd moments, a sense of proximity to a vastness that was the mathematical opposite of the vastness of space— abundant, willed, joyful. These thoughts were too private to share even with his brother. He ate another mouthful of noodles. "The boss-man's gonna be pissed."

"No, he isn't."

"He'll probably threaten to space me."

"No, he won't. Come have a look at this."

Jun vanished his noodles and floated over to the refrigerator, which stood in a corner between the head and the disused comms officer's desk. He clicked his fingers at the screen on the refrigerator door that would normally display its contents.

The screen turned death blue.

"Oh my God," Kiyoshi said. He snatched the refrigerator open. Inside were bread and fruit and vegetables from their Karl Ludwig City grocery run; soft-drink pouches; a half-used thing of Zilk imitation milk; an opened pouch of nasi goreng that had been there for months; and a failed experiment in homemade natto. The same health hazards as usual.

Kiyoshi closed the refrigerator door. He stared at Jun.

"I didn't want you to freak," Jun said. "That's why I put it in the fridge. You never go in there."

"I'm throwing all that stuff out. Now."

"As Mom would say, *mottai nai*—what a waste. Anyway, it would be the first case in history of demonic possession of a cucumber."

"That thing is dangerous." Kiyoshi sounded like their father. There were times you needed to sound like your father.

"It's isolated. In the fridge," Jun said patiently.

"Have you been poking at it?"

Jun's silence was a confession.

Kiyoshi folded his arms.

Jun gabbled, "Coming from our background, you learn how to do a lot with a little, right? And on the *Unicorn*, I've learned to do more with less. Specifically, I can run a mean sim on minimal processing power. That turns out to be the key. The Heidegger program is dangerous, but it's also kind of dumb. I've given it the illusion that it's taken possession of a small ship. It doesn't know any different ...In all honesty, Kiyoshi, this fridge is as smart as the rest of my subsystems put together."

"So we've got a demonically possessed refrigerator."

"Yeah," Jun said, not catching the humor. "But it's totally going to be worth it. Based on the way it's trying to customize its imaginary ship, I've already picked up a few clues about the PLAN's stealth technology."

"OK," Kiyoshi said. "OK."

Their eyes met in a shared acknowledgment of what this

meant ... and how very, very pleased the boss-man was going to be.

★

Elfrida walked down to Lac Léman, past the ivied palaces of the WTO, IMF, CERN, WHO, WEF, and the rest. Grandest of all, isolated behind high-security barriers in Parc Moynier, UNSSCHQ (United Nations Select Security Council Headquarters) thrust its glass spires into the cerulean autumn sky. Tourists vidded each other in front of the famous gates. You'd never know that SSC was just a front for the smaller, even more select organization that really ran things: the President's Advisory Council.

Elfrida limped along the lakeshore. Colors were painfully crisp. A breeze blew, but the sweater she had bought at the mall on UNLEOSS kept her toasty. People swam in the crystalline water. On the far bank, forested slopes eased out of the water to become the Alps. The mountains ringed the city like a bank of low-lying clouds. Compared to Rheasilvia Mons, they were toy-sized. Human-scale.

Elfrida leaned against a tree, closed her eyes, and turned her face up to the sun.

In a minute she'd text her parents, let them know she'd landed safely. In a minute. Cydney had been texting her, too. Maybe to make up; more likely, to continue their fight. *In a minute.* Right now, Elfrida just wanted to feel the sun on her face, listen to the children splashing in the lake, and breathe ... breathe ... breathe.

She was home.

THE END

THE ADVENTURE WILL CONTINUE...

The Solarian War Saga continues in *The Mercury Rebellion* and *The Luna Deception*.

Sign up for my mailing list to be the first to know about new releases in the series! You'll also get FREE books, and access to exclusive content including giveaways, contests, and pre-launch reader's copies

http://felixrsavage.com/signup

Books by Felix R. Savage

The Solarian War Saga, in chronological order:

Crapkiller
The Galapagos Incident
The Vesta Conspiracy
A Very Merry Zero-Gravity Christmas (short story)
The Mercury Rebellion

The Elfrida Goto Trilogy (includes *The Galapagos Incident*, *The Vesta Conspiracy*, and *The Mercury Rebellion*)

The Luna Deception

Stand-alone

Finity (A Story of Mars Exploration)
Mercy (A Fantasy Novella of Revenge)

... and more to come!

Made in the USA
Middletown, DE
12 January 2019